Pimpernel and Rosemary

By

Baroness Orczy

D1601634

Cover Photograph: woodleywonderworks, h3_six, xxxrmt

ISBN: 978-1-78139-245-4

© 2012 Oxford City Press, Oxford.

Contents

CHAPTER I

To Peter Blakeney, Rosemary Fowkes' engagement to his friend Tarkington seemed not only incredible but impossible. The end of the world! Death! Annihilation! Hell! Anything!

But it could not be true.

He was playing at Lord's that day; Tarkington told him the news at the luncheon interval, and Peter had thought for the moment that for once in his life Tarkington must be drunk. But Tarkington looked just as he always did-grave, impassive, and wonderfully kind. Indeed, he seemed specially kind just then. Perhaps he knew. Perhaps Rosemary had told him. Women were so queer. Perhaps she did tell Tarkington that he, Peter, had once been fool enough to--

Anyway, Tarkington was sober, and very grave and kind, and he told Peter in his quiet, unemotional way that he considered himself the happiest man on God's earth. Of course he was, if Rosemary---But it was impossible. Impossible! IMPOSSIBLE!!

That afternoon Peter hit many boundaries, and at the end of play was 148 not out.

In the evening he went to the Five Arts' Ball at the Albert Hall. He knew that Rosemary would be there; he had designed the dress she would be wearing, and Tarkington told him, sometime during that afternoon that he was taking his fiancée to the ball.

His fiancée! Dear old Tarkington! So kind, so unemotional! Rosemary's husband presently! Ye gods!

At the Albert Hall ball Peter wore that beautiful Hungarian national dress that had belonged to his grandfather, a wonderful dress of semi-barbaric splendour, with the priceless fifteenth-century jewellery which he had inherited from his mother-the buttons, the sword-belt, the clasp for the mantle-they had been in the Heves family ever since it was fashioned by Florentine workmen imported into Hungary by a medieval queen. Peter dressed himself with the greatest care. If a thing was worth doing at all, it was worth doing well, and Rosemary had said once that she would like to see him in the dress.

But during that hot afternoon at Lord's while he dressed, and now inside the crowded, stuffy Albert Hall, Peter did not feel as if he were really alive. He did not feel like a personage in a dream, he only felt that the world as he had seen it since luncheon time, was not a real world. Someone had invented something altogether new in opposition to the Creator, and he, Peter, being no longer alive, was permitted a private view of the novelty.

It appeared to be a very successful novelty. At any rate, the numberless puppets who raised shrill voices so that Peter might hear what they said, all declared that this ball was incontestably the most successful function of the season.

Just as in the real world, Peter thought, where every function is always incontestably the most successful function of the season.

Other shrill voices declared in Peter's hearing that this function had been more than usually well-managed. It had been splendidly advertised, and the tickets had sold like the proverbial hot cakes.

And Peter was quite sure that somewhere in the dead, forgotten world of long ago he had heard such an expression of opinion over and over again.

Anyway, in this Albert Hall of the newly invented world things were much as they had been in the old. It was crowded. At one time there was hardly room enough to move, let alone to dance. Certain contortions of the body being called dancing, now as then, and certain demoniacal sounds made on hellish instruments by gentlemen of colour being called dance music, the floor of the hall, raised to the level of the lower-tier boxes, was given over to the performance of various gyrations more or less graceful, whilst Peter looked on, strangely familiar with this new world of unrealities which had only been invented a few hours ago, when Tarkington told him of his engagement to Rosemary Fowkes.

He knew just how it would be!

In to-morrow's issue of the Morning Star or the Talk of the Town, the thousands who gyrated here or who looked on at the gyrations of others would be referred to as being "also present."

He, Peter Blakeney, the famous cricketer and distinguished V.C., would be referred to as being "also present," and there would be a photograph of him with a set grin on his face and his eyes staring out of his head like those of a lunatic at large, in all the illustrated weeklies.

2

This was as it should be. It was well worth paying two guineas (supper included) for the privilege of being referred to as "also present" in this distinguished company of puppets that included both home and foreign royalties.

Of course there were others, the select few who would be referred to in the columns of the Morning Star or the Talk of the Town with charming familiarity as Lord Algy Fitznoodle, or Miss Baby Tomkins, or simply as Lady Poots or Lord Tim.

"While I was chatting with Lady Poots, etc."

"Lady Vi Dartmouth, with her beautiful hair shingled, etc. etc."

"The Marchioness of Flint came with her girls, etc."

All of which Peter knew by intuition would be vastly interesting to the suburban little madams who read Talk of the Town in this world of unrealities, that the puppets named Miss Baby or Lady Vi, would not think of being absent from the Five Arts' Ball. It was the acme of smartness, of Bohemian smartness, that is to say: the smartness of Chelsea and fashionable studios, which is so much smarter than the smartness of Mayfair.

And Peter-a kind of disembodied Peter-watched the throng. Ye gods! what a motley and a medley!

Polychromatic and kaleidoscopic, iridescent and prismatic, ceaselessly on the move, mercurial, restless, ever stirring, fluttering fans, fingering clothes, adjusting coiffures, lapels, frills, hair-ornaments and feathers! And talking! Talking incessantly, with voices hard and high-pitched trying to rise above other voices that were harder and higher of pitch. Dazzling to eye and ear; exciting to nerves and sense, the atmosphere and mixture of odours: of powders, cosmetics, perfumes, heat, gas, and a score of other indefinable scents.

The picture quite brilliant; not without touches of unconscious humour: Marie Antoinette flirting with Robespierre, Russian moujik in familiar converse with a jewelled Catherine, Queen Elizabeth condescending to pre-historic man. And then Pierrots, Pierrots everywhere, of every conceivable motley and shape. Blue Pierrots and yellow Pierrots! white or black, purple with orange frills, and orange with purple frills, black skull caps and tall white peaks. Pierrots of satin, and Pierrots of gingham! Cool and active! Ye gods! how active! Bohemian smartness, it seems, demanded that its Pierrots should be bright and amusing and active.

From his point of vantage on the floor of the hall Peter scanned the semicircle of boxes where sat more puppets, hundreds of them, watching the thousands down below.

What was the good of them? Peter thought. Why has God made them? What use were they in his new world which some wanton sprite had fashioned in opposition to the Creator? They fluttered their fans, they laughed, they jabbered, and did not seem to know that they, just like Peter, had become unreal and disembodied at the precise moment when Rosemary Fowkes promised to become Jasper Tarkington's wife.

And then suddenly the puppets all faded away. The new world ceased to be, there was no hall, no dancing, no music, no more puppets, no more Pierrots. There was only Rosemary, and she came up to Peter and said quite gaily, naturally, in a voice that belonged to the old world, not the new:

"Won't you ask me to dance, Peter?"

After that-well, dancing permits, necessitates, holding the partner in one's arms. And Peter danced with Rosemary.

CHAPTER II

Lady Orange always had a box for the big functions at the Albert Hall. It was chic, it was right and it was convenient. It gave her an opportunity of entertaining distinguished foreigners de passage in London in a manner that was both original and expensive.

Lady Orange prided herself on her internationalism, and delighted to gather distinguished foreigners about her; members and attaches of minor embassies invariable graced her dinner parties. She often referred to her attainments as "bi-lingual," and in effect she spoke French with a perfect Geneva accent. She thought it bon ton to appear bored at every social function except those which took place at her house in Belgrave Square, and now when a procession made up of bedizened unities marched in double file past her box she remarked languidly:

"I think they show a singular lack of imagination. One would have thought Chelsea artists would have invented something unique, picturesque for themselves."

"They only thought of comfort, perhaps. But it is they who gave the impetus to the imagination of others. Not?"

The man who sat next to Lady Orange spoke with certain gestures of hands and arms that would have proclaimed him a foreigner ever apart from his appearance-the somewhat wide expanse of white waistcoat, the ultra-smart cut of his evening clothes, the diamond ring on his finger. He had large, mellow dark eyes, which he used with great effect when he spoke to women, and full lips half-concealed under a heavy black moustache. He had a soft, rich voice, and spoke English with that peculiar intonation which is neither Italian nor Slav, but has the somewhat unpleasant characteristics of both; and he had large, well-shaped, podgy hands all covered with a soft dark down that extended almost to his finger-tips.

Lady Orange, who had pale, round eyes and arched eyebrows that lent to her face a perpetual look of surprise, gazed intelligently about her.

"Ah, oui!" she sighed vaguely. "Vous avez raison!"

She would have liked to continue the conversation in French, but General Naniescu was equally determined to speak English.

As Lady Orange was going to Bucharest shortly, and desired an introduction to august personages there, she thought it best to humour the general's whim.

"How well you express yourself in our barbarous tongue, M. le General!" she said kindly.

"Ah, madame," the general replicd, with an expressive shrug, "we in our country are at such disadvantage in the social life of great cities like London and Paris, that we must strive to win our way by mastering the intricacies of language, so as to enable us to converse freely with the intelligentsia of the West who honour us by their gracious acceptance."

"You are a born courtier, Monsieur le General," Lady Orange rejoined with a gracious smile. "Is he not, ma chere?" And with the edge of her large feather fan she tapped the knees of an elderly lady who sat the other side of M. le General.

"Oh, Mademoiselle Fairfax was not listening to my foolish remarks," General Naniescu said, turning the battery of his mellow eyes on the somewhat frumpish old maid.

"No," Miss Fairfax admitted drily. "Monsieur de Kervoisin here on my left was busy trying to convert me to the dullness of Marcel Proust. He is not succeeding."

"Ah!" exclaimed Naniescu suavely, "you English ladies! You are so intellectual and so deliciously obstinate. So proud of your glorious literature that even the French modernists appear poor in your sight."

"There, you see, ma chere," Lady Orange put in with her habitual vagueness, "always the courtier."

"How can one help being a courtier, dear lady, when for hours one is thrown in a veritable whirlpool of beauty, brilliance and wit? Look at this dazzling throng before us," the general went on, with a fine sweep of his arm. "The eyes are nearly blinded with its magnificence. Is it not so, my dear Kervoisin?"

This last remark he made in French, for M. de Kervoisin spoke not a word of English. He was a small, spare man, with thin grey beard neatly trimmed into a point, and thin grey hair carefully arranged so as to conceal the beginnings of baldness. Around his deep-set grey eyes there was a network of wrinkles; they were shrewd, piercing eyes, with little, if any, softness in them. M. de Kervoisin, whose name proclaimed him a native of Brittany, was financial adviser to a multiplici-multiplicity of small, newly created states, all of whom were under the tutelage of France. His manner was quiet and self-effacing when social or political questions were on the tapis, and he only appeared to warm up when literature or the arts were being discussed. He fancied himself as a Maecenas rather than a financier. Marcel Proust was his hobby for the moment, because above all things he prided himself on modernity, and on his desire to keep abreast of every literary and artistic movement that had risen in the one country that he deemed of intellectual importance, namely his own.

For the moment he felt vaguely irritated because Miss Fairfax-a seemingly unpretentious and socially unimportant elderly female-refused to admit that there was not a single modern English prose writer that could compare with Proust. To the general's direct challenge he only replied drily.

"Very brilliant indeed, my good Naniescu; but you know, I have seen so much in my day that sights like these have no longer the power to stir me."

"I am sorry for you," Miss Fairfax retorted with old-maidish bluntness. "I have been about the world a good deal myself, but I find it always a pleasure to look at pretty people. Look at Rosemary Fowkes now," she went on, addressing no one in particular, "did you ever in all your life see anything so beautiful?"

She made lively little gestures of greeting, and pointed to a couple on the dancing-floor below. Lady Orange turned her perpetually surprised gaze in that direction and General Naniescu uttered an exaggerated cry of admiration. Even M. de Kervoisin appeared interested.

"Who is the lady?" he asked.

"She is Rosemary Fowkes," Miss Fairfax said, "one of the most distinguished-"

"Ah! I entreat you, mademoiselle, tell us no more," the general exclaimed with mock protest; "a lovely woman needs no other label but her own loveliness. She is distinguished amongst all because she is beautiful. What else should a woman be when she is the finest work the Creator ever produced-an enchantress?"

"Well." Miss Fairfax rejoined drily, "I would scold you, general, for those lyrical effusions if they were intended for anybody else. Pretty women are usually silly, because from childhood upwards they have been taught to use their intellect solely for purposes of self-contemplation and self-admiration. But Rosemary Fowkes is an exception. She is not only beautiful, but brilliantly clever. Surely you re-remember those articles in the International Review on the subject of 'The Evils of Bureaucracy in the Near East'? They were signed 'Uno,' and many doubted at the time that the writer was a woman, and a young one at that."

"Uno?" General Naniescu exclaimed, and threw a significant glance at M. de Kervoisin, who in his turn uttered an astonished "Ah!" and leaned over the edge of the box in order to take a closer view of the lady under discussion.

CHAPTER III

Indeed no lyrical effusion would seem exaggerated if dedicated to Rosemary Fowkes. She was one of those women on whom Nature seemed to have showered every one of her most precious gifts. There are few words that could adequately express the peculiar character of her beauty. She was tall, and her figure was superb; had hair the colour of horse-chestnuts when first they fall out of their prickly green cases, and her skin was as delicately transparent as egg-shell china; but Rosemary's charm did not lie in the colour of her hair or the quality of her skin. It lay in something more undefinable. Perhaps it was in her eyes. Surely, surely it was in her eyes. People were wont to say they were "haunting," like the eyes of a pixie or of a fairy. They were not blue, nor were they green or grey, but they were all three at times, according as Rosemary was pleased or amused or thoughtful; and when she was pleased or amused she would screw up those pixie eyes of hers, and three adorable little lines that were not wrinkles would form on each side of her nose, like those on the nose of a lion cub.

Her chestnut-coloured hair lay in luscious waves over her forehead and round her perfectly shaped little head, and when she smiled her small white teeth would gleam through her full, parted lips.

Eschewing the fantastic pierrot costumes of the hour, rosemary Fowkes was dressed in a magnificent Venetian gown of the fifteenth century, the rich crimson folds of which set off her stately figure as well as the radiant colouring of her skin and hair. She wore a peculiarly shaped velvet cap, the wings of which fastened under her chin, thus accentuating the perfect oval of the face and the exquisite contour of forehead and cheeks.

"A woman so beautiful has no right to be clever," General Naniescu remarked with an affected sigh. "It is not fair to the rest of her sex."

"Miss Fowkes is certainly very gifted," Lady Orange remarked drily, her enthusiasm apparently being less keen on the subject of Rosemary than that of Miss Fairfax.

"And who is the happy man," M. de Kervoisin put in in his dry, ironic tone, "with whom the enchantress is dancing?"

"Peter Blakeney," Miss Fairfax replied curtly.

"Qui ça, Peter Blakeney?"

"Peter Blakeney, Peter Blakeney! He does not know who is Peter Blakeney!" Lady Orange exclaimed, and for this supreme moment she departed from her habitual vagueness of attitude, whilst her glance became more markedly astonished than before.

Two or three young people who sat at the back of the box tittered audibly, and gazed at the foreigner as if he were indeed an extraordinary specimen lately presented to the Zoo.

"Remember, dear lady," General Naniescu put in, wholly unperturbed by the sensation which his friend's query had provoked, "that M. de Kervoisin and I are but strangers in your wonderful country, and that no doubt it is our want of knowledge of your language that causes us to seem ignorant of some of your greatest names in literature or the Arts."

"It is not a case of literature or the Arts, mon cher general," Lady Orange condescended to explain. "Peter Blakeney is the finest cover-point England ever had."

"Ah! political sociology?" M. de Kervoisin queried blandly.

"Political what?"

"The Secret Points, no doubt you mean, dear lady?" the general went on, politely puzzled. "Advanced Communism, what? M. Blakeney is then a disciple of Lenin?"

"I don't know what you are talking about," Lady Orange sighed. "Peter Blakeney is the finest cricketer Eton and Oxford have ever produced."

"Cricket!" exclaimed the general, while M. de Kervoisin uttered a significant "Ah!"

There was a moment of quite uncomfortable silence. Naniescu was thoughtfully stroking his luxurious moustache, and a gentle, indulgent smile hovered round the thin lips of M. de Kervoisin.

"It is interesting," Naniescu said suavely after a moment or two, "to see two such world-famous people given over to the pleasure of the dance."

"They are excellent dancers, both of them," Lady Orange assented placidly, even though she had a vague sense of uneasiness that the two foreigners were laughing surreptitiously at something or at her.

"And we may suppose," the general continued, "that a fine young man like Mr. Blakeney has some other mission in life than the playing of cricket."

"He hasn't time for anything else," came in indignant protest from a young lady with shingled hair. "He plays for England, in Australia, South Africa, all over the world. Isn't that good enough?"

"More that enough, dear lady," assented Naniescu with a bland smile. "Indeed, it were foolish to expect the greatest-what did you call him?-secret point to waste his time on other trifling matters." "Cover-point, mon general," Lady Orange suggested indulgently, whilst the young people at the back broke into uproarious mirth. "Cover-point, not secret."

"Peter Blakeney rowed two years in the 'Varsity eights," one of the young people interposed, hot in the defence of a popular hero. Then he added with characteristic English shamefacedness when subjects of that sort are mentioned, "And he got a V.C. in the war."

"He is a jolly fine chap, and ever so good-looking," rejoined the pretty girl with the shingled hair. She shot a provocative glance in the direction of the two ignorant dagoes who had never even heard of Peter Blakeney, and then she added, "He couldn't help being jolly and fine and all that, as he is the great-grandson--"

"No, kid, not the great-grandson," broke in one of her friends.

"Yes, the great-grandson," the young girl insisted.

There was a short and heated argument, while General Naniescu and M. de Kervoisin looked courteously puzzled. Then Miss Fairfax was appealed to.

"Miss Fairfax, isn't Peter Blakeney the great-grandson of the 'Scarlet Pimpernel'?"

And Miss Fairfax, who knew everything, settled the point.

"Peter," she said, "is the great-grandson of Jack Blakeney, who was known as the Little Pimpernel, and was the Scarlet Pimpernel's eldest son. In face and in figure he is the image of that wonderful portrait by Romney of Sir Percy Blakeney."

"Hurrah for me!" exclaimed the one who had been right whilst the pretty girl with the shingled hair threw a glance at the handsome Roumanian which conveyed an eloquent "So there!"

General Naniescu shrugged amiably.

"Ah!" he said, "now I understand. When one gets the youth of England on the subject of its Scarlet Pimpernel, one can only smile and hold one's tongue."

"I think," Miss Fairfax concluded, "that Peter is the best-looking and the best-dressed man in the hall to-night."

"You stab me to the heart, dear lady," the general protested with mock chagrin, "though I am willing to admit that the descendant of your national hero has much of his mother's good looks."

"Did you know Mrs. Blakeney, then?"

"Only by sight and before her marriage. She was a Hungarian lady of title, Baroness Heves," General Naniescu replied, with a shrug that had in it a vague suggestion of contempt. "I guessed that our young cricket player was her son from the way he wears the Hungarian national dress."

"I was wondering what that dress was," Lady Orange remarked vaguely, thankful that the conversation had drifted back to a more equable atmosphere. "It is very picturesque and very becoming."

"And quite medieval and Asiatic, do you not think so, dear lady? The Hungarian aristocrats used to go to their Court dressed in that barbaric fashion in the years before the war."

"And very handsome they must have looked, judging by Peter Blakeney's appearance to-night."

"I knew the mother, too," Miss Fairfax remarked gently; "she was a dear."

"She is dead, then?" M. de Kervoisin asked.

"Oh, yes, some years ago, my dear friend," the general replied. "It was a tragic story, I remember, but I have forgotten its details."

"No one ever knew it over here," was Miss Fairfax's somewhat terse comment, which seemed to suggest that further discussion on the subject would be unwelcome.

General Naniescu, nevertheless, went on with an indifferent shrug and that same slightly contemptuous tone in his voice. "Hungarian women are most of them ill-balanced. But by your leave, gracious ladies, we will not trouble our heads any longer with that man, distinguished though his cricket-playing career may have been. To me he is chiefly interesting because he dances in perfect harmony with Venus Aphrodite."

"Whose Vulcan, I imagine, he would gladly be," M. de Kervoisin remarked with a smile.

"A desire shared probably by many, or is the one and only Vulcan already found?"

"Yes, in the person of Lord Tarkington," Miss Fairfax replied.

"Qui ça Lord Tarkington?" the general queried again.

"You are determined to know everything, mon cher general," Lady Orange retorted playfully.

"Ah, but Mademoiselle Fairfax is such a wonderful encyclopedia of social science, and since my attention has been purposefully drawn to Aphrodite, my curiosity with regard to Vulcan must be satisfied. Mademoiselle, I beg you to tell me all about him."

"Well," Julia Fairfax resumed good-humouredly, "all I can tell you is that Jasper Tarkington is one of the few rich peers left in England; and this is all the more remarkable as his uncle, the late Lord Tarkington, was one of the poorest. Nobody seems to know where Jasper got his money. I believe that he practically owns one of the most prosperous seaside towns on the South Coast. I forget which. Anyway, he is in a position to give Rosemary just what she wants and everything that she craves for, except perhaps--"

Miss Fairfax paused and shrugged her thin shoulders. Taunted by General Naniescu, she refused to complete the sentence she had so tantalizingly left half spoken.

"Lord Tarkington is a great friend of your country, General Naniescu," she said abruptly. "Surely you must know him?"

"Tarkington?" the general mused. "Tarkington? I ought to remember, but--"

"He was correspondent for the Daily Post at the time that your troops marched into Hungary in 1919."

"Surely you are mistaken, dear lady. Tarkington? I am sure I should remember the name. My poor misjudged country has so few friends in England I should not be likely to forget."

"Lord Tarkington only came into the title on the death of his uncle a year ago," Lady Orange condescended to explain.

"And he was called something else before that," the general sighed affectedly. "Ah, your English titles! Another difficulty we poor foreigners encounter when we come to your wonderful country. I knew once an English gentleman who used to come to Roumania to shoot with a friend of mine. He came four times in four years and every time he had a different name."

"Delicieux!" Lady Orange murmured, feeling that in this statement the Roumanian general was paying an unconscious tribute to the English aristocracy. "Do tell me who it was, mon cher general ."

"I cannot exactly tell you who he was, kind lady. When first I knew the gentleman he was Mr. Oldemarsh. Then somebody died and he became Lord Henly Oldemarsh. The following year somebody else died and he was Viscount Rawcliffe, and when last I saw him he was the Marquis of Barchester. Since then I have lost sight of him, but I have no doubt that when I see him he will have changed his name again."

"Vous etes vraiment delicieux, mon cher," Lady Orange exclaimed, more convinced than ever that there was only one aristocracy in the whole of Europe, and that was the English. "No wonder you were puzzled."

She would have liked to have entered on a long dissertation on a subject which interested her more than any other-a dissertation which would have embraced the Domesday Book and the entire feudal system; but Naniescu and Miss Fairfax were once more discussing Rosemary Fowkes and her fiancé.

"I suppose," the Roumanian was saying, "that Lord Tarkington has given up journalism altogether now?"

"I don't know," Miss Fairfax replied. "Lord Tarkington never talks about himself. But Rosemary will never give up her work. She may be in love with Jasper for the moment, but she is permanently enamoured of power, of social and political power, which her clever pen will always secure for her, in a greater degree even than Tarkington's wealth and position."

"Power?" the general said thoughtfully. "Ah, yes. The writer of those articles in the International Review can lay just claim to political power. They did my unfortunate country a good deal of harm at that time, for they appeared as a part of that insidious propaganda which we are too proud, and alas! also too poor, to combat adequately. Over here in England people do not appear to understand how difficult it is to subdue a set of rebellious, arrogant people like the Hungarians, who don't seem to have realized yet that they have lost the war."

Lady Orange gave a little scream of horror.

"Pour l'amour de Dieu," she exclaimed, "keep away from politics, mon cher general."

"A thousand pardons, gracious friend," he retorted meekly, "the sight of that lovely lady who did my poor country so much harm brought words to my tongue which should have remained unspoken in your presence."

"I expect you would be interested to meet Rosemary," said the practical Miss Fairfax, with her slightly malicious smile. "You might convert her, you know."

"My only wish would be," General Naniescu replied with obvious sincerity, "to make her see the truth. It would indeed be an honour to pay my devoirs to the lovely 'Uno'."

"I can arrange that for you easily enough," rejoined Lady Orange.

She leaned over the edge of the box, and with that playful gesture which seemed habitual to her she tapped with her fan the shoulder of a man who was standing just below, talking to a friend.

"When this dance is over, George," she said to him, "tell Rosemary Fowkes to come into my box."

"Tell her that a distinguished Roumanian desires to lay his homage at her feet," Miss Fairfax added bluntly.

"Do you think Sir George will prevail on the divinity?" the general asked eagerly.

Just then the dance was over, the coloured musicians ceased to bawl, and there was a general movement and confusion down below through which Sir George Orange, ever obedient to his wife's commands could be seen vainly striving to find a beautiful needle in a tumbled and unruly haystack. He came back to the side of his wife's box after a while.

"I can't find her," he said apologetically. "She has probably gone to get an ice or something. Tarkington was also looking for her."

"Well," said Lady Orange placidly, turning her surprised gaze on General Naniescu, "suppose you and M. de Kervoisin take us up to supper in the meanwhile. We'll capture Rosemary later, I promise you."

The party in the box broke up. The young people went downstairs to dance whilst the two foreigners gallantly escorted the elderly ladies up innumerable flights of stairs to a cold and cheerless upper story, where an exceedingly indigestible supper washed down with salad dressing and coloured soda-water was served to Pierrots, Marie Antoinettes, Indian squaws, and others who crowded round the tables and fought eagerly for unwashed forks and glasses of doubtful cleanliness.

The Five Arts' Ball was indeed a huge success.

CHAPTER IV

"Would you like anything?" Peter Blakeney asked of his partner while he steered her clear of the crowded dancing floor.

"I am rather thirsty," Rosemary replied, "but I could not stand that awful supper upstairs."

"Well, look here," he urged, "you slip into one of the empty boxes and I'll forage for you."

They found a box on the upper tier, the occupants of which had probably gone off to supper. Rosemary sat down and pulled the curtain forward; thus ensconced in a cosy corner of the box she drew a contented little sigh, glad to be in the dark and alone. Peter went to forage and she remained quite still, gazing-unseeing-on the moving crowd below. She was hot and felt rather breathless, her chestnut hair, below the velvet cap, clung against her forehead, and tiny beads of moisture appeared round the wings of her delicately modelled nose. The last dance had been intoxicating. Peter was a perfect dancer. Rosemary sighed again quite involuntarily: it was a little sigh of regret for those golden minutes that had gone by all too rapidly. Jasper, she reflected, would never make a dancer, but he would make a kind, considerate, always thoughtful husband. The kindest husband any woman could wish for.

Her eyes now sought the dancing floor more insistently. She had just become aware of Jasper's tall figure moving aimlessly amidst the crowd. Dear, kind Jasper! He was looking for her, of course. Always not physically and actually, then with his thoughts, trying to find her, to understand her, to guess at an unspoken wish.

"Dear, kind Jasper," Rosemary sighed and closed her eyes, in order to shut out that sudden glimpse she had just had of Jasper's anxious gaze scanning the crowd-in search of her. She pulled the curtain an inch or two farther forward, pushed back her chair deeper into the shadow.

Peter returned, carrying a bottle of champagne and a tumbler.

"Will this do?" he asked, and busied himself with the cork.

"Delicious," she replied, "but what about you?"

"Me?"

"Yes; you have only brought one glass."

"The only one I could get. There's a regular fight up there for crockery."

She laughed. "It must be horrible up there." She exclaimed.

"Dante's Inferno," he assented laconically.

He filled the glass till the froth bubbled over and then gave it to her to drink, which she did with delight.

"Lovely," she exclaimed.

He watched her as she screwed up her eyes and those tantalizing little lines appeared at the sides of her nose.

"I hear you did splendidly at Lord's this afternoon, Peter," she said. "There's a wonderful article about you in the Evening Post."

Then she held the glass out to be refilled. "Your turn next," she said.

"Won't you have some more?"

"Not just now, thank you."

He put the bottle down on the floor, then put out his hand to take the glass from her. As he did so his fingers closed over hers. She tried to withdraw her hand, and it the brief struggle the glass fell between them and was smashed to smithereens.

"Our one and only glass," Rosemary exclaimed. "Please, Peter," she went on with a nervous little laugh, "will you release my hand?"

"No," he replied, and increased the pressure on her struggling fingers. "I have often been allowed to hold your hand before. Why not now?"

She shrugged her shoulders and ceased to struggle.

"Am I never to be allowed to hold your hand again?" he insisted.

But her head now was turned away; she was apparently deeply interested in the crowd below.

"Oh, Peter," she exclaimed lightly, "do look at Mrs. Opert in that girlish 1840 costume. Did you ever see anything more ludicrous? Do look at her huge feet in those wee sandals. There's Jimmy Ransome talking to her now-"

Again she tried to withdraw her hand and still he held her fast. She turned to him with a frown.

"Peter," she said, "if you are going to be foolish, I'll go."

"What do you call being foolish?" he retorted. "Holding your hand? I held you in my arms just now while we danced."

"I call it being foolish, Peter," she retorted coolly. "Would you rather I called it disloyal?"

"You are too clever to do that, Rosemary," he rejoined, "disloyalty being so essentially a feminine attribute."

"Peter!"

"Oh, I know! I know!" he went on, quite slowly, and then suddenly released her hand. "Presently you will be Jasper's wife, the wife of my best friend. And if I happen to hold your hand just one instant longer than convention permits I shall be called disloyal, a cad-any ugly word that takes your fancy or the moment. So I must become less than a friend-less than a distant cousin-I must not hold your hand-the others may-I may not. They may come near you, look into your eyes-see you smile-my God! Rosemary, am I never to look into those glorious eyes of yours again?"

For a moment it seemed as if she was going to give him a direct answer, a soft flush rose to her cheeks, and there was a quick intake of her breath as if words would tumble out that she was determined to suppress. The struggle only lasted for a second. The next she had thrown back her head and burst into a peal of laughter.

"Why, Peter," she exclaimed, and turned great, serious eyes upon him, "I never knew before that you read Browning."

Her laugh had half sobered him. But evidently he had not grasped her meaning, for he frowned and murmured puzzled: "Browning?"

"Why, yes," she said gaily. "I forgot exactly how it goes, but it is something like this: 'I will hold your hand, just as long as all may, Or so very little longer.'"

He made no sign that her flippancy had hurt him; he sat down beside her, his hands clasped between his knees.

"Why should you hate me so, Rosemary?" he asked quietly.

"Hate you, my dear Peter?" she exclaimed. "Whatever put that quaint notion into your head? The heat must have been too much for you this afternoon. You never will wear a cap."

"I know that I am beneath contempt, of course," he insisted, "but when one despises a poor creature like me, it seems wanton cruelty just to kick it."

"I did not mean to hurt you, Peter," Rosemary rejoined more gently, "But when you are trying to talk nonsense, I must in self-defence bring you back to sanity."

"Nonsense? Would to God I could talk nonsense, act nonsense, live nonsense. Would to God my poor brain did refuse to take in the fact that you have promised to become Jasper's wife, and that I like a fool, have lost you for ever."

"Lost me, Peter?" she retorted, with just the faintest tremor of bitterness in her voice. "I don't think you ever sought me very seriously, did you?"

"I have loved you, Rosemary," Peter Blakeney said very slowly and very deliberately, "from the first moment I set eyes on you."

Then, as the girl shrugged her shoulders with an obvious attempt at indifference, he said more insistently: "You knew it, Rosemary."

"I know that you often said so, Peter," she replied coldly.

"You knew it that night on the river when you lay in my arms just like a lovely pixie, with your haunting eyes closed and your lips pressed to mine. You knew it then, Rosemary," he insisted.

But now she would no longer trust herself to speak. She had drawn herself farther back within the shadows. All that Peter could see of her was the exquisite oval of her face like a cameo carved against the dark, indefinite background. Her eyes he could not see, for they were veiled by the delicate, blue-veined lids, but he had a glimpse of her breast like mother-of-pearl, and of her small hand clinging tightly to the protecting curtain. The rest of her, swathed in the rich folds of her brocaded gown, was merged in the shadows, her auburn hair hidden by the velvet cap. Just by looking at her face, and on that clinging hand, he knew that everything within her was urging her to flee, was warning her not to listen, not to allow her memory to recall that wonderful night in June, on the river, when the tall grasses bending to the breeze, and a nightingale in the big walnut tree sang a lullaby to its mate. Intuitively he knew that she wished to flee, but that a certain something held her back, forced her to listen-a certain something that was a spell, an enchantment, or just the arms of her sister-pixies that clung around her and would not let her go.

"Don't let us talk about the past, Peter," she murmured at last involuntarily, with a pathetic note of appeal in her voice.

"I mean to talk about it, Rosemary," he retorted quietly, "just this once more. After that I will fall out of your life. You can cast me out and I will become one of the crowd. I won't even take your hand, I will try not to see you, not even in my dreams. Though every inflection of your voice makes my bones ache with longing, I shall try not to listen. Just now I held you while we danced; you never once looked at me, but I held you closer than any man ever held woman before. I held you with my soul and heart and body-just now and for the last time. And though you never looked at me once, Rosemary, you allowed me to hold you as I did-not your body only, but your soul-and whilst we danced and your sweet breath fanned my cheek you belonged to me as completely as you did that night on the river, even though you have pledged your word to Jasper. Though why you did that," he added, with a quaint change of mood, "God alone knows."

"Jasper wants me," she murmured. "He loves me. He sets me above his ambition-"

Peter Blakeney gave a harsh, mirthless laugh.

"Dear old Jasper," he said, "even he would laugh to hear you say that. Ambition! There's no room for ambition in the scheme of Jasper's life. How can a man be ambitious when all the beneficent genii of this world presided at his birth and showered gifts into his lap? It is we, poor devils, who have ambitions-and see them unfulfilled."

"Ambitions which you set above your love, above everything," Rosemary broke in, and turned to look him straight in the eyes. "You talk of love, Peter," she went on with sudden vehemence, while the sharp words came tumbling out at last as if from the depths of her overburdened heart. "What do you know of love? You are quite right, I did lay in your arms that night, loving you with my whole being, my soul seeking yours and finding it in that unforgettable kiss. My God! How I could have loved you, Peter! But you? What were your thoughts of me the next day, and the next day after that, whilst I waited in suspense which turned to torture for a word from you that would recall that hour? What were your thoughts? Where were you? I was waiting for you at the Lascelles as you had promised you would come over from Oxford the very next day. You did not come-not for days-weeks--"

"Rosemary!"

"Not for days-weeks--" she insisted, "and I waited for a sign-a letter--"

"Rosemary, at the time you understood!"

"I only understood," she retorted with cold irony, "that you blamed yourself for having engaged my young affections-that you had your way to make in the world before you could think of asking a girl to share your poverty-and so on-and so on-every time we met-and in every letter you wrote-whilst I--

"Whilst you did not understand, Peter," she went on more calmly. "Whilst you spoke of the future, of winning fame and fortune--"

"For you, Rosemary!" he cried involuntarily, and buried his head in his hands. "I was only thinking of you--"

"You were not thinking of me, Peter, or you would have known that there was no poverty or toil I would not gladly have shared with the man I loved."

"Yes! poverty-toil-on an equal footing. Rosemary; but you were rich, famous: already you had the world at your feet--"

"And you did not care for me enough, Peter," she said with a note of fatality in her voice, "to accept wealth, comfort, help in your career from me--

"Peter Blakeney the cricketer," he declaimed with biting sarcasm; "don't you know, he is the husband of Rosemary Fowkes now. What a glorious career for a man, eh, to be the husband of a world-famous wife?"

"It would only have been for a time," she protested.

"A time during which youth would have flown away on the wings of life, taking with it honour, manhood, dignity--"

"And love?"

"Perhaps."

There was silence between them after that. The last word had been spoken, the immutable word of Fate. Peter still sat with his head buried in his hands, his elbows resting on his knees-a hunched up figure weighed down by the heavy hand of an inexorable past.

Rosemary looked down at the bent head, and there, in the shadow, where no one could save the immortal recorder of sorrows and of tears, a look of great tenderness and of pity crept into her haunting eyes. It was only for a moment. With a great effort of will she shook herself free from the spell that for a while had held possession of her soul. With a deliberate gesture she drew back the curtain, so that her face and figure became all at once flooded with light, she looked down upon the kaleidoscopic picture below: the dusky orchestra had once more begun to belch forth hideous sounds, and hellish screams, the puppets on the dancing floor began one by one to resume their gyrations. Several among the crowd, looking up, saw and recognized Rosemary: she smiled and nodded to them, waved her fan in recognition. She was Rosemary Fowkes once more, the most talked-of woman in England, the fiancée of Jasper Tarkington, queen of her set, admired, adulated, the comet of the past two seasons.

"There's that tiresome George Orange," she said in her coldest, most matter-of-fact tone. "He is making desperate and ludicrous signs.

I strongly suspect him of making straight for this box. Shall we try to give him the slip?"

Her quiet voice seemed to act like an anodyne on Peter's jangled nerves. He straightened out his tall figure, quietly pulled the chairs away, to enable her to pass. She, too, rose and prepared to go. It seemed difficult not to say another word, or to look him once more straight in the eyes; and yet to speak words now, after what had just passed between them, seemed more difficult than anything. His hand was on the door handle. The other side of the door people were moving up and down, talking and laughing. Another second or two and she would pass out of his sight-pass out of his life more effectually even than she had done when she gave her word to Jasper Tarkington. Another second. But just then she raised her eyes, and they met his.

"Rosemary!" he said.

She shook her head and smiled gently, ironically perhaps, indulgently also as on a rebuked child.

"I had better go now, Peter," she said quietly. "I feel sure George Orange is on his way to drag me to his wife's box."

Just for another second he did not move.

"It is no use, Rosemary," he said, and in his turn smiled as on something very dear, very precious, wholly unattainable. "It is no use, my dear."

"What is no use, Peter?" she murmured.

"Thinking that all is over."

"In six months' time, if I am alive," she rejoined coolly, "I shall be Jasper Tarkington's wife."

"I know it, dear. Jasper is my friend, and I would not harbour one disloyal thought against him. But you being the wife of an enemy or of my best friend is beside the point. I cannot shut you out of my life, strive how I may. Never. While I am as I am, and you the exquisite creature you are, so long as we are both alive, you will remain a part of my life. Whenever I catch a glimpse of you, whenever I hear the sound of your voice, my soul will thrill and long for you. Not with one thought will I be disloyal to Jasper, for in my life you will be as an exquisite spirit, an idea greater or less than woman. Just you. If you are happy I shall know it. If you grieve, Heaven help the man or woman who caused your tears. I have been a fool; yet I regret nothing. Sorrow at your hands is sweeter than any happiness on earth."

It was quite dark where they stood side by side in this moment of supreme farewell. Each felt the inevitableness of it all-the fatality. Pride on either side had built a barrier between them: honour and loyalty would consolidate it in the future. Too late! Everything was too late!

Peter bent his knee to the ground and slowly raised the hem of her gown to his lips. But Rosemary did not move: for that one instant her limbs had become marble, and in her soul she prayed that her heart, too, might turn to stone.

Then Peter rose and opened the door, and she passed out into the world again.

CHAPTER V

Outside in the corridor Rosemary met Sir George Orange, who claimed her then and there and dragged her willy-nilly to his wife's box. She never looked back once to see what Peter was doing. He had become merged in the crowd, and, anyway, this was the end.

She found herself presently being talked to, flattered, adulated by the distinguished Roumanian who turned the full battery of his mellow eyes and his persuasive tongue upon her, bent on making a breach in the wall of her prejudices and her thinly veiled enmity.

She told no one, not even Jasper, the gist of her conversation with Naniescu. He had put a proposal before her-a proposal which meant work for Rosemary Fowkes-the Uno of the International Review. He had proposed that she should go to Transylvania, study for herself the conditions now prevailing in the territory occupied by Roumania, and publish the result of her studies in the English and American Press. And this was just the sort of work that Rosemary longed for, now, more than at any other time of her life. Naniescu had played his cards well. He had known how to flatter, insidiously, delicately, this popular writer who had captured the public fancy, and whose influence with pen and personality was paramount with a vast section of review and newspaper readers in England. What he had proposed could in no way hurt the most delicate scruples of an over-sensitive conscience, and the proposal came as a veritable godsend to Rosemary at this moment when her whole soul was in a turmoil of remorse, longing, and rebellion. That her love for Peter Blakeney was not dead, she had known well enough all along, but she had little dreamed until this hour how completely it still possessed her, what power his glance, his touch, his nearness still had over her. She had thought of her love as a heap of smouldering ashes, and lo! it had proved itself to be a devastating fire that burned fiercely beneath.

And Peter?

Peter had set the future above the present; his pride above his love, and she, wounded to the quick, had allowed ambition and pride to throw her into Jasper Tarkington's arms. It was all done now. Irrevocably done. But even at the moment when she most bitterly regretted the past, she was resolved to keep her word loyally to Jasper. Sitting beside him in the car that took her home from the Albert Hall ball, she allowed her hand to rest contentedly in his. His arm was round her, and her cheek rested against his shoulder. She did not speak, for she was very tired, but she listened, unshrinking, to the tender words which he whispered in her ear. Dear, kind Jasper! He had thoughts only for her. From the moment when she finally promised that she would be his wife, he had loaded her with delicate attentions and exquisite gifts. Every word he spoke was soothing and restful, so different from Peter's tempestuous outbursts, his unrestrained, passionate eloquence that would leave her limp and bruised, unable to understand his next mood, his sudden indifference to everything save his own future pursuits.

CHAPTER VI

It was only a couple of days later that Rosemary broached to Jasper Tarkington the subject that was uppermost in her mind. She had lunched with him at the Ritz, and they walked together across St. James's Park to her flat in Ashley Gardens It was one of those rare days of June which make of England one of the most desirable countries to be alive in. The air was soft, with just that delicious feeling of moisture in it that gives additional fragrance to the scent of the hawthorn: it vibrated with the multitudinous sounds of bird-song, a twitter and a singing and a whistling that thrilled the ear with their heavenly melodies.

Rosemary Fowkes was very nearly as tall as her fiancée, and Jasper Tarkington had a slight stoop which brought his eyes on a level with hers. Scoffers were wont to say that Tarkington's stoop was nothing but affectation; it certainly was a characteristic of him as is a monocle with some men. His whole appearance was one of super-refinement: he essentially gave the impression of a man who had seen so much of the world that he had become surfeited with it, and thoroughly weary. The weary expression was never absent from his eyes, which were very dark and set rather close together, and though he was quite a young man-still on the right side of thirty-there were a good many lines round them-as well as round his expressive mouth and firm chin. He had slender, beautifully shaped hands which, when he walked, he kept behind his back holding a malacca cane that was adorned with a green tassel. There is no doubt that there was a hint of affectation about Jasper Tarkington's appearance and manner, although in conversation he spoke with true Anglo-Saxon directness. He was always dressed with scrupulous correctness, and affected the Edwardian rather than the ultra-modern modes. On the whole an arresting personality, whose kindly expression attenuated the somewhat harsh Wellingtonian features, and the hard outline of the narrow hatchet face.

Rosemary Fowkes, walking beside him in her irreproachably cut tailor-made looked like a young Diana, radiant with youth and health. Her skin, her eyes, her hair, the jaunty little hat she wore, the trim shoes and neat silk stockings appeared strangely out of harmony with the stooping figure of this disillusioned man of the world, with that vague air of Buckingham Palace about his grey frock coat and silk hat.

It was whilst walking through the park that Rosemary spoke to her fiancé about Naniescu's proposal. Jasper listened attentively and without interrupting her, until she herself paused, obviously waiting for him to speak. Then he said:

"And you have fallen in with General Naniescu's views?"

"Yes!" she replied, after an instant's hesitation. "The whole thing appeals to me very much, and I am flattered by the confidence which the Roumanian Government apparently has in my judgement. And of course," she added, "I am not bound in any way."

"Have you made any definite promises to Naniescu?"

"Not quite definite. I wanted first of all to consult your wishes."

"Oh, my dear!" Tarkington interjected, and for one instant a light of youth and folly illumined his tired eyes. "Did I not promise you when you made me so immeasurably happy that you should be absolutely free to follow your career in whatever manner you choose? I am far too proud of you to wish to hamper you in any way."

"You have always been the dearest, kindest, most considerate creature on God's earth," Rosemary rejoined, and in her eyes there came a look so soft, so tender, so womanly, that the man on whom it fell hardly dared to meet it. "But you are not forgetting, are you, Jasper," she went on earnestly, "that politically we don't always see eye to eye, you and I?"

"So long as we see eye to eye in other things," he said, "what does it matter? When I asked you, my dear, to be my wife, I knew that I would not be mating with a silly doll. I am not fatuous enough to imagine that you would change the trend of your beliefs in order to harmonize them with mine."

Rosemary made no reply for the moment. Probably had they been alone she would have put out her hand and given his a grateful and understanding squeeze. As it was, the tears gathered in her eyes, for Jasper had spoken so naturally, and at the same time so nobly, that her heart was more than ever touched by those splendid qualities in him which his actions and his words were constantly revealing to her. Perhaps she was nearer to being in love with Jasper Tarkington at this hour that she had been since first he asked her to be his wife; and when the glory of this June afternoon, the twittering of birds, the scent of syringa and lilac in the air brought back with nerve-racking insistence memories of Peter's voice and Peter's touch, it was by mentally comparing the character of the two men as she knew them that she succeeded in casting those memories away.

"You are wonderfully good to me, Jasper," she sighed.

"One cannot," he retorted simply, "be good to that which is most precious in life: one can only worship and be grateful. But now tell me something more about your plans. I feel a little bewildered, you know, at the suddenness of them."

"I have not yet made any definite plans," she replied, "and as I told you, I have made no definite promise to General Naniescu. As a matter of fact, I intend writing him a final acceptance or refusal to-night."

"But you incline towards an acceptance?"

"Frankly, yes!"

"That would mean--?" he queried.

"That I start for Budapest within the next few days."

"What about your passport?"

"General Naniescu assured me that he would see to that."

"But you would not stay long in Budapest?"

"No, only a couple of days. I shall go straight on to Transylvania. I have been there before, you know."

"No, I did not know."

"Peter's mother was a great friend of mine. You know I was a motherless kid, and she took me under her wing on many, many occasions. At one time I travelled with her a good deal, and she took me several times with her when she went to Transylvania to stay with her relations. I know them all. They are dears."

"And, of course, they are extraordinarily hospitable over there," Tarkington admitted dryly.

"Hospitable to a fault! Mrs. Blakeney's sister, who is Countess Imrey, was kindness itself to me when I was in Transylvania two years ago for the International. In any case, I should go to her first. The Imreys have a beautiful chateau not far from Kolozsvár."

"I am afraid we must call it Cluj now," Jasper interposed with a smile.

"Yes," Rosemary retorted hotly. "Aren't those little pin-pricks damnable? Changing the name of a city that has been Hungarian for centuries, and that has been the centre of some of the most epoch-making movements in Hungarian history. It is mean and petty! You must admit, Jasper," she insisted, "that it is mean and far more galling to a proud, if conquered, nation than other more tangible deeds of oppression. Why, even the Germans when they took Alsace-Lorraine from France did not re-name their towns!"

Jasper Tarkington smiled at her vehemence.

"Naniescu, I perceive," he said, "has set himself a difficult task."

"He has," she admitted with a merry laugh. "But I left him no illusions on the subject. He knows that at the present moment, and with all the knowledge which—as I reminded him—I gathered at first hand two years ago, I am just as severe a critic of his government as I was then. He, on the other hand, declares that if I will divest myself of every prejudice and go to Transylvania with an open mind, I shall understand that Roumania is acting not only in her own, very obvious, interests, but also in the interests of European peace. Well," Rosemary concluded gaily, "I am going to accept General Naniescu's challenge, and I am going to Transylvania with an open mind. I am to have a perfectly free hand. Not a word in any article I choose to write is to be censored: he declares that he will show me the truth, and nothing but the truth, and that his government is only too ready to accord me every facility for investigation and for placing the case before the British public."

She paused to draw breath after this long peroration. As she walked so freely along, the eyes of many a passer-by were cast with undisguised admiration on the graceful girlish figure, the face aglow with youth and animation, the sparkling eyes, the lips which Nature had so obviously framed for a kiss. Jasper Tarkington said nothing for the moment; when she had finished speaking he sighed, involuntarily perhaps, and his tired eyes took on a still more wearied look. Was it that he felt he could not altogether follow this exquisite woman along the path of ambition which she trod with so youthful a step? Was he just a little too old, a little to blasé, to share all that enthusiasm, that pride, that burning desire to live every moment of the span of life, to fill every hour with deeds and spoken thoughts which would abide when youth had gone?

Who shall say? Jasper Tarkington had never been communicative; his best friends knew little of his life, and though he, too, in his day had used his unquestioned mental gifts for political journalism, he had never been the ardent propagandist that this beautiful apostle of lost causes desired to be. His silence now acted as a slight damper on Rosemary's enthusiasm.

"I am sorry, dear," she said gently. "I always seem to forget that you and I are in opposite camps over this one thing."

"We shan't be that for long," he retorted lightly, "if Naniescu's hopes are fulfilled."

Strangely enough, just as he spoke he saw General Naniescu and M. de Kervoisin, who were entering the park at Queen Anne's Gate as they themselves were coming out of it. The three men raised their hats, and Rosemary gave Naniescu and his friend a pleasant nod.

"I don't think," Tarkington said after a moment of two, "that our friend Naniescu will be very fond of me after this."

"Why?" On the contrary, "he should be grateful that you have not tried to oppose him in any way."

"I am going to oppose him in one way, though," Jasper resumed earnestly. "I don't intend to interfere with his plans or yours, my dear, as I said before; but there is one thing I am going to ask you, Rosemary."

"What is it, dear?" she asked impulsively. "I am so glad you are going to ask me for something. All the giving has been on your side up to now."

"Not so fast, little one. You mayn't be ready to do what I want."

"Is that likely?" she retorted. Then added with gentle earnestness: "There is nothing in the world I wouldn't do for you, Jasper."

"Will you marry me," he asked abruptly, "before you go away?"

She did not reply immediately, for in truth she was very much taken aback. Her engagement to Jasper Tarkington was very recent, and up to now he had not once spoken of a definite date for the marriage. She felt herself placed in an awkward position, for the fact that only a few seconds ago she had assured him that there was nothing she would not do for him. And now this request for an immediate marriage. She certainly was not prepared for it. Everything in her urged her to refuse. The memory of that hour in the box at the Albert Hall, her talk with Peter, her realization that Peter still held her heart, still ruled over her thoughts; everything, in fact, except a sense of gratitude urged her to refuse. And yet she could not-not after what she had said, not after all that Jasper Tarkington had done for her. While all these thoughts were whirling in her brain as she walked along, mechanically now, all the spring gone out of her step, something of the joy of living gone out of her spirits, she vaguely heard Jasper's quiet, gentle voice.

"You mean so much to me, Rosemary," he was saying, "that life here in England while you were God knows where, in tribulation, perhaps, perhaps in danger, needing me too, perhaps without knowing it, would be unendurable. I could not do it. I should follow you, anyway, and come as near to you as I dared, yet without the right to look after you as closely as I would wish. Well, my dear, you are far to womanly and kind to inflict such torture upon me. For it would be torture, and I would go under through it all. I don't know if you quite understand, but--"

There was an unusual vibration in his voice; it seemed as if, for once, passion would get the better of his habitual restraint. Tarkington always spoke slowly and directly, but for once words appeared to be failing him. However, just then they turned into Victoria Street, and the noise and bustle of traffic, his meticulous care of Rosemary while they crossed the road, brought him back to the prosiness of life. Nor did he speak again till they had reached the quietude of Ashley Gardens.

"Will you come up?" Rosemary asked, pausing at the entrance of one of the blocks of flats.

He shook his head.

"I think I would like you to think it all over quietly," he said. "I want you to remember that when I am asking you to hurry on our marriage, I only do it because I want to have the right to look after you. I won't interfere with you in any way whatever. I give you my word that as my wife you will be every bit as free as you are now-more so, really, because in that part of Europe a married woman can claim an independence which convention absolutely denies to a girl. In Budapest you will meet people of your own nationality, and of your own set. I could not bear the thought that your loveliness would leave you a ready prey to gossip or malice. There now," he added, with a self-deprecatory smile, "I have said more than I meant to. My first excuse is that you are more than life to me, and as you are so precious, I foresee dangers where perhaps none exist. My second is that I am pleading for my own happiness-I was almost going to say for my life. you are not like other women, Rosemary; you are above the petty conventions of trousseaux and crowded weddings. As soon as I have your answer I will get the special licence and we'll be married in your parish church without fuss and ceremony. So think it over, my dear, and let me have your answer as early to-morrow morning as you can. Remember that I shall scarcely live until I have your answer."

She made no reply; only put out her hand, which he took in his. There was no glove on it, and for a moment it seemed that in spite of passers-by, in spite of the conventional atmosphere of this part of London, he would raise that little hand to his lips. His eyes rested on her with a look of passionate desire; so intense was his gaze that suddenly she felt almost afraid. Rosemary had never seen Jasper's eyes look quite like that. As a rule they were so gentle, sometimes mildly ironical, at others only weary. But now it almost seemed as if, in order to bend her will to his, he was striving to exert some kind of power that was outside himself, as if he had called to his aid forces that would prove more invincible than those that were within him. The spell-it seemed like a spell-only lasted a couple of seconds; the next instant his look had turned to one of infinite tenderness. He patted her hand and reiterated gently:

"Think it over, my dear, when you are alone."

Instantly she felt the tears gathering in her eyes. His gentleness, his tender care of her, appealed to all that was truly womanly in Rosemary Fowkes. Self-reliant, brilliantly clever, independent in thought and actions as she was, she responded all the more readily to a man's desire for the right to protect as well as to cherish. Her independence had found its birth in loneliness. Fatherless, motherless in very early life, she had soon enough shaken herself free from any trammels that well-meaning relations desired to put over her actions. Her genius had consolidated her independence, but it had never stifled those vague longings for submission and self-abnegation which are the sublime satisfaction of a true woman's soul.

After Jasper Tarkington left her, and when she was alone in her flat, Rosemary Fowkes turned to the one thing that had never failed her in the great moments of her life. She turned to prayer. On her knees, and with her heart filled with longing and a sorrow that she dared not face, she prayed for help and for guidance. She had no one to turn to but Him who said with infinite understanding and love: "Come unto me all ye that travail and are heavy laden and I will refresh you."

In the midst of worldly joys, satisfied ambition, hopes for the future and pride in the past, Rosemary Fowkes would to-night have felt desperately lonely and lost in bewilderment before a divided duty-duty to self, duty to Jasper-but for the comfort of prayer, the thought of all that lay beyond this world of ours, a world that is so sordid and petty even at its best.

CHAPTER VII

The next two or three weeks were like a dream for Rosemary Fowkes. She left herself no time to think. The future beckoned to her with enticing arms, holding prospects of activities, of work that would fill the mind to the exclusion of memory. That evening when she rose from her knees, she rose with a resolve, and never for one moment after that did she allow herself an instant of regret. She wrote a line to Jasper to tell him that she would do as he wished; she was prepared to marry him as soon as his own arrangements were completed.

She also wrote to General Naniescu, agreeing to his proposal. She reserved to herself complete freedom of action to send any articles or reports she chose to English or foreign Press; all that she desired from him was a confirmatory letter, promising that nothing she ever wrote would pass through the censor's hands. This he at once sent her. Nothing could be more fair, more straightforward. Rosemary's chivalrous mind responded whole-heartedly to Naniescu's generosity, and the feeling that it would probably be in her power to do real good, not only to individuals but to peoples, acted as a soothing balm upon her bruised heart.

On the other hand, nothing could have exceeded Jasper's kindness and consideration during the days immediately preceding her marriage It almost seemed as if his super-sensitive soul had received a faint ink-ling of what was going on in Rosemary's mind. Nothing appeared too onerous, no sacrifice too great where Rosemary's comfort and desires were at stake, and at times-such are the contradictions of a woman's nature-she felt almost impatient with him for his magnanimity, almost obsessed by the unselfishness of his love.

She only saw Peter Blakeney once before she and Jasper left for Budapest, and that was on the day of her wedding. By one of those involuntary blunders so peculiar to dim-sighted lovers, Jasper Tarkington had asked Peter to be his best man. What it was that had induced Peter to accept, Rosemary could not conjecture. His impulses had always been strange and unaccountable, and this one was more unaccountable than most. Perhaps he merely wished to pander to his own mad desire to see her once again, perhaps it was just a semi-barbaric instinct in him that pushed him to self-torture. Rosemary by now had sufficient hold over herself to meet him calmly; not one line in her beautiful face, not one look in her haunting eyes, betrayed what she felt, after the wedding ceremony, when she accepted Peter's warmly expressed good wishes for her happiness. Even her sensitive ear could not detect the faintest note of irony or bitterness in his voice. After that he said a few words about the projected journey to Hungary, about which Jasper had spoken to him. She would be seeing his relatives there-the Imreys, the Heves. Elza Imrey was his mother's sister and such a dear, and Philip used to be a jolly boy; but Rosemary knew them all. She knew she would be made very welcome. Peter ended by speaking with great earnestness about his little cousin Anna Heves; her father, who had been Mrs. Blakeney's only brother, was dead, and Peter had an idea that Anna was not altogether happy.

"She has left home for some reason I can't quite fathom," he said, "and lives now at Kolozsvár-I mean Cluj. She writes to me sometimes, and when I know the exact day when you will be in Cluj, I will write and tell her to go and see you. I suppose you will put up at the Pannonia?"

Rosemary nodded and Peter went on talking about little Anna, as he called her. "I know you will be kind to her," he said. "You remember her as a child, of course; in a way she is still a child, and so pretty and enthusiastic. Give her a kiss from me when you see her."

Which Rosemary, of course, promised to do. Then she gave him her hand, without saying anything, for she could not trust herself to speak much, and he kissed it just above the wrist, but more like a knight doing homage to his lady than a lover who gazed, perhaps for the last time, on the woman he worshiped.

It was after the marriage ceremony that the dream-land in which Rosemary had moved these past days became more intangible, more of a spirit-world than before. The brief days in a dreary hotel at Folkestone would have been unendurable but for her state of mind, which almost amounted to semi-consciousness. Then came the weary journey to Budapest, the sleepless night in the train, the awful meals in the crowded, stuffy restaurant-car, the ceaseless rub-a-dub-dub, rub-a-dub-dub of the wheels that bore her away farther-ever farther from that bygone world which had become the might-have-been. And through it all, like a ray of light, so persistent that it ceased to impress, was Jasper's constant, unwearying care of her. He never seemed too tired to minister to her wants, to arrange cushions for her, a footstool, to open or close the window, the thousand and one little attentions, in fact, which most travellers are too self-engrossed to render.

And as Rosemary sat in her corner seat during those two wearisome days gazing out of the window with eyes that failed to take in the beauties of successive landscapes, her mind gradually became at peace with her heart. Her youth, her buoyancy of spirits, reasserted themselves, made her envisage life in all its brightest aspects, as it presented itself before her with cornucopia filled to the brim with all that made it worth the living. Work and a noble mate! What more could heart of woman desire? And Rosemary closed her eyes, and in a quickly fleeting dream sighed for the one thing that would have made her life a paradise, and-still dreaming-she felt hot tears of regret trickle slowly down her cheeks.

She woke to feel Jasper's arms around her and his lips kissing away her tears.

CHAPTER VIII

Budapest had been baking all day under a merciless sun in late July. But at this hour the coolness of a clear moonlit evening sent everyone out of doors. The Corso was crowded.

Rosemary Tarkington, on the terrace of the café sat sipping delicious coffee and lazily watching the throng. Now and then she would look straight out before her, and her eyes would lose all sense of fatigue as she gazed on the incomparable panorama before her: the ornate palace of the Hapsburgs, and the cathedral of St. Matthias, and on the left, towering above all, high upon the rock, the great grim fortress that for over a century had held the Turks at bay and saved Europe from the hordes of Islam. One by one tiny lights began to wink and to blink in the houses that rose tier upon tier on the slopes across the river, whilst down below gaily illuminated boats flitted to and fro upon the turbulent waters of the Danube, carrying a burden of merrymakers home from the shady island of Ste. Marguerite close by. The whole scene before Rosemary's eyes was one of unrivalled picturesqueness and animation. No town in Europe presents quite so enthralling a spectacle, and one whose charm is still further enhanced by the strains of those half-sad, half-voluptuous Hungarian melodies which come to the ear from out the shadows, or from the passing river boats, gentle as a caress, soothing to nerves and senses by their sweet melancholy rhythm, or exhilarating when they break into their peculiarly harmonious syncopated cadences.

Rosemary had specially elected to put up at the Hungaria rather than in one of the more modern, recently built hotels. For her the "Hungaria" was full of associations, of joyous times spent there when she was still a schoolgirl in the days before the war. She had travelled in Hungary and Transylvania under ideal conditions with Mrs. Blakeney, Peter's mother, seeing the best this romantic country had to offer, welcomed always with that large-hearted hospitality peculiar to these kindly people. But memory recalled more strenuous times, too, those in the early days of her journalistic career, when her heart was filled with pity for the sufferings of a proud and ill-starred country, whose fairest lands had been flung like rags by thoughtless politicians as a sop to those who had been her associates in the war until the hour when self-interest prompted them to throw in their lot with the other side.

"You must be very tired, Lady Tarkington," a pleasant voice said close to her elbow.

"Not tired," Rosemary replied, "but rather dazed. The journey over from England is slower and much more fatiguing than it used to be."

Captain and Mrs. Payson were sitting beside her at the table. Recently attached to the British Military Mission in Hungary, Captain Payson and his young wife lived at the "Hungaria." It had been a great pleasure for them to see Rosemary again, whom they had known for several years, and after supper they had all foregathered on the terrace over their coffee. Some few minutes before this Jasper had elected to take a turn on the Corso, to stretch his legs and to smoke a cigar, but Rosemary felt too lazy to move, and she like to talk to the Paysons, who were genial and intellectual, and with whom she had a great deal in common in the way of associations and friends.

"The place has not altered much," Rosemary went on after a while. "The people here are always gay and cheerful-in spite of-of everything."

"Yes," little Mrs. Payson assented lightly. "Give then their music, their delicious wines and perfect cooking, and nine out of ten Hungarians won't care if they are ruled by King or Emperor, by foreign tyrant or Bolshevist ruffian."

"I always think Ruth is wrong when she says that." Captain Payson put in earnestly. "The Hungarians are sportsmen, as we are, and they are taking their punishment like sportsmen. They are not going to let the world see how much they suffer. In that way they are very different from the Germans."

"They behaved with unparalleled folly," Rosemary remarked.

"Yes," the captain retorted, "and with commendable loyalty. The Hungarians are a nation of gentlemen, just as the British. They, like ourselves, are worshippers of tradition. They are royalists in their hearts, almost to a man. Just thing what their feelings must be whenever they look across the river and gaze on that gorgeous palace over there, whence their anointed King has been driven by petty foreign politicians who scarcely knew where Hungary was situated on the map."

Before Rosemary could pursue the subject she caught sight of her husband forging his way towards her between the crowded tables of the terrace.

"Naniescu is down below," Jasper said as soon as he had reached his wife's side. "I told him you were up here, and he said he wished to pay his respects. He is talking to some friends for the moment, but he will be here directly."

"Then Ruth and I had better run," Captain Payson said lightly. "He and I are always on the verge of a quarrel when we meet."

He and his wife rose and took their leave; there was much talking and laughing and promises to meet on the morrow. When they had gone Rosemary said to her husband: "I would rather not have seen General Naniescu to-night. I am very tired, and honestly I don't feel at my best."

"I am so sorry," Jasper replied at once, full of contrition. "I did my utmost to put him off. I knew, of course, that you must be very tired. But he leaves Budapest early to-morrow morning. He is going to Cluj--"

"Cluj?" she asked, puzzled, then laughed lightly. "Oh, ah!" she went on. "I always forget that dear old Kolozsvár is Cluj now."

"Naniescu was anxious to see that our passports were quite in order, and as this is important--"

"You did quite right, dear," Rosemary rejoined gently, "as you always do. I don't suppose the general will keep us long-though he is a terrible talker," she added with a sigh.

A moment or two later the handsome Roumanian came up to Rosemary's table.

"Ah, dear lady," he said, and with habitual elaborate gesture he took her hand and raised it to his lips. "What a joy it is to see that you have fulfilled your promise and that you are here at last."

He sat down at the table but declined Jasper's offer of a liqueur or cup of coffee.

"I am only here for a moment," he said, "Overwhelmed with work and with engagements. But I thought it would save you trouble if I just looked at your passports and saw that they were entirely in order."

"That is more than kind," Rosemary rejoined, whilst Jasper went immediately to fetch the passports. For a moment or two Rosemary remained silent and absorbed. An indefinable something had caused her to shrink when she felt General Naniescu's full lips upon her hand-something hostile and portentous. The next moment this feeling had gone, and she was ready to chide herself for it. Naniescu was earnest, persuasive, elaborately polite in manner and florid of speech just as he had been in London, when first he put his proposal before her, and certainly there was not a hint of anything sinister about him.

"I am looking forward to my visit to Transylvania," Rosemary said quite gaily.

"You will find every official there ready to welcome you, dear lady," Naniescu assured her. "You need only express a wish, to find it met in every possible way. And if you should do me the honour of requiring my personal services, needless to say that I should fly immediately to obey your commands."

Rosemary shrugged her pretty shoulders.

"I don't anticipate any such call upon your valuable time," she said coolly.

"Ah, one never knows. You, dear lady, are going amongst a strange people," he added with a sigh. "People whose supposed grievances have made bitter."

"I have old friends in Transylvania, and will feel as safe with them as I should in my flat in London."

"You will stay the whole time with the Imreys?" the general asked.

"Who told you I was going to stay with them?" she retorted quickly.

"You yourself, dear lady," he replied, unperturbed, "or did I merely make a shrewd guess? Anyway, on that unforgettable evening at the Albert Hall, when first I had the honour of an introduction to you, I saw you dancing with Mr. Blakeney. The Countess Imrey is his mother's sister-you told me that you had friends in Transylvania-the inference surely was obvious. I trust I have not offended you," Naniescu went on in his most mellifluous tone, "by the suggestion."

"No, no," Rosemary replied, already vexed with herself for having unwittingly provoked the Roumanian into one of those elaborate speeches which irritated her and gave her a vague feeling that malicious irony lurked behind so much blandness. "Mrs. Blakeney was a dear friend of mine; she and I travelled a great deal together, and I stayed more than once with the Imreys, not only at Kis-Imre, but in their beautiful house at Kolozsvár."

"Ah, then," the general rejoined, "if you know the house at Cluj, you would-in the scarce probable likelihood of your wishing to command my services-know where to find me?"

"What do you mean?"

"I am living in the Imreys' house now."

"But-how can that be?" Rosemary retorted, somewhat puzzled, for she knew that in this part of Europe the idea of letting their house to strangers would never occur to proud, wealthy people like the Imreys, as it does so readily to those of their caste in England. But when General Naniescu, with an indifferent shrug, replied dryly: "Oh, the house was a great deal too big for the occupation of a small family. On public grounds we cannot allow the many suffer for the whims of a few," Rosemary frowned, no longer puzzled. She felt rather than saw that the Roumanian's dark, mellow eyes rested on her for an instant with a look of quiet mockery. But it was a mere flash. The next moment he was as suave as before, and said with that perfect deference which he had always affected when speaking to her about her work:

"That question, dear lady, will be one which I earnestly hope you will approach with an open mind, and on which your brilliant intellect will, I trust, shed the light of truth."

Jasper's return with the passports brought on a fresh train of thought. Naniescu pronounced them to be in perfect order. He added a special note and signature to the visa which had been obtained from the Roumanian Consul in London. Rosemary was feeling very tired and longed to go to bed, but Naniescu stayed on, talking desultorily to Jasper about politics and social conditions, all matters which Rosemary did not feel sufficiently alert to discuss. Her thoughts wandered away and she scarcely heard what the two men were saying; she was, in fact, just meditating on a polite-form of abrupt leave-taking when something that Naniescu said arrested her attention.

"My Government," the Roumanian was saying, obviously in reply to a remark from Jasper, "is quite alive to the evil wrought by those pernicious articles which appear from time to time in English and American newspapers. . . ."

"Then why doesn't your censor stop them?" Jasper queried bluntly.

"He would, my dear Lord Tarkington," Naniescu rejoined blandly, "he would. But those devils are so astute. How they manage to smuggle their articles through the post I for one cannot for the life of me make out."

"Ah," Rosemary put in with a smile, as quietly ironical as Naniescu's had been a while ago, "you still carry on a strict censorship, then? You do not believe in liberty of speech or of the Press."

"We do, dear lady, indeed we do. But unfortunately the English and American Press are so easily captured by sentimentality. Put a case before them of supposed wrong, however preposterous and palpably false, and they will revel in it, print it with capital head-lines, and so capture the imagination of their sentimental, unthinking readers that these will no longer listen to the voice of reason or of truth. We are too proud-or perhaps not clever enough-to combat such barefaced propaganda; a strict censorship may be a crude weapon, but it is the only one at our command. What would you? A man who is attacked defends himself as best as he can."

"But in this case your weapon is failing you?" Jasper queried in his quiet, incisive way. "Whoever sends those articles to England and America is apparently too clever for you."

"For the moment-yes," Naniescu admitted. "But," he went on more lightly and at last rose to take his leave, "I fear my irresponsible prattle is keeping Lady Tarkington away from the rest she so much needs. Dear lady, pray accept my humble homage, and my earnest wish that your stay in our poor country will afford you all the delight that you anticipate."

He raised Rosemary's hand to his lips with the same show of gallantry that marked his every action in her presence. Just before he finally released it he looked up with deep earnestness into her eyes:

"Let me once more assure you, dear lady, that as far as you are concerned every word you write will be transmitted in its entirety and with all possible speed to its destination. All that you need do is to send your articles and letters in a sealed packet undercover to me. I give you my word of honour that you will be satisfied."

CHAPTER IX

Until the moment of her arrival in Cluj, Rosemary had felt nothing but exhilaration whenever she thought of her work and of the good which she proposed to do, thanks to the facilities so magnanimously accorded her by Naniescu. Just for one moment at Budapest, when she first met the handsome Roumanian, she had been conscious of a slight feeling of mistrust, an instinctive dislike of the man's fluent speech and affected gestures. But on reflection she had persuaded herself that this sudden aversion was bound to arise at first contact with those elaborate manners which pass for gallantry in most of the Latin and Slav countries of Europe. The contrast between Naniescu's exaggerated politeness and Jasper's unobtrusive consideration had naturally reacted on her sensibilities to the detriment of the Roumanian.

Anyway, the sensation soon wore off. She had a very happy time in Budapest. The Paysons were charming; she met several friends, both English and Hungarian, who made her very welcome, and Jasper was, as usual, thoughtfulness itself. The journey across Hungary filled her with that gentle melancholy which those limitless expanses of earth and sky engender in the mind of imaginative people. It was close on harvesting time, and to right and left of the permanent way the great fields of corn stretched out like a sea of ruddy gold to the purple line of the horizon far away. Rosemary loved to gaze on these measureless stretches of country, whereon for mile upon mile nothing showed above the line of waving corn save, at rare intervals, the thatched roof of a tiny homestead peeping from behind a clump of grey-green willow, or an isolated well, with one gaunt arm stretched skywards, around which a herd of young horses had halted for the midday rest. Her eyes followed with loving intensity the winding ribbon of the dust-laden road, bordered by tall, slender poplars or twisted acacia trees, and at intervals the great patches of vivid green amidst the gold, where row upon row of water-melons turned their huge, shimmering carcases to the warmth of the sun.

A faint perfume of heliotrope and mignonette hung in the air, and just for one moment Rosemary's dreamy gaze caught a glimpse of an exquisite mirage on the far distant horizon-a vision of towers and minarets and of a cool, shady stream painted with fairy brush upon the moisture-laden atmosphere. It was a phantom picture that vanished almost as soon as it appeared, but upon the watcher's super-sensitive mind it left in its swift transit an impression as of a magic land, a paradise the gates of which had for one brief second been opened by celescelestial hands, so that she might glimpse the garden of Eden beyondthe world of happiness and of love which for her must ever remain elusive and unattainable.

The arrival at Cluj was dreary and disappointing. From Budapest she herself had telegraphed to the hotel she knew so well, and had sent a letter at the same time asking the proprietor to have a hot supper ready for herself and Lord Tarkington. The hotel appeared unfamiliar when she stepped out of the little cab which had brought them from the station. The smiling hall-porter who used to greet Mrs. Blakeney with respectful familiarity on arrival was no longer there; an out-at-elbows, ill-dressed, unwashed porter took charge of their luggage. The proprietor, he said, was not in the house, and he himself was in charge of the place. He bluntly explained in broken German that under the new management no meals except early morning coffee were served in the hotel, the restaurant being now under separate ownership. The lady and gentleman could get something to eat there, no doubt.

It was all very cheerless, and to Rosemary very strange. The gay little town of Kolozsvár, usually so full of animation at this late evening hour, seemed already asleep. The streets were ill-lighted; there was an air of desolation and melancholy about this place. The hotel itself had become stuffy, dirty and ill-lighted. The furniture looked dilapidated, the bed-linen was coarse and the rooms none too clean. Rosemary spent a wretched night; but she was a hardened traveller and had before now put up with worse inconveniences that these. There was always the comforting thought that it was the only night that she would spend in Cluj. The next day Count Imrey's carriage and horses (he was not allowed to have a motor-car) would be taking her and Jasper to Kis-Imre, where a big welcome and every conceivable luxury awaited them both.

All that she was waiting for now was to see Anna Heves; little Anna, as Peter called her, the pretty, enthusiastic child to whom

Rosemary had promised to give a kiss for Peter's sake. And in the morning, just as Rosemary had finished putting up her hair and slipped into a dressing-gown preparatory to going in to breakfast with Jasper, there was a knock at the door and Anna came in. Sweet, enthusiastic Anna, who gazed at her shyly with Peter's eyes and then smiled with Peter's smile. She would have been pretty, too, but for the unhealthy pallor of her cheeks and the dark rings that circled her eyes-Peter's eyes!

"I am so ashamed, Miss Fowkes," Anna murmured shyly; but at once Rosemary broke in, stretching out her arms:

"Aren't you going to kiss me, Anna?"

With a pathetic little cry the girl ran into Rosemary's arms, and, her head buried on her friend's shoulder, she burst into tears. Rosemary let her cry for a moment of two; her own eyes were anything but dry, for with a quick glance she had taken in the girl's changed appearance, also the shabby clothing, the worn boots, the unmistakable air of grinding poverty and, worse still, of insufficient food. Poor little Anna! If Peter saw her now!

After a few moments the girl raised her head and dabbed away her tears. Rosemary led her to the sofa, made her sit down beside her, and took both her thin little hands in hers.

"To begin with you must not call me Miss Fowkes, Anna," she said. "I was always Rosemary, wasn't I?"

Anna nodded, and a wan little smile struggled round her lips.

"And, you know, I am married now," Rosemary went on. "Hadn't you heard?"

Anna shook her head. She could not yet trust herself to speak.

"Of course," Rosemary said gaily, "how stupid of me. Jasper and I were married very quietly in London, and we are not people of such importance that your Hungarian papers would chronicle the fact. My husband is Lord Tarkington, the best and kindest of men. I'll tell him presently that you are here. He would love to see you."

"No, no, Rosemary dear!" Anna broke in quickly, "don't tell Lord Tarkington that I am here. I-I never see strangers now. You see, I have no decent clothes, and--"

"Jasper would look at your sweet little face, Anna, and never notice your clothes. And you are not going to call my husband a stranger, are you?"

Then, as Anna was silent, and with head bent appeared to be staring into nothingness, Rosemary continued lightly, even though her heart felt heavy at sight of the havoc wrought in this young thing by miseries at which she could still only guess.

"By the way, little 'un," she said, "I don't yet know what you are doing in Kolozsvár-or Cluj-tiresome name, I never can remember it! Your cousin, Peter Blakeney, told me I should find you here, and that he had written to tell you I should be at the Pannonia to-day; but that is all I know. Where is your mother?"

"She is still in Ujlak, of course," the girl replied more calmly, "looking after the place as best she can. But, of course, it is very hard and very, very difficult. They have taken away so much of the land, some of the best pasture, over twelve hundred acres; mother has only about two hundred left. There is not enough for the horses' feed. Mother had to have ten brood mares destroyed this spring. It was no use trying to keep them, and she could not bring herself to sell them. Imagine mother having her mares killed! It would have broken her heart, only she has had so much to endure lately she--"

Once more the girl broke down; a lump in her throat choked the bitter words. Rosemary frowned.

"But, then, why are you not at home with your mother, Anna? she asked.

"I earn a little money here, and Marie is at home. She is younger than I, you remember, and she was always mother's favourite."

"How do you earn money, Anna? At what?"

Anna hesitated for a moment. She looked up and saw Rosemary's eyes fixed questioningly upon her, and those eyes were so full of kindness that the girl's reticence, even her bitterness, melted under the warmth of that gaze.

"I help in the shop of Balog, the grocer," she replied simply.

"Balog, the grocer? You?"

The cry of surprise, almost of horror, had come involuntarily to Rosemary's lips. She thought of Mrs. Blakeney, the exquisite grande dame who, after her marriage to Peter's father, the eminent scientist, had won her position in English society by her charm, her tact and that air of high breeding which is becoming so obsolete these days. She thought of Peter himself, who had inherited so much of his mother's charm and all her high-souled notions of noblesse oblige, of what was due to birth and descent. Did Peter know what little Anna was suffering under this new regime brought about by a treaty of peace that was to bring the millennium to all the peoples of Europe? With a sudden impulse Rosemary put her arms once more round the shrinking little figure.

"Anna," she said earnestly, "I think you are absolutely splendid! I admire your pluck more than I can say. But surely, surely you could find more congenial work than selling groceries!"

She paused a moment, her active brain at once turning to projects that had little Anna's welfare for their aim. Little Anna could not go on selling groceries in an obscure Roumanian town. It was unthinkable! Surely Peter did not know. And how could Rosemary face him with the news that she had found little Anna selling groceries at Cluj?

Something must be done, and quickly, to alter such an awful state of things. While she remained silent, thinking, and Anna, equally silent, fidgeted with long, thin fingers the tassel of her friend's dressing-gown, Rosemary became conscious that Jasper was watching her from the doorway of the next room. How long he had been standing there she did not know. She looked at him over Anna's bent head, and, as usual, she read in his expressive face a divination of her thoughts. It almost seemed as if, with a slight nod of his head, he was actually approving of what she had not yet put into words. Then he stepped back into the other room and quietly closed the door.

"Listen, little one," Rosemary said eagerly. "I am here at the invitation of the Roumanian Government; that is to say, General Naniescu, who, I understand, is military governor of Transylvania, has asked me to come over here and study the conditions, both social and political. I shall be writing several articles for English and American papers, and I simply must have a secretary for my ordinary correspondence, and--"

Anna shook her head.

"I don't know how to type," she said rather curtly, "and I can't do shorthand."

"Neither of which is necessary," Rosemary retorted.

Anna looked her straight in the eyes. "You don't imagine," she said quietly, "that if your articles revealed even a particle of the truth they would ever be allowed to pass the censor, and if they concealed the truth you would not expect my father's daughter to associate herself with them."

"That's a brave patriotic speech, Anna," Rosemary rejoined with a triumphant little laugh, "but you need not be the least afraid. My articles will contain the truth, and the censor will have not power over them. I give you my word."

But Anna was unconvinced.

"Rosemary dear," she said earnestly, "don't think me ungrateful or obstinate. Just imagine what it would mean to me to give up this awful grinding routine that wearies me at times to such an extent that I go into the cathedral and beg and pray to God that I might soon die and escape from it all. But you know, dear, when one's country is as unfortunate as ours has become, one must do one's utmost to help and serve her, mustn't one?"

"Why, of course," Rosemary assented, puzzled by the girl's strange earnestness, the glow of ardent patriotism that all at once emanated from that drooping, slender figure; "but I don't quite see how you are serving your country by selling groceries in Balog's shop."

"No! no! not by that," Anna went on eagerly. "Oh, I know that I can trust you, Rosemary, and you can't imagine what a relief it is to me to have someone to talk to. I have not spoken like this to a soul for nearly two years. And sometimes I feel as if I must choke. But one dare not talk to anyone these days, for government spies are everywhere. You never know who will betray you; the concierge of your house, the woman who washes the stairs, or the beggar to whom you give alms. Oh! I could tell you things---However all of us who are suffering unspeakably under our new tyrants are determined that the outside world shall hear the truth, but there is such a strict censorship that one dare not send anything through the post except what is absolutely banal and meaningless."

The girl paused a moment, her eyes wandered searchingly around the room, rested for an instant first on one door, then on another, as if in fear that those spies whom she so dreaded were lurking behind them, then, satisfied that she was alone with her English friend, whom she knew she could trust, she said abruptly:

"You remember my cousin, Philip Imrey?"

"Of course."

"He always had a great talent for writing. When he was quite a boy he used to write poetry and little stories. He is only nineteen now; next year he will have to do his military service in the Roumanian army, and that is a perfect hell for every Hungarian! Just think, Rosemary, if an Englishman had to serve in the German army! Isn't it unthinkable? But still, that cannot be helped! We are the vanquished race, and we have to pay the price. But we are determined that the nations of the West shall know the truth! So Philip and I, between us, thought of a plan. We thought of it for two years, and it took some time to organize. At last I obtained what I wanted, mother's consent that I should come to Cluj to earn my living, and a post in Balog's grocery shop. Balog sends Transylvanian goods regularly to Budapest: mustard, cheese, vegetable seeds; I have to pack them. Now do you understand?"

Rosemary nodded. "Yes, I think I do! Philip writes those articles which appeared in the Evening Post and caused such an outburst of sympathy for the Hungarians of Transylvania throughout Great Britain. And you--?" she added, and her eyes full of tenderness and com-compassion rested with undisguised admiration on the shrinking little figure of Anna Heves.

"He rides over from Kis-Imre," the girl continued simply, "and brings me the articles which he has written, and I consign them inside the grocery parcels to the firm at Budapest, who, of course, are in entire sympathy with us, and post them on to England. Oh! it is splendid, Rosemary dear," the girl continued with glowing eyes, "to be able to do all this. Now you see, don't you? that I could not possibly give it all up."

"Yes, Anna, I do see that. But you are running terrible risks, little 'un."

"I know I am, and so does Philip; but you don't know how happy it makes us. The days when an article of his goes to Budapest is a fete day for us both. It is usually a Saturday when the parcels are sent off, and," the girl went on with pathetic naivete, "on the Sunday morning when I go to Mass, I no longer bother God with my troubles and with senseless prayers, I just thank Him, and thank Him for letting me do something for Hungary."

Rosemary said nothing for the moment. Indeed, what could she say? To try and dissuade this young fanatic from all her high-souled foolishness was an attempt foredoomed to failure. Rosemary had far too keen a knowledge of human nature, and held far too high an opinion of patriotism as a virtue not to understand the intense happiness that this constant sacrifice brought into Anna's dreary life. To have suggested that the girl give up this joy-these constant risks-would have been futile.

"You are a splendid, brave thing, Anna!" was all that she could say, and her voice sounded quite harsh as she spoke, because she was fighting against emotion.

She gazed with real admiration on the poor wizened little figure of this girl, in whose soul burned a flame of ardent patriotism. Anna had counted the cost of what she was doing; with her eyes open, envisaging every risk, she was accomplishing quietly and unostentatiously what she believed to be her duty to her poor native land. A heroine of the peace, she risked more than the thousands of heroines of the war had done-save perhaps one. Like Edith Cavell, she faced and risked death for an ideal, happy in her quiet way for the privilege of doing it, enduring a life of grinding routine, of dreary monotony more trying for the young to bear than active sorrow or physical pain.

The two girls had not spoken for some time, they sat side by side on the sofa with hands clasped, and eyes fixed upon one another. Anna, with nerves weakened by privations, was on the verge of giving way to an emotion which would have eased the tension that for the past months was threatening to break down her spirit. Rosemary, on the other hand, felt for the moment almost ashamed of her robust health, her virile brain, the contentment-if not happiness-in life which was her portion since she had married Jasper, and her compassionate heart longed for the power to comfort and to help this gentle, high-souled girl who looked at her with Peter Blakeney's eyes, and whose lips when she smiled were so like his. Anna was running her head against a stonewall. Rosemary felt that inevitably she would sooner or later be crushed in the process. Her thoughts flew to her husband, the man on whom she knew that she could always rely when knotty problems of life threatened to be beyond her powers to unravel. Jasper would be of good counsel: selfless, generous to a fault, his unerring tact would perhaps find a way into the innermost recesses of Anna's heart, and find the means to save the child from further fanatical folly without wounding the susceptibilities of her high-mettled patriotism.

"And now, Anna," Rosemary said after that moment of silence which had sealed a bond of sympathy between herself and Peter's kinswoman, "you are going to have a cup of hot coffee with me and Jasper. No! No!" she went on determinedly, and took hold of the girl's wrist. "I shall not let you go till you have seen Jasper. He will just love you, and you and he will get on splendidly together. You two fine creatures are made to understand one another."

She dragged the obviously unwilling Anna with her into the next room. Jasper was there, waiting. His hand was on the bell-pull at the moment, and his kind, grave, eyes at once sought those of Anna, who, reluctantly, allowed herself to be drawn toward him.

Rosemary effected a quick introduction. In a moment Jasper's kind words had gained the victory over Anna's shyness; less than two minutes later they were seated side by side at the table, while Rosemary ordered coffee of the slatternly chambermaid who had come in answer to the bell.

It was wonderful how splendidly Jasper and Anna got on; he seemed in a few seconds to have caught the knack of gaining the girl's confidence. She became animated, quite pretty, with shinning eyes and full red lips that had lost for the moment their pathetic droop. She did not refer to her cousin, Philip Imrey, or to the dangerous game he and she were playing together, but she talked of her mother and of Ujlak, of the horses and the farm and the difficulties that beset the Hungarian landowners at every turn.

"I dare say that to a great extent it is our fault," she was even willing to admit in response to gentle criticism from Jasper. "We did not make ourselves beloved by the peasantry; they spoke a different language from ours, theirs was a different religion, and they were the alien race. We did little, if anything, for them. But tell me," she went on, and fixed her shrewd glance upon Jasper, "do you think that you landowners over in England, who do so much for your tenantry and your villagers, cricket-clubs, football, concerts-oh! I don't know what else, but things that you pay for and that they enjoy-well! do you think that in their hearts they love you any better than the Roumanian peasantry loved us Hungarians? And do you really believe that if you were in trouble, as we are now, and they were given a certain power over you, they would use it to show their gratitude for past generosity? Do you really believe that, Lord Tarkington?" she insisted.

And Jasper, with a smile at her vehemence, could only shrug his shoulders.

He was evidently very much taken with little Anna.

CHAPTER X

It was a week later and Jasper and Rosemary had been spending that time at Kis-Imre. No one who has not travelled in that part of the world can form a conception of the large-hearted hospitality that welcomes the stranger in a Hungarian chateau.

And Rosemary at once took the Imreys to her heart. She had known them before, of course, in the days before the war, when they dispensed that same wonderful hospitality, light-heartedly, gaily, as a matter of course.

But most of that had become a thing of the past. So much of it had gone, been irretrievably lost in the cataclysm of war and alien occupation. The will to give was still there, the love of the stranger, the boundless hospitality, but giving now meant a sacrifice somewhere, giving up something to give to others. All the sweeter, all the more lovable for being tinged with sadness. To Rosemary, Elza Imrey now was a woman' before that she had been just like a child, naïvely proud of her home, her table, her horses, without a hint of ostentation in her display of the rich gifts the good God had showered upon her. Now Elza's large, prominent blue eyes had become a little dim with constant weeping, and her mouth, when at rest, drooped slightly at the corners. Elza was still a very handsome woman, with her hair of ruddy gold like the cornfields of her native land, but all around the temples there was now a sprinkling of silver, a sprinkling that softened the face as powder does when applied lightly to the hair.

Though in outward appearance she was very unlike her sister, yet she constantly reminded Rosemary of Mrs. Blakeney; it was a question of movements, a gesture here and there, and also the tone of the voice. Elza, too, like her sister, had a magnificent figure, and the perfect hands, arms and wrists peculiar to her race. She had suffered, of course: badly during the war, terribly since the peace. At all times a maîtresse femme, it was she who had carried on the administration of her husband's estates, she who used to interview bailiffs, lawyers, tenants. She had always been looked up to by the local officials and by the surrounding peasantry as the head of the house. Maurus Imrey had always been neurasthenic, and the privations of the war, and the humiliations consequent on the alien occupation of his country, had exasperated his nervous system and further embittered his quarrelsome disposition. In the happy days before the war his contribution to the management of his estates consisted in grumbling daily at his chef and swearing unremittingly at those of his servants who came to him for orders in anything pertaining to the house. Malicious tongues were wont to say that Maurus Imrey had gipsy blood in his veins; more likely it was an Armenian strain. Certain it is that his face and hands were swarthy, his nose hooked and his eyes very dark and piercing; characteristics which he had transmitted in a softened degree to his son Philip. But he was a man of culture for all that. He had read a great deal and thought over what he had read. Jasper Tarkington found him at the outset an interesting, if not very genial, companion.

Then there was Philip, worshipped by his mother, adored by his father, handsome, a splendid dancer, an accomplished musician. Philip was very attractive; if there was gipsy blood in his veins it had given him nothing but physical beauty and the highly developed musical talent of that race. He had dark, curly hair, and large mellow eyes, fringed with long lashes that would have been a gift of the gods to a girl. Jasper at first sight pronounced him effeminate, but Rosemary-knowing what she did about him-would not allow this for a moment. How could a boy be called effeminate who staked his life time and again, every time he rode into Cluj with those newspaper articles of his in his pocket?

But this, of course, Jasper did not know.

CHAPTER XI

Elza Imrey talked very freely with Rosemary, and often referred to her husband having taken the oath of allegiance to the King of Roumania. It was all because of Philip. "What I am working for," she said, with the light almost of a fanatic in her eyes, "and what I shall work for so long as I have breath left in my body, is to save Philip's inheritance. The Roumanians are lying in wait for us, watching for an excuse to expel us from Transylvania. Many have had to go. Nothing would induce them to be false to the oath that they had sworn to the anointed King of Hungary. So they had to go. Sometimes at twenty-four hours' notice, bag and baggage, turned out of the home their forbears had owned for hundreds of years. But I would not do that. I had to think of Philip. The Roumanian occupation is now an accomplished fact, and we are too helpless, too friendless, not to accept it. But we must be very careful. One false step and we are done. Imagine how I tremble every time Maurus lets himself go. You know how unguarded he always is in his speech."

Rosemary felt an actual physical pain in her heart when she thought of this devoted mother's brave struggle to guard her son's inheritance, and how little she guessed that Philip himself was jeopardizing his future and risking his life in a cause that she was proclaiming hopeless. Those rides to Cluj! The meeting with Anna Heves! The dispatch of those newspaper articles of his! And Government spies lurking everywhere!

But during meals all unpleasant subjects were vetoed. Rosemary would have none of them, and her wishes, as the honoured guest, were law in this hospitable house. These good people, with their mercurial temperament, had a wonderful gift of casting aside trouble and giving themselves over to the pleasures of the moment. And so at dinner in the evenings the gipsy band not yet driven forth out of the neighbouring village would discourse sweet music, the tender, sad Hungarian refrains that appeal to the stranger almost as much as they do to the native.

Rosemary, who was an exquisite dancer, longed to tread the measure of the csàrdàs, the Hungarian national dance, which begins with a dreamy, languorous slow movement, and then suddenly breaks into a wild, mad whirl, wherein the dancer's eyes glow with excitement, their cheeks burn like fire, and their breath comes and goes through quivering, parted lips. Surely the merriest, maddest, most intoxicating dance devised by a passionate people-probably for the letting off of some inward steam that must find vent in such rapturous movements from time, or it would consume them with its glow.

"I think Lady Tarkington is quite splendid," Maurus Imrey said to Jasper, in the intervals of beating time with hand and foot to the ever-quickening measure of the dance. "Hey, you confounded gipsy!" he cried, shouting to the swarthy, perspiring leader of the band. "Quicker! Quicker! Can't you hear me speak? Do you think you are playing a funeral march?"

"I think," Jasper put in, with his quiet smile, "if the musicians put on anymore speed, Rosemary for one will be crying 'Mercy!'"

But for the moment Rosemary showed no sign of crying any such thing. Her nimble feet had quickly caught the quaint, syncopated rhythm, and Philip was a magnificent teacher. Perhaps there was some truth in saying that he had inherited a strain of gipsy blood, for indeed when he danced the csàrdàs there was something barbaric about his movements. They were full of grace and perfect in rhythm, but all the time they gave the impression of wild roamings through desert lands, of a will that brooked to fetters and was a law unto itself. Rosemary gave herself wholly to the pleasure of being whirled round, turned and twisted, sometimes lifted off her feet. All intellectuality fell away from her for the time being: she was just like a young and beautiful animal in enjoyment of the senses kind Nature had given her, the sound of that intoxicating music, the feeling of unfettered movement, the scent of dying roses in huge vases, that sent their sweet indefinable fragrance through the heat-laden air.

Faster, ever faster! Little hoarse cries escaped her throat as Philip seized her with one arm round the waist, and, lifting her off her feet, twirled her round and round till the golden lights of the shaded candles swam like the trail of comets before her eyes.

Faster! Always faster! She could hardly see now out of her eyes; all that she saw was Philip's dark, curly hair waving around his forehead.

The music seemed now a part of the universe, not played by one band of musicians, but the very atmosphere itself vibrating and resounding, forcing her to tread the measure and not to leave off, to go on-and on-and on-always hearing the music-always lifted off her feet and whirled round and round--

Then suddenly everything ceased all at once. The music, the movement, everything. Rosemary would have fallen, giddy, dazed, but for the fact that Jasper, quick as lightening, had caught her in his arms. Her instinct was to laugh.

"What happened?" she asked, rather wildly.

Then only did she look about her. First she saw Jasper's face bending over her, but he was not looking at her: he was gazing straight across the room. Rosemary's eyes followed his gaze. And all at once she gave a gasp, which she smothered instantly by clapping her hand to her mouth. The whole aspect of the room had changed. The gipsies seemed to have shrunk into a dark corner, with their instruments tucked hastily under their arms; they seemed to be trying to make themselves invisible. Two of them had crawled under the piano; only their feet, in shabby, down-at-heel shoes, protruded under the folds of rich brocade that covered the instrument.

And in the centre of the room there was a group of men, some half-dozen, in the uniform of the Roumanian army. One of them had his hand on Philip's shoulder. Philip stood in the midst of them; his dark face was still flushed with the dance, his curly hair clung to his streaming forehead. He was still panting with the movement and excitement of a moment ago, and his eyes, dark and glowing, wandered ceaselessly from one soldier's face to another.

Under the lintel of the great double doors that gave on the hall a couple of men servants stood, scared.

Rosemary's ears were buzzing and she saw everything through a veil; the room had not yet quite ceased whirling about her, but through the din in her ears and the hammering in her head she heard the ominous words: "Resistance will do you no good. You had best come quietly." They were spoken in Roumanian, which Rosemary understood.

Then there came a cry like that of a wounded beast, and Maurus Imrey jumped to his feet. With head down he charged into the soldiers just like an infuriated bull. Of course, he was seized at once, dragged back, forced down into a chair, where, with arms gripped by the soldiers, he launched forth a torrent of invective and abuse, and now and then, when he succeeded in freeing one of his arms, he hit out to right and left with his fist.

One of the soldiers, who appeared to be in command, spoke to him with cold deliberation:

"You are behaving like a fool, M. le Comte," he said. "For let me tell you that if you interfere with my men in the execution of their duty I will take you along, too."

Maurus's answer to this sound piece of advice was a fresh torrent of vituperation. He shook himself free from the hands that held him down, raised a menacing fist, and cried hoarsely:

"If you dare to touch me, you miserable--"

But suddenly stronger arms than those of the soldiers were thrown around him and forced him back into the chair. They were his wife's arms. Elza Imrey throughout all this had thought of nothing but the danger to Philip. The humiliation of this descent upon her house, the insolent attitude of the soldiers, this bringing home the fact of alien occupation and alien government, hardly affected her. Her one thought was Philip. The danger to Philip doubled and trebled by his father's ungoverned temper. And, my God, if he should strike one of the soldiers! So she held Maurus down, held her hand across his mouth; and Rosemary could hear her whispering in a thick, choked voice:

"Maurus, in God's name! Maurus, keep quiet! Maurus, for Philip's sake, hold your tongue!"

He struggled desperately, but she held him as only a mother can hold that which threatens her child. The soldier looked on with a sardonic smile. When Maurus at last was forced into silence, he shrugged his shoulders and said dryly:

"You are very wise, madame, to keep M. le Comte's temper in check for him. My orders are that if any resistance is offered to take all three of you along. I need not tell you that after that you two will be sent packing out of the country, and your son--"

A cry from Elza broke into his complacent speech. At once she became humble, cringing, all the pride of the aristocrat was submerged in the devastating anxiety of the mother. She still held Maurus down, for she dared not loosen her hold on him, but she turned a tear-stained face, pathetic-looking in its expression of appeal, toward the Roumanian.

"You must not take any notice of his lordship, captain," she said, trying in vain to speak lightly and to steady her voice. "You-you have known him for years, haven't you? You remember-he was always a little excitable-you used to amuse yourselves-you and your brother officers-by making him angry with one of the peasants, and seeing the men's terror of him? You remember," she reiterated, with the same pathetic effort at conciliation, "when we were at Tusnàd and you were in garrison at Sinaia, you used to motor over for luncheons and balls and--"

"It is not a part of a soldier's duty, madame," the young soldier broke in curtly, "to remember such incidents. If M. le Comte will cease to insult my men, we will leave him in peace. Otherwise you both come with me."

He turned sharply on his heel and spoke with one of his men. Apparently he was willing to give Maurus Imrey time to make up his mind what he would do. Rosemary still could hear Elza's voice thick and hoarse with anxiety:

"Maurus, in the name of Heaven--" The same refrain, the same reiterated prayer for submission, the one thing that would help to make Philip's lot easier. They could not do anything to Philip, of course. What had the poor lad done? Nothing. The mother racked her brain, thinking, thinking what he had done. Nothing. He had taken the oath of allegiance to the new King. Next year he would do his military service, a perfect hell; but Philip had never grumbled. And he had never joined in with those senseless political groups who met at night in out-of-the-way places about Cluj and dreamed dreams of freeing Hungary one day, Philip had never done anything so foolish. This cloud, therefore, would blow over. It was all a mistake, a misunderstanding. With silence and submission it would all blow over.

But Philip all along had never said a word. The first inkling that he had of this sudden danger that threatened him was the grip of a heavy hand upon his shoulder. Breathless with the dance, he had not made a movement or uttered a word of protest. His great, dark gipsy eyes wandered defiantly from the captain's face to those of the men, but he asked no questions. He knew well enough what had happened.

Two days ago he had ridden over to Cluj with certain newspaper articles in his pocket. He had given them to Anna. Together the cousins had spent one of those happy days which seemed to compensate them for all the risks they ran. Well, he had been suspected, spied upon and followed. The strain of fatalism which ran through his veins with the gipsy blood of his forbear bade him to accept the inevitable. Slowly his dark face became composed, his lips ceased to twitch, and the roaming glance of his dark eyes became fixed. Rosemary, looking up, saw the glance fixed upon her. In it she read the word: "Anna!" Philip was pleading to her mutely, desperately, for Anna. And this intuition which came to her when she met Philip's glance gave her the power to shake off the torpor that had invaded her limbs when the dance ceased so suddenly and she had fallen backwards into Jasper's arms.

Like Philip himself, she saw what had happened. The spies, the ride to Cluj, the articles given to Anna. And now the arrest of Philip and the deadly peril that threatened the girl.

"Can we do anything?" she whispered hurriedly to Jasper, and with quick, nervy movements she patted her hair into place and readjusted her tumbled gown.

Jasper shook his head. "We should do no good by interfering," he said gravely.

But Rosemary was in no mood to listen. She remembered Naniescu and his promises, the powers he had given her, the request that she should speak the truth. She felt that she was a force to be conciliated, and here was the moment to test her own power.

Without another word she ran out of the room and then through the great hall to the outer vestibule, where stood the telephone. While she took down the receiver and hurriedly gave the number of the Imrey palace at Cluj, she prayed in her heart that a few minutes' respite would be granted her before the soldiers marched Philip away.

"Hallo! Hallo! His Excellency General Naniescu! Lady Tarkington wishes to speak with his Excellency at once!! Say it is urgent-most urgent. Yes, Lady Tarkington, the English lady at Kis-Imre. No, no, never mind the name, please. Just say the English lady from Kis-Imre."

Another moment or two of agonizing suspense, then Naniescu's mellow voice. Thank God! He was at home, and she was through to him.

"General Naniescu? Lady Tarkington speaking! Thank you, I am well-very well, yes, my first article goes early next week. Yes, quite happy so far. General Naniescu, Philip Imrey has been summarily arrested. . . . I don't know. . . . There's a captain in charge. No, he did not say. . . . Yes, I am sure it is a mistake, but the mistake may prove fatal unless---Yes, yes! You will? Really? To-morrow morning? You are kind. I hardly liked to ask you. Of course, I shall be here. Will you speak to the captain yourself now? I thank you with all my heart. Will you hold the line? I'll send the captain to you. I don't know how to thank you. No, nothing else to-night; but I am looking forward to thanking you myself to-morrow morning. About ten o'clock. Yes! Thank you a thousand times. Good night!"

She had hardly finished speaking when she heard the tramping of feet coming from the drawing-room and then across the hall, and glancing round, she saw the soldiers filing out two by two, with their captain beside them and Philip in their midst. There was no other sound except this tramping of feet. No protests, no shrieks. Philip in the midst of the soldiers, and behind them Elza creeping along, silent, watchful, her great eyes fixed upon what she could see of her son-the dark, curly hair and sometimes the top of his shoulder.

Rosemary waited until the captain was quite close to her. He saluted and was about to pass, when, like a triumphant goddess, she turned and faced him.

"His Excellency the Governor, on the telephone." she said curtly, and held the receiver out to the young soldier. "He desires to speak with you."

The Roumanian, obviously very much taken aback, looked at her for a moment or two, frowning before he took the receiver from her. The group of soldiers had halted, waiting for further orders. Behind them Elza hovered, her white face and golden hair alone visible in the gloom.

After that instant's hesitation the captain put the receiver to his ear.

"Yes, Excellency. No, Excellency. Yes, Excellency." Then a long, long wait, while the captain stood with the receiver against her ear, and Elza came nearer, watching, hoping, mutely questioning; and Rosemary, with glowing eyes and an enigmatic smile, put a finger up to her lips. Finally: "I quite understand, Excellency. Quite! Absolutely!" And the captain hung up the receiver.

Then he turned to Elza, who had drawn close to Rosemary, quite close; he clicked his heels together and touched his képi with his right hand.

"By order of his Excellency General Naniescu," he said, "Count Philip Imrey is free to remain under this roof. He will give his word of honour that he will not attempt to leave the castle until after the arrival of his Excellency in the course of the morning."

And thus the incident was closed. Philip gave the required parole, and with more clicking of heels and salutes the young captain marched out of the house, followed by his men. Then only did Elza break down, when she put her arms round Philip's shoulders and sobbed her heart out against his breast. He appeared more dazed than relieved, and kept his eyes fixed on Rosemary, whilst with his long, thin hand he stroked and patted his mother's hair. Rosemary gave him an encouraging glance. "It was for Anna's sake," her glance said mutely. "In any case, Anna will be safe."

And the incident being closed, she went back to the drawing-room. Jasper held out a hand to her, and when she placed her hand in his he raised it to his lips. She took it as a sign of his approval, and bending down, she gave him her forehead to kiss. He just took her face between his two palms and gazed long and intently into her eyes.

He had often done that before; he loved to take hold of her face, to feel the soft velvety cheeks against his hands, and Rosemary would turn her pixie eyes to his and in one glance express all the affection, the sincere regard and fervent gratitude which she felt for him. But somehow this time it all seemed different, more intense, almost terrifying. To a sensitive woman a man's passion, if she cannot respond to it, is always terrifying; and of course, Rosemary's nerves were stretched now almost to breaking point. Else why should she be conscious of a sense of fear?

Jasper's gaze was not so much searching her soul as striving to reveal his. Something in him seemed imprisoned, and he was asking her to set that something free. A force, a power, greater even than his love, so great that love itself became its slave. And this Rosemary could not understand. She had experienced something of the same sensation that afternoon in London when he had asked her to marry him before she left for Hungary. Then, as now, she had caught a glimpse of a whirlpool of passion which seethed beneath her husband's grave, gentle manner. Then, as now, it had seemed to her as if he were trying to exert some supernatural power outside himself, to rouse an echo of his own passion in her heart. And with that glimpse into the depths of a man's soul came the knowledge that never would it be in her power to give soul for soul or passion for passion. And yet the day would come-she felt it, knew it at this moment-when the man, wearied of sentimental doles, would demand her whole surrender-body, brain, soul, everything, soul above all-which she would not be prepared to give.

Strange that this realization, this vague feeling akin to fear, should come to her again at this moment, when both she and Jasper were only minor actors in the drama that had just drawn to its close. Like most great moments in the inner life of the soul, it only lasted for one brief flash. It left its indelible mark on Rosemary's memory, but it lasted less than one second. The very next she tried to recapture it, but it was gone. Jasper looked grave and kind, as he always did, busy now with getting her comfortably ensconced in a capacious arm-chair, with plenty of cushions behind her back. Elza came in with Philip, and

Maurus roused himself from his apathy to hurl invectives against those damnable, impudent Roumanians.

And the gipsy musicians, reassured, crawled out of their hiding-places, and their leader, shouldering his violin, began to play a dreamy melody. One by one the others fell in in harmony, the 'cello, the bass, the clarinet, and the inimitable czimbalom. "There is but one beautiful girl in all the world" was the tune that they played; its soft, languorous cadence rose and fell in the air wherein the dying roses once more sent up their voluptuous fragrance. Forgotten was the danger just past, the peril still ahead. Music, the never-failing expression of emotion in these romantic people, soothed their nerves and uttered the words which would not rise to their lips. Elza sat with Philip's hand in hers. Rose-mary, with eyes fixed far away, caught herself gazing on the memory picture of a dark recess in a box in the Albert Hall, with the noise and whirl of a big social function about her, but with the complete isolation there in the darkness; and through the deafening noise memory conjured up a man's voice that murmured with passionate earnestness: "It is no use, my dear, thinking that all is over."

CHAPTER XII

The morning was as clear as crystal, the sky of a translucent turquoise blue. Away on the right the masses of soft-toned purple hills stretched their undulating lines like waving veils, hiding the mysteries of the horizon.

Rosemary had thrown open the windows of her bedroom and stepped out upon the balcony. With arms outstretched she drank in the intoxicating air, laden with the scent of heliotrope and lilies. She had the delicious feeling of having accomplished something, of having tested her power and found it absolute. Naniescu, on the telephone, had been almost apologetic when she told him about Philip's arrest. He declared that there was some mistake, and that he himself would come over in the morning and inquire into the matter. Rosemary was young enough to feel a naïve pleasure in her work. That Philip Imrey was restored then and there to his mother's arms was her work, the outcome of her position in the journalistic and political world. And the knowledge that this was so was as intoxicating as the fragrant air on this perfect late July morning.

A moment or two later she heard the pleasant noise of the rattling coffee-cups in the room behind her. She turned in, ready to embrace the little housemaid who looked after her so cheerfully. In fact, Rosemary was in a mood to embrace the whole world. Contrary to her usual happy way, however, the little housemaid did not look up when Rosemary came in. As a rule she would run and kiss the gracious lady's hand, according to the pretty custom of her country. To-day she just rattled the coffee-cups, and Rosemary noticed that her hands were shaking and that she turned her head very obviously away.

"What is it, Rosa?" Rosemary asked in her best Hungarian, of which she had learned quite a good deal at different times. "Why don't you come and say good morning?"

The kind voice and the necessity to respond to the gracious lady's inquiry broke down the barrier of Rosa's self-control. She raised her apron to her eyes and burst into a flood of tears. The next moment Rosemary was by her side, her arms round the girl's shoulders.

"Rosa!" she said, "Rosa! what is it? Tell me, little thing. What is it? Who has made you cry?"

But Rosa only went on sobbing, and murmuring between her sobs: "Oh, gracious lady! gracious lady! What a calamity! What a dreadful calamity!"

After a few seconds of this Rosemary began to lose patience. She was English and practical; Rosa's continued sobbing and incoherent mutterings got on her nerves. She gave the girl a good-humoured shake.

"What calamity, Rosa?" she queried. "Bless the girl! I'll smack you, Rosa, if you don't speak."

Now this was a language that Rosa understood far better than a string of kindly inquiries. She had been smacked by her mother, almost as soon as she was born, she had been smacked by her elder sister, by her grandmother, by her aunt and by her father while she grew up, and when she started service in the chateau and was silly or tiresome she had been smacked by the gracious Countess. Being smacked did not hurt, but it acted as a tonic, and braced up Rosa's slackened nerves. The threat of it by the gracious English lady at once dried the well of her tears, she wiped her nose and eyes with her apron and murmured:

"The gracious Count Philip-they have taken him away."

At first Rosemary did not take it in. She did not trust her ears, or her knowledge of Hungarian. She must, she thought, have misunderstood Rosa, or else Rosa was talking like a fool But Rosemary's grasp tightened on the girl's arm, her fingers buried themselves in the young, firm flesh.

"What do you mean, Rosa?" she queried. "What do you mean about the gracious count? Who has taken him away?"

"The soldiers, gracious lady," Rosa murmured.

"What soldiers?" which was a foolish question on Rosemary's part- and she knew it. There were no soldiers now in Transylvania except the Roumanian soldiers. But somehow the thing would not penetrate into her brain-she felt that, too, and wanted to give it time to sink in slowly, slowly.

Rosa now ventured to look the English lady in the face. Her big, blue eyes were still swimming in tears.

"The Roumanian soldiers, gracious lady," she said, "the ones who came last night."

"But they went away again last night, Rosa," Rosemary explained deliberately and patiently, "they went away and the gracious Count Philip remained at home, he went to bed as we all did. Anton must have waited on him, as he always does."

But Rosa gave a deep sigh and gulped down a fresh flood of tears that threatened to choke her.

"Anton did wait on the gracious count when he went to bed. But soon after midnight the soldiers returned. Feri the night watchman at the gate, had to let them in. They ordered him not to make a noise, only to rouse the gracious count's valet. So Feri went to call Anton, as quietly as he could, for the soldiers kept threatening him that if he made a noise they would beat him. Poor Anton nearly fainted with terror-you know, gracious lady, Anton always was a coward. What would you?" Rosa added with a shrug. "A gipsy."

"Yes! Yes!" Rosemary urged impatiently. "Go on, girl, go on."

"The soldiers would not even allow Anton to dress himself. Just as he was he had to go and rouse the gracious Count Philip. The soldiers were threatening to burn the house down if anyone made a noise, but I am sure that Feri and Anton were too scared to think of screaming. The gracious count jumped out of bed: the soldiers stood by while he dressed, but they would not allow him to take anything with him except just the clothes he put on-no money-not his watch-not a letter-nothing. Feri says that the soldiers were in the house and out again in less than a quarter of an hour. They took the gracious count with them, but four of them remained behind; they made Feri and Anton sit together in the lodge and kept guard over them until an hour ago. Then they went away and Anton ran in with the news. Oh! you should have seen the gracious countess! It was pitiable-pitiable, though she said nothing and she did not cry. By God! My God! What is to become of us all?"

The girl started wringing her hands, and her voice became loud and shrill with the sobs that would no longer be suppressed.

"Be quiet, Rosa, be quiet!" Rosemary said once or twice quite mechanically. She had taken it all in at last: the trick, the awful treachery, the cruelty of it all. She stood there beside the sobbing girl, with hands tightly clenched and a deep frown between her brows. She wanted to think. To think. Something would have to be done, and done quickly. But what? Naniescu? What role did he play in this mean trickery? Rosemary was a woman who thought straight and acted straight: so consistently straight, in fact, that she never could visualize treachery in others. In the wide, wide would that attitude of mind is called the attitude of a fool. Yet Rosemary Tarkington was anything but a fool. Per-Perhaps she was lacking in the intuition of evil: certain it is that at this moment she would not allow herself to think that Naniescu was a party to the abominable deed. The young officer, perhaps, or the local commandant who might have a grudge against the Imreys. But Naniescu? No!

She sent the girl away; Rosa's round, pink face with the round, blue eyes and round-tipped nose was getting on her nerves. The girl was comical in her grief, and when Rosemary looked at her she felt an uncontrollable desire to laugh. And this would have horrified Rosa. So she sent Rosa away.

A moment or two later Jasper came in, ready for breakfast. Once glance at this face and Rosemary knew that he, too, had heard the news.

"What do you think of it?" Rosemary asked after she had given him a morning kiss.

"My darling," Jasper replied in his cool, British manner, "I only think that you are making a grave mistake in throwing yourself headlong into the politics of these out-of-the-way countries. . . ."

"It is not a question of politics, Jasper," Rosemary broke in, protesting.

"I know, my dear, I know. Your warm heart prompts you to interfere there where prudence would dictate the wiser course of closing one's eyes. You would not be the adorable woman that you are if you acted differently. But, believe me, my darling, it is not wise. You will only run your lovely head against a stone wall, and in the end do no good. You must let these people fight out their quarrels in their own way. They are not our kind; we don't understand them. My firm conviction is that you will only do harm by interference. Mind you, I haven't a doubt that young Imrey has done something stupid. They are a hot-headed lot, these Hungarians, especially the young ones, and, of course, they don't like the present regime. The government in power has a perfect right to protect itself against conspiracy and rebellion, even though we outsiders may think that those conspiracies are futile, and the measures of repression unduly harsh. Leave them alone, my dear," Jasper concluded more lightly, with a shrug, "and have a cup of hot coffee."

He settled himself down on the sofa and tried to draw her down to him. But Rosemary was not in the mood for sentiment. Reason whispered to her that Jasper was right-he was always right, worse luck!-she knew that Philip Imrey had acted foolishly-very, very foolishly-and that, as a matter of fact, in this case the commandant (or whoever was responsible for Philip's arrest) was entirely within his rights. She certainly, as an impartial spectator of events, brought here for the express purpose of seeing the truth and nothing but the truth, could not in conscience make capital of this incident. She had come out here determined not to act on impulse, but to judge coolly and without bias, and thus to consolidate her reputation as one of the foremost women journalists of the day. With Sir Philip Gibbs as her master, and model, she could not go back on the ideal of justice and impartiality which she had set herself. But she did want to save Philip Imrey from the consequences of his own folly. And, above all, she wanted to know what had become of Anna.

"I cannot leave them alone, Jasper," she said slowly "I cannot. All this petty tyranny makes my blood boil."

Jasper sighed somewhat impatiently. "I know, my dear, I know," he reiterated vaguely.

Rosemary did not continue the discussion for the moment; Jasper was so right in everything he said, and Philip Imrey had been desperately foolish. Now she blamed herself for not having worked on Anna's mind and dissuaded her from lending herself to her cousin's mad schemes. She mentioned Anna's name to her husband, but Jasper, knowing nothing of the girl's dangerous activities in Balog's grocery stores, could not, of course, see that Anna was in any kind of danger.

"But," Rosemary argued, "Anna and Philip are first cousins, they see a great deal of one another--"

"Do they?" Jasper ejaculated. "But even so, my dear, you surely are not going to suppose that the Roumanian Government is going to lay hands on all Philip Imrey's relations, just because he has run his silly head into a noose."

"No! No!?" Rosemary protested vaguely.

But she could not say anything more on the subject of Anna. Anna had told her everything in confidence: "I know I can trust you, Rosemary," the child had said, and Rosemary could not betray that confidence-not even by speaking of it all to Jasper-not even by hinting at it. If the peril became more imminent-if Anna herself was in danger-then perhaps. But not now.

Rosemary tried to swallow some breakfast, just to please Jasper, for his kind, grave eyes looked quite sad, and she did not want to add to his anxiety. But her thoughts were dwelling on Elza.

66

"I wonder if she could bear to see me," she said presently.

"You can always ask," was Jasper's wise suggestion.

Rosemary found Elza Imrey outwardly quite calm and resigned. That woman had a marvellous fund of common sense and self-control. What she suffered no one should know. Only when she read true understanding and mute sympathy in Rosemary's eyes, she gave an answering look which contained such a depth of sorrow and anxiety that Rosemary's heart was overwhelmed with pity. In these few hours Elza had aged twenty years. Anton had brought the news across from the lodge to the chateau in the early morning as soon as the Roumanian soldiers had gone away. The gracious countess had received the news with extraordinary indifference, was the verdict on the incident below stairs; Rosa was crying her eyes out, all the men-servants went about cursing and swearing and threatening to kill someone, but the gracious countess had not shed one tear. When she had heard Anton's report, she asked a few questions: what suit had the gracious count put on? did he take an overcoat? what shoes did he wear? and so on; but never a tear. Then she said: "Very well, Anton, you may go!" and that was all. No! No! It was not natural. But then these great ladies! . . . One never knew!

No one ever did know to what height a mother's heroism could go. Elza, with her heart nearly broken, thought only of what was best for Philip.

"Of course, he has done nothing!" she reiterated over and over again, "so they can't do anything to him."

Then her voice would break on a note of pathetic appeal; she would seize Rosemary's hands and search the depths of her English friend's eyes, with the look of a poor stricken animal begging for sympathy.

"Can they?" she asked, and Rosemary would shake her head, not trusting herself to speak. It was no use now rending the mother's heart, adding another load of anxiety to the heavily burdened soul. Elza would know soon enough. Soon enough! And she could do nothing even if she knew now.

Maurus was shut up in his own apartments, tearing up and down like a beast in its cage, raging and swearing. That was his temperament, Elza said philosophically, with a shrug; the Armenian blood in him. (She never would admit the gipsy strain.) Fortunately the servants were all Hungarian; faithful and discreet. They knew him. When he was in one of those moods they fled from him; but not one of them would betray him. Now he was threatening to kill every Roumanian that ever crossed his path. Well, fortunately there was no one to hear him-only the servants, and they would hold their tongues.

"Maurus won't understand," Elza explained to Rosemary, "that our chance is submission. If they turn us out of here it will be the end of Philip's inheritance. We must save that at all costs. What is the sacrifice of a little pride when it means so much for Philip's future. Things can't go on as they are-not for long, and if only I can keep Maurus quiet, we shall have Philip back here in a week."

Then she harked back on the old refrain. "He has done nothing. They can't do anything to him. Can they?"

CHAPTER XIII

Naniescu arrived soon after ten-o'clock. Rosemary heard the hooting of his motor when it turned in at the gate, also the general bustle, clatter, running about that ensued. Her rooms, with the balcony overlooking the park, were on the other side of the house, so she saw nothing of this; but somehow, after the arrival of his Excellency, the stately chateau appeared to have lost something of its dignified quietude. Loud voices resounded from end to end of the galleried hall, footsteps that sounded almost aggressive echoed along the corridors.

Jasper had gone down some time ago for a stroll in the park, while Rosemary dressed. She was sorry now that she had not asked him to be sure to come back so as to support her in her interview with Naniescu. However, this wish was only a momentary weakness. She had been accustomed for years past to stand on her own feet, to act for herself, and to take swift decisions without outside advice. So now, with a careless shrug, she turned back to the important task of dressing; this she did with deliberate care, then surveyed herself critically in the glass, and, having satisfied herself that Rosemary Tarkington was in no way less beautiful than Rosemary Fowkes had been, she settled herself down in her boudoir with a book and waited.

A very few minutes later one of the men came to announce that his Excellency General Naniescu desired to pay his respects to Lady Tarkington.

He came in looking breezy and gallant. He kissed Rosemary's hand, sat down on the chair she indicated to him, inquired after the state of her health, her journey, her work, all in a mellifluous voice and in execrable English. In fact, for the first five minutes of this momentous, visit he was just a pleasant, cheerful man of the world, exchanging banalities with a pretty woman.

"Et ce cher Tarkington?" he queried. "How is he?"

"My husband will be in, in a moment or two," Rosemary replied, trying to bring the conversation round to the all-important subject. "He will, of course, make a point of not failing to see you." She made a slight, insignificant pause, then she went on more seriously: "I can assure you, M. le General, that Lord Tarkington's interest in our dear host and hostess is just as keen as mine."

"Of course, of course," Naniescu rejoined vaguely, with a sweep of his well-manicured hand. "They are very foolish people, these Imreys. And that young man! Dear lady, you have not an idea what trouble we have with these Hungarians! They are all a little toqué! What you call so admirably in your picturesque language: they have a bee in their bonnet. What?"

He laughed, very pleased with himself for what he apparently considered a little joke.

"A bee in their bonnet," he reiterated, still waving his white, podgy hands about. He set his teeth together and made a sound to represent the buzzing of bees. "Buzz-z! Just like that! But bees," he added curtly, "are apt to be tiresome. Is it not so?"

"You choose to look upon the matter lightly, M. le General," Rosemary rejoined, with a touch of impatience, "but to these unfortunate people the summary arrest of their only son is anything but a light matter. On the telephone last night--"

"Oh, the telephone!" the general broke in with an affected sigh. "A marvellous invention! What? But it is difficult on the telephone to give those little nuances which are the essence of conversation. It was wonderful to hear your melodious voice on the telephone last evening. I was not expecting to hear it, and it was delightful! Like a spirit voice coming from a place unseen to soothe me to pleasant dreams."

He tried to capture her hand, and when she snatched it away with obvious irritation he gave a soft, guttural laugh and gazed with a look of bold admiration into her eyes. Rosemary felt her temper rising, and nothing but her knowledge that this distinctly unpleasant personage had supreme power over those she cared for kept her impatience in check.

"General Naniescu," she said, quietly determined, "you must forgive me if I cannot enter into your playful mood just now. The only son of my very dear friend is under arrest for an offence of which he knows nothing, and, moreover, he was arrested under circumstances that are entirely unjustifiable, seeing that this country is not, I presume, under martial law."

"Not under martial law, certainly, dear lady," Naniescu was willing to admit, and did so with a certain measure of seriousness, "but under strict disciplinary law, framed by a suzerain state for the protection of its own nationals in occupied territory. But let that pass. You graciously informed me over the telephone last night that young Imrey was arrested, and I gave orders to the captain in charge for his immediate release. As I intended to come over here in the course of the morning, I was willing to let the matter stand until I had investigated it myself."

"Count Philip Imrey was released at ten o'clock yesterday evening, and rearrested in the middle of the night; he was not even given the chance of saying goodbye to his parents, or of providing himself with the necessary clothing and money. I imagine, M. le General," Rosemary went on coldly, "that this was done by your orders, or at any rate that you were not kept in ignorance of it."

For the fraction of a second Naniescu hesitated; then he said cynically:

"Yes; certainly I knew of it. I may even say that it was done by my orders."

Rosemary suppressed a cry of indignation.

"Well, then?" she exclaimed hotly.

But Naniescu, not in the least taken aback, only retorted blandly:

"And how am I to interpret that enigmatic query, dear lady?"

"As a challenge to justify your actions," was Rosemary's bold reply.

Then, as he gave no immediate answer but allowed his mellow dark eyes to rest with a distinctly mocking glance on her face, Rosemary felt at a disadvantage. She was obviously not in a position to demand explanations from a man who belonged to the governing classes in his own country. With every belief in the power of the press, Rosemary had far too much common sense not to realize that a man in Naniescu's position would not put up with being dictated to, or cross-examined, by a stranger, however influential he or she might be. So once again she swallowed her resentment, determined that whatever chance she had of helping the Imreys should not be wrecked through want of tact on her part. Diplomacy, good temper, and, if necessary, seeming complaisance, would be more likely to win the day than any attempt at threatening.

"Monsieur le General," she resumed, after a while, "I know that you will forgive me for my seeming ill-humour. I have witnessed so much sorrow these last few hours that I suppose my nerves are rather jarred. I know, of course, that it is not my place to criticize the measure which your Government chooses to impose on a subject race. As a suzerain state Roumania has a perfect right to defend what she believes to be her own interests, and in a manner that she thinks best. Will you forgive me the sharp words I allowed to slip just now?"

And with a return of that charm of manner which even more than beauty held most men in thrall, Rosemary put out her hand. The gallant Roumanian, without a trace of mockery now in his large, dark eyes, took it in both his own; then he stooped and kissed the dainty finger-tips.

"And now," Rosemary went on resolutely, "that I have made amende honorable, will you allow me to plead the Imrey's cause in all earnestness-in the name of humanity, Monsieur le General? The boy is only nineteen."

The general leaned back in his chair, his well-manicured fingers gently stroking his silky moustache, his eyes no longer attempting to conceal the satisfaction which he felt at seeing this exquisitely beautiful woman in the role of a suppliant before him. Now when she paused he gave an indifferent shrug.

"Dear lady," he said, "my experience of this part of the world is that boys and girls of nineteen who give up jazzing and have not started making love, but who choose to meddle in politics, are veritable pests."

"But Philip Imrey does not meddle in politics," Rosemary protested.

"Are you quite sure of that?" he retorted.

As he said this his eyes became quite small, and piercing like two little flaming darts; but though his sudden challenge had sent a stab of apprehension through Rosemary's heart, her glance never faltered, and she lied straight out, lied boldly without hesitation, without a blush.

"I am quite sure," she replied.

And the only compunction she felt over that lie was when she realized-as she did at once-that the Roumanian did not believe her.

"Little Anna Heves did not confide in you?" he asked, with perfect suavity.

"What do you mean?"

"Just what I said, dear lady. Anna Heves and Philip Imrey are two young hotheads who have given us an infinity of trouble. For a long time we could not find out how certain pernicious articles, injurious to the good reputation of Roumanian, found their way into the English and American press. Now we know."

"Your spy system seems more efficient than your censorship," Rosemary retorted bitterly.

"That is beside the point."

"Yes; the point is that those two are mere children."

"I dare say the judges will take that into account and deal leniently with them."

"With them?" Rosemary exclaimed, and suddenly a new terror gripped her heart. "With them? You don't mean--?"

"What, dear lady?" he queried suavely.

"That Anna--?"

"Anna Heves, yes; the late Baron Heves' daughter, now a saleswoman in the shop of Balog the grocer. I often wondered how she came to demean herself in that way. Now I understand."

"But surely, surely," Rosemary protested, striving in vain to steady her voice, which was quaking with this new, this terrible anxiety, "you have not arrested Anna Heves? The child has done nothing--"

Naniescu put up his hand with a gesture of protest.

"Dear lady," he said, with quiet irony and in a tone one would use to an obstinate child, "let me assure you once and for all that the accusations against Philip Imrey and his cousin do not rest upon assumptions, but upon facts. Anna Heves was arrested and she will be brought to trial because she was found-actually found, mind you-smuggling newspaper articles, defamatory to the Government of this country, for insertion in foreign journals. English sense of justice is reputed to be very keen; your own must tell you that it is hardly fair to bring the battery of your charms as a weapon to break down my sense of duty. I lay, as always, my homage at your feet, but I should be a traitor if, whilst gazing into your adorable eyes, I were to forget what I owe to my country."

Gradually he dropped the irony out of his tone, and his voice became once more mellifluous and tender while he leaned forward, almost touching Rosemary's knees with his, and striving to hold her glance with the challenge of his own. Rosemary shrank back. Suddenly something of the truth had dawned upon her. Not all of it just yet. It was only presently-in a few more days-that she was destined to realize the extent to which this man-half Oriental in his capacity for lying-had hoodwinked and cajoled her. It was his mien, the thinly veiled insult that lurked behind his suave speech and expressive eyes, that suddenly tore the veil from before her own. And yet reason fought for a moment against this wave of aversion. The man was right, unquestionably right. Philip and Anna had been very foolish. And, what is more, they were technically guilty of treason: there was no getting away from that; and Rosemary could not shut her eyes to the fact that the very lives of those she cared for were in the hands of this soft-toned liar. At one moment she longed passionately for Jasper, the next she would dread his coming, for she knew well enough that he, with his straight matter-of-fact mode of thinking, would inevitably give Naniescu his due, insist that the general was within his rights, and advise his wife to keep clear of these imbroglios, which were so contrary to the lenient, sportsmanlike English attitude toward a beaten enemy.

On the whole she felt glad that Jasper was not here. He would hate to see her plead. Yet plead she must. There was nothing else to do. She must plead with fervour, plead with all the strength that she possessed, all the eloquence that she could command.

"In the name of humanity!" That was her chief plea; and with anxious eyes she searched the man's face for the first trace of pity.

"Anna and Philip are so young," she urged. "Mere children."

But Naniescu smiled, that fat, complacent smile of his which she had quickly learned to loathe.

"You would not like me," she said at one moment, "to send an account of it to all the English and American papers. Two children, one under eighteen, the other not yet twenty, arrested in their beds at dead of night, brought to trial for having smuggled a few newspaper articles through the post. If you do not deal leniently with them--"

"Who said we would not deal leniently with them?" Naniescu broke in blandly. "Surely not I. I am not their judge."

"General Naniescu," she retorted, "I have been in Transylvania long enough to know that your powers here as military governor are supreme. Leniency in this case," she urged insistently, "could only redound to your credit, and to the credit of the country which you serve."

"But frankly, dear lady, I don't see what I can do. The case has passed out of my hands-"

"Send these children home with a caution, Monsieur le General," Rosemary went on pleading. "That is what we would do in England in a like case."

"To hatch more treason," he retorted, with a shrug. "Give us more trouble-more buzzing of bees and pestilential backbiting--"

"No!" she protested hotly. "Not for that, but to be immensely grateful to you for your generosity, and show their gratitude by striving to work for the good of their country, hand in hand with yours."

"Ah, what noble sentiments, dear lady!" General Naniescu said with a sigh, and clapped his white, fat hands together. "I wish I could believe that some of them will sink into those young hotheads."

"They will, general, they will." Rosemary asserted eagerly. "If you will send those two children back to their parents, I will not leave Transylvania until you yourself are satisfied that I have brought them to a reasonable frame of mind."

"A hard task, dear lady," Naniescu said, with a smile.

"I would undertake a harder one than that," Rosemary rejoined, with an answering smile, "to show my appreciation of your generosity."

"Words, dear lady," he said softly. "Words!"

"Try me!" she challenged.

He made no immediate reply, and suddenly his eyes again narrowed as they had done before, and their piercing glance rested upon Rosemary until she felt that through those heavy lids something inimical and poisonous had touched her. She felt a little shiver running down her spine, an unaccountable sense of apprehension caused her to glance rapidly toward the door, where she hoped to perceive Jasper's comforting presence. She was not afraid, of course, nor did she regret her enthusiasm, or her advocacy of the children's cause; but she had the sudden, vague feeling that she had come to the brink of an abyss and that she was staring down into unknown depths, into which unseen forces were urging her to leap.

Slowly Naniescu's eyes reopened and the mellow expression crept back into them; he gave a sigh of satisfaction, and settled himself down once more comfortably on the cushions of the chair.

"I am happy indeed, dear lady," he began, "that you yourself should have made an offer, which I hardly dared place before you."

"An offer? What do you mean?"

"Surely that was your intention, was it not, to do something in return for the heavy sacrifice you are asking of me?"

"Sacrifice?" Rosemary queried, frowning. "What sacrifice?"

"Sacrifice of my convictions. Duty calls me to very insistently in the matter of those young traitors whom you, dear lady, are pleased to refer to as children. I know that I should be doing wrong in giving them the chance of doing more mischief. I know it," he reiterated emphatically, "with as much certainty as I do the fact that they will not give up trying to do mischief. But-"

He paused and fell to studying with obvious satisfaction Rosemary's beautiful eager eyes fixed intently upon him.

"But what, Monsieur le General?" she asked.

"But I am prepared to make the sacrifice of my convictions at your bidding, if you, on the other hand, will do the same at mine."

Rosemary's frown deepened. "I don't think I quite understand," she said.

"No," he retorted; "but you will-soon. Let me explain. You, dear lady, have come to Transylvania wrapped in prejudice as in sheet-armour against my unfortunate country. Oh, yes, you have," he went on blandly, checking with an elegant gesture the cry of protest that had risen to Rosemary's lips. "I am even prepared to admit that nothing that you have seen in these first few days has tended to pierce that armour of prejudice. Well, well!" and the general sighed again in that affected way of his. "You have one of your wonderful sayings in England that exactly meets this case: 'East is East,' you say, 'and West is West.' This is the East really, and you Occidentals will never think as we do. But I am wandering from my point, and you, dear lady, are getting impatient. Having admitted everything that you would wish me to admit, I now will come forward with my little proposition-what?"

"If you please," Rosemary replied coldly.

"The children, as you are pleased to call them," Naniescu went on with slow deliberation, shedding his affected manner as a useless garment no longer required to conceal his thoughts, "the children have done us an infinity of mischief, in the eyes of the British and American public, by the publication of articles defamatory to our Government; for this they have deserved punishment. Now, I propose to remit that punishment if you will undo the mischief that they have done."

"I?" Rosemary exclaimed, puzzled. "How?"

"By publishing newspaper articles that will refute those calumnies once and for all," the general said blandly. Then, as Rosemary recoiled at the suggestion as if she had been struck in the face, he went on cynically: "You are such a brilliant journalist, dear lady, endowed with a vivid imagination. It will be easy for you to do this for the sake of those two young traitors in whom you take such a kindly interest. You may, in your articles, begin by stating the truth, if you like, and say that my Government invited you to come over to Transylvania in order to investigate the alleged acts of tyranny that are supposed to be perpetrated against the minority nationals. Then you will proceed to state that after impartial and exhaustive inquiry you have come to the conclusion that practically all the charges brought against us are unfounded, that with the exception of a few inevitable hardships consequent of foreign occupation, the minority nationals in Transylvania are enjoying the utmost freedom and security under the just laws of an enlightened country. You will-"

But here the flow of the worthy general's eloquence received a sudden check in the shape of a rippling outburst of laughter from Rosemary. He frowned; not understanding her mood, his knowledge of women being superficial, his thoughts flew to hysteria. He had known a woman once-

As a matter of fact there was something hysterical about Rosemary's laughter. She checked it as soon as she regained control over herself. It was as well that she could laugh, that her sense of humour, never absent in an Englishwoman of intellect, had at once shown her the folly of giving way to the indignation which had been her first impulse. Frankly she could not see herself as an outraged tragedy queen thundering forth an emphatic "Never!" to the Roumanian's impudent proposals; and when Naniescu marvelled at the strange moods of women and vainly tried to guess what there was in the present situation to make this pretty woman laugh, he little knew that Rosemary was laughing at an imaginary picture of herself, with head thrown back and flaming eyes, and gestures that rivalled those of the general himself in their elegant and expressive sweep.

"You must forgive me, Monsieur le General," she said presently, "but your proposition is so funny!"

"Funny, dear lady!" he protested. "Frankly I do not see-"

"No," she broke in, "you would not."

"Will you be so gracious as to explain?"

"No," Rosemary went on lightly, "I don't think I will. You would not understand-even then."

"Then," he said coolly, "there is nothing left for me to do but to take my leave, and to deplore that you should have wasted so much of your valuable time in conversation with a clod."

He rose, and bowing low, he put out his hand in order to take hers, but Rosemary did not move.

"You cannot go, Monsieur le General," she said firmly, "without giving me a definite answer."

"I have given you a definite answer, dear lady. It is my misfortune that you choose to treat it as ludicrous."

"But surely you were not serious when you suggested--"

"When I suggested that the mischief wrought by two traitors should be remedied by one who takes an interest in them? What could be more serious?"

"You seriously think," she insisted, "that I would lend myself to such traffic? that I would put my name to statements which I could not verify, or to others that I should actually believe to be false? Ah ça, Monsieur le General, where did you get your conception of English women of letters, or of English journalists?"

Naniescu put his finger-tips to his breast, then spread out his hands with a broad gesture of protest.

"I was wrong," he said suavely, "utterly wrong. I admit it. Forgive me, and permit me to take my leave--"

"Monsieur le General--"

"At your service, dear lady."

"Young Imrey," she pleaded, "and Anna Heves!"

He shrugged his shoulders.

"I am truly sorry for them," he said unctuously; "but surely you do not think seriously that I would lend myself to any traffic where the safety of my country is concerned. Ah ça, dear lady," he went on, not only mocking the very words she had used, but even the inflexion of her voice. "Where did you get your conception of a Roumanian officer or of a Roumanian gentleman?"

"It is you who proposed an infamous traffic," she retorted, "not I."

"Pardon me," he protested. "All that I suggested was that the mischief done should be remedied in the simplest way, before those who had wrought it could hope for pardon. The mischief was done through the public Press; it can only be made good through the public Press, and only through the medium of one as influential as yourself. My suggestion has not met with your approval. Let us say no more about it."

Before she could prevent it he had taken her hand and raised it to his lips. She snatched it away as if her finger-tips had come in contact with something noxious; the indignation which she had tried so hard to keep under control flamed for an instant out of her eyes; and Naniescu, seeing it, gave a soft, guttural laugh.

"I had a suspicion," he said cynically, "that the situation was not entirely ludicrous. And now," he went on, "have I your permission to take my leave?"

He bowed once more, hand on breast, heels clicking, and was on the point of turning to go when an impulsive cry from Rosemary brought him to a halt.

"That is not your last word, General Naniescu?"

"Indeed," he replied with utmost gallantry, "but the last word rests with you, dear lady. I am ever at your service. Only," he continued very slowly and very deliberately, "let me assure you once and for all that young Imrey and Anna Heves will appear before the military courts on a charge of treason unless a series of articles written in the spirit I have had the honour to outline before you, and bearing your distinguished name, appear in-shall we say The Times?-within the next month. But, just to show you how greatly I value your regard, I will be as lenient as my duty permits. I will even allow those two young traitors to return, temporarily, to their homes. Philip Imrey and Anna Heves will be brought here in the course of a day or two. They will be free, within certain limitations, to move about among their friends. I need not add, dear lady, that you, on the other hand, are ab-solutely free, without any limitations, to come and go as you choose. On the day that the last of your brilliant articles will have appeared in The Times Imrey and his cousin will receive a free pardon from the Government which they have outraged."

He paused a moment, then raised one hairy, manicured finger and added with theatrical emphasis:

"But not before."

Rosemary had listened to his long speech without moving a mus-cle. She stood straight as a sapling, looking unflinchingly at the man, striving to shame him, yet knowing that in this she would not succeed. There was no room for shame or compunction in that bundle of con-ceit and depravity.

Fear, too, appeared to be one of the tortuous motives which had suggested this ignominious "either-or." How far the Roumanian Gov-ernment was a party to the mishandling of Transylvania, Rosemary had not yet had the opportunity of ascertaining.

She strongly suspected Naniescu of having over-stretched his pow-ers, and of dreading an exposure at Bucharest more, perhaps, than in London or New York. Now, when he had finished speaking, and while his mellow eyes still rested with gentle mockery upon her, she could not keep back the final taunt which she hoped would sting him as much as his urbanity had stung her.

"What proof have I," she queried slowly, "that if I fulfil my share of the bargain you will not in the end repudiate yours?"

He smiled, quite undisturbed.

"You mistrust me. It is only natural," he said unctuously. "But what can I do?"

"Write me a letter," she replied coldly, "embodying your terms for the release of Philip Imrey and Anna Heves, and your promise to keep to the bargain if I accept those terms."

"Will that satisfy you?" he asked.

"It would hold you to your word, at any rate. For if it did not--"

He gave his soft, throaty laugh, and a glimmer of satisfaction shot through his eyes.

"You Englishwomen are truly marvellous," he observed. "So business-like. Everything in black and white-what?"

"Preferably," she rejoined drily.

"Well, then, you shall have the letter, dear lady," he concluded blandly. "And I promise you that I shall so tie myself down to my share of this interesting transaction that you will not hesitate any longer to fulfil yours."

And the next moment, even while Rosemary turned towards the window in order to look for one brief moment, at any rate, on something clean and pure, Naniescu had gone, softly closing the door behind him and leaving in his wake a faint odour of Havana cigar and eau de Cologne, and an atmosphere of intrigue which Rosemary felt to be stifling. She threw open the window and inhaled the clean air right down into her lungs. Her thoughts were still in a whirl. The situation was so impossible that her brain at present rejected it. It could not be. Things like this did not occur. It was not modern. Not twentieth century. Not post-war. Civilized men and women did not have interviews such as she had just had with this smooth-tongued Roumanian. There was something medieval about this "either-or," this impasse to which in very truth there was no issue.

Rosemary now started pacing up and down the room. She was alone and could indulge in this time-tried method of soothing jangled nerves. With both forefingers she tapped her temples, as if to stimulate the work of a jaded brain. Issue? There must be an issue to this impasse. She was a British subject, the wife of an English peer. She could not be bullied into doing things against which her sense of honour rebelled. She could not be made to lend her name to falsehoods, knowing them to be falsehoods. Of course not. Of course not. She could not be compelled. That was a fact. An undisputable, hard, solid fact. What then? Well, then there were Philip and Anna, who would be brought before the military courts on a charge of treason. And the military courts would condemn them-to what? To death? No! No! No! Not to death! Philip and little Anna: children whom she knew and loved! Condemned to death! Shot! like Edith Cavell, or Captain Fryatt! Shot! But that was in war time! Now the world was at peace! The Treaty of Versailles was the millennium that would bring peace on earth, goodwill toward men! Peace! This was peace! Foolish, thoughtless children could not in peace time be shot as traitors!

Tap-tap went Rosemary's fingers against her temples. Peace, ye gods! Philip and Anna had rendered themselves liable to human justice, and human justice in this half-forgotten corner of God's earth knew but one law-revenge! Philip and Anna would be condemned-and shot, unless she, Rosemary Tarkington, gained a free pardon for them at the price of truth, honour and the welfare, perhaps, of thousands of innocents.

And as gradually this awful alternative penetrated into the innermost recesses of her brain, the girl looked wildly about her like an animal suddenly fallen into a trap. Her knees all at once gave way under her, and she fell up against the sofa, with arms outspread upon the cushions. With head thrown back, she gazed unseeing up at the ceiling, and this time it was a real hysterical outburst that caused her to laugh and to laugh, until laughter broke into a sob, and burying her face in her hands she burst into a flood of tears.

CHAPTER XIV

Rosemary, being very human and very young, felt all the better after she had had a good cry. Better mentally, that is to say. Physically she was tired, hot, overstrained; her eyes ached, her limbs ached, her head ached, but mentally she felt better.

Presently she struggled back to her feet, dabbed her eyes with cold water, put powder on her nose and a comb through her hair. She did not want to look a sight when presently Jasper came back from his walk and she told him all that had happened.

By the way, where was Jasper?

Rosemary was just aching to review the whole situation with him. No need now for secrecy with regard to Philip and little Anna's foolish conspiracy. Soon the whole world would know of it, friend and foe alike. And Jasper would be able to help, of course, or at any rate to advise. He had done so much for the Roumanian Government in the past, there was just a chance they might do something at his request—out of gratitude.

Gratitude? Rosemary smiled ironically to herself at thought of connecting so gentle an emotion with men like Naniescu. Still, Jasper might think of something, of some way out of the situation, which Rosemary still persisted in thinking unreal. It was, of course, the climax of a plan formed as far back as the Five Arts' Ball at the Albert Hall, when Naniescu first proposed to her that she should come to Transylvania. To get her here, then to close on Philip and Anna a trap which had no doubt long ago been set, and finally to use them as a lever in order to force her, Rosemary, to write those articles which would sooth the vanity of Roumanian bureaucrats and throw dust in the eyes of the sentimental public.

As if in response to Rosemary's wish for his presence, Jasper presently walked in, courteous, chivalrous, full of apologies for having left her to face Naniescu alone.

"I must have been dreaming," he said contritely, "while I wandered out of the park, for, all of a sudden, I found myself away upon the mountain-side, thinking of you. Your dear face peeped at me through the trees, and then I realized that I was leaving you in the lurch, and that you might be wanting me-and I not there! Can you, I wonder, forgive me?"

He sat down beside her on the sofa and took her hand, and one by one he kissed each rosy finger-tip.

"Wherever I am, little one," he said softly, "I always see you. Your presence beside me this morning was so real that I was never wholly conscious that you were not actually there. Will you forgive me?" he asked again.

Rosemary turned to him with a smile. There was no one in the world quite so kind as Jasper; his kind, grave eyes were fixed on her with such a look of adoration that instinctively Rosemary nestled closer to him like a trusting child, and on an impulse she told him everything: the arrest of Philip Imrey and of little Anna, and Naniescu, and his mind appeared to wander, as if he were thinking of something else, and Rosemary harkened in vain for a word of indignation from him when she told him about Naniescu's abominable "either-or." Yet she studied his face very closely, those fine aristocratic features with their somewhat affected wearied expression, and the dark eyes set closely together like those of an eagle or a hawk. He said nothing. He only looked as if he were thinking hard. Pondering over something that puzzled and worried him. Rosemary wondered what it was. And later on, when she pressed him with questions, he seemed to drag himself back to the present situation with a great effort of nerve and will, and even then he did not appear to have a firm grasp of it. He put irrelevant counter-questions, and once or twice answered at random. His chief concern seemed to be that she, Rosemary, knowing the foolish game Philip and Anna were playing, had not succeeded in putting a stop to it.

"The girl appeared sensible enough," he said almost irritably. "I believe she would have listened to you. That sort of thing is just romantic nonsense. It never does any good, and more often than not it brings trouble on the innocent rather than on the guilty. The same thing applies to the Germans, the Austrians and to the Hungarians. They have been beaten and they have got to take their punishment. All these political intrigues are just folly!"

Of course Jasper was right. Of course he was sensible, and just and clear-thinking. But while Rosemary paid ungrudging tribute to his judgement, she felt more and more chilled by his total lack not only of sympathy but even of attention, as if the matter of Philip and Anna's life and liberty hardly interested him. Now Rosemary hardly liked to ask him for advice, for fear he might tell her to assent to Naniescu's wish-and to write those articles against which her sense of right and wrong, of truth and professional honour rebelled.

She could almost hear Jasper saying:

"You can get quite near the truth in your articles and satisfy Naniescu and you will save those two hotheads from the consequences of their own indiscretion. Believe me you would be doing far more good that way to this miserable country than Philip ever did with his ill-considered articles."

Perhaps Jasper had actually said all this. Rosemary could not be sure. For the last few minutes her mind had been absent from her body. It had flown over mountains and seas, right across the great plains of Hungary and the fields of waving corn, to a small, dark corner in the crowded Albert Hall, with noisy jazz music buzzing in the distance like phantom melodies, with laughter and chatter all around, glittering jewels, fantastic clothes and waving fans; and here Rosemary's mind came to a halt and insistently beckoned to memory. She recalled every moment of that night, every incident stood out like a picture before her now: the dance with Peter, and then the box with the heavy curtains that shut her right out of the world-alone with Peter. She recalled every line of his face, those fine white hands made to wield brush or pen rather than a cricket-ball, the fair, curly head, the tense dark eyes.

What sympathy she would have got from Peter if only he were here! His judgement, perhaps, would not have been so sound as Jasper's: Rosemary would not feel that she could rely on Peter to say or do only what was right, what was just and reasonable. He would be guided by his heart and not by his head; he would be wrong, no doubt-utterly wrong-in his judgements, in his advice. But oh! he would be so human, so full of pity, so understanding! And for the first time since her marriage to Jasper, Rosemary allowed herself to think of Peter, to long for Peter, to mourn that which Peter had meant in her life: youth, humanity and enthusiasm.

And suddenly she was brought back to Kis-Imre and to the reality of the present situation by a direct question put to her by Jasper:

"Why didn't you tell me, dear, that Peter Blakeney was in Transylvania?"

Jasper had put the question quite gently and kindly. He never put on with Rosemary any airs of martial authority, nor was there even a hint of reproach in his tone. But the question did bring Rosemary's mind back in a second from the Albert Hall to Kis-Imre. She frowned, very much puzzled, and turned to look straight at Jasper. He, too, appeared to have come back to Kis-Imre from the land of nowhere. He still had on a puzzled and pondering expression, but with it a certain look of hardness, which he seldom had when his wife was nigh.

"Peter Blakeney?" Rosemary asked slowly. "What in the world do you mean?"

"Don't look so scared, little one," Jasper rejoined, his stern face breaking into a smile. "As a matter of fact the whole thing has puzzled me to such an extent that I am afraid I must have appeared very unresponsive just now--" He paused, and, leaning forward, he rested his elbows on his knees, and instead of looking as if he wished to avoid making her feel uncomfortable by staring directly at her.

"A moment ago," he resumed presently, "as I was crossing the hall, General Naniescu came out of the smoking-room into the outer vestibule. He did not see me, and I was just debating in my mind whether I would speak to him when he turned to a young officer who was evidently in attendance, and what he said to him was this: 'Ring up Mr. Blakeney at once and tell him I will see him about the business at five o'clock his afternoon; you may tell him that on the whole I think I have been successful."

"Impossible!" Rosemary exclaimed impulsively.

"So I thought at the time," Jasper rejoined. "Therefore I recrossed the hall and spoke a few words to Naniescu. He appeared vexed when he saw me, and I distinctly saw him make a sign to the officer, who did not then go to the telephone, although a moment ago Naniescu had ordered him to ring up at once. I kept the general talking for a few minutes in the hall. He did not refer to his conversation with you, nor did he refer in any way to Peter."

"You must have misunderstood the name," Rosemary insisted.

"I thought so at first, but I had confirmation of it later on. Naniescu very obviously and very clumsily maneuvered me toward the dining-room, the doors of which were wide open. As soon as he had got me into the room he closed the doors. Now, I happened to have very sharp ears, and although Naniescu talked to me at the top of his voice I distinctly heard what was going on in the hall. The officer called up the Hotel New York at Cluj, after which there was a pause. I tried to take my leave of the general, for I wanted to come up to you, but he would not let me go. He talked incessantly and always at the top of his voice on all sorts of irrelevant topics. He dragged me to the window at the farther end of the room to show me the view. He tried to persuade me to go out with him for a turn in the park. Finally fortune favoured me; my sharp ears caught the ring of the telephone bell. I gave Naniescu the slip and just had the door open when I heard the officer say quite distinctly in French:

"'Is that you, Mr. Blakeney? Mr. Blakeney, his Excellency will see you--' At this point," Jasper went on, "Naniescu with a loud guffaw took hold of my arm and made some facetious remark which I did not catch. However, he had made it so obvious that he did not wish me to hear the telephone message, and, on the other hand, I had heard the officer name Peter so distinctly that I allowed myself to be dragged back into the room, and made no further attempt to pry into Naniescu's-or Peter's-secrets."

"But this is all nonsense," Rosemary broke in warmly. "Peter is not in Transylvania. I am sure he is not. He would have told me. He would have let me know. It is some other Blakeney whom Naniescu was calling up."

Jasper shrugged. "Perhaps," he said quietly.

"I am sure," Rosemary insisted.

Jasper said nothing more after that, and Rosemary was conscious of a feeling of irritation against him because he was so obviously convinced that Peter was in Transylvania and in secret communication with that odious Naniescu. How could he imagine such a thing? Peter! Peter with the lovely Hungarian mother! Peter? Nonsense! But Rosemary could not sit still. She jumped to her feet and began fidgeting about the room, arranging her dress, her hair, fidgeting, fidgeting. She would not look at Jasper, and she was determined not to say anything more. He would discover his mistake soon enough, and if she said anything now she might use words, phrases, expression which later on she would regret.

Peter intriguing with a Roumanian! Nonsense! And yet her nerves were terribly on edge, more so now than they were after her interview with Naniescu. And she could not bear to look at Jasper. She was afraid that she would hate him for his thoughts about Peter. Fortunately after a little while the luncheon-bell sounded. Jasper jumped to his feet. He too seemed relieved that the subject of Peter could now be conveniently dropped.

"Will you see Elza?" he said abruptly.

"Elza?" Rosemary asked. "Why?"

"Naniescu and his suite are in the house," Jasper replied drily. "They will stay to lunch. I don't know what Elza will feel about it."

"She will feel as I do," Rosemary retorted hotly, "that the man's presence at her table is an outrage."

"But he told me that Philip and Anna will be allowed to come home."

"Yes. Provisionally. Until I--"

"Elza need not know about that," Jasper broke in hurriedly. "That is why I thought you would see her. She need not know that Philip's release is only-conditional--"

Rosemary thought the matter over for a moment. As always, Jasper was right. Elza need not know. Not yet.

"Shall I go to her now," she said, "and tell her?"

"I think it would come best from you. It will be such news for her, poor thing."

"Poor darling!" Rosemary sighed; then she added more coldly: "But what about me?"

"What do you mean?"

"Am I expected to sit at table with that mealy-mouthed Roumanian?"

Jasper smiled. "How else would you explain the situation to Elza?" he asked.

All this had brought about a fresh train of thought, and Rosemary was quite thankful that Jasper was showing such sympathy for Elza. He was quite right. Elza need not be told that the release of Philip and Anna was only conditional. There was a month still ahead before Elza need be told the truth.

"Will you keep Naniescu talking," Rosemary said finally, "while I see Elza?"

She looked quite cool and self-possessed now, beautifully dressed, one row of perfect pearls round her neck, circles of diamonds in her ears, a great lady conscious of her own beauty. "How wonderful you are!" came as an involuntary exclamation from her husband's lips, and his dark, deep-set eyes lit up with a sudden flash of passionate admiration as they rested on the vision of loveliness before him.

Then together they went out of the room, Rosemary just a step of two in front of her husband. She still could not bear to look at him, and when she caught his look of bold admiration she coldly turned her head away. Obedient to her wish, he went downstairs to keep Naniescu talking, while she went to break the good news to Elza. But walking along the stately gallery that led to her hostess's rooms, Rosemary's thoughts were not with Elza, her lips were murmuring almost audibly:

Peter intriguing with a Roumanian?

What nonsense!

Jasper must be mad!

CHAPTER XV

The moment that Rosemary came into the room she guessed that Elza somehow or other had heard the news. She had tears in her big, kind eyes, but they were tears of emotion, not of sorrow or anxiety.

"Philip is coming home with Anna!" she cried as soon as she caught sight of Rosemary.

"Who told you?" Rosemary asked.

"General Naniescu sent his captain to tell me. I only knew it five minutes ago. But oh, my dear, they have been such five minutes!"

Rosemary kissed her with tender affection. She did not feel somehow as if she could say much.

"Isn't it wonderful?" Elza went on while she put a few finishing touches to her toilet. "And has not Naniescu been kind? Of course I knew that they could not do anything to Philip because he has done nothing, and I don't believe that Anna did anything either. But you know, my dear, these days some awful mistakes do occur. But," she added lightly, "I have so often experienced it in life that men are not nearly so cruel as they are credited to be. One is so apt to pass judgement on insufficient evidence. Give a man the chance of doing a kind act, that is my motto, and he will nearly always do it."

Fortunately Elza was rather fussy for the moment, fidgeting about the room and obviously trying to calm her nerves, so she did not notice Rosemary's silent, unresponsive way.

"When do you expect Philip and Anna?" Rosemary said at last.

"This afternoon," Elza exclaimed, her words rang out like a little cry of joy. "And you know Maurus is so happy that he has actually gone down in order to say something civil to Naniescu, who, of course, is staying for lunch. Well," she added after a moment or two, when she had gathered up her keys, her rings, her handkerchief, and given a final tap to her hair, "shall we go down too?"

Without a word Rosemary followed her. She felt as if she must choke. Elza's happiness was going to be the most severe trial of all during this terrible month that lay ahead of her.

"Oh, and I was almost forgetting," Elza resumed, while she tripped lightly along the gallery towards the stairs, "the smaller joy beside the greater-the greatest one! I have heard from Peter Blakeney."

"From Peter?"

"Yes. He is at Cluj, at the New York. He is over here about some arrangement he wants to make for a cricket match or something silly of that sort-you know what Peter is: quite mad about that silly cricket. I had a letter from him this morning, but when it came I had no thought for anything except Philip. I must let you read it presently. I don't really know what he says, but if he is at Cluj we are sure to see him very soon."

She prattled on as merry as a bird. She seemed twenty years younger all of a sudden-her step was light and springy, her eyes were bright, her voice was fresh and clear. Rosemary kept on repeating to herself:

"She need not know for at least three weeks. She need not know, and I must pretend-pretend-at any cost. She will know soon enough, poor darling."

And Rosemary did manage to pretend; for the next three hours she was just an automaton, wound up to play a certain part. To everyone she had to pretend-to Elza, to Maurus, to that odious Naniescu, and even to Jasper. The worst of all was pretending to Jasper, for from this she got no reprieve. Jasper's kind, anxious eyes were on her all the time, but she would not let him see that she was anxious about Peter. Somehow the episode about Peter had made everything so much worse. Not that she harboured the thought for a moment that Peter was intriguing with Naniescu. That, of course, was out of the question. He had come to arrange something about a cricket match, and, of course, he had to see Naniescu about it, get his permission, and so on. There were ten chances to one that Peter had written to her and told her all about it, and that his letter had gone astray. No, no, no! There could be no thought of an intrigue between Peter and these Roumanians; but Rosemary felt that Jasper thought there was, and was vaguely pitying her because of some unknown treachery on Peter's part. It was odious!

And with it all Elza's obvious happiness was almost intolerable to witness, and even Maurus departed from his habitual ill-temper to exchange facetious remarks with Naniescu. Time seemed leaden-footed. The interminable luncheon dragged on wearily, as did the hour of coffee and liqueurs, of endless small talk and constant pretence. But even the worst moments in life must become things of the past sooner or later, and when Rosemary began to feel that she could not stand the whole thing any longer, she found that Naniescu and his officers were actually taking their leave.

After luncheon Jasper was quite charming. He had thought the whole matter over, he said, and decided that it was in his power to make a personal appeal to the King in favour of Philip and Anna. He had certainly rendered more than one signal service to Roumania during and after the war, and he thought that in these countries personal influence counted a great deal. At any rate, there would be no harm in trying, and he would start for Bucharest immediately. He had spoken about the proposed journey to Elza and Maurus, alleging official business, and Elza had already arranged that he should be driven into Cluj in time for the afternoon express. Rosemary's heart was at once filled with gratitude; she felt angry with herself for having mistrusted him. She threw herself whole-heartedly into the preparations for his journey, lolled her troubled soul with the belief that it would prove to be the happy issue out of this terrible situation. When it was time for him to go she wished him God-speed with more fervour and affection than she had shown him for days.

"Bar accidents," he assured her, "I shall be back in a fortnight. If I have definite good news to report I will wire. But even if you don't hear from me, I shall be back, as I say, in fifteen days."

"I shall count the hours until your return," she said.

"And in the meanwhile," he urged with deep earnestness, "you will do nothing without consulting me."

She smiled at this want of logic, so unlike her methodical husband.

"I could not consult you, dear," she said. "You won't be here."

"No, no, I know," he insisted; "but I want you to promise that you will leave things as they are until my return. I don't want you to give anything away to Elza, or to Philip or Anna. Promise me."

"Of course I'll promise," replied readily. "God knows I don't want to be the one to break the awful news to them."

"Or to Peter," he added gravely.

"Peter?"

"I want you to promise me-to promise, Rosemary, that you will not speak of this miserable affair to Peter Blakeney."

Then, as she seemed to hesitate, vaguely puzzled at his desperate earnestness, he again insisted:

"Promise me, Rosemary, whatever you may hear, whatever you may see, whatever may be planned by Elza or anybody else, promise me that you will not speak of it to Peter."

"But Jasper," she exclaimed, "why? Of course I will promise, if you wish it, but frankly I don't understand why you insist, so solemnly too," she added, trying to assume a lightness of heart which she was far from feeling. Then she went on more gravely: "I could trust Peter as I would myself."

"You can put it down to nerves," Jasper said, with the ghost of a smile, "to intuition or foreboding, or merely to jealousy and my wretched character, to anything you please, my dear one. But promise me! Promise me that everything in connexion with this miserable affair will remain just between you and me. Let the others talk, guess, plan. Promise me that you will never speak of it with Peter. Promise me, or I will throw up the sponge, remain here to look after you, and let Naniescu do his worst with the lot of them."

Thus, alternately demanding, entreating, threatening, he extracted the promise from her, even though her heart cried out against what she felt was treachery to Peter. Jasper's insistence filled her with a vague sense of foreboding not unmixed with fear; and yet, the very next moment, as soon as he had her promise, he became tender, soft, loving, as if trying to make her forget his solemn earnestness of a while ago. He took her in his arms and gazed into her eyes with an intensity of longing which made her own heart ache with self-reproach.

"If God there be," he whispered softly, as if to himself, "it was cruel of Him to make you so beautiful-and so desirable."

Again his mood had changed. Tenderness had turned into passion, fierce, almost primeval, and he held her now more like a man defending the greatest treasure he possessed on God's earth than like a husband taking affectionate leave of his wife.

"If I should lose you, Rosemary," he murmured, "because of this."

She tried to laugh and to speak flippantly. "Lose me?" she said. "You have little chance of doing that, my dear, for this or any other cause. Naniescu has not the power of life and death over me," she added more seriously.

There was something about Jasper at this moment that she could not entirely fathom. Twice before she had seen him in these moods of violent passion akin almost to savagery, when she felt utterly helpless and absolutely in his power. She had the feeling that when he was in one of these moods he was capable of any violence against her if she dared to disobey or resist. Not that Rosemary was afraid; she had never in her life been afraid of anyone; but she had always been mistress of herself, and at this moment, held tightly by the man to whom she had sworn love and fealty, she felt like a slave of olden times in the grip of her lord.

"You-you will care for me some day, Rosemary?" he asked with passionate earnestness. "Say that you will some day, when all this-all this is forgotten, and we are back again in England, free to live our own lives, free to love. You will care for me then, Rosemary, will you not? For I could not live beside you for long, feeling all the time that you did not belong to me with your whole soul. You have such haunting eyes-eyes such as pixies and fairies have-maddening eyes. I should go crazy presently if I failed to kindle the love-light in those eyes."

He kissed her eyes, her mouth, her throat. Rosemary would have struggled, would have screamed if she dared. Fortunately a knock at the door and the entrance of one of the menservants, who came to fetch milord's luggage, put an end to a situation which Rosemary found very difficult to endure. After the man had gone the spell appeared to be broken. Jasper became once more the courteous, grave man of the world he had always been. The episode of a moment ago did not seem to have occurred at all, as far as he was concerned, and while Rosemary felt her teeth chattering and the palms of her hands were covered with a cold sweat, Jasper moved about the room and spoke to her about his proposed journey, his certain return in a fortnight, as if nothing had happened.

CHAPTER XVI

The carriage which took Jasper to Cluj brought back Philip and Anna. After that the house was full of animation, like a beehive in May. Rosemary only saw the two young people for a moment. She felt a stranger in this family gathering, and her heart was so heavy that she soon found a pretext for going up to her room. Later on she pleaded a headache. Kind and hospitable as were these dear people, Rosemary felt that they must wish to be alone amongst themselves after the terrible time they had all gone through. They would have so much to talk over that the presence of a stranger, even so welcome as one as Rosemary Tarkington, must of necessity be irksome. It was clear to her from the first that Philip and Anna knew little, if anything, of the conditions attached to their release. Philip talked lightly of their being under surveillance for a time, and then added quite gaily that he would gladly lead the life of a hermit in Kis-Imre and never go outside the gates until the present clouds blew over. He gave himself up wholly to the joy of watching his mother's happiness and seeing her dear eyes beaming on her returned boy. Altogether he was more like a schoolboy who by a fluke has escaped punishment than a man conscious of a deadly peril that had not ceased to threaten him.

They all sat up talking late into the evening, and when Rosemary found herself at last alone in her room, trying to think things out before she went to bed, little Anna came up to her. The child looked hollow-eyed and grave; the joy that had been on her face when she first found herself in this second home of hers had all gone. She looked old, wan and tired out.

Rosemary put out her arms, and Anna ran up to her and snuggled up close to her, just like a child. For a long time she was quite silent, with her head against her friend's shoulder, her little thin hands held in Rosemary's kind, firm grasp. Now and again a hot tear would fall on

Rosemary's hands. Anna was crying quietly to herself, and Rosemary waited until the girl was calm enough to speak.

"I don't understand the whole thing, Rosemary," were the first words that Anna spoke.

"What is it you don't understand, dear?" Rosemary asked.

"It is not like them to be lenient, is it?" the girl retorted, looking up with quick, eager inquiry into her friend's face.

"Oh, in this case," Rosemary rejoined vaguely, "you are both so young!"

Anna shook her head vigorously.

"That wouldn't worry them," she said, "after all the trouble they must have taken to track us down."

"You were caught in the act, I suppose?" Rosemary queried.

Anna nodded.

"Yes," she said. "And that was strange too. I had all my parcels ready-the usual ones for Budapest, and Philip's manuscript at the bottom of a box of vegetable seeds. Half a dozen soldiers and an officer came into the shop and walked straight up to the place where the parcels were stacked. They seemed to know all about everything, for the officer just ordered his men to undo all the parcels, and, of course, there was Philip's manuscript."

"There is nothing strange in all that, Anna," Rosemary said. "I have no doubt in my mind that you both have been watched for some time by secret service men, and at last they closed their trap on you."

But once more Anna shook her head.

"I can't explain what I mean," she said, and puckered her fine straight brows together. "It is a kind of intuition that came to me when I saw those soldiers walk in. I am absolutely convinced that we were not denounced by regular Government spies. They are too clumsy, and we were too careful. I am certain," she reiterated obstinately, "that we were not denounced by one of them."

"By whom, then?"

"Ah, that I don't know. It is an awful feeling I have. You know I never believed in all that so-called psychic nonsense which is so fashionable just now, but the feeling I have is not just an ordinary one. It is so strong that I cannot fight against it. It is a feeling that eyes-eyes-are always watching me and Philip-cruel eyes-eyes that wish us evil-that will us to do something foolish, unconsidered, something that will get us again into trouble, and for good this time."

"You are overwrought, Anna dear," Rosemary put in gently. "And no wonder! Of course, we all know that there are Government spies all over the place, and you and Philip will have to be doubly careful in the future' but here in Kis-Imre you are among friends. Your aunt Elza's servants are all of them Hungarian and thoroughly to be trusted."

Anna said nothing. She was staring straight out in front of her, as if trying to meet those mysterious eyes which were for ever watching her. An involuntary cry of horror rose to Rosemary's lips.

"Anna!" she exclaimed, "you don't think that I--"

But before she could complete her sentence Anna's arms were round her.

"Of course not. Of course not," the girl murmured tenderly. "Rosemary darling, of course not!"

"I never spoke about your affairs to a single soul, Anna," Rosemary said gravely. "I give you my solemn word of honour that I never even mentioned the thing to my husband until after your arrest, when, of course, all the facts became public property."

"I know, Rosemary, I know," Anna repeated. "I would trust you with every secret. I would trust you with my life-with Philip's life."

"And you did not trust anyone else?" Rosemary asked.

"I never breathed a word about it to a living soul, except to you and Peter Blakeney."

"Peter knew?"

"Yes, Peter knew."

"You wrote to him?" Rosemary insisted. "Ah, then I understand. Your letters were held up by the censor, and--"

"No, I never wrote to Peter what Philip and I were doing; but you know he arrived in Cluj the day before I was arrested. He came to arrange some cricket match or other between Roumanians and Hungarians. I don't know anything about cricket, but, of course, Peter was full of it. He came to see me at my lodgings quite unexpectedly. I was so surprised to see him, and so happy, as I am very, very fond of Peter. We talked till late into the evening, and somehow I had to tell him everything. But except for that one talk with Peter, and the one I had with you, I never breathed a word about what Philip and I were doing, not to a living soul!"

Rosemary said nothing for the moment. Indeed there was nothing much that she could say. Little Anna had got hold of the idea that some mysterious agency had been at work and brought about her and Philip's arrest. But, after all, what did it matter? Professional spies or insidious traitor? What difference did it make in the end? Anna was frightened because she feared a fresh denunciation. She did not know that her poor life was already forfeit, that she was just a mouse whom the cat had allowed to run free for a moment or two, and that she would be pounced upon again unless her friend Rosemary whom she trusted with her whole soul, bought freedom and life for her.

But it was not thoughts of Anna that sealed Rosemary's lips at this moment and left her mute, motionless, like an insentient log, with Anna's cold little hand held tightly in her own. Anna had not spoken of her activities or her plans to anyone except to Peter. And Jasper had extracted a promise from her, Rosemary, that she would not speak of Philip's or Anna's affairs to Peter. What connexion was there between Jasper's insistence and that other awful thought which, strive as she might, would haunt Rosemary's brain like a hideous ghoul risen out of hell? What mystery lurked in the denunciation of these children, in their release, in the alternative which Naniescu had placed before her? What hidden powers were at work, threatening her with shame and the children with death?

Rosemary felt stifled. Rising abruptly, she went to the window and stepped out on the balcony. The moon was up, a honey-coloured, waning moon that threw its cool, mysterious light on park-land and lake and the distant pine forest beyond. Immediately below the balcony a bed of tuberoses, with wax-like corollas that shimmered white and spectral, sent their intoxicating odour through the balmy air. And against the background of dense shrubberies a couple of fireflies gleamed and darted aimlessly, ceaselessly, in and out of the shadows. Rosemary, seeing them, was reminded of what Anna had said just now-that eyes were for ever looking at her, cruel eyes, eyes that were on the watch, spying, spying.

Suddenly she clapped her hand to her mouth, smothering a sharp cry that had risen to her throat; and instinctively she stepped back into the room and hastily closed the window.

"What is it, Rosemary darling?" Anna asked.

"Nothing, dearie, nothing," Rosemary replied quickly. "The smell of those tuberoses made me feel queer. That's all."

She could not tell Anna that while she watched the fireflies, and the air was so still, so still that not a blade of grass shivered, and even the leaves of the aspen were at rest, she had perceived a tremor amongst the laurel bushes and seen some of the tall branches held back by a hand, each finger of which was outlined by the silvery light of the moon. And above the hand she had sensed a pair of eyes that were looking up at her.

She tried to talk lightly with Anna, to infuse into her some of the buoyancy of mind which she was far from feeling herself. She was

Pimpernel and Rosemary

sure that Anna had a vague consciousness of the danger that hung over her and those she cared for; the only thing she could not know was that her fate and theirs lay in the hands of the friend whom she trusted. How would she-how would they all-bear the knowledge when it came to them, as come it must? How would she, Rosemary, face the reproach which, even if unspoken by them, would haunt her to the end of her life: "You might have saved us, if you would."

CHAPTER XVII

And it was that spectre which from that hour haunted Rosemary; it would not allow her to rest at night; it dogged her steps by day. When she walked in the park and the soft summer breeze stirred the branches of Lombardy poplars or the stately plumes of maize, ghostly voices would seem to be whispering all around her: "Life and liberty for Philip and Anna! Life and liberty for those two children who love and trust you, who know nothing of the fate that hangs over them!" And when she was in the house at meals or in the family circle, with Elza radiating happiness and even Maurus unbending, with Philip almost feverishly gay and Anna thoughtful, the eyes of all these kind, dear people whom she loved seemed full of reproach to the one woman who could save them-if she would.

Then Rosemary, unable to pretend any longer, would run up to her room; and she-one of the most sane, most level-headed women in this neurotic age-would throw herself on her knees and pray to be taken out of it all. Oh! to be out of it-underground-anywhere! Just to be out of it, not to see those smiles, that happiness, that contentment which she knew must presently end in a devastating catastrophe. To be out of it when the time came-in a few weeks-days-hours!

Hour followed hour, dull and leaden-footed. And they were all so happy at Kis-Imre! Suspecting nothing, knowing nothing, whilst Rosemary felt her self-control slipping away from her day by day. At times she felt as if she could not endure the situation and longer, as if she must tell one of them. Tell Elza or Maurus, or the children! Surely they should know! There comes a time when a doctor, knowing that his patient cannot recover, is bound in all humanity to tell him. Then surely it was Rosemary's duty to say to them all: "You don't know! You have not guessed! But you are doomed. Doomed! Philip and Anna to death! You Elza and Maurus to worse than death--limitless sorrow. Now you are just living on a volcano. In another few days-twenty, nineteen, eighteen-the flames will break through, the earth will totter under your feet, and everything you care for in the world will be engulfed. You will perish. Yes, you! All of you! And then you will know about me! How I might have saved you and did not. And you will hate me as no woman has ever been hated before. And I shall go forth into the vast wilderness which is called the world. And I, too, shall perish of sorrow and endless regret!"

She had not again seen those mysterious eyes which that evening, while little Anna was talking, had peered at her from behind the laurel bushes; and she was far too sensible to dwell on what might only, after all, have been the creation of overwrought nerves.

The time was drawing near for Jasper's return. "Fifteen days" he had said; and she knew that, bar accidents, he would keep his word. But she had no news of him, and after the first week she ceased to expect any. She would not own, even to herself, that she had already ceased to build hopes in that direction. Jasper had promised to wire as soon as he heard anything definite, so in this case no news was bad news. Dear, kind Jasper! he knew how miserably anxious she was! He would not keep good news from her-not one hour.

It was on the tenth day that Peter arrived at the castle. He had announced his coming twenty-four hours previously, and in a moment there was excitement from attic to cellar in the house. Everybody seemed to be arranging something, planning something. Tennis excursions, dancing! Peter was such a good dancer! They would have the gipsies over from Bonczhida. That was the finest band in the whole of Transylvania; and they would ask the Keletys over from Hajdu and the Fejérs from Henger, and perhaps Aunt Charlotte could be persuaded to come and bring Marie. There was some talk of private theatricals, of tableaux, a tennis tournament, perhaps a cricket match, English fashion. Peter was so clever at all that sort of thing! Rosemary was consulted about the cricket match and the tournament, for these were to be done on English lines! But the dancing and the acting and the picnics, these were to be truly and entirely Hungarian-pre-war Hungarian, the gayest, merriest things darling Rosemary had ever seen.

How much she had looked forward to Peter's coming, Rosemary did not know until after she had seen him. What hopes she had built on his mere presence, on his nearness, she did not own to herself until afterwards. He had not been in the house many hours before she realized that he had changed. Not changed for the worse, of course not-but changed.

He seemed younger, more boyish-more English in many ways. At one time the Hungarian strain had been very conspicuous in Peter-his tempestuous love-making, his alternating moods of fatalism and rebellion had always reminded Rosemary of those barbaric chieftains-his forbears about whom she loved to read-who had been up and fought the Turks, while the rest of Europe only trembled at thought of their approach.

But now Peter was much more like the conventional young English athlete: not very loquacious, very placid, ashamed of showing emotion or excitement, standing about for the most part with his hands in his trousers pockets contemplating the toes of his boots, and smoking innumerable cigarettes. He had not seemed like this at first. He arrived in the late afternoon, and Rosemary was downstairs in the paved courtyard when the carriage drove in through the gates, with its four spanking greys shining with lather, for the day had been very hot and the roads were dusty. Peter was on the box, having dislodged the coachman, who sat beside him, the groom being relegated to the cushioned seat of the victoria.

There was such a halloing and a shouting, everyone screaming a welcome, grooms rushing to hold the horses, the greys pawing and champing and shorting, that Rosemary hardly saw Peter when he threw the reins to the coachman, jumped down from the box, and was lost in a forest of welcoming arms that hid him completely from view.

It was only after dinner, when the whole company went out into the garden to get a breath of air, that Rosemary found herself for a few moments alone with him. It had been desperately hot indoors, and the noise of all these dear people all talking and laughing at the same time had been overpowering. Fortunately everyone thought it would be lovely in the garden, and still laughing and chattering they trooped out like a brood of chickens let out of a coop. Rosemary had wandered on ahead of the others, and presently she turned down the path that ran along the perennial border, now a riot of colour and a tangle of late lilies, crimson pentstemons and evening primroses.

Rosemary did not hear Peter coming. No one ever dressed for dinner at Kis-Imre, and Peter had his tennis shoes on, and the rubber soles made not the slightest sound upon the smooth gravel path. She had stopped to look at a clump of tiger lilies, when suddenly a wonderful sense of well-being seemed to descend upon her soul. It was as if she had stepped out of a boat that had been tossed about a stormy sea, and had all of a sudden set her foot upon firm ground. The first words he said were so like the foolish, lighthearted Peter she knew.

"You wonderful pixie!" he said, "I can't believe that it is really you!"

She did not immediately turn to look at him, but went on studying the markings on the lilies; then she said, as indifferently as she could:

"Why didn't you let me know sooner, Peter, that you were coming to Transylvania? In fact," she went on coolly, "you never did let me know at all. I first heard through-others that you were here."

"Who told you?" he asked.

"I think Jasper did first," she replied. "He had heard the news from General Naniescu."

Then only did she turn and look at him. She had to look up, because, though she herself was very tall, one always had to look up at Peter, who was a young giant. At this moment she certainly did not think that he was changed. He looked just the same, with his very boyish face and laughing grey eyes, and his fair hair that so often looked as if it had been Marcel-waved. He was looking down at her when she turned to him, and suddenly he said:

"You don't look happy, Rosemary!"

Of course she laughed and told him not to make silly remarks. How could she help being happy here with these dear, kind people? Never, never in all her life had she met with such kindness and hospitality. Peter shrugged his shoulders. He thrust his hands in the pockets of his flannel trousers and looked down at the toes of his shoes.

"Very well," he said lightly, "if you won't tell me, you won't. And that's that. But let me tell you this: though I dare say I am a bit of a fool, I am not quite such an ass as not to see the difference in you. You've gotten thinner. When I first arrived and shook hands with you, your hand felt hot, and your eyes--"

He broke off abruptly, and then with sudden irrelevance: "Where's Jasper?"

"Gone to--," she began, and suddenly came to a halt. When she promised Jasper not to breathe a word of Philip's and Anna's affairs to Peter, she had not realized how difficult this would be. Would she be breaking her promise if she now told Peter that Jasper was in Bucharest. He would ask questions, more questions which Rosemary's promise bound her not to answer.

"He has been called away on business," she said curtly.

Her hesitation had only lasted a second or two; she hoped that Peter had not noticed it. Anyway, when he asked: "To Budapest?" she replied, without hesitation this time: "Yes, to Budapest." And she added quite gaily: "He'll be back at the end of the week. You can't think, Peter, how I miss him when he is away! Perhaps that is why I am looking thin, and why my hands are hot."

"Perhaps," Peter assented laconically.

Then somehow the conversation flagged, and all the happy feeling that Rosemary had experienced when Peter first stood near her slipped away from her. She suddenly felt cold, although the evening was so hot that a little while ago she had scarcely been able to breathe. At some little distance behind her Philip's voice sounded cheerful and homely, and Maurus Imrey's throaty laugh and Elza's happy little giggle rang through the sweet-scented evening air. Poor Rosemary shivered.

"Shall we walk on," she asked, "Or wait for the others?"

"Let's walk on," Peter replied; then added in a clumsy, boyish fashion: "Rather!"

They walked on side by side. Rosemary, at a loss what to say next, had thrown out an inquiry about the cricket match. This set Peter talking. All at once he threw off his abrupt, constrained air, and prattled away nineteen to the dozen. The cricket match was going to be a huge success. Didn't Rosemary think it was a grand idea? Talk about the League of Nations, or whatever the thing was called! In Peter's opinion, there was nothing like a jolly good cricket or football match to bring people together. Make them understand one another, was Peter's motto. Of course, all these dagoes over here had got to learn to be proper sports. No sulking if they got beaten. Peter would see to that. Anyhow, the old General What's-his-name had been a brick. He had helped Peter no end to get the Roumanian team together, and had given them all free passes to Hódmezö, where the match would take place. Hódmezö was in Hungary, and old What's-his-name-meaning Naniescu-said he would rather the Roumanian team went to Hungary than that the Hungarian team came over here. Well, Peter didn't mind which. It was going to be a topping affair. He was going to captain the Roumanian team, and Payson was captaining the Hungarians. Did Rosemary know Payson? Jolly chap with a ripping wife-done splendid work in the Air Force during the war. He had something to do with the Military Commission on disarmaments. He was at Budapest now, and Jasper would probably see him while he was there. Payson was coming over to Hódmezö by aeroplane. Wouldn't that create a sensation. There was a splendid landing ground quite close to Hódmezö fortunately. Payson's wife was coming with him. She was so keen on flying. Ripping couple, they were! Didn't Rosemary think so? Oh! and Peter had had telegrams of good wishes from no end of people, and a jolly letter from dear old Plum Warner. Did Rosemary know Plum Warner? There was a cricketer if you like! No one like him, in Peter's opinion. The science of the man! Well, the dagoes should learn that cricket is the finest game in the world! Didn't Rosemary agree with him?

Rosemary gave monosyllabic replies whenever Peter gave her the chance of putting in a word. She could not help smiling at his enthusiasm, of course. It was so young, so English, so thoroughly, thoroughly fine! But somehow she could not recapture that lovely feeling of security, that sheer joy in having Peter near her, and she kept asking herself whether it was really Peter who had changed-who had become younger, or she who had grown old. In this youthful athlete with his self-assurance and his slang, she vainly sought the wayward, sometimes moody, always captivating Peter, whose tempestuous love-making had once swept her off her feet.

At one moment she tried to lead the conversation into a more serious channel: "How do you think Anna is looking?" she asked abruptly.

"A bit peaky." Peter replied lightly, "poor little mole! When you go back to England," he went on more gravely, "you ought to take her with you. It would do her all the good in the world. Take her out of herself, I mean."

"She wouldn't come," Rosemary replied earnestly.

"Don't you think so?"

"Why, Peter," she retorted, feeling exasperated with him for this air of indifference even where Anna was concerned, "you know Anna would not come. For one thing," Rosemary added impulsively, "I don't suppose she would be allowed to."

"You mean her mother wouldn't let her?"

"No," she replied laconically. "I didn't mean that."

"Well, then?" he retorted. Then, as Rosemary, shocked, angry, remained silent, holding her lips tightly pressed together, almost as if she were afraid that words would slip out against her will, Peter shrugged his broad shoulders and rejoined flippantly:

"Oh, I suppose you mean old What's-his-name-Naniescu-and all that rubbish. I don't think he would worry much. He has been a brick, letting Anna and Philip out like that. I expect he would just as soon see them both out of the country as not. Jolly good thing it would be for both of them! They would learn some sense, the monkeys!"

He paused and looked round at Rosemary. Then, as she seemed to persist in her silence, he insisted:

"Don't you agree with me?"

"Perhaps," she replied, with a weary sigh.

"Anyway, you'll think it over, won't you?" Peter went on. "I am sure you could fix it up with old Naniescu. He admires you tremendously, you know."

It was all wrong, all wrong. Peter used to be so fond of little Anna. "Give her a kiss for me," were almost the last words he had spoken to Rosemary on the day of her wedding. His own affairs evidently pushed every other consideration into the remotest corner of his brain; and cricket matches were apparently of more importance than the danger which threatened Anna and Philip. Nor had Rosemary any longer the desire to break her promise to Jasper. She no longer wished to speak to Peter about Anna and Philip, or about the horrible alternative which Naniescu had put before her. Peter-this Peter-would not understand. Jasper had not understood either-but he had misunderstood in a different way. Rosemary realized how right he had been to extract that promise from her. Was not Jasper always right? And was it intuition that had prompted him, after all, rather than an attack of jealousy of which Rosemary, in her heart, had been so ready to accuse him?

Suddenly she felt a longing to get away from Peter, from this Peter whom she neither knew nor trusted. "I'll go in now, I think," she said abruptly; "the dew is rising, and my shoes are very thin."

And she started to walk more quickly. Slowly the shades of evening had been drawing in. Rosemary had not noticed before how dark it was getting. The line of shrubbery behind the perennial border was like a solid wall; and on the other side of the path the stretch of lawn, with its great clumps of pampas grass and specimen trees, became merged in the gathering shadows. Beyond the lawn glimmered the lights of the chateau, and the veranda in front of the drawing-room was like a great patch of golden light, broken by the long, straight lines of its supporting columns. There was no moon, only an infinity of stars; and in the flower border the riot of colour had faded into the gloom, leaving just the white flowers-the nicotiana, the Madonna lilies, a few violas-to break the even mantle spread by the night.

From the direction of the chateau there came a loud call of "Hallo!" to which Peter gave a lusty response. A voice shouted: "We are going in!"

"Right-o!" Peter responded. "We'll come in too!"

Then suddenly he gave a bound, and in an instant had leaped the border and disappeared in the shrubbery beyond. Rosemary, taken completely by surprise, had come to a halt. From the shrubbery there came a loud cry of terror, then a swear-word from Peter, and finally a string of ejaculations, all in Hungarian, and of distressful appeals for mercy in the name of all the saints in the calendar. The next moment Peter's white flannels glimmered through the foliage, and a second or two later he reappeared lower down, coming up the path and half dragging, half pushing in front of him a huddled-up mass, scantily clothed in ragged shirt and trousers, and crowned with a broad-brimmed hat, from beneath which came a succession of dismal howls.

"What is it?" Rosemary cried.

"That's what I want to know," was Peter's reply. "I caught sight of this blighter sneaking in the shrubbery, and got him by the ear, which he does not seem to like, eh, my friend?"

He gave the ear which he held between his fingers another tweak, and in response drew a howl from his victim, fit to wake the seven sleepers.

"Mercy, gracious lord! Mercy on a poor man! I was not doing anything wrong; I swear by holy Joseph I was not doing anything wrong!"

The creature, whoever he was, succeeded in wriggling himself free of Peter's unpleasant hold. At once he turned to flee, but Peter caught him by the shoulder, and proceeded this time to administer something more severe in the way of punishment.

"Leave the man alone, Peter," Rosemary cried indignantly. "You have no right to ill-use him like that!"

"Oh, haven't I? We'll soon see about that!" Peter retorted roughly. "Now then, my friend," he went on, speaking in Hungarian to the bundle of rags that had collapsed at his feet, "listen to me. You have tasted the weight of my boot on your spine, so you know pretty well what you can expect if you don't tell me at once what you are doing at this hour of the night in the gracious count's garden?"

The man, however, seemed unable to speak for the moment; loud hiccoughs shook his tall, spare frame. He held his two hands against the base of his desperate contortions in a vain attempt to get his right shoulder out of Peter's grip.

"Peter," Rosemary cried again, "let the poor wretch go. You must! Or I shall hate you."

But Peter only retorted harshly: "If you weren't here, Rosemary, I'd thrash the vermin to within an inch of his life. Now then," he commanded, "stop that howling. What were you doing in their shrubbery?"

"I only wanted to speak with the gracious countess," the man contrived to murmur at last, through the hiccoughs that still seemed to choke the words in his throat. "I have a message for her!"

"That's why I caught you with this in your belt, eh?" Peter queried sternly, and drew something out of his pocket, which Rosemary could not see; he showed it to the man who promptly made a fresh appeal to the saints.

"The roads are not safe for poor gipsies, gracious lord. And I had the message--"

"Who gave you a message for the gracious countess?" Rosemary asked him gently.

"I-I don't know, gracious lady. A fine gentleman on a horse called to me when I was gathering wood over by the forest of Normafa. He gave me a letter. 'Take it,' he said, 'to the gracious countess over at Kis-Imre, but do not give it into any hands but hers, and only give it to her when she is alone.'"

"Where is the letter?"

"It is here, gracious lady," the man replied and fumbling with the belt that held his ragged trousers round his waist, he drew from underneath it a oiled and crumpled rag that effectively looked like a letter in a sealed envelope. Peter would have snatched it out of his hand, but Rosemary interposed.

"Peter," she said gravely, and stretched a protecting arm over the gipsy's hand, "the man was told not to give it in any hand but Elza's!"

"The man is a liar," Peter riposted harshly.

Just then Philip's voice reached them from across the lawn.

"What are you two doing over there?"

"Philip, is your mother with you?" Rosemary shouted in response.

"Yes! We are just going in."

"Ask her to wait a moment then."

"What has happened?" Elza called.

"Nothing, darling," Rosemary replied. "Send the others in and wait for me, will you?" Then she turned to the gipsy, and said kindly: "Walk beside me, and don't try to run away; the gracious lord will not hurt you if you walk quietly beside me."

And so the three of them walked across the lawn toward the chateau, Rosemary in front, and beside her the gipsy, whose long thin hands almost swept the grass as he walked with bent knees and arched back, throwing from time to time anxious glances behind him. But Peter was lagging behind.

When they were close to the chateau, they saw Elza coming down the veranda steps. Rosemary ordered the gipsy to wait, and ran to meet Elza; in a few words she told her what had occurred. Elza then came across the gravel path, and said to the gipsy: "I am the Countess Imrey. You may give me the letter!"

The man's back became more curved than ever; he nearly touched the ground with his forehead. In the darkness Rosemary seemed to see his long, thin body curling itself up almost into a ball.

"I was told," he murmured meekly, "to give the letter into the hands of the gracious countess only when she was alone."

Instinctively Rosemary turned to look for Peter. To her surprise she saw him just above her, going up the veranda steps. He had his hands in the pockets of his trousers, and he was whistling a tune.

The gipsy whom he had so maltreated a little while ago no longer seemed to interest him. Rosemary called to him rather impatiently:

"Peter!"

He paused and looked down at her. "Hallo!" he said coolly.

"Do you think it is all right for Elza to talk with this man alone?"

Peter shrugged his shoulders. "Why not?" he said, with a laugh.

Then he called out to Elza:

"I say, Aunt Elza, if the wretch should try to kiss you, sing out, won't you?"

Elza laughed good-humouredly.

"Of course I am not afraid," she said. "And I do want to know about this mysterious letter."

Rosemary would have liked to argue the point. She could not understand how it was that Peter took the matter so lightly all of a sudden. However, as Elza was playfully pushing her out of the way, whilst Peter calmly continued to stroll up the stairs, she only said with a final note of earnestness: "I shall be quite close, Elza. You have only to call, you know."

"I know, I know," Elza rejoined, still laughing. "You don't suppose that I am frightened of a gipsy, do you?"

She waited a moment or two until Rosemary was out of sight, then she turned back to the man, and said:

"I am alone now. You may give me the letter."

CHAPTER XVIII

Rosemary went slowly up the veranda steps. She did not feel that it would be loyal to pry into Elza's secrets, but at the same time she wanted to remain well within call. From where she was she could see Peter's broad shoulders blocking the French window which gave on the drawing-room. From somewhere in the house, both above and below stairs, came the sound of laughter and song.

A moment or two later she heard Elza's footsteps behind her on the gravel walk, and presently Elza was there, going up the veranda steps beside Rosemary. She did not say a word, and Rosemary asked no questions. She could see that Elza was preoccupied. She also noticed that the letter-or whatever it was-was not in Elza's hands.

Peter stood aside to allow the two ladies to step into the drawing-room. He asked no questions either, and Elza did not volunteer any information. It seemed as if the incident of the mysterious gipsy had never been. Later on Peter sat down at the piano and played a csàrdàs, for Philip and Anna to dance. They were beautiful dancers, both of them, and it was a pleasure to watch them swaying and bending to the syncopated cadences of the beautiful Hungarian music. Peter, too, had evidently that music in the blood. Rosemary had no idea he could play it so well. He seemed just as excited as the dancers, and accelerated the movements of the csàrdàs until little Anna called for mercy, and even Philip seemed ready to give in. For the time being Rosemary forgot her troubles in the joy of seeing those two enjoying themselves, and the delight of listening to Peter. What a pity, she thought, as she had often done, that he should waste all the poetry, the talent that was in him, and only devote his mind to cricket. She drew close up to the piano, to watch his slender fingers flying over the keys, and as she did so, her glance at one moment wandered to the small what-not in the corner by the piano. There, in the midst of a miscellaneous collection of cigarette boxes, ash-trays, match-boxes, lay a small automatic.

Peter caught her eye, which at the moment expressed a mute inquiry. He shrugged his shoulders and smiled. He had a cigarette in a long holder in the corner of his mouth, but he contrived to murmur:

"Yes, the blighter; wasn't I right to thrash him?"

Rosemary looked across at Elza. She sat quite placidly, as she always did, close to her husband's chair, watching her Philip-her soul in her eyes. She was smiling, and now and then she turned to say a word or two to Maurus; but to Rosemary she still looked preoccupied, and once she caught Elza's large kind eyes fixed upon her with a curious, scrutinizing gaze.

An hour later when Rosemary was in her room and beginning to undress, there was a knock at her door, and Elza came in, with that kindly smile of hers still on her face, but with a troubled look in her eyes.

"May I come in for a moment, darling?" she asked.

Rosemary made her comfortable on the sofa, and sat down beside her. Elza took hold of both her hands and fondled them, stroking them up and down, and she began talking about Philip and Anna, and the dancing and the plans for future parties, and picnics and so on. Rosemary let her prattle on; it was her turn to scrutinize Elza's face closely. That something was troubling this dear, kind creature was obvious. She was, as it were, gathering her moral forces before she broached something unpleasant that she had come to say. It was no use brusquing the matter, and Rosemary entered into Elza's plans, discussed the coming dinner-parties, the proposed lists of guests, talked about Anna's future, and made some remarks about Peter.

This brought the main subject on the tapis.

"Where did you and Peter first see that gipsy?" Elza asked presently.

"He was hiding in the shrubbery," Rosemary replied, "behind the flower border. I didn't see him. Peter saw him and pounced upon him, and dragged him out on to the path."

"Funny he did not just go to the service door and ask for me, wasn't it?"

"That's what Peter thought. I am afraid he treated the poor wretch rather roughly."

"I am sorry he did that," Elza mused, and thoughtfully stroked Rosemary's slender fingers between her own. "The man really had a message for me."

110

"I know," Rosemary rejoined; "a letter."

"No, it wasn't a letter," Elza said, and looked Rosemary now straight between the eyes. "You know these gipsies are queer people. They have curious gifts of divination and prophecy. This man--"

She seemed to hesitate, her glance wavered, and once more she started mechanically stroking Rosemary's hands.

"But the man had a letter for you, Elza dear," Rosemary insisted. "I saw it in his hand."

"Oh, that was only a blind; and so was his story about the gentleman on a horse. He told me that he had come all the way from Ujlak to speak with me. Ujlak is where I was born, and my dear brother and Peter's mother. My sister-in-law lives there still. Anna was born there, and little Marie. It was my father's home and my grandfather's before him, and our ancestors' for many generations. Well, this gipsy came from there."

"In order to speak with you?"

"So he said."

"Well, and what did he have to tell you?" Rosemary asked.

"That he had had a vision. My father had appeared before him in a dream, and told him that he must start at once and seek me. He was to tell me that he whom I love best in all the world is in immediate danger of death."

Rosemary never moved; she was looking straight at Elza. Only when Elza paused, seeming to wait for some word from her, Rosemary said:

"That-wretched creature told you that?"

Elza nodded. She went on simply:

"I see by your face, dear, that he told the truth, not only in that, but in what he said was to follow."

"What was that?"

"He said that the stranger now within our gates knows of this danger, and would confirm what he said. Well, my darling, I only need look at your sweet face to see that that miserable wretch spoke the truth. He was inspired by a dream to come and speak with me. But I would not question him further. Those gipsies often lie, and they will tell you any tale in order to get a few coppers. But I saw your look when I told you what he said, and it is from you that I want the truth. What is the danger that threatens Philip?"

"Elza, darling--" Rosemary murmured.

"I am his mother, you know," Elza interposed, with her gentle, quiet smile. "I must know. He is all the world to me. And as soon as you knew that something threatened him, you should have told me, my darling."

Then, as Rosemary was still fighting with herself, alternately praying to God for guidance, and striving to swallow the tears that were choking her, Elza went on quite quietly:

"It is difficult for you, of course," she said, and patted Rosemary's cheek like an indulgent mother, "but it would have been better to tell me at first. I have had a very, very happy week since the children came home, but looking back on it now, I don't think that I was ever quite free from a vague sort of doubt. I was always a little uneasy, and whenever Philip kissed me, I could not help crying."

Elza had spoken in a curious, dreamy manner, her round blue eyes fixed somewhere on vacant space. But now she seemed to pull herself together, she looked once more at Rosemary, gave her an encouraging smile, and said in a perfectly quiet, matter-of-fact tone:

"Well, now tell me all about it. Philip's release and Anna's is only a temporary one. Is that it?"

Rosemary nodded. She could not trust herself to speak. Elza gave a little gasp, but her voice was still quite steady as she went on questioning Rosemary:

"What is the charge against them?"

"Philip wrote certain newspaper articles," Rosemary replied, and her voice sounded mechanical, like that of an automaton, "which have appeared in the English and American press. Anna used to send those through in the parcels she packed up in Balog's shop."

"I knew about those articles," Elza rejoined simply. "Everybody in Transylvania knew about them, but I did not guess that Philip had anything to do with them, or Anna. Then," she went on with a little catch in her throat, "it means a charge of treason against the State?"

"Yes!"

"Military tribunal?"

"Yes."

"And-if they are found guilty-a-sentence-of death?"

"No! No! No!" And Rosemary was on her knees with her arms round Elza's shoulders, her tear-stained face turned up to her, protesting vigorously, strenuously, that which she knew was false. But Elza's big, round eyes were tearless; she looked a little wildly perhaps, but quite kindly into the beautiful face that expressed such a world of love and sympathy. Then, gently but firmly, she disengaged herself from Rosemary's arms.

"Well now, my dear," she asked, very quietly, "all this being so, why did Naniescu let those children come home at all? Why should he postpone their trial, their-their punishment?"

Rosemary's head fell upon her breast.

"I don't know," she murmured.

But Elza put her podgy finger under Rosemary's chin, and forced her to look up.

"Don't lie to me, darling," she pleaded softly; "tell me the truth."

"I have told you the truth, Elza," Rosemary protested through her tears.

"Then I must believe you, if you say so. And yet it is all very mysterious. Why should Naniescu wait? Why should he play with those poor children, like a cat does with a mouse? You know, Rosemary darling, what they gipsy said in the end?"

Rosemary shook her head.

"He said that the stranger within the gates had the power to save my son from death. Have you that power, Rosemary?"

"No! No!" Rosemary protested wildly. "If it were in my power, don't you think that I would do anything in the world to save Philip and Anna?"

Elza nodded.

"Yes, dear," she said gently. "Of course I do think it; but when the gipsy said that, I could not help feeling hopeful, for he was right in everything else he said--"

Then suddenly she took Rosemary's face between her two hands, and she gazed into her eyes with a look of almost fierce intensity in her own, as if she would wrest a secret from the depths of the younger woman's soul.

"Swear to me, Rosemary," she said, and her gentle voice sounded raucous and harsh, "swear to me that there is nothing in the world that you can do to save Philip!"

And Rosemary, returning her gaze, replied steadily:

"I swear to you that it is not in my power to save Philip and Anna. If it were, I would do it."

Even then Elza did not cry. She just sat there quite, quite still, her big, round eyes quite dry, her mouth without a quiver, but sitting there so still, so still with her beautiful golden hair all round her face, the soft streaks of grey all about her temples, her fine features rigid, her podgy white hands resting on her knees; she looked such a tragic figure of despair that Rosemary could hardly suppress the cry of anguish that rose insistently to her throat.

"And so we can do nothing," Elza said, with a note of quiet finality in her voice.

"Don't say that, dear," Rosemary protested. "Jasper, as a matter of fact, has gone to Bucharest to try and see the King personally. The Roumanian Government owes some gratitude to my husband, as you know. I am quite sure that he will bring strong pressure to bear upon the authorities, and get a full pardon for Philip and Anna on the score of their youth."

But Elza slowly shook her head.

"You don't believe yourself, darling," she said, "in what you say. The children have committed the unpardonable crime of being born Hungarians, and of resenting foreign tyranny in their native land. The King himself would be kind, I am sure, but Bucharest is a long way off, and the bureaucrats over here do not know the meaning of the word 'mercy'."

"But we know the meaning of the word 'hope,' Elza dear," Rosemary said steadily, and struggled to her feet. "We are not going to give up hope. You talk about your gipsies having the gift of prophecy. Well, it is my turn to prophesy now. Philip and Anna are in God's hands, and you and I are going to pray so hard and so ceaselessly that God will help us, I am sure. I know," she added firmly.

Elza gave a short, quick sigh.

"Oh, yes," she said, "you are lucky, you English! Your religion means a great deal to you. But we, over here, are so different. We go to convent schools when we are too young to understand. Then we are all fire and enthusiasm, but we do not understand. After that we marry and live in those remote villages where the poor curé is only an illiterate peasant with whom we have nothing in common, whose habits are often such that we could not possibly make our confession to him. And so we soon forget what we learned in our childhood, and we come to trusting in ourselves rather than in God."

She rose and, with the same motherly gentleness which she always showed to Rosemary, she folded the girl in her loving arms.

"Good night, my dear," she said placidly. "I ought not to have kept you up so late. Good night, dear. Pray to your God for us all. The God of the English is more merciful, I think, than ours."

"Elza," Rosemary insisted, "promise me that you will not give up hope. Jasper comes back to-morrow. He may bring the best of news. Promise me that in any case you will not give up hope."

The ghost of a smile appeared on Elza's face.

"I will promise," she said, "not altogether to give up faith."

Rosemary kissed her tenderly. After that she escorted her as far as her room, and at the door she kissed her once more, and then she said, with solemn earnestness:

"Elza darling, will you believe me if I say that if I could give my life for those two children I would do it? If it were in my power to save them, I would. But it is not in my power to save them, to do anything, but to leave them in God's hands."

Elza returned her kiss with gentleness and affection.

"Dear, kind Rosemary," she murmured; "go to bed, dear, you must be so tired."

Then she quietly slipped into her room and closed the door. And Rosemary was left to face the night alone.

CHAPTER XIX

What puzzled Rosemary was the gipsy.

What was the mystery of that vagabond found lurking in the park at nightfall with a revolver in his belt? What connexion had he with the eyes that had watched Rosemary the night that she was talking with little Anna? And how had he come in possession of the inner history of Philip's and Anna's temporary release?

There was a mystery here. Somewhere. A disquieting, a terrifying mystery, not altogether to be accounted for by the spy system or other secret organization of the Roumanian Government.

All night Rosemary struggled with the puzzle. All night she wrestled with herself for the right to break her promise to Jasper and to lay all the facts of this case before Peter. She wanted to do this before Jasper's return, and, anyway, he must release her-he must-from that promise which placed her in a false and disloyal position towards Peter. When Rosemary fell asleep the dawn was breaking, and she had almost made up her mind to tell Peter everything.

But the next morning when she went downstairs she found the whole house in a turmoil. Servants rushing to and fro, Elza in close conversation with the chef, Maurus shouting contradictory orders across the galleried hall. Peter was in the drawing-room playing a jazz tune this time, and Philip and Anna were fox-trotting, infusing even into this ugly so-called dance some of their own native grace.

As soon as Rosemary appeared she was greeted with regular warwhoops of delight. In a moment she was drawn into the whirlpool of excitement. Philip and Anna dragged her to the sofa, and they and Maurus and Elza all talked to her at once, while Peter, with the inevitable cigarette in the corner of his mouth, continued to pound away at the jazz tune.

From the deafening hubbub of conversation Rosemary gathered, in the first instance, that the gipsy band from Bonczhida were coming over the next day, and the gipsies of Bonczhida were the finest in Transylvania. Then that the Keletys were driving over from Hajdu, and the Fejérs from Henger; that perhaps Aunt Charlotte would come too and bring Marie; that the Keletys were bringing the Poltys, and the Fejérs having the Kékesy boys staying with them would of course bring them along. They reckoned that there would be ten or a dozen couples to dance, and with the mammas and papas they would be thirty to supper. They expected most of the guests to arrive in time for luncheon, and in the afternoon they could have some tennis; then in the evening they would have a ball to which the officers from the garrison at Cluj had already been invited, and they had accepted by telephone. Among them were those who were going to play cricket with the Hungarians at Hódmezö under Peter's direction.

At this marvellous statement Peter came to a pause in the music with a crashing chord, took the cigarette out of his mouth, and throwing up his hands, exclaimed:

"Going to play cricket with the Hungarians under Peter's direction! Oh, blessed People! Ye ghosts of Fitzgerald, Pycroft, and of Lillywhite, do ye hear them and writhe up there in Heaven?"

Then he struck up the "March of the Men of Harlech."

"If anyone says anything more about cricket," he said solemnly, "I shall force them to play with warped bats and golf-balls on a ploughed field."

Not a trace of anxiety or even preoccupation on any of those dear, beaming faces. Elza was as excited as any of them, worried to death because the carp they had got out of the lake for this evening's supper were not really fat.

"They're no bigger than a good-sized goldfish," she said to Rosemary with a note of real tragedy in her voice, and her blue eyes at once looked anxious and troubled, as if the matter of the carp was the only thing that could worry her.

Rosemary made a great effort not to be a wet blanket in the midst of all this gaiety. In this she succeeded admirably. All she had to do was to smile and to nod her head, and now and then to cry out, "How splendid!" The others did all the talking, and when conversation subsided for a moment Peter came down with a fresh, crashing jazz tune.

Rosemary would have thought the whole scene a phantasmagoria-illusive images that would presently be dispelled-only that she had known these people ever since she was a child. She had studied their

117

curious psychology, half barbaric, with all the primitive disregard of danger and the passion for pleasure, even at the point of death. She gave ungrudging admiration to Elza-Elza who had sat in her room last night, rigid, dry-eyed, a living statue of despair. What went on behind that smooth, white brow of hers? What projects? What hopes? And little Anna? Anna knew. Anna guessed. She had spoken of her fears to Rosemary. Spoken of eyes that watched her, of eyes that were willing her to do something foolish that would compromise her irretrievably this time. Elza and Anna! What an example of self-possession, of self-control! Rosemary was almost ready to persuade herself that something had happened to reassure them both-that, in fact, they knew the danger to be past.

Only that Elza avoided her glance, and that the dear soul, usually so placid, so stable, was just a thought more restless than usual, and her gentle voice would from time to time become shrill.

At last, genuinely tired and bewildered by so much noise, Rosemary jumped up and, laughing, declared that she must escape out of the bear-garden for a moment and get a breath of fresh air in the park. In order to reach the glass door that gave on the veranda, Rosemary had to go past the piano. Quite close. Peter looked up when she was near him, and she said to him as she went past: "They are very gay, aren't they?"

"Elza has a perfectly mad plan in her head," Peter replied, and struck a few loud chords so that no one save Rosemary should hear what he said. "For God's sake, if you have any influence over her, get her to give it up."

Then he shouted merrily: "I've had enough of those horrible American tunes. Who wants a csàrdàs?"

But he did not play a csàrdàs. For a moment or two his fingers wandered aimlessly over the keys, whilst his eyes followed Rosemary as she stepped through the glass door on to the sun-bathed veranda. And as Rosemary felt the sun, the clear, luscious air, the scent of flowers and of distant pines, envelop her as in a warm mantle, there came wafted to her ears the soft strains of that exquisite Hungarian love-song: "There is but one beautiful girl in all the world." The piano now seemed to sing under Peter's delicate touch and Rosemary paused and stood quite, quite still, letting the music sink into her, yielding to its voluptuous cadence, and allowing her thoughts, her desires, her longings, to soar upwards to that infinity to which music alone can convey the soul on its magic wings.

CHAPTER XX

Rosemary had wandered beyond the confines of the park, and roamed about in the woods, having lost all sense of time. When presently she came back to the reality of things she looked at her watch and saw that it was close on twelve o'clock. Luncheon at the chateau was at half-past. It meant stepping out briskly so as to be in time.

As soon as she reached the flower-garden, it struck her as strange that the château suddenly appeared to be so quiet. No sound reached her as she came near to the veranda steps, either of shrill, excited voices, or of laughter or song.

She found the family assembled on the veranda-Maurus, Elza, Philip and Anna. Only Peter was not there. A first glance at them all revealed to Rosemary what had occurred. Elza had told them what the gipsy had said. Maurus sat in his chair like a man in a trance, his dark face flushed, his hair towzled, his large, dark eyes staring out before him, with a look in them that was not entirely sane.

Philip, on the other hand, was pacing up and down the veranda floor, whilst Anna stood quite still, leaning against a column, looking for all the world like a little martyr tied to the stake, her small, thin hands clasped together, a faint flush on her cheeks. These two children looked excited rather than horror-filled. Anna's face suggested that of an idealist-not altogether resigned, but nevertheless eager to suffer for the cause. But Philip looked like a fighter, seeking for a chance to hit back, a combatant not yet brought to his knees.

Elza's round, blue eyes just wandered from one to the other of these faces all dear to her.

They were dry eyes, anxious eyes, but there was nothing in them to-day of that tragic despair which had been so heart-breaking to behold the evening before.

Rosemary's first thought had been: "They know. Elza has told them!" The second was "Elza has a plan. Peter said it was a mad one. A plan for Philip and Anna's escape." She wondered if they would tell her.

"I hope I am not late for lunch," she said, rather breathlessly, as she had been walking very fast. Then she added casually: "Where is Peter?"

"He is busy packing," Elza replied.

"Packing?" Rosemary exclaimed, puzzled. "He is not going away - already?"

"Yes," Elza said, "to-night."

"But he did not say anything yesterday," Rosemary insisted, "about going away again so soon. Or even this morning."

"I don't think he knew yesterday," Elza rejoined. "It seems he had a telephone message half an hour ago. He says he must go."

Anna now appeared to wake out of her trance. Rosemary was standing close to her just then; she took Rosemary's hand gently in hers and said:

"You see, darling, it is like this: one of Peter's cricketers has telephoned to him to say that they have such a lot of trouble about their rooms at Hódmezö. Roumanians are not exactly popular in Hungary," she went on with a wan little smile, "and I suppose that hotel-keepers don't care to put them up. So Peter had to promise to go and put things right for his cricketers."

"He will come back, of course, after the cricket match," Elza concluded placidly. "But it is a great nuisance for him, packing and unpacking all the time."

Rosemary made no further remark. Everything seemed terribly puzzling. That Elza had told the children, had told Maurus, all she knew, was beyond the question. That Peter also knew everything, and that he knew and disapproved of some plan which Elza had made, Rosemary supposed, for the escape of Philip and Anna was, to her mind, equally certain. But even if Peter disapproved, how could he go away at this critical time, and leave Elza to plan and contrive alone, hampered by a half-crazy husband, and surrounded by spies? However, no one apparently meant to say anything more just then, and it was quite a relief when the luncheon-bell sounded and the little party on the veranda broke up and everyone trooped downstairs for luncheon.

Peter was already in the dining-room, waiting for the others. Elza in her kind, gentle way asked him about his packing, and whether she could help him to get ready. But Peter declared that he wanted nothing, only the carriage this evening to take him to Cluj.

He grumbled terribly at having to go away. He hated the idea of missing the ball and all the friends who were coming; but when Elza or Maurus tried to persuade him to stay, he was very firm. "I've got to go, Aunt Elza. You don't know what complications might occur if those Roumanians got to Hódmezö and were not properly treated. Good God!" he added, with mock horror, "it might land you all in another war! And all through my fault!"

Rosemary had never seen Peter so gay or conversational. He appeared entirely unconscious of the undercurrent of tragedy that flowed through Elza's pathetic attempts at conversation, and Maurus's equally tragic silences. He talked incessantly, chiefly about the cricket match and chiefly to Philip, who made desperate efforts to appear interested. Rosemary did her best, too, but she was anxious and puzzled, and frankly she did not believe in the story of the telephone message.

She tried now and then to catch Elza's eye, but in this she never once succeeded. Elza was avoiding her glance. She meant to say nothing about her plan-this mad plan of which Peter disapproved so thoroughly that he preferred to be out of the way. Did these dear, kind people mistrust her then, because of what the gipsy had said? Or was this reticence merely the natural outcome of a sense of supreme danger that mistrusted everything and everybody?

Rosemary felt the mystery deepening around her. She could not understand Peter.

Sometime after luncheon she found Elza and Anna sitting together in the small brick-built summer-house at the farther end of the lake. Rosemary had wandered as far as there with a book, anxious as she was to be out of the way. It was hot, and the air was very still, and the scent of tuberoses and heliotrope was almost too heady. In the perennial border a number of humming-bird moths were busy about a bed of sweet sultan; the soft whirring sound of their wings could be heard quite distinctly in the extreme stillness of this late summer's afternoon. From time to time distant sounds of village life came in quick, short waves to Rosemary's ear, as well as the sharp click of tools wielded by the gardeners at work somewhere in the park. Close beside the summer-house one man was busy hand-weeding the path. As Rosemary drew nearer, he looked up for an instant, and then he shuffled rapidly away. In the long, stooping figure, the dirty rags and the dark skin, Rosemary thought that she recognized the gipsy of the previous night.

It was just like Elza, she thought, to give the poor wretch work on the estate.

When Rosemary saw Elza and Anna sitting together in the summer-house, her instinct was to pass discreetly on, with just a hasty, cheery word, but Elza called to her.

"Come and sit here a minute, Rosemary darling," she said. "Anna and I want to tell you everything."

Everything! Rosemary without a word stepped into the little pavilion. Anna pulled a wicker chair forward between herself and Elza, and Rosemary sat down, a little anxious, a little fearful, wondering what these dear, enthusiastic hotheads had devised, and how she herself would act when she knew. Elza at once took hold of her hand and fondled it.

"You asked me last night, darling," she began, "not to give up hope, didn't you?"

Rosemary nodded acquiescence.

"And I promised that I would not give up faith," Elza went on quietly. "Well, I have kept my faith all through last night, which was very trying. With the dawn, hope came to me, and after that I once more felt in charity with all the world."

Rosemary gave Elza's podgy white hand a tender squeeze. "Dear!" she whispered.

"We have a plan, darling," Elza said triumphantly. "A splendid plan! To-morrow night Philip and Anna will be in Hungary, safely out of the way."

Rosemary had known all along what was coming. She looked at Anna, who gave an excited little nod.

"Tell Rosemary, Aunt Elza," she said. "All from the beginning. There's no one in the world you can trust as you can Rosemary."

"Listen then, darling," Elza said, speaking quite quietly at first, then allowing excitement to get hold of her voice, making it tremble while she spoke, and husky with eagerness, while her command of the English tongue became less and less pronounced.

"It has all been made possible by this cricket business, for which I thank God and Peter Blakeney. As I told you this morning, Peter's cricket people are all coming here to-morrow for the ball. They have to be at Hódmezö the following day for the cricket. So they will bring their luggage, and make a start from here after the ball-I suppose about midnight-in three motor-cars which the Governor, General Naniescu, has himself placed at their disposition. Hódmezö is, as you know, in Hungary, just the other side of the frontier. It will be about four or five hour's drive from here, as there is a short cut-quite a good road-which avoids Cluj. In two of those motor-cars the cricket people themselves will go; they are mostly young Roumanian officers and men of the better class. General Naniescu has, of course, given them all free passes for the occasion. Fortunately he has also given them passes for four servants to accompany them. These four men will go in the third motor, and they will also go in the motor all the way to Hódmezö. Now two of these servants, whom the local commissary of police has himself chosen and to whom passes have been given, are the two sons of János the miller, who is devoted to us all. His two sons have certainly served in the Roumanian army because they were obliged, but they have remained Hungarian at heart and would do anything for me and for Philip."

Elza paused. Her eager, round eyes searched Rosemary's face. Rosemary, of course, had already guessed the rest, her own excitement while she listened was as tense as Elza's. She gripped the white podgy little hand of her friend, and looked from her to Anna-a mute question in every glance.

"You can guess, of course?" Anna said.

Rosemary nodded: "I can guess," she said, "but do go on."

"I sent for János early this morning," Elza went on. "All I had to tell him was that Philip and Anna were in great danger, and must be got out of the country at any cost. He understood! We Hungarians in this occupied territory all understand one another. We understand danger. We live with danger constantly at our door. And János was so clever, so helpful. I only had to outline my plan, he thought out all the details. The mill is about a kilometre from here, the last house in the village; as soon as the first two motors have gone with the cricket people and the Roumanian officers, Philip and Anna will at once run round to the mill, and János will give them clothes belonging to his sons. The clothes they will put on. In the meanwhile the third motorcar will have collected the two other men in the village who are going as servants to Hódmezö-one is the brother of the Jew over at the inn, and the other the son of the Roumanian storekeeper. Then it will call at the mill. János will ask the two men to come in. He and his two sons will give them some strong spirit to drink. The brother of the Jew and the son of the storekeeper are both of them great drunkards. When they have become what you English call, I think, blotto, János will take them back into the motor. There they will sit; and will probably at once go to sleep. But Philip and Anna will also get into the motor. They will be dressed in peasant's clothes, and they will have the free passes which Naniescu has given to János' sons. They will get to Hódmezö about five o'clock in the morning. And once they are in Hungary they are safe. Rosemary darling! they are safe!"

Rosemary had remained silent. The whole thing certainly at first glance appeared so easy, so simple that she found herself wondering why she or Jasper-or Peter-had never thought of such a plan. She also wondered why Peter should have spoken of it as a mad plan, and begged her if she had any influence with Elza to dissuade her from it. What had been in his mind when he said that? Of what was he afraid? Spies, of course. But spies, like the poor, were always there, and, after all, Philip and Anna would only be risking what already was forfeit-their lives.

Rosemary sat there in silence, her fingers closed over Elza's soft, warm hand. She gazed straight before her, thinking. Thinking; her mind already following Philip and Anna's flight through this hostile, cruel country, to the land which would mean freedom and life for them. She saw them in her mind's eye, like a vision floating before her across the lake, which in this daydream had become a wide, dusty road with a motor-car speeding along toward life and toward freedom.

It seemed a solution. It must be a solution. Thank God Jasper would be there to help with counsel and with suggestions. Elza was talking again now. In her quaint English, which became more and more involved, she continued to talk of her plan, as a child will talk of some event that made it happy. She harped on the details, on János' devotion, the two sons who would make their way to the frontier in their father's bullock cart, and then cross over to Hungary on foot, through the woods and over a mountain pass where there would be no fear of meeting Roumanian sentinels. At Hódmezö they would find Peter and the cricket people. They would get back their passes, and return quite gaily with the others, having saved the lives of Philip and Anna. Such devotion! Wasn't it splendid?

Rosemary only nodded from time to time, and from time to time she squeezed Elza's hand. It was so hot and so airless here in the little pavilion with those clusters of climbing heliotrope all over the roof and half-blocking up the entrance. The bees and humming bird moths were making such a buzzing and a whirring; it was just like the hum of motor-car wheels on the dusty road. And through it all came the swishing sound of a garden broom upon the gravel path, between the summer-house and the stone coping around the ornamental lake. Rosemary caught herself watching the broom swinging backwards and forwards across the path, and across; she saw the two hands-very dark lean hands they were-that wielded the broom, and finally the gipsy's tall, thin figure bent almost double to his task. It seemed just right that the man should be there at this hour, sweeping the path for Elza to walk on presently, for Philip also and for Anna. It was right because it was the gipsy who had told Elza what she, Rosemary, had not had the courage to say. There was very little mystery about the gipsy now; he was just a ragged, dirty labourer, bending to his task. Did the strange intuition-or was it divination-that had brought him all the way from his native village to speak with Elza whisper to him that his warning had already borne fruit, and that the gracious lady whom he had come to warn had found in faith and hope the way out of dark destiny?

"Oh, that's all right, darling! We spoke English all the time!"

Elza said this with a light laugh. Rosemary woke from her day-dream. She must have been speaking in her dream-about the gipsy who haunted her thoughts.

"Did I say anything?" she asked.

"Yes, darling," Anna replied, "you have been very silent for the last minute or two, and then suddenly you said: 'The gipsy, the gipsy,' twice, like that. It sounded so funny."

"I thought," Elza put in, "that perhaps you were afraid that the dirty old gipsy had heard what we said. But gipsies in Hungary don't speak English, you know. For one thing they never go to school."

Elza appeared quite light-hearted now.

"I knew," she said, "that you would approve of my plan."

She said this, but Rosemary herself was quite unconscious that she had spoken. She had dreamed and dreamed, and seen a motor-car speeding along the dusty road. But through it all, she had approved, approved of the plan. It was so feasible, and so simple. She only wondered why Peter disapproved.

"What does Peter Blakeney say to all that?" she asked presently.

"Peter?"

Elza asked wide-eyed.

"Yes. You told him about your plan, didn't you?"

"No! No!" Elza asserted firmly. "We have told no one but you. Peter is going away. Why should we tell Peter?"

"I thought--" Rosemary murmured.

"It will be time enough to tell him," Anna put in gaily, "when Philip and I turn up at the hotel at Hódmezö. Won't he be surprised when he sees us?"

How strange it all was! Peter knew, since he spoke of a mad plan in Elza's head, and begged Rosemary to dissuade her from it. Peter knew, though no one had told him. Another mystery added to all those which had of late filled Rosemary with such a torturing sense of foreboding. Another mystery that seemed to surround Peter's changed personality, that seemed a part of this new personality of his, flippant and indifferent, so unlike the Peter she had known.

Now she longed passionately for Jasper-dear, kind Jasper, around whom there hung no mystery-the strong hand that would guide her through this maze of intrigue which bewildered as much as it terrified her. Fortunately her promise to Jasper had been kept. With this new mystery about Peter that she vaguely dreaded, she would have been racked with anxiety if she had confided in him. And yet, how disloyal was this thought, this fear! Fear of Peter! Mistrust of Peter! A very little while ago she would have staked her soul that Peter was true, loyal, the soul of honour, an English gentleman, an English sportsman! A Blakeney! A Scarlet Pimpernel of to-day! What was there in the atmosphere of this unfortunate country groaning under a foreign, hated yoke to taint his simple soul with the foul breath of intrigue?

CHAPTER XXI

Walking across the lawn toward the château half an hour later, Rosemary found herself once more laughing at her suspicions of Peter. Peter!! Heavens above! what turn were her suspicions taking?

Did she really believe for one moment that Peter was intriguing with these crafty Roumanians for the undoing or the persecution of his own kith and kin? The very thought was preposterous. The suggestion untenable. Whatever Jasper might think, whatever he might fear, she, Rosemary, was nothing but a traitor if she allowed herself for one moment to harbour such thoughts of Peter.

He was changed, certainly he was changed. But between that and Jasper's suspicions--! It was Jasper who had first put thoughts into Rosemary's head by extracting that strange promise from her. Not to talk to Peter. Not to discuss the situation with Peter. Otherwise she would never for one moment--

Of course, of course, the thought was preposterous. Peter and intrigue! Peter and crafty Machiavellism! Peter and a double game he was ashamed to avow! Why, reason should have rejected the first hint of such a possibility, even if loyalty did not.

"Hallo, Rosemary!"

Peter's voice brought Rosemary back to reality. She had wandered up the veranda steps, hardly conscious of where she was. Thank Heaven, after her musings she was able to look Peter loyally in the face. He had his hands buried as usual in the pockets of his trousers, and the inevitable cigarette between his lips. Rosemary felt hot and tired; the sun had been baking the lawn while she walked across it, and she had no parasol. With a contented little sigh she sank into the basket chair that Peter pulled forward for her.

"I suppose," he said abruptly, "that they have been telling you about the nonsense that's going on in their dear, silly heads."

And with a nod he indicated the summer-house where, against the creeper-clad entrance, Elza's white dress gleamed in the sunshine. Rosemary made no reply. Peter's words had somehow acted like a douche of cold water upon her sense of rest and well-being. It was true then! He did know. Though Elza and Anna had told him nothing, he knew. How? Rosemary would have given worlds for the right to ask him, but suddenly her promise to Jasper loomed before her with paramount importance, and put a seal upon her lips.

"Won't you tell me?" Peter insisted.

Of course there was a simple explanation for the whole thing. Those dear people, Elza, Maurus, even Anna, were not models of discretion. Their voices were loud and penetrating, and, when they were excited about any project or event, they would discuss it here, there and everywhere at the top of their voices, and with a total disregard of possible eavesdroppers. Peter's knowledge of Elza's plans may have come about quite innocently. Rosemary was quite sure it had come about innocently. But somehow she longed for that perfect security and trust in Peter which she used to feel even when he was most capricious and his love-making most tempestuous. Why hadn't he told Elza that he knew? Why, instead of discussing the plan over with Elza or one of the others, did he feign ignorance with them, and suddenly elect to go away on an obviously futile excuse?

Oh, how Rosemary hated all this mystery! And how she feared it! And how, above all, she hated that promise which she had made to Jasper, and which prevented her at this moment from having a straight talk with Peter.

"So you won't tell me?" he reiterated, and his voice sounded curiously harsh, quite different to his usual very pleasant, musical tones. Peter had the voice of a musician. It was deep in tone and beautifully modulated. Peter's voice had been one of the things about him that had captivated Rosemary's fancy in the past. Now, he spoke through his teeth, with that hateful cigarette in the long holder held between the corners of his lips. Rosemary tried to be flippant.

"Dear me!" she exclaimed, with a little broken laugh, "are you trying to play the role of the heavy father, Peter, or of the silent strong man? And now you are frowning just like the hero in one of Ethel M. Dell's books. When are you going to seize me by the wrist and whack me with a slipper?"

It was very easy to make Peter laugh. He was laughing now, and the scowl fled for the moment from his face.

"Don't play the fool, Rosemary," he said in his slangy, boyish way. "Tell me what Aunt Elza has been saying to you out here?"

"But you silly boy," she riposted, "There's nothing to tell."

Back came the scowl on Peter's face, darker than before.

"So," he said curtly, "I suppose that you and Aunt Elza and Anna have been discussing frocks for the past hour and a half."

"No, dear," she replied coolly, "only the arrangements for to-morrow's ball."

Whereupon Peter said "Damn!" and swung round on his heel, as if he meant to leave her there without another word. But for this move of his Rosemary was unprepared. She did not want Peter to go. Not just yet. She was perfectly loyal to him in her thoughts, and she was irrevocably determined not to break her promise to Jasper, but she was not going to let Peter go off to-day without some sort of explanation. She might not see him again after this-for weeks, for months, for years! So she called him back.

"Peter!" she cried.

He swung back and returned to her side. His deep, changeful eyes, which at times were the colour of the ocean on the Cornish coast, and at others recalled the dark tints of his Hungarian ancestors, looked strangely resentful still. But as his glance rested on Rosemary, wandered from her delicate face in the pearly shadow of her garden hat, along the contour of her graceful shoes, the resentful look fled. And Rosemary, glancing up, caught a momentary flash of that soul-holding gaze which had taken her captive that lovely night in June by the river, when she had lain crushed and bruised in his arms, the gaze which that other night in the Albert Hall box had filled her soul with abiding regret.

"What do you want me to tell you, Peter?" she asked in that stupid way that comes to the lips when the soul is stirred and the mind commands self-control.

"Nothing," he replied roughly, "that you don't want to."

"Peter," she retorted, "why are you so strange with me? One would think I had done something to offend you. You scarcely will speak to me; when you do you are so rough and so abrupt, as if-as if---Oh, I don't know," she went on rapidly, and her voice shook a little as she tried to avoid that memory conjuring glance of his. "It seems as if something had come between us, almost as if we were enemies."

Peter laughed at this, but his laugh sounded rather forced and harsh.

"Enemies!" he exclaimed. "Good God, no!"

"But something has happened, Peter," she insisted. "I cannot tell you how I find you changed."

"Well," he said curtly, "something did happen, you know, when you married Jasper."

"I don't mean that, Peter. I saw you in London after I was engaged, and you had not changed then. It is here-in this place-that you seem so different."

"You must admit the place gets on one's nerves," he said with a shrug.

"You must make allowances, Peter," she rejoined gently. "They are in such trouble."

"Are they?" he retorted.

"Why, you know they are!" And her voice rang with a note of indignant reproach. "How can you ask?"

"I ask because I don't know. You say that they-I suppose you mean Aunt Elza and Maurus and the kids-are in trouble. How should I know what you mean? Since I've been here they have done nothing but shout, dance and make plans for more dancing and shouting, and when I ask you anything you only tell me lies."

"Peter!"

"I beg your pardon, dear," he said with sudden gentleness. "I didn't mean to be caddish. But you know," he went on, harshly once more, "you did tell me that Jasper had gone to Budapest on business."

"Well?" she queried.

"Well! Knowing you to be truthful by nature, I am wondering why you should have told me such an unnecessary lie." Then, as Rosemary was silent, he insisted: "Won't you tell me, Rosemary?"

"You are talking nonsense, Peter," she replied obstinately. "There is nothing to tell."

"Which means that Jasper has told you-or insinuated-that I am not to be trusted."

She protested: "Certainly not!"

"Then," he concluded, "the mistrust comes out of your own heart."

"That again is nonsense, Peter. There is no question of trust or mistrust, and I have no idea what you mean. It is you who try to deceive me by feigning ignorance of what is going on in this house. If Aunt Elza has not spoken openly with you, it certainly is not for me to enlighten you. There," she added, as she caught a look of eager questioning in his eyes, "I have already said more than I have any right to say. Elza and Anna are coming across the lawn. If you want to know anything more, you had better ask them."

And abruptly she rose and left him and went into the house. She felt hurt and angry and not a little ashamed. She felt hurt with Peter, angry with Jasper, and ashamed of herself. Peter was quite right. She had told him lies-unnecessary lies. And Jasper had forced her to tell them and to be disloyal to Peter. The present situation was a false one. Utterly false. It was Peter who should take over the direction of Elza's plan. With his help the chances of Philip's and Anna's escape would be increased tenfold. It seemed an awful thing-it was an awful thing-that he should be shut out of Elza's councils, that he should go away on a futile and trivial errand while those his own kith and kin were in such terrible danger, and running into dangers that were worse still.

For the last time the temptation returned, and with double violence, to break her promise to Jasper and go straight back to Peter and tell him everything. She paused in the centre of the drawing-room and looked back through the wide-open glass doors. Peter was still on the veranda. He had picked up a stick and a tennis ball and was hitting the one with the other and humming a tune. He caught Rosemary's eye as she glanced back to look at him.

"Hallo!" he called gaily.

Rosemary went deliberately back to the glass door. She paused under the lintel; then she said earnestly:

"Don't go to Hódmező to-day, Peter. I am sure there is no necessity for you to go. You can book rooms by telephone, and, anyway--" She paused a moment and then went on more earnestly still: "Wait another twenty-four hours, Peter. Don't go till-till after the ball."

Peter did not look at her. He was taking careful aim with the stick and the tennis ball. He made a swinging hit and watched the ball fly away over the lawn. Then he threw the stick down and turned to Rosemary.

"Sorry," he said lightly, "but I have promised."

She gave an impatient sigh, and after another second's hesitation once more turned to go.

"I say," he called after her, "what about a game of tennis. There's just time for a set before I need make a start."

But by now all temptation to talk openly with Peter had vanished. What would be the use of telling this irresponsible boy anything? Jasper was right. Elza was right. Only she, Rosemary, was foolish, and her vaunted knowledge of human nature nothing but vanity. She had only sufficient self-control left to call back lightly to him:

"No, thank you, Peter, I am rather tired."

Then she fled precipitately out of the room.

CHAPTER XXII

Rosemary did not see Peter again before he left. Somehow that last vision which she had of him, hitting at a rubber ball with a stick, and his utterly callous suggestion of a game of tennis at an hour which he must have known was fateful to all his kindred, had caused a revulsion in Rosemary's heart. She felt that never again would she feel tempted to break her word to Jasper. Indeed, she felt how right Jasper had been all along in insisting that she should not discuss the grave events that affected the lives of all the inmates of Kis-Imre with such a callous, empty-headed, irresponsible young jackanapes as Peter had lately become.

So she had gone upstairs to her room, and with a curious heartache, for which she was unable to account, she listened to the familiar bustle and noise that always filled the château whenever visitors came or went. Somehow she could not bring herself to say "Good-bye" to Peter. Elza had told her that he would be coming back within the next week or so, but Rosemary, who felt too tired for introspection, could not have told you whether she was glad or sorry at the prospect of seeing him again quite so soon.

The rest of the day, as well as the long, interminable evening, were taken up with the discussion of household affairs-the luncheon, the dinner, the ball, and even into these Philip and Anna entered wholeheartedly and with apparent complete disregard of what that fateful morrow might bring them. As for Elza, she was perfectly marvellous! Kind, fussy as usual, her menus and the airing of the guest-rooms being, to all appearances, the most important matters in her mind.

After everyone had gone to bed little Anna came to Rosemary's room and sat for a while beside her on the sofa, holding the Englishwoman's hand as if she wished to transfuse through those slender fingers strength and courage into her soul. When Rosemary made a passing allusion to the wonderful stoicism that could allow trivial matters to seem so important at a moment when life and worse were at stake, Anna explained quite gently:

"We are made like that, we Hungarians. We hold our lives cheap, I think, because throughout our history we have always had to sacrifice them for our country. And also, I think, that we have a certain Oriental fatalism in us. Not the fatalism of the Moslem, who abdicates free will, but the faith of the Christian who believes that God ordains everything and that it is useless to fight his decrees."

"And yet you are not a religious people," Rosemary riposted, thinking of what Elza had said to her the night before.

"Only in the sense that children are religious," Anna rejoined. "We accept blindly what some kind nuns and ignorant priests have taught us, and we believe in an Almighty God more absolutely and ingenuously than the more thoughtful people of the West."

Long after Anna had gone Rosemary thought over what the child had said. Well, perhaps it was true. There certainly was an exquisitely beautiful passage in the New Testament where the Divine Master enjoins his disciples to become as little children. And, recollecting Anna's words, Rosemary caught herself wondering whether the childlike faith of these people would not open the Kingdom of Heaven more easily for them than would a more considered, more rational religion-a compromise between a very erring human reason and the Divine Mysteries which no human thought could fathom.

As for the next day, it was just a whirl, a jumble of gaieties and talk, of arrivals and merry greetings, of meals and tennis and walks, and of talk, talk, talk and endless laughter. Rosemary, when she rose, had made up her mind that she would just shed her real personality for the whole of the day. She would cease to be Rosemary with the aching heart, the soul rent by conflicting duties, by anxieties, determination and sorrow; she would become the "dear Lady Tarkington," the "Rosemary darling" of all these kind, hospitable, wonderful people. She would laugh with them, play with them and with them lay aside for the next few hours the torturing anxiety of the day.

She would forget, she would laugh, she would talk. The effort would do her good, and when the hour came when the fate of all those she cared for would have to be decided, when on one word, one smile, would perhaps hang the destiny of Philip and of Anna, then she would be strong enough to play the part allotted to her in the tragic farce--the farce that had found birth in the brain of a heart-broken mother.

CHAPTER XXIII

And it had been a wonderful day. The weather was perfect. Everyone was in the highest possible spirits. The chef surpassed himself; everyone pronounced the lobster à l'Américaine perfect and the Charlotte Russe Créole quite inimitable.

All afternoon tennis balls were flying, and there was coffee, ices and iced drinks going all day on the lawn. At five o'clock the gipsy musicians from Bonczhida arrived, and after that music never ceased. Rosemary learned something of gipsy endurance that day, for this band of twelve musicians never left off playing form the moment they arrived until-until midnight, when time ceased to be and Fate began to swing her long pendulum.

But between five o'clock and midnight there was music, ceaseless music. While the guests arrived, while everyone played tennis, croquet, drank coffee, walked, flirted, dressed, dined and danced there was music-music all the time.

After dinner the young Roumanian officers from the garrison at Cluj came over in several motors. Among them were the eleven cricketers, very proud of themselves, feeling quite English and real sportsmen, delighted to have been chosen to play in the historic match. Fine-looking young men, most of them, with the unmistakable swaggering air of the conqueror about their whole attitude towards the subject race. Elza was invariably a perfect hostess; but Maurus, after a curt greeting, nursed his wrath in a corner of the ballroom, surrounded by his own friends. He had been drilled to keep his temper in check, and love for his own son, anxiety for him and knowledge of danger gave him for this one evening a certain amount of self-control. Rosemary admired him as much as she did the others, for she knew what it cost Maurus to have these alien conquerors in his house.

Anna's mother and sister had come over from Ujlak. The mother was a hard woman, obviously selfish and unsympathetic. Her own grievances, the confiscation of a great deal of her property, seemed to have smothered every soft, womanly instinct in her. Apparently she knew nothing of the danger that hung over her daughter, and Rosemary had the feeling that if she had known she would not greatly have cared. Her eyes, which were dark and set very wide apart in a flat, colourless face, only softened once, and that was when she spoke about her husband, who had died just before the war.

As for persecutions, humiliations, petty tyrannies, she dismissed them with a shrug of the shoulders. "The Roumanians are the scum of the earth," she said in her quiet, unemotional manner, through her thin, colourless lips, "just a horde of uneducated peasantry; you can't expect anything from a pig but a grunt. I am only thankful that Béla is not here to see it all."

On the other hand, the young people who filled the stately château of Kis-Imre with their flutterings like an army of gaily painted butterflies did not worry about political grievances. For them the Roumanian officers were just dancing-partners, and their worth was only measured by their proficiency in the latest steps. The mammas and papas either played bridge or sat on the chairs that were ranged against the walls all round the beautiful ballroom placidly admiring the evolutions of their own progeny.

Rosemary, not to be outdone in self-discipline, was outwardly as gay as any of them. She danced impartially with the Hungarians and the Roumanians, and talked cricket knowledgeably with the team. For her the atmosphere was electrical. At times it seemed to her overstrained senses as if she could hear the whir of the spinning-wheel driven by the Fates, the hum of the spindle, and the click of their scissors as they made ready to cut the thread of these people's destiny.

Just before midnight the young Roumanian officers who formed the cricket team left in the two motor-cars which were to take them direct to Hódmezö, a matter of ninety odd miles. Rosemary found herself saying good-bye to them like an automaton--counting them over as if they were ninepins. A kind of mist was before her eyes through which their good-looking faces seemed to be grinning at her, and their moustaches bristling like Alice's Cheshire cat.

Elza, wonderful as ever, fussed around them, stuffing delicacies into the cars at the last moment, fruit, bottles of wine, cakes, chocolates, and lending them rugs and cushions.

"It is a long drive," she said, as she shook hands one by one with the young officers, who clicked their heels together, jingled their spurs and declared that they had had a very pleasant evening. "You will be hungry when you get to Hódmezö," she added, "and all the restaurants will be closed. You will be glad of a glass of wine and some of my home-made cake."

Rosemary was standing next to Maurus Imrey at the time. She heard him mutter between his teeth:

"And may it choke you when you eat and drink."

But even Maurus was wonderful. Wonderful! He shook hands. He smiled--wryly; but he smiled. Wished them all God-speed. He had been well drilled, and he was fully conscious of the danger to Philip and Anna if he lost control over his temper now.

So he, too, gave directions for putting provisions into the cars. He had four bottles of French red wine in his cellar and he insisted that the young officers should have those. "It will make them play that silly cricket better," he said. "And I hate the stuff myself."

The four men who were going with the team as servants were there arranging the rugs, stowing the wine and fruit and cake in the cars. Rosemary knew the two sons of János, the miller, by sight. They were fine, well-set-up young fellows, obviously of the stuff that heroes are made of, for they were going to risk their lives for the children of their feudal lords.

Anna, equally self-possessed, flitted among the guests like a little fairy. She had on a pale blue dress, and out in the open her slim figure was hardly distinguishable in the gloom; only her small, white face told as if carved out of alabaster: that dear little face, with the big eyes that were so like Peter's. When she was saying good-bye to one of the young officers, who had been her dancing-partner, she said with a pout:

"I think it was horrid of you to telephone to Peter Blakeney yesterday and take him away from us. I don't believe you would have had any difficulty with the hotel people about your rooms. And, anyway, you might have let Peter have another day's enjoyment."

The young man appeared genuinely bewildered.

"Will the gracious lady deign to explain?" he asked.

"Oh, there is nothing to explain," Anna said, with a light laugh. "We were all of us very angry with you for sending that telephone message which took Peter Blakeney away from us."

"But pardon me, dear lady," the officer rejoined, "we didn't send any telephone message to Monsieur Blakeney. As a matter of fact, we fully expected to find him here."

"But about your rooms--?" Anna insisted.

"Our rooms at Hódmezö have been arranged for ages ago. Everything there is in perfect order and--"

"Anna, dear," Rosemary broke in quickly, "Peter didn't say who sent him the telephone message. He only said that he had one. It may have come from Hódmezö-from one of the hotel people-he didn't say--"

What had prompted Rosemary to interpose at this moment she did not know. It was just an instinct: the blind instinct to protect, to shield Peter from something ugly and vague, that she had not yet had time to see clearly, and Anna then went on lightly:

"Oh, of course he didn't say. Anyway, when you see Peter, tell him he was very silly to go away, and that he missed a great deal by not being here to-night. You can tell him that Marie never danced so well in all her life, and the gipsies from Bonczhida simply surpassed themselves."

Whereupon the young officer clicked his heels and promised that he would deliver the message.

"But we shan't see Monsieur Blakeney," he said, "until the evening. You know the match is not until Thursday. Monsieur Blakeney arranged to meet us in Hódmezö on Wednesday evening, and this is only Tuesday.

"It will be Wednesday morning before we start," one of his friends broke in lightly, "if you don't hurry, you old chatterbox."

After that, more "good-byes" and waving of hands as the motorcars rounded the courtyard and finally swung out of the gates. Rosemary looked round to catch sight of Elza. She was quite placid, and on her dear, round face there was a set smile. Evidently she was unconscious of the fact that something stupendous had happened, something that had hit Rosemary like a blow from a sledge-hammer. No, no! Elza had not noticed. Elza's mind was no longer here. It was way out upon the dusty road, watching a motorcar travelling at full speed over the frontier away from this land of bondage, to Hungary to freedom. Elza had noticed nothing. Anna and Philip were still laughing and chattering, Maurus muttering curses. No one had noticed anything. Only for Rosemary had the world-her own beautiful world of truth and loyalty-come to an end. Peter had lied. Peter was playing a double game. It was no use arguing, no use hoping. The only thing to do was to go on

Pimpernel and Rosemary

groping in this mystery that deepened and deepened, until it became tangible, material like a thick, dark fog through which glided ghouls and demons who whispered and laughed. And they whispered and laughed because Peter had lied and because she, Rosemary, saw all her hopes, her faith, her ideals lying shattered in a tangled heap at her feet. Peter had lied. He had acted a lie. He told her that he had promised to go to Hódmező to see about rooms for the cricket team. Well, that was not true. Rosemary had interposed, made some excuse for Peter. She wouldn't have those Roumanians think that Peter was a liar. They would have smiled, suggested some amorous intrigue which Monsieur Blakeney wished to keep dark. At the thought Rosemary's gorge rose, and she put in a lame defence for Peter. But all the time she knew that he had lied. If Peter did not go to Hódmező yesterday, where was he now? Why all this secrecy? These lies?

Why? Oh, God, why?

Rosemary had found a quiet corner in the hall where she could sit and think for a moment. Yet thinking was the one thing she could not do. Always, at every turn she was confronted with that hideous query: Why had Peter lied? After a while she had to five up trying to think. Fate's spindle was whirring, the scissors clinking. She, Rosemary, a mere atom in the hands of Fate, must continue to play her part.

A quarter of an hour must have gone by while she sat-trying to think-in the dark. Perhaps more. Anyway, when she returned to the ballroom she found the company much diminished in numbers. All the Roumanian officers had gone, also one large party who lived just the other side of Cluj. Only a few remained whose châteaux were too far away for a midnight start, seeing that motors were forbidden to the conquered race. They were going to spend the night at Kis-Imre, and probably make a start in the morning. The young people had already resumed dancing; the gipsies were playing the latest fox-trot. The mammas and papas were placidly admiring their respective progeny.

All this Rosemary took in at a glance.

Then she looked round for Elza. But neither Elza nor Maurus was there. And Philip and Anna had also gone.

138

CHAPTER XXIV

A few minutes later Elza came back. To Rosemary, who had been watching for her by the door, she just whispered as she entered:

"It is all right. They have gone."

She still was wonderful. Quite calm and with that set smile on her face. Only her round, blue eyes had an unusual glitter, and the pretty silvered hair clung matted against the smooth white brow. Rosemary watched the scene, now entranced. She had never seen anything like it. It did not seem reality at all. It could not be. All these people here were just puppets and they were play-acting. They could not have behaved as they did if they had been real.

There were no longer any Roumanians there. They were all Hungarians together-just a few of them, all from Transylvania, the wretched, occupied territory, in which everybody was something of a slave, never allowed to forget for an instant that they were the defeated, and that they must submit. All were relatives or else very intimate friends. And after a while they began to notice that Philip and Anna were not there. At first they asked questions. Where were Philip and Anna? Elza said nothing. She only gave an answering look here and there, a quiver of the eyelid and certain setting of the lips. She did not say anything, but it was remarkable how everybody understood.

Rosemary watched every face and knew that they understood. They asked no more questions. They accepted the situation. Philip and Anna had gone. They had to go as countless others, who had to fly at dead of night, get the other side of the frontier as quickly as possible, to escape from military tribunal, chicanery, persecution, or even death.

It was late now, long past midnight. The gipsies had been sent downstairs to get some supper. The mammas and papas declared that it was time to go to bed. The young people thanked dear Aunt Elza for such a happy time, the young men kissed her hand. One or two of the older people whispered: "Good luck!" Others said reassuringly: "Don't fret, they will be all right." Never a question about Philip and Anna. Never a comment. They knew. They understood.

Orders were given for the carriages to be ready at nine o'clock the next morning. With the innate delicacy that underlay so much apparent pleasure-loving, they wished to relieve as soon as practicable this house of sorrow from the burden of their presence.

By half-past twelve ballroom, hall, reception-rooms, were all empty. Elza waited downstairs till the last of the servants had gone. Rosemary helped her at the last to put the gold service away in the strong cupboard. It consisted of half a dozen pieces of great artistic beauty and equally great value. Each piece had to be wrapped up in cotton wool and green baize. Elza did it all, and Rosemary could see that her podgy white hands did not tremble, and that she put every piece away with her usual meticulous care. Only when her task was accomplished and there was nothing more to do but switch off the light did Elza's stoicism give way. She sank into a chair, her head fell back against the cushions, and a leaden tint spread over her cheeks and lips. Rosemary quickly poured some brandy into a glass, and kneeling beside her tried to get her to drink some of it. To please her, Elza sipped a few drops. A wan smile spread over her face.

"Don't worry about me, Rosemary darling," she said, "I am quite well."

She jumped up at once and added: "I must see how poor Maurus is."

"Come into my room afterwards," Rosemary suggested, "and rest there on the sofa. I know you won't sleep."

"Yes," Elza replied, "I will come as soon as I can get Maurus to sleep. I think he may get to sleep presently. But I don't think I shall. You see, we ought to get a telephone message through from Hódmező the first thing in the morning. Philip and I agreed on a code. If everything is all right he is to give Peter Blakeney's name and say that the weather is beautiful in Hungary, and every arrangement for the cricket match splendid. After I get that message I shall probably sleep."

She had toiled up the stairs while she was talking, and Rosemary followed close behind her, ready to catch her if she swooned.

"I won't say 'good night' now," Elza said when she near her bedroom door. "You go to bed, Rosemary darling, and I will come in presently for a little talk when Maurus is asleep."

Rosemary went into her room. She undid her hair and slipped into a dressing-gown. It was no use going to bed; she knew she would not be able to go to sleep. It was just a case of waiting. Of watching, of praying, and commending those two young creatures to God. Watching and praying, with eyes fixed upon the hands of the clock, following in imagination every phase of to-nights adventures. Every detail. At this hour they would be at the mill, all the actors in the drama which poor Elza had invented. Philip and Anna would be there, changing into peasant's clothes, and János the miller would be setting out the mugs and the spirit, which would make the Jew's son and the brother of the Roumanian storekeeper blind to the world. Old Emma would be there too, the miller's wife, the mother of the two boys who were going to risk so much for Philip's sake and Anna's Emma would be fussing round with cloth and duster. Grumbling and fussing. Knowing nothing of the drama on which the curtain would ring up in the parlour of her cottage, and in which her two sons would be playing leading roles. János would not have told her. He, the father, had agreed to it all; had even suggested it. But the mother? No! If she knew she would protest. Weep, of course. Weaken the resolution of the two boys who just had to go through with it all.

And now the motor would be drawing up at the mill, and János the miller would ask the company to walk in and have a drink. Even the motor-driver would be persuaded. Just a drop of spirit, as it was a long drive all the way to Hódmezö. Time was moving leaden-footed up here in the château. But not so at the mill, while János was telling funny stories and plying his guests with drink. Leaden-footed! My God! how slowly did those clock hands move! Only half an hour gone by since Elza had switched off all the lights, and the whole château was plunged in darkness, and every sound was stilled.

So still! Only the ticking of the clock, and at times the click of the scissors of Fate, ready to cut the thread of two young lives--of more perhaps--if anything went wrong, if the slightest mistake was made, if any one man proved disloyal--or a liar.

Rosemary shuddered although the night was hot. She could not sit still. At times she felt that she could not breathe. She went out upon the balcony and listened. Listened. The air was so still that she felt she must hear presently the whir of the motor when it made a fresh start from the mill half a mile away. Far away on the hillside a fox gave a cry, and from the old thatched barn close by came the melancholy hoot of an owl.

Then the village church clock struck the half-hour. Half-past one. More than an hour since Rosemary, going into the ballroom, had noted that Philip and Anna were no longer there. In one of the homesteads on the outskirts of the village a cock crew. In another two hours dawn would be breaking, and the motor was to be in Hódmezö before sunrise. And suddenly Rosemary heard right through the stillness a crepi-crepitation and then a whir. And then the whirring died away very gradually, and stillness reigned once more. Absolute!

"They've started!"

It was Elza's voice close to Rosemary's elbow. Rosemary had not heard her timid knock, and Elza had slipped into the room and now stood by the open window, listening. The voice was quite calm, with just a ring in it of exultation rather than excitement. Rosemary took her hand. It was quite cold. She fondled it and warmed it between her own.

There was a wicker chair on the balcony and some cushions. Rosemary made Elza sit down, and then she piled up the cushions and squatted on them at Elza's feet, fondling her hands and caressing them by laying her young velvety cheek against them.

The night was exquisitely beautiful, with the waning moon mysterious and honey-coloured in a firmament shimmering with stars. In the borders the flowers slept, the evening primroses had folded their golden petals, the scarlet pentstemons hidden their brilliance in the gloom; only the heliotrope and the nicotiana swung their censers, lazily sending their heady perfume through the night, and the white tufted pansies shone like numberless tiny mirrors, reflecting the stars.

"Did Maurus get to sleep?" Rosemary asked after a while.

"Yes," Elza replied. "I gave him a cachet of aspirin. It quietened his nerves, and after a while he went to sleep."

"Won't you just close your eyes, Elza, and try to rest a little? The night is young yet, and I am afraid you'll be ill if you don't get a little rest. You've gone through so much!"

"Presently, darling," Elza said quietly. "I dare say I shall drop to sleep, as I am very tired. But not just yet. I would like to stay here a little longer-unless I am bothering you." Then, as Rosemary gave her knees an affectionate hug, she went on gently: "I love the smell of flowers in the night, don't you? They smell quite differently from what they do in the daytime." And presently she went on à propos of nothing at all:

"There is just one difficult place where the driver might miss his way. That would delay them a little, but even so they should be very near the frontier by now."

"Have you arranged to get any news?" Rosemary asked.

"Philip is to telephone from Hódmezö as soon as the office is open."

"You won't hear before then?"

"Yes. I told János to say to the motor-driver that if he will drive straight back here from Hódmezö there will be a thousand leis for him, and if he gets here before eight o'clock then he will get two thousand."

After the village church clock had struck three Elza became very still, but Rosemary did not think that she was actually asleep. Her hands were very cold, and her breath came and went more rapidly than usual. Rosemary rose noiselessly to her feet, she got the eiderdown from her bed and wrapped it round Elza's knees. Elza did not move. Her pretty, round face showed very white in the light of the waning moon, and all her hair seemed to have lost its golden tint and shimmered like threads of silver.

Rosemary went back into the room and lay down on the sofa. The air was very close, and she was very tired, so tired that she must have fallen asleep. Presently something roused her and she opened her eyes. The room was flooded with the golden light of dawn. She jumped to her feet and went to the window. Elza was not on the balcony; but Rosemary, looking over the balustrade, saw her on the veranda about to descent the steps.

"Elza," she called down softly, "wait for me."

Elza nodded acquiescence, and Rosemary ran down-stairs just as she was, in dressing-gown and slippers, with her hair all hanging loosely round her shoulders. Elza had waited on the veranda for her quite patiently; she linked her arm in Rosemary's.

"You were able to sleep a little, darling," she said. "I am so glad."

"And what about you, Elza?" Rosemary retorted.

"Oh, I slept quite nicely," Elza replied in her quiet, simple way, "until the dawn closed the eyes of the night one by one, and the moon went down behind the old acacia trees."

"I quite forgot to look at the time," Rosemary rejoined.

"It was half-past four when I left your room. I went to have a peep at Maurus. He is still asleep."

"Thank God for that. He will only wake to hear the good news."

Rosemary could no longer keep the excitement out of her voice. Another two or three hours and this terrible suspense would be over. She hardly dared to look at Elza, for she felt the dear creature's body quivering against hers. The first glance had shown her Elza's face the colour of ashes, with swollen eyelids and red hectic spots on her cheek-bones. But outwardly she was still quite calm, and when together they reached the dew-wet lawn she threw back her head and with obvious delight drank in the sweet morning air.

"It is astonishing," she said, "that one should be able to sleep when-when things happen like they did to-night."

"You were dog-tired, Elza, and the air was so wonderfully balmy and soothing. I think," Rosemary went on gently, "that God sent down a couple of his guardian angels to fan you to sleep with their wings."

"Perhaps," Elza assented with a tired smile.

"Do you feel like a walk, as far as the perennial border?"

"Why, yes. I should love it. And we still have hours to kill."

Already sounds of awakening village life filled the morning with their welcome strains. The fox and the owl were silent, but two cocks gave answer to one another, and from the homesteads and the farms came a lowing and a bleating and a barking, the beasts rousing the humans to activity and calling them to the work of the day.

As Elza's and Rosemary's footsteps crunched the gravel of the path, Mufti, the big sheep-dog, and Karo, the greyhound, came from nowhere in particular, bounding across the lawn, and threw themselves, in the exuberance of their joy, upon these two nice humans who had shortened the lonely morning hours for them.

"Let's go and see the moss-roses," Rosemary suggested, "see if they smell as sweet as they did in the night."

They walked on to the end of the perennial border, where two or three clumps of moss-roses nestled at the foot of a tall crimson Rugosa laden with blossom.

"Dear little things," Elza said. "They are my favourite flowers. I like them so much better than all those wonderful new roses that get the prizes at the horticultural shows."

She stooped to inhale the fragrance of the roses, and while she was stooping a faint, very distant whirring sound became audible, which grew in volume every moment. Just for the space of one second Elza did not move; she remained just as she was, stooping and with her face buried in the roses. Then she straightened out her fine figure and grasped Rosemary's hand.

"The motor," she said huskily. "Let us go."

The end of the perennial border where they were was nearly a quarter of a mile away from the house; and then there was the house to get round, the courtyard to cross---The whirring grew louder every moment, then slower, and then it ceased. The car had come to a halt, but not in front of the gates, which were still closed. Rosemary and Elza

144

were in the courtyard with Mufti and Karo jumping about them and getting in the way. The motor was not in sight.

"Down, Mufti! Karo, down!" Elza kept repeating mechanically.

She was rather breathless after that race across the garden. Rosemary ran to the lodge to call Feri, the night-watchman, who had the keys of the gate. He had heard the dogs barking and the voice of the gracious countess, so he was on the doorstep wondering what had brought the ladies out at this hour of the morning.

"Quick, Feri, open the gates!" Rosemary called to him.

It took Feri a few moments to get the keys to unlock the gates. An eternity.

From the direction of the village there had come a loud cry, followed after a few seconds by shouts and the sound of men running. Running and shouting, and now and then another shrill cry.

"Run ahead quickly, Feri," Rosemary whispered to the watchman. "Quickly, see what it is."

She held Elza's hand in the tight clutch, and under her arm. But even so Elza succeeded in breaking free, and while Feri ran on ahead, she did not lag far behind. Past the thick clump of acacias, the village street came in sight. At the end of it, a quarter of a mile away, in front of the inn which was kept by the Jew, a motorcar had come to a halt, and some half-dozen peasants stood round it, gesticulating and arguing. Down the street, from one or two of the cottages, men, women and children came running out to see what was happening, and when they caught sight of the gracious countess and the gracious foreign lady they paused, bewildered. The gracious countess-at this hour in the village! Such a thing had never happened before. The men doffed their hats, the women hastily bobbed a curtsy, the children stood stock-still, finger in mouth, staring. A few, bolder than the rest, ran forward to kiss the ladies' hands. But Elza hastened on, seeing nothing, heeding nothing, whilst Rosemary kept close by her side. Feri, as he drew near to the inn, shouted to the people to make way. But as soon as he came in close sight of the car he turned and hastened back to Elza. He clasped his hands together and cried:

"Don't come, gracious countess. Don't come! It is nothing, nothing, just an accident, a--"

Silently, with lips tightly pressed together, Elza pushed past him, but Rosemary now had once more taken hold of her hand. She held Elza tight, with one arm round her waist and the other clutching her hand. Struggle as she might, Elza could not free herself this time.

The next moment they stood together by the side of the motor. It was a large, rather shabby touring car, painted a dull grey and fitted with leather cushions. It was smothered in dust. There was no one in the back seats, but the innkeeper was just in the act of climbing in beside the chauffeur. The chauffeur appeared to be asleep; he sat like a huddled-up heap, wrapped in a dirty, military coat, and with his peaked cap pulled down over his face. The innkeeper appeared rather scared. He took hold of the military coat and pulled it open, and immediately he clapped his hand to his mouth, smothering a scream. The cap rolled off the chauffeur's head, and his right arm dropped down the side of the car. One man who stood quite near, not knowing probably that the two ladies were there, cried excitedly:

"God in heaven! The man has been shot-dead!"

CHAPTER XXV

There was no one there quite so self-possessed as Elza. Even Rosemary had some difficulty in smothering a cry. The innkeeper jumped down from the seat as if he had been driven away by a whip; the peasants gesticulated and jabbered in an undertone. Rosemary looked at Elza and clutched her hand more tightly against her own body. Elza's face was the colour of lead, her lips looked purple, even her large, blue eyes appeared colourless. Her hand was as cold as ice and shook in Rosemary's strength-giving clasp. But to the eyes of all these peasants and subordinates she appeared perfectly calm, and after a moment or two she turned to the group of jabbering, gesticulating peasants and asked quite quietly:

"Which of you first saw the motor draw up?"

"I heard the noise, gracious countess," the Jew volunteered, "as the car drew up outside the door, and--"

"And I saw the soldier jump down," a young labourer broke in excitedly. "He ran--"

"Very well," Elza said coldly. "Now you, and you," she went on and pointed to the innkeeper and to the labourer, "come inside and tell me what you have seen. Will you come, too, darling?" she asked Rosemary.

Finally she turned to her own man Feri:

"One of you," she said, "had better go to the gendarmerie. They ought to have been here by now."

Then she went into the inn; the Jew and the labourer followed, and the peasants, having looked their fill at the car, or else scared by that lifeless bundle in the chauffeur's seat, crowded together in the doorway of the inn. But Rosemary lagged behind for a moment, examining the car as if she expected the huge, shabby thing to yield up the key of its own mystery. But in the body of the car there was nothing, except the cushions and the dust and the huddled figure of the dead chauffeur, with the head fallen forward on the breast, and the arm hanging over the side of the car. Rosemary turned away from it at first with a shudder, but almost despite her will her eyes turned back to gaze again at that huddled-up heap and the limp arm, from beneath the coat-sleeve of which a thin filet of blood trickled drop by drop to the ground.

And suddenly something white and crisp fell from the lifeless hand into the dust at Rosemary's feet. She stooped and picked it up. Fortunately the jabbering peasants were not looking this way, and Feri had walked off to the gendarmerie. What Rosemary had picked up was a letter addressed to "Lady Tarkington." She tore open the envelope and read:

"A very clumsy attempt, dear lady. As you see, it has led to no good. Your two protégés are now under my direct care, and you have little more than a fortnight in which to write the newspaper articles which I want."

The letter was signed "Naniescu." Rosemary slipped it into the pocket of her gown, and then she went into the inn. The peasants all made way for her, and then crowded again in the doorway, trying to hear what was going on. Rosemary thought the long, low room one of the stuffiest and most evil-smelling places she had ever been in. It was very dark, the light only feebly penetrating through two tiny, impracticable windows, the panes of which were covered in dust. The only breath of fresh air that could possibly find its way in would have been through the door, but that was blocked now by a solid bundle of perspiring humanity. From the low raftered ceiling hung strings of onions and maize, and in a corner of the room, on a low table which was apparently used as a counter, were numerous bottles and a number of pewter mugs. The odour in the room was a mixture of dirt, onions and silvorium. But Elza, who sat beside the table with the innkeeper and the peasants before her, appeared quite unconscious of smells or dirt. She was questioning the labourer, who apparently was the only man who had actually witnessed the arrival of the motor-car into the village.

"I saw it come, gracious countess," he said, with obvious pride in his own importance, "and I saw it draw up outside here. There was a soldier sitting near the chauffeur."

"And he was in the driving seat?" Elza asked.

"Yes, gracious countess, the soldier was driving when I first saw the car come along the road."

"And the other man?"

"Well, gracious countess, I saw a sort of heaped-up bundle beside the chauffeur. I did not know there was another man."

"Well, then what happened?"

"The car slowed down, gracious countess, and drew up outside here. Then the soldier jumped up; he stepped over the heaped-up bundle and got out of the car."

"Yes, and then?"

"He took the thing which I thought was just a bundle covered with a military coat, and pushed it into the driver's seat. After that he ran away as fast as he could."

"In which direction?"

"Where he had come from, gracious countess. There was another car waiting for him there about half a kilometre away."

"Another car?"

"Yes; I didn't see it come, but I heard it slow down and come to a halt. The soldier ran all the way. He jumped into that other car, and it drove away in the direction of Cluj."

After that another man stepped in from the doorway and volunteered the information that he had seen the second car standing about half a kilometre away. He had seen the soldier running, and had seen the car drive off. He thought there was another soldier in that car.

By that time a couple of gendarmes were on the scene. They were conducting their own investigations of the case in a casual, perfunctory manner. At first they took no notice of Elza or of Rosemary, talked over their heads in a proper democratic manner; then one of them asked curtly of Elza:

"Did you see the car drive up?"

Elza said: "No!"

"Do you know anything about it?"

Again she replied: "No!"

Whereupon the man queried roughly: "Then what are you doing here?"

Elza's face flushed a little, but she replied quite courteously: "We all hoped at the castle to hear that the miller's two sons had arrived safely at Hódmezö, and I thought that this was the car that drove them in the night."

The man gave a sneer and a shrug of the shoulders.

"You seem mightily concerned," he said, with a harsh laugh, "about the miller's sons, to be out of your bed at this hour of the morning."

He spat on the ground, turned on his heel, and once more addressed the peasants.

"Now, then," he said, quite genially, "all of you get back to your homes. The Government will see about this affair, and it is no concern of anybody's. Understood?"

The two gendarmes waved their arms and drove the people out of the inn and away from the door as if they were a flock of sheep. They obeyed without murmur, only with an occasional shrug of the shoulders, as much as to say: "Well, well, these are strange times, to be sure! But it is no concern of ours."

The gendarmes then went out of the inn. They moved the body of the dead chauffeur into the body of the car; one of them got in beside it, the other took the driver's seat, and the next moment the mysterious car had disappeared up the village street in the direction of the gendarmerie.

When the last of the crowd had dispersed, Elza rose and, white-faced, wide-eyed, she turned to Rosemary.

"There is nothing more," she said, "that we can do here. Shall we go home?"

She nodded to the Jew, and, leaning heavily on Rosemary's arm, she went out into the street. It was past six now, and the village was flooded with sunlight. Elza's tired, aching eyes blinked as she came out into the open. Rosemary would have put an arm round her to support her, for she felt that the poor woman was ready to swoon; but mutely and firmly Elza refused to be supported. Her pride would not allow her, even now, to show weakness in sight of these cottages, behind the windows of which the eyes of Roumanian peasants might be on the look-out for her.

"They are outwardly obsequious," she said, as if in answer to a mute remark from Rosemary. "Call me gracious countess and kiss my hand, but at heart they hate us all, and triumph in our humiliation."

Strange, wonderful people! Even at this hour of supreme anxiety and acute distress, pride of caste fought every outward expression of sorrow and conquered in the end. Elza walked through the village with a firm step and head held quite erect. It was only when she was inside the gates of her own home that she spoke, and even then her first thought was for her husband.

"How to break the news to Maurus!" she murmured under her breath. "My God, how to break the news."

In the hall, where Rosemary saw that they were quite alone, she put her arms round Elza and drew her down into a low-cushioned seat.

"Elza, darling," she said gently, "have a real cry, it will do you good."

Elza shook her head.

"It won't bring Philip back," she said dully, "nor Anna. Will it?"

Her big, round eyes gazed with pathetic inquiry into Rosemary's face. She seemed to have some sort of intuition that her English friend could help-that she could do something for Philip, even now. Rosemary, her eyes swimming in tears, slowly shook her head. And with a low moan, Elza buried her face in the cushions, convulsive sobs shook her shoulders, and little cries of pain broke intermittently from her lips. Rosemary made no attempt to touch her. She let her cry on. Perhaps it was for the best. There was nobody about, and tears were sometimes a solace. The quietude, the stoicism of the past two hours, had been unnatural, racking alike to heart, nerves and brain. There was a limit to human endurance, and Elza had reached it at last.

When the worst of the paroxysm was over, Rosemary suggested gently: "Would you like me to break the news to Maurus? I'll do it most carefully, and I am afraid the strain would be too much for you."

But already Elza had struggled to her feet. She was wiping her eyes, then breathing on her handkerchief and dabbing them with it.

"No, no, my dear," she said between the dry, intermittent sobs that still shook her poor weary body, "not on any account. I understand Maurus. I know just what to say. Poor, poor Maurus! He has so little self-control. But I shall know what to say. You go and get your bath now, darling," she went on, gently disengaging herself from Rosemary's arms, "and get dressed. It will refresh you. I will do the same before I speak to Maurus. Rosa shall bring your coffee in half an hour. Will that do?"

She forgot noting, thought of everything-Rosemary's bath, her breakfast, the guest. Ah, yes, the guests! Rosemary had forgotten all about them. It was long past six now; they would soon be up. All of them wanting breakfast, baths, attention. Elza forgot nothing. Thank God that she had so much to think about!

"You go up, darling," she said to Rosemary. "I shall be quite all right. Don't worry about me."

One or two servants came through the hall, busy with their work. Elza had something to say, some order to give to all of them.

"Tell the chef," she said to Anton, "to come and speak to me here. And don't go into the gracious count's room until I call you."

Rosemary lingered in the hall a moment or two longer, until the chef, in immaculate white, tall linen cap in hand, came for his orders. Elza immediately entered into a long conversation with him on the subject of milk rolls for breakfast. And Rosemary at last went slowly up the stairs. Almost without knowing it, she found herself once more in her room, the pretty, old-fashioned room with the huge bedstead and the curtains embroidered in cross-stitch. How pretty it looked, and how peaceful! Through the open window came the sound of bird-song; a blackbird was whistling, a thrush was singing, a hundred sparrows were chirruping, and on the large lily leaves on the ornamental lake a frog was sitting croaking. So peaceful, so still! And, heavens above, what a tragedy within these walls!

For a while Rosemary stood at the open window gazing out upon the beautiful panorama laid out before her, the prim, well-kept garden the flower borders, the shady park, and out, far away, the wooded heights, the forests of oak and pine which the morning sun had just tinted with gold.

And with a sudden impulse Rosemary fell on her knees, just where she was, at the open window, and she stretched out her arms towards the Invisible, the Unattainable, the Almighty, and from her heart there came a cry, forced through her lips by the intensity of despair:

"Oh God! My God! Tell me what to do!"

CHAPTER XXVI

If Rosemary had been gifted with second sight!

She would have seen at the moment when she, in despair, turned to the great Healer for comfort, General Naniescu and his friend M. de Kervoisin enjoying their petit déjeuner in one of the palatial rooms of the Imrey's house in Cluj. M. de Kervoisin had arrived the night before. He was the guest of the general, and after a night's rest was enjoying the company of his host, as well as the luxury of these beautiful apartments so thoughtfully placed at the disposal of the military Governor of Transylvania by the Roumanian Government.

M. de Kervoisin was also enjoying the anxieties to which his friend was a prey in his capacity of Governor of this unruly country. There is something in a friend's troubles that is not altogether displeasing to a philosopher. And M. de Kervoisin was a philosopher. He had come over to give advice to his friend, and the role of adviser in a difficult situation was one which he knew how to fulfil with infinite discretion and supreme tact. Just now, while sipping a cup of most excellent café-au-lait, he listened with every mark of sympathy to Naniescu's account of the terrible trouble he was having with a certain obstinate lady journalist who would not do what he wanted.

"I have only asked her," he lamented, "for a few articles to be published in The Times which would put us right with the British and American public; but you know what women are. They never see farther than their noses. And this one, damn her, is like a mule. So far I have not been able to move her."

He had finished his breakfast, and with a pungent havana between his fingers, was waving his podgy, hairy hands to emphasize his words.

Kervoisin smiled. "And you want those newspaper articles?" he asked. "Seriously?"

"Seriously," Naniescu assented. "My Government has become suspicious. They are treating me very badly, you know. They began by giving me a free hand. 'No more plottings and counter-plottings in Transylvania,' they said to me when they sent me out here. 'It is your business to see that things work smoothly out there. How you do it is your affair.' Well," the general went on in an aggrieved tone, "you would construe that order into a free hand for me, would you not?"

M. de Kervoisin carefully spread butter on a piece of excellent fresh roll before he answered: "Yes, I think I should."

"Of course," Naniescu retorted; "so would anyone. And I was doing very well, too, until that young fool Imrey managed to send his newspaper articles over to England. And at once my Government got restive. You know those articles were pretty hot!"

"Yes, I know. But I always thought you attached too much importance to them. Mon Dieu! Confiscations, perquisitions, arrests and even executions, they are the inevitable consequences of foreign occupation." And M. de Kervoisin took a little honey with his bread and butter, and poured himself out another cup of coffee. "And you know," he went on with a shrug, "the British and American public are really very indifferent to what goes on out here. Cluj is such a long way from London or New York. For a time the public is interested, a few are indignant, one or two make a fuss and ask questions in their Parliament, but, after all, you are one of the Allies; you must not be too openly criticized. The man who asks uncomfortable questions in Parliament is rebuked: et puis voilà!"

"I know all that," Naniescu rejoined with some impatience, "but unfortunately my Government does not think as you do. Their vanity suffers when they are attacked in English newspapers, and then they vent their spleen on me."

M. de Kervoisin said nothing for a moment or two; then he remarked blandly: "I think I understand the position-now."

"There is a talk of my resignation," the general added curtly.

M. de Kervoisin smiled. "And you don't want to resign?" he asked.

"Of course not. Five thousand sterling a year; it is a fortune in this miserable country; and then there are the perquisites."

M. de Kervoisin had finished his breakfast. He pushed his cup and plate on one side, and resting both his elbows on the table, looked intently at his friend, while a sarcastic smile curled round his thin lips.

"So," he said, "you imagined this little scheme for putting yourself right before your Government-and before the world-by getting the beautiful Uno to write glowing accounts of your marvellous administration of Transylvania, for the benefit of English and American readers? Is that it?"

"Well, wouldn't you?" Naniescu retorted.

"Yes. But you are not succeeding, my friend," M. de Kervoisin added with the suspicion of a sneer. "What?"

"I shall succeed in the end," Naniescu rejoined. "With the help of my friend--" But at this point he was silenced by a peremptory gesture of his friend's hand.

"S-sh!" de Kervoisin broke in quickly. "I shouldn't mention his name-not even here."

"Oh, we are safe enough."

"Walls have ears, my friend," the other riposted, "even in this perfectly administered land. And our friend's work would be futile if his identity was suspected. I introduced him to you as Number Ten. Number Ten let him remain."

"I suppose I can trust him," Naniescu mused. "You assured me that I could. But bah!" he added with a contemptuous shrug. "Can one trust those English?"

"You can trust this one," Kervoisin retorted curtly. "He was the best spy we had during the war."

"During the war-yes! The man might think he was serving the entire Allied cause by serving you. But now! And here! Frankly, I don't understand the man's motive. He is rich, well born, and he is playing a terribly risky game for us, who are nothing to him."

"He is not running terrible risks for you, my friend, don't you worry," de Kervoisin retorted with a mocking smile. "Though he may have reasons which we don't know for hating the Hungarians, he certainly has none for loving you; and you are one of the Allies, and to a large section of the British public his work would not be called very heinous, seeing that it is in your service and directed against ex-enemies. However, let that pass. I attribute to Number Ten a very different motive for his actions than the mere desire of serving you."

"And what is that?"

"Money, for one thing. He is not as rich as you think, and has extravagant tastes. But that is not all. I know the English better than you do, my friend, and I can tell you that Number Ten would just call his work sport; and for sport, adventure-what?-a certain type of Englishman will do anything, dare anything, risk everything. A hundred and fifty years ago they had their Scarlet Pimpernel, who gave the Revolutionary Government of France a deal of trouble at the time. Now they have their Number Ten. The same spirit animates this man that animated the other-one for good, the other, perhaps, for evil. Just the spirit of adventure. A cycle of years has woven a halo of romance round the personality of the Scarlet Pimpernel, and to us Number Ten still appears as sordid, just a miserable paid spy in the service of an alien Government. But believe me that many Englishmen and even women will forgive him when they know him for what he is, because they will put it down to a love of adventure-to sport, which is the only motive the English appreciate."

He took his cigarette-case out of his pocket, carefully selected a cigarette, thrust it between his lips and lighted it. All the while Naniescu had remained thoughtful. "You may be right," he said finally. His was not an analytical mind; he was quite content to accept de Kervoisin's explanation of the mystery that had vaguely puzzled him; and, anyway, he did not care. Whatever motive animated the mysterious spy, the man was very useful, and in the matter of Philip Imrey and Anna Heves and of the obstinate lady journalist he had had one or two brilliant ideas.

De Kervoisin smoked on in silence for awhile, then he said:

"Our friend does not seem to be coming. I hope there has been no hitch."

"There could be no hitch," Naniescu asserted. "But it is two hours' drive to Kis-Imre and two hours back here. Will you wait a moment?" he went on, and rose to his feet. "I'll see if they've any news downstairs in the office. I told Number Ten to telephone from Kis-Imre when he got there."

Downstairs in the office they had nothing definite to report. No message had come through from Kis-Imre. But even whilst Naniescu was storming and fuming, blaming his subordinates, who obviously were not responsible for the delay, a man wrapped, despite the heat, in a huge stained and worn military coat, and wearing a soiled képi, crossed the courtyard from the direction of the entrance gates towards the principal staircase of the house. Naniescu saw him from the window and ran out into the hall. He met the man just as he was entering the house, and at once greeted him with the greatest effusion.

"Is everything all right?" he asked hurriedly.

"All right," the man answered curtly. "Of course."

"Kervoisin is upstairs," Naniescu went on. "Come and tell us all about it."

He ran upstairs two at a time; the man in the military coat followed more slowly.

"Here is Number Ten," Naniescu announced, as he ushered the man into the room where Kervoisin was patiently waiting and smoking cigarettes. Kervoisin rose at once, a word of welcome on his lips. But at sight of the man he paused and frowned, obviously mystified, until gradually his face cleared and he exclaimed:

"Bon Dieu! I should never have known you."

"I do look a disgusting object, don't I?" the man retorted. He shook hands cordially with Kervoisin; then he threw off his heavy coat and sank, obviously exhausted, into a chair.

"A cup of coffee?" Naniescu suggested.

"Thanks!" the other replied.

He drank the coffee, then took a cigarette from the case which de Kervoisin offered him. He looked a regular vagrant, with face and neck stained both with grease paint and with grime, his hands were soiled with motor grease, and his hair hung lank and matted into his eyes. He had what looked like a two weeks' growth of beard on his chin and upper lip, and his clothes-if indeed what he wore could be called clothes-were a mere bundle of rags.

"Number Ten," de Kervoisin said with conviction, "you are an artist. I have seen our friend here," he went on, turning to Naniescu, "in any number of disguises, but never two alike, and every new one a surprise!"

"You flatter me, sir," Number Ten said with an almost imperceptible sneer.

"But I am afraid you must be very tired," de Kervoisin resumed affably. "I told the general last night that he might just as well have sent one of his subordinates on this errand."

"I like to finish my work myself," Number Ten rejoined curtly.

Whereupon Naniescu threw up his hairy, fat hands and exclaimed in wonderment:

"Ils sont impayables, ces Anglais!"

"Then we may take it," de Kervoisin went on, "that the work is finished?"

"Yes, finished," Number Ten replied. "We spotted the car on the road about five kilometres from Cluj. The patrol summoned the driver to stop, but the man had obviously had his orders; he swerved sharply to the right and put on speed to try and rush through, so I shot him."

"Ah! these English," Naniescu exclaimed complacently; "they are wonderful!"

But de Kervoisin only expressed the mildest possible surprise by a very slight lifting of his eyebrows.

"Yourself?" was all he said.

"Yes," the other replied. "The patrol was on the other side of the road, but I guessed what would happen, so I had brought my horse to a halt about two hundred metres higher up."

"And," Naniescu asked blandly, "you killed the chauffeur?"

"Of course," the other sneered. "I was not likely to miss him, was I?"

But Naniescu could only smile, and sigh, and murmur: "Oh, those English! Voyez-moi çà!"

"There were two men in the body of the car," Number Ten continued coolly, "they were dead drunk. Philip Imrey and the girl were on the front seats. I gave my horse in charge of the patrol and took the wheel. We were in Cluj outside the gaol soon after two o'clock. I saw the chief superintendent and gave the three men and the girl in his charge."

"Yes! Yes!" Naniescu broke in glibly, and turned to de Kervoisin, "he had all instructions. Everything was ready. I have seen him since. Philip Imrey and Anna Heves are in separate cells, and the two drunken oafs he dispatched by train to Hódmezö. They did not seem to know what had happened, and it was no use detaining them."

"None whatever," Number Ten said dryly. "They were just drunken oafs, as you say. With the miller and his two sons you will have to deal presently-that is, if your second patrol succeeded in capturing the sons. I couldn't be in two places at once, and they may have crossed the frontier. Anyway, that's your affair, not mine."

"Of course, of course," Naniescu said airily. And de Kervoisin put in rather impatiently:

"What about the car and the dead chauffeur?"

"I drove both out to Kis-Imre," Number Ten replied deliberately. "The best way to let people there know what had happened. The General agreed to it."

"Was that your brilliant idea?"

"Mine!" Number Ten replied curtly.

And suddenly through the paint and the grime a look of almost inhuman cruelty distorted his face: the thin lips drew back tight above the red gums, and the sharp teeth gleamed white like those of a wolf. It was the recollection of a note which Naniescu had scribbled at his dictation, and which he, Number Ten, had thrust into the hand of the dead chauffeur for the perusal of an obstinate woman, that brought that wolf-like look into his face. His eyes almost disappeared beneath the strand of false eyebrows and the thick layers of paint upon the lids, and his hands opened out and were clutched again like the talons of a bird of prey.

For the space of a second or two Number Ten looked hideous. De Kervoisin, who was watching him, was conscious of an uncomfortable shudder: Naniescu fortunately was looking another way, and the whole episode was over in a moment; the next, Number Ten was once more leaning back in his chair, looking weary, grimy and ill-tempered, but there was nothing supernatural about him, except perhaps his amazing change from one personality to another.

"How did you get back here?" Kervoisin asked after a moment's pause.

I have a car which our friend the general has placed at my disposal, with a soldier-driver. I ordered him to follow me to within half a kilometre of Kis-Imre."

"No one stopped you?"

"No one."

"I suppose you got to Kis-Imre before anyone was astir?"

"I won't say that. The ladies at the château were astir."

"And they saw you?"

"No. I had reached my own car, and was on the point of driving off when I saw them coming through the gates of the château."

"You would not have liked them to see you, I imagine," Naniescu put in with a chuckle.

"They wouldn't have known me," Number Ten retorted quietly.

"Heu! heu!" the general rejoined with a shrug. "There are certain eyes that are reported to be very sharp."

"Anyway," Number Ten broke in coolly, "no one saw me except an oaf from the village, so why discuss the point?"

And strangely enough General Naniescu, usually so dictatorial and so arrogant, did not seem to resent the gruffness of this man who was in his pay. On the contrary, he laughed good-humouredly and rested his fat hand with a gesture of almost affection on the shoulder of the spy.

"Ah, ces chers 'Anglais!" he sighed fatuously whilst de Kervoisin turned quite politely to Number Ten with the bland question: "And what is your next move, my dear friend?"

"To get those articles out of the fair Uno," Naniescu interposed hurriedly before the other had time to reply. "That point must not be lost sight of."

"I am not likely to lose sight of it," the other riposted dryly, "seeing that I am to get ten thousand pounds sterling for them. I suppose you think they are worth it?" he added, turning with his habitual sneer to Naniescu.

"I think," the general replied slowly, "that with the arrest of Philip Imrey and Anna Heves, which, when it becomes known, will deter other young fools from playing the same game--with that, I say, as a make-weight, I think the articles will be worth the money--to my Government and to me."

"Well," Number Ten rejoined coolly, "I shouldn't have done your dirty work for less."

And Naniescu once more gave a fatuous sigh and murmured:

"Ils sont impayables, ces Anglais!" whilst de Kervoisin smiled as a philosopher smiles on follies and stupidities with which he has no concern. Then he asked Number Ten: "And when do you return to civilization, my friend-to decent clothes and a bath?"

"At once," the other replied, "unless I am wanted for something else."

"No, no, my dear man," the general rejoined, with perfect affability. "I am quite content to leave everything in your hands."

"And when do you want those articles?"

"Shall we say within the week?

"You shall have them," Number Ten said coolly as he rose from his chair. He nodded to Kervoisin, who responded cordially: "A bientôt, mon ami!" Then he turned to go; but already Naniescu was on his feet.

"I'll escort you," he said hospitably, "in case you meet anyone on the stairs. In your present get-up," he added with his oily, guttural laugh, "it might be awkward."

"Thank you," the other assented coolly, and, gathering up the dirty old military coat, he strode to the door. Naniescu was already there, holding it open for him.

"You will stay and have lunch with M. de Kervoisin and me, I hope," he said.

"I think not, thank you," the other replied.

"Ah! You are going to Hódmezö, perhaps-or to Kis-Imre?"

And Number Ten replied, with his habitual curtness:

"That is my affair."

De Kervoisin, who still sat smoking, chuckled at this. A scene such as this was part of a philosopher's enjoyment. Naniescu threw him a look, and shrugged his shoulders. De Kervoisin could almost hear him reiterating his stock phrase: "Ils sont impayables, ces Anglais!"

After that the two men went out of the room and de Kervoisin remained, sitting and smoking, with a thin smile on his colourless lips-the smile of a philosopher who sees the humour of a situation which to a less keen mind would only appear obscure and topsy-turvy, and after a while he murmured softly to himself:

"They certainly are remarkable, these English!"

Memory had brought back to his mind that cruel, wolf-like look which for one unguarded moment had distorted the features of the spy. There was, then, some motive other than greed or love of sport, that had pushed the Englishman into doing this dirty work. Hatred? Love? Perhaps. Passion? Certainly.

"I wonder now!" mused M. de Kervoisin.

And being a Frenchman as well as a philosopher he was deeply interested in this new problem.

CHAPTER XXVII

But Rosemary was not gifted with second sight, and she saw nothing of this while she knelt at the open window of her pretty room at Kis-Imre. She was in such an agony of mind, that for a time she became almost insentient. Presently, dressed as she was, she threw herself upon the bed, because she was dog-tired and had no longer the power to feel or to suffer. Even the well of her sympathy appeared to be dry. She could not bring herself to think of Elza or of Maurus, or to feel for them; even Philip and Anna seemed blotted from her mind. An intense self-pity absorbed every other sensation for the moment. She felt herself in such a hopeless impasse that she had not even the strength to beat her hands against the walls that had so completely closed her in.

And so she lay there for an hour and more while life in the château went on, unheeded by her. Long afterwards she heard that, as arranged, the guests all departed soon after nine o'clock, that Elza had been there to see them off, looking after their comforts, bidding them good-bye and tendering hospitable little invitations for the future. Wonderful as always! Rosemary saw nothing of that. She only heard of it afterwards, when she saw Elza again an hour or two later. For the time being she was just a log-neither thinking nor feeling; conscious only of that intense self-pity which was so humiliating, because her senses were so numb that she had not the power to trace that self-pity to its source. While she lay on her bed, blind, deaf, dumb, she did not know that she suffered; she did not know that she lived.

But this state of coma was the one concession to weakness. A giving in. It was not the least like Rosemary; and as consciousness slowly returned and with it the power to feel, she felt humiliated on account of that weakness which was foreign to her. Fortunately no one had witnessed it. Dear, wonderful Elza had had her hands full, and the departing guests had only thought of being discreet and tactful and of leaving this stricken home without putting too great a strain upon the self-control of their hostess. They did not know, of course, that tragedy had followed on the exciting events of last night; but they asked no questions, well knowing that good news spreads like wildfire, and guessing perhaps by Elza's set face and expressionless eyes that something was not altogether right.

Anyhow, they went away, and after their departure the house became still-very still. Presently Rosemary had her bath and dressed, then left the room to go and search for Elza. So far she had not been able to gather anything from Rosa's stolid, round face. The girl went about her work as if nothing special had happened; only when Rosemary was ready to go downstairs and gave Rosa a final nod, the girl suddenly said with an excited little gasp: "The gracious count Philip and the Baroness Anna will be in Hungary by now, won't they, gracious lady?"

Rosemary nodded. "We hope so," she murmured.

She waited in the hall for a little while, hoping that Elza would presently be coming downstairs; but a quarter of an hour later Anton came running down and made straight for the telephone.

"What is it, Anton?" Rosemary asked.

"The gracious count," the man replied hurriedly. "He is ill. I am telephoning to Cluj for the doctor."

"What is it, do you know?"

"No, gracious lady, the countess did not say, but I think it is the heart. The gracious count has fainted, and--"

After that Anton was busy with the telephone, and Rosemary wandered aimlessly into the drawing-room and out upon the veranda.

Maurus ill! Yet another calamity striking that unfortunate woman! Indeed, there was no room for self-pity in this house. Every feeling of love, of sympathy and of pity must be concentrated on Elza. She stood alone, just as Rosemary stood alone. Two women, each with their burden. Elza with a load of boundless sorrow and anxiety, and Rosemary with a terrible responsibility to face. Elza was helpless; she could only watch and pray. But Rosemary had the choice between waiting and acting. Sentiment on the one side; Philip, Anna, Elza and Maurus, people she knew and loved; and duty on the other, duty to others, to countless of unknown innocents, to mothers, to father, to wives. "What are they to me?" cried sentiment. "The few for the many," was the command of duty. Heart and brain in direct conflict and no one to advise, no one to help, save God, and He was silent! The affairs of men are so futile in face of the Infinite.

Later on in the day the doctor came over in his motor from Cluj, and after his visit Elza escorted him down into the hall. This was the first glimpse that Rosemary had of her since the morning, and the sight of her was a terrible shock; Elza was aged, her hair had lost its lustre, her eyes their colour, her cheeks were the colour of lead, and even her magnificent figure had shrunk. Elza looked an old woman, wide-eyed and scared as if Fate was a tangible being standing perpetually before her with flail upraised, striking, striking incessantly, until the poor, weak shoulders bent under the blows, and the last vestige of youth fled, chased away by pain.

As soon as the doctor had gone Elza came back to Rosemary.

"Poor Maurus," she said. "Have you heard?"

"What is the matter?" Rosemary asked.

Elza hesitated a moment, then she said:

"As a matter of fact, it was a fit. He had had them before, and you know he was always peculiar. And now the shock! The doctor says we shall have to be very careful with him. He must be watched and kept very quiet."

"Had you told him?"

"Yes; it is that which brought on the fit. The doctor asked me if he had been more than usually agitated the last day or two."

"But he is in no danger?" Rosemary insisted.

"The doctor says not. But then he does not know. If--if the worst happens with--Philip, I don't think that Maurus will live it through."

Elza had allowed Rosemary to lead her into the drawing-room. She sank down against the cushions and Rosemary knelt beside her, with her arms round the poor woman's shoulders.

"Darling," she murmured, "is there anything I can do?"

"No, dear, nothing. What can you do? We are only atoms. So help-less! We can only suffer. I suppose that God wants some of us to suffer, and others to be happy. It seems strange and unjust, but we cant help it. We must just get through with it." Elza spoke jerkily, in a dry, cracked voice, without the slightest ring or modulation in its dull mo-notony.

"Am I in the way, Elza darling?" Rosemary went on, trying with loving eyes to probe the secret thoughts that lay hidden behind that set, expressionless face. Elza turned large, round eyes upon her, and for an instant a gleam of tenderness shot through them.

"You are not in the way, darling," she said. "I don't know what I should have done this morning if you had not been there to brace me up. But it is miserable and dull for you here. Fancy you coming all the way from England into this house of misery!"

"If you sent me away now," Rosemary said, "I should break my heart with longing to be near you. But-I didn't know whether you would not rather be alone--"

"Alone? I should indeed be alone if you went away. Now that the children are not here . . . and Maurus must be kept very quiet-I should be very lonely if you went."

Rosemary gave her hand a little squeeze.

"But Jasper will be coming soon," she said. "I am sure you won't want him."

"Lord Tarkington is so kind," Elza replied gently, "and he would be company for you. The doctor is sending me a couple of nursing sisters from Cluj, but you know what Maurus is. He gets so impatient if I am not there. So we shall not see much of one another. But it would be a comfort to me to know that you are in the house."

"You are an angel, Elza, and I am glad that you are not sending me away. If you did I should not go very far. Probably to Cluj. I could not exist far away from you whilst I had a glimmer of hope. In my heart, darling," Rosemary went on earnestly, "I am still convinced that God will not permit this monstrous injustice. Something will happen. You will see. You will see."

"It would have to be a miracle, my dear," Elza said dully.

"God has accomplished greater miracles before this," Rosemary retorted firmly.

Elza smiled. She, poor dear, obviously did not believe in miracles.

After a moment or two she said:

"By the way, I quite forgot to tell you-so stupid of me-this morning, while you were resting there came a telephone message for you from Lord Tarkington."

"From Jasper?"

"He said he was coming some time in the afternoon."

"Where was he speaking from?"

"I am not quite sure, and, stupidly enough, I did not ask. When I understood that it was Lord Tarkington speaking I asked if I should send the carriage to meet him at Cluj. But all I heard in reply was: 'No, no,' and then we were cut off. These telephone people are so tiresome, they cut one off sometimes in the middle of a conversation. I am so glad, darling," Elza continued gently, "that Lord Tarkington is coming back. For your sake," she added, "and also mine."

After that she rose and gave Rosemary a final kiss.

"I have one or two little things to see to before lunch," she said, "but I understood from Lord Tarkington that he would not be over before the afternoon."

And she went off with her bunch of keys jingling in her hand, outwardly quite serene, and presently Rosemary could hear her calling to the servants, giving orders, scolding for something left undone. She was still wonderful, even though the elasticity had gone out of her step; and her back was bent like an old woman's, her voice had lost its metallic ring, and all the glorious colour had gone out of her hair.

CHAPTER XXVIII

Jasper arrived in the late afternoon, unheeded and unannounced. Elza and Rosemary were in the garden at the time, and he was in the house for over a quarter of an hour before they heard that he had come. Then she and Elza hurried to greet him. He was in the drawing-room waiting patiently. Rosemary thought him looking tired or perhaps travel-stained.

He kissed Elza's hand first, then his wife's, no more. But Rosemary knew her Jasper. He could not have kissed her in front of anyone, and Elza for once did not seem surprised at the cold, formal greeting between husband and wife. She asked a few questions: "Will you have something to eat, dear Lord Tarkington?" and "How did you come?"

Jasper gave the required explanations.

He had jumped out of the train at Apahida, which is the next station before Cluj, to get a drink, and whom should he see in the station restaurant but General Naniescu, who had driven out in his motor on some business or other. Hearing that Jasper was on his way to Kis-Imre, he offered to drive him over. It was a kind offer, as Jasper was sick of the train journey. He had only hand-luggage with him, and this he transferred, together with himself, to Naniescu's motor. And here he was-very glad to be back.

Elza asked him what had become of the luggage, and where the motor was.

Jasper explained that he had put the motor and the chauffeur up at the inn. General Naniescu had only driven in as far as Cluj, and after that had graciously put the motor and chauffeur at his, Tarkington's disposal, not only for the day but for as long as he and Rosemary would care to use it. The chauffeur was bringing the luggage over presently and would give it to Anton.

"The car might be very useful," Jasper went on, turning to his wife, "so I accepted the offer gladly. I thought it kind of old Naniescu."

Of course, he knew nothing of what had occurred, but even so his mention of Naniescu's name hurt Rosemary. She had already read failure in her husband's eyes-complete failure, and all of a sudden she realized how much hope she had built on this mission of Jasper's, and how it had dwelt at the back of her mind whenever she tried to comfort Elza. Now there was nothing left to hope for, nothing to believe in. Even faith appeared shipwrecked in this new tidal-wave of despair.

Rosemary had always found it difficult to extricate herself from Jasper's arms once he held her tight, and this he did a few moments later, when, at Elza's suggestion that Rosemary should see him up to his room, he found himself alone with her. He took her breath away with the suddenness, the almost save strength of his embrace.

"Jasper!" she murmured once or twice. "Jasper! Please!"

"I was so hungry for you, my Rosemary," he said. "Ten days-my God, ten days without your kiss!"

He looked her straight between the eyes and whispered huskily:

"I've been in hell, little one."

Rosemary tried to smile: "But why, my dear? We can't expect to be always, always together, every day for the rest of our natural lives."

"I don't know what you expect from life, little one, but I do know that if you send me away from you again, I should not come out of that hell again alive."

"But I did not send you away, Jasper," she argued, a little impatient with him because of his wild talk. "Your going to Bucharest was entirely your own idea."

"And I have lamentably failed," he muttered with a shrug.

She gave a little gasp that sounded like a sob.

"There was nothing to be done?" she asked.

"Nothing."

"The King?"

"Indifferent. He trusts Naniescu, has confidence in his judgement, and believes in his patriotism and sense of justice."

"Then there is absolutely nothing to be done," she reiterated slowly in a dull dream-voice.

She was keying herself up to tell him all that had happened in the past four-and-twenty hours. But she was so tired, almost on the verge of breaking down. She did not think that she would have the strength to go through with the long tale of hope and despair. But Jasper made her sit down on the sofa and arranged a couple of cushions round her head. Then he sat down on a low chair beside her.

"Now tell me, little one," he said quietly.

"Why, Jasper," she exclaimed, "how did you guess that there was anything to tell?"

"Don't I know every line of your adorable face," he retorted, "every flicker almost of your eyelid? Before I touched your hand I knew that something was amiss. After that I was sure."

"Dear," she murmured, and nestled her hand in his. Wasn't Jasper wonderful too? With his marvellous understanding and that utterly selfless love for her, who, alas! gave so little in return. He bent his head and pressed his lips upon her wrist.

"You guessed right," she said. "Something is very much amiss."

Then she told him everything. He listened to the whole tale without a comment, and even after she had finished speaking he sat in silence with her hand held between his own, only bending his head now and again in order to kiss her wrist.

"There's nothing to be done!" she reiterated, with a pitiable little catch in her voice.

And after awhile he said quite quietly and deliberately:

"The only thing to be done, my dear, is to comply with Naniescu's wish."

But against this she at once exclaimed, hot with indignation, and he went on with a sigh: "I know, I know. You are such a sweet, enthusiastic creature, and you have embraced the cause of these good people whole-heartedly, injudiciously. I don't want to influence you, of course--"

"You promised me that you would not," she retorted.

"I know! I know! You would not be the adorable creature that you are if you were not unreasonable sometimes. But-I put it to you-what harm would you do in writing the articles that Naniescu wants?"

This question roused Rosemary's indignation once more.

"How can you ask?" she queried. "To begin with I should alienate from these wretched people over here all the sympathy which Philip Imrey's articles have aroused for them abroad. Never again after that could any friend raise a voice on their behalf. Naniescu or his kind would have a free hand. He knows that well enough. Not only he, but all the waverers, all the selfish and the indifferent could in the future point to The Times and say: 'Hardship! Nonsense! Why, here was an independent lady journalist-and a woman at that-with every opportunity for getting at the truth, and she writes at full length to tell the entire world that the administration in Transylvania is a model of equity and benevolence.' And mothers like Elza would cry in vain because their sons had been torn from them, families would be sent into exile, fathers, brothers murdered, oppression, confiscation, outrage would go unpunished, all because one woman had been too great a coward to smother sentiment under the mantle of justice."

Jasper had not uttered a word, hardly made a sign, while Rosemary spoke her impassioned tirade. Only from time to time his dark eyes flashed with a glance of admiration on his beautiful wife, who, with flaming cheeks and slightly dishevelled hair, looked perhaps more desirable in her indignation than she had ever done in repose.

When she paused for want of breath he slowly shook his head.

"And do you really think, my darling," he said softly, "that you can permanently influence English and American opinion by a few newspaper articles, even if these are written by a well-known person like yourself? Dear heart, in order to do that you would have to go at your subject hammer and tongs, never allow one article to be forgotten before you write another; you must be at your subject all the time if you want to create an impression-hammer away at the newspaper-reading public until its stupid wooden head is saturated with the stuff you give it. Naniescu thinks a great deal of these articles which he wants you to write. Well, in my opinion their effect would last just one week after the last of them has appeared. After that some philanthropist or other will have his say on the maladministration of Transylvania, and you are not bound to refute that again, are you? But in the meanwhile Philip and Anna will be comfortably out of the country, and even Elza and Maurus will have settled down somewhere in Hungary to await better times; you will have saved the lives of two young things whom you love, and spared these good people here a terrible sorrow."

While Jasper spoke Rosemary could not do anything but stare at him. His sophistry amazed her. That there was a modicum of common sense in his argument was not to be gainsaid, but that the suggestion of such bargaining with truth and honour should come from Jasper, her husband, horrified Rosemary and revolted her. And men often accused women of a feeble sense of honour! From the first Rosemary had turned away from Naniescu's proposal as from something unclean. She had never dwelt on it, not for a moment. Even this morning, when first she felt herself sinking into an abyss of despair, she had not dwelt on that. But Jasper had not only dwelt on it; he had weighed its possibilities, the "for" and "against" which, with unanswerable logic and not a little sarcasm, he had just put before her. And even now, when she could not keep the look of horror out of her eyes, he only smiled, quite kindly and indulgently, as if she were just an obstinate child who had to be coaxed into reason; and when indignation kept her dumb he patted her hand and said gently:

"You will think over it, I am sure!" Then he rose and started pacing up and down the room, as was his custom when he was irritated or worried, with his head thrust forward and his hands clasped behind his back.

"You will think over it," he murmured again.

"Never!" she retorted hotly.

"You have another fifteen days before you."

"Never!" she reiterated firmly.

He looked at her for a moment or two with an indefinable smile on his lean, dark face, then he shrugged his shoulders.

"How much longer can you stand the mother's tears," he asked, "and the father's despair?"

"Elza, if she knew," Rosemary rejoined, with an obstinate toss of her head, "would be the first to wish me to stand firm."

"Try her!" Jasper retorted laconically. Then as Rosemary, reproachful, indignant, made no attempt to reply, he went on with harsh insistence: "Have you tried her? Does she know that the life of her son is entirely and absolutely in your hands?"

Rosemary shook her head.

"No!" she murmured.

Jasper gave a harsh laugh. "Then," he said, "I can only repeat what I said just now. Go and tell Elza everything, the see if her arguments will be different form mine!"

"Jasper!" Rosemary exclaimed, flushed with bitterness and resentment.

He paused in his restless walk, looked at her for a moment or two, and then resumed his seat beside her. For an instant it seemed as if he wanted to take her hand, or put his arms round her, but whether she divined this wish or no, certain it is that she made a slight movement, a drawing back away from him. A curious flash, like a veritable volcano of hidden fires, shot through the man's deep, dark eyes, and, as if to control his own movements, he clasped his hands tightly together between his knees. Strangely enough, when he next spoke his voice was full of tenderness and almost of humility.

"I am sorry, dear," he said gently, "if I hurt you. God knows that I would rather be broken to pieces on a rack than do that. But things have come to a pass," he went on more harshly, "where my duty-and my right-as your natural friend and protector command me to get you out of this impasse before all this damnable business has affected your health, or, God help us! clouded your brain."

"The impasse, as you very justly call it, Jasper," she riposted, "will not cloud my brain, so long as you do not seek to make right seem wrong and wrong right."

Then suddenly he dropped on one knee close beside her; before she could prevent him his two hands had closed upon hers, and he looked up into her face with a glance full of love and entreaty, whilst every tone of harshness went out of his voice.

"But child, child," he urged, "don't you see, can't you understand, that it is you who make right seem wrong? What good will you do, by letting those two wretched young idiots suffer the extreme penalty for their folly? Will you ever afterwards know one moment's peace? Won't you for ever be haunted by the ghosts of those whom you could so easily have saved? Won't your ears ring for ever with the whole-hearted curses of these wretched people, who will look upon you as the murderer of their son? And, honestly, my dear, your articles in The Times won't do more than flatter the vanity of Naniescu. Those people in England and America who have really studied the question won't think any the better of Roumanian rule or misrule in Transylvania because a lady journalist-eminent, I grant you-chooses to tell them that everything is for the best in the best possible occupied world. Think of all those articles in The Times on the subject of the French occupation in the Ruhr and their misrule in the Palatinate-did it prevent the very readers of that same paper from joining the League of the Friends of France and proclaiming at the top of their voices their belief in the un-selfish aims of M. Poincaré? You attach too much importance to the Press, my dearest. Roumania and Transylvania are very, very far away from Clapham and Ealing. People don't trouble their heads much what goes on there. A few do, but they are the ones who will stick to their opinions whatever you may say."

Unable to free them, Rosemary had yielded her hands passively to Jasper's clasp. She lay back with her head resting upon the cushions, her eyes obstinately evading his glance and fixed upon the ceiling, as if vainly seeking up there for some hidden writing that in a few terse words would tell her what to do. Jasper thus holding her captive by her hands made her feel like an imprisoned soul bruising itself against the bars of an unseen cage. She felt fettered, compelled, unable to see, to visualize that rigid code of honour which had ruled her actions until now. Jasper had talked at great length; she had never heard him talk so long and so earnestly and with such unanswerable logic. And Rosemary, who up to this hour had seen her line of action before her, crystal-clear, was suddenly assailed with doubts, more torturing than any mental agony which she had suffered before. Doubt-awful, hideous, torturing doubt. How could she fight that sinister monster "compromise" if the one man whom she could trust tilted on its side? She had never dreamed of such a possibility. And now, suddenly, Jasper had made such a thing possible-worse, imperative!

Rosemary felt her eyes filling with tears. She was so tired and could not argue. She dreaded argument lest she should give in. It was all so utterly, utterly hopeless. Jasper was out of sympathy with her, and Peter--Peter--

She must unconsciously have murmured the name, for all of a sudden Jasper jumped to his feet with a loud curse.

"If you mention that devils' name--" he began. Then once more he started on his restless pacing, with lips firmly set almost as if he were afraid that words would come tumbling out of them against his will.

"Jasper!" Rosemary exclaimed, "why do you hate Peter so?"

"Hate him?" Jasper retorted harshly. "Does one hate a snake-or a worm?"

"That is unjust," she riposted, "and untrue. You forced a promise from me not to confide in Peter. But I wish to God I had spoken to him, asked for his help. Peter half belongs to these people; he would have helped us if he had known."

But Jasper only threw his head back and broke into a harsh, sardonic laugh:

"Peter?" he exclaimed. "Peter Blakeney help you? Heavens above! Don't you know, child," he went on, and once more came and sat down beside her, "that Peter Blakeney is nothing but a paid spy of the Roumanian Government? I warned you; I told you. You remember that day, when you did not even know that he was in Transylvania, he was in Cluj in touch with Naniescu. I warned you then as much as I dared. I could not say much because-because--" He paused, perhaps because he had felt Rosemary's eyes fixed upon him with a curious, challenging look. A second or two later he went on coldly: "And the denunciation of Anna and Philip? How did it come about? Who knew of their folly except you and Peter Blakeney? And what about last night? I warned you not to confide in Peter, not to speak with him of the whole thing while I was away. Are you quite sure, quite, quite sure that Peter knew nothing of the plan? Are you quite sure that he--"

"Jasper! Stop!" Rosemary cried; and with a great effort she pushed Jasper away from her and rose to her feet. She wanted above all to get away from him. She would not listen. She would not hear, because-because every word that Jasper spoke was a dart that hit straight at her heart, and every dart was marked with the word "Truth." All that Jasper said she had heard whispered about her by unseen demons who had tortured her for days with these horrible suspicions. She had rejected them, fought against them with all her might; but no sooner had she silenced one tempter than another took his place and whispered, whispered awful words that, strung together, became a fearful, and irrefutable indictment against Peter. But this, she would not admit; not now, not before anyone, not even before Jasper.

"I won't believe it," she said firmly. "I have known Peter all my life, and what you suggest is monstrous. There have been strange coincidences, I admit, but--"

"Strange," Jasper broke in with a sneer. "You are right there, little one. It is a strange coincidence, shall we say, that has made Peter Blakeney the new owner of this house."

"Whatever to do you mean?"

"That Peter Blakeney has bought an option on the château and property of Kis-Imre from the Roumanian Government."

Rosemary frowned in bewilderment.

"Jasper," she said, "will you please tell me clearly what you do mean?"

"I have told you, dear heart, as clearly as I could. But perhaps you have not realized that if Philip and Anna are brought before a military tribunal and convicted of treason against the State, these estates, together with the château, will be confiscated. It will then be sold for the benefit of the State and the owners will be expelled from the country."

Rosemary felt herself shuddering. "No," she said slowly; "I had not realized that."

"I am afraid that it is so. And in the meanwhile, some who are in the know have already cast covetous eyes on this admirable château and beautiful park and garden, and our friend Naniescu has hit on the happy idea of selling the option of them to the highest bidder. And it seems that Peter Blakeney was the lucky man. He has paid a few hundred thousand leis for a first option on Kis-Imre and its dependencies, should it come in the market after the conviction and presumably the death of his cousins for treason against the State."

"Who told you all that?" Rosemary queried coldly.

"Our friend Naniescu."

"And you believed it?"

"I could not help believing; Naniescu showed me the contract for the option. It was signed 'Peter Blakeney'."

"If Peter has done that," Rosemary went on slowly, "it is because he wants to secure the place ultimately for Elza."

Jasper smiled tenderly. "You are a loyal friend, sweetheart," he said.

"The accusation is so monstrous," Rosemary retorted, "it defeats its own ends."

"I wish I could think so," he rejoined with a sigh. "Unfortunately, ever since Peter's arrival in Cluj I have seen nothing but one calamity after another fall upon these wretched people here. I only wish I had your belief in coincidences. I only wish I could explain satisfactorily to myself how those two children, how Elza, Maurus, all of us, have come to this terrible pass, at the end of which there is nothing but chaos. But there," he went on with his usual gentleness and patience, "I won't worry you any longer. I have said my say. I have put my case before you. Perhaps I look at it too much from a selfish point of view. I am heart-broken to see you so wretched, and feel like hitting out right and left to set you free from this awful impasse. So now, sweetheart, try and forgive me, and think over it all from my point of view a little. The people here are nothing to me, you are everything. All the world and more. Even Heaven would be nothing to me without you, and this place is a hell when you are not here."

Rosemary was standing close by the open window. The sky was grey. Great banks of cloud rose and tumbled about the mountain tops. The pine trees on the hill-side appeared like ghostly sentinels standing at attention in the mist. The heat was oppressive. From far away came the dull rumble of distant thunder. The tuberoses beneath the window sent a heady, intoxicating scent through the storm-laden air. Rosemary felt terribly wearied, and for the first time in her life discouraged. She had striven for right, smothered every sentiment for the sake of abstract justice, and in the end right was proclaimed to be wrong, at best a fantasy born of her own vanity. Was Jasper right, after all? He had rather a way of being always right. Anyway, he was English and practical; sentiment had no part in his organization. Even his love, deep as it was, was not sentiment. Rosemary had found this out before now. It was not sentiment-it was elemental passion. But his views of life were built neither on sentiment nor passion. He looked at things straight, as Englishmen of a certain type do, who despise sentiment and whose unanswerable argument is: "Well, it is the right thing to do."

But, heavens above! what was the right thing now? Rosemary felt sick and faint; the heat and the scent of the tuberoses made her head ache and her eyes smart. Jasper was saying something, but she hardly heard him, and she hardly felt his nearness when he took her hand and pressed it against his lips.

CHAPTER XXIX

But a moment or two later a curious thing happened.

Jasper had gone out of the room, and Rosemary, leaning against the window frame, was looking out into the approaching storm. She had not heard what Jasper had said just before he kissed her hand; but her mind must have registered it, must have made a kind of record of it, like that of a gramophone, because now some of his words came back to her quite distinctly through the rumblings of distant thunder. She had not heard him then, but she heard him now quite distinctly-every word.

"I have jotted down a few ideas. You, of course, will put them into your own picturesque language. Just a few notes of what Naniescu would like to see in The Times. I thought it would save you the trouble to think. I don't think that you will find anything glaringly impossible in my suggestions."

Then he had put something down on the table. Memory had registered a kind of swishing sound. And Rosemary, now turning slowly away from the window, caught sight of that something on the table. Half a dozen loose sheets of paper covered with Jasper's clear, minute handwriting. Like a sleep-walker Rosemary went to the table and picked up the sheets. The shades of evening were drawing in, and the heavy grey clouds in the sky blotted out the remaining rags of daylight. With the papers in her hand Rosemary went out on the balcony. She had the feeling that while she read she must have the pure, storm-laden air about her. She had not turned away from these notes of Jasper's in horror. She had not closed her ears to the record of his words. She knew quite well what was written on these sheets of paper, and deliberately she sat down and began to read.

The political and economic situation of Transylvania was stated in these brief notes with remarkable lucidity. Jasper's clear, unemotional outlook on the administration of the conquered country was set forth without any imagery or attempt at style. Even the obvious bias in favour of the ruling Government was tempered by sound logic and a certain measure of indulgent toleration for the other side. Rosemary read the notes through twice very carefully. She could hear Jasper's voice in every sentence, feel his presence while she read. Long after she had finished reading she sat there quite still, with the sheets of paper lying on her lap and her hands folded over them. She marvelled whether she was quite sane. Jasper had said at one moment that this terrible impasse might overcloud her brain. Well, perhaps it had done that already, and she could no longer distinguish right from wrong through the clouds.

Evening closed in about her. The garden down below became a blur, through which white, starry flowers blinked up at her, and with their placidity mocked the turmoil which was rending her soul. The thunder-clouds were drawing nearer; they hung like lead over the mountains. The pine trees, like dark sentinels, shivered at times under a sudden gust of wind, and from time to time a pale reflex of distant lightning lit the sky above the valley.

Rosa came presently into the room and turned on the lights; she inquired anxiously whether the gracious lady would not come in, as it was raining already and the storm would be breaking very soon. Then only did Rosemary become conscious that her hair and her dress were wet. Heavy drops, the size of a shilling, were falling, but she had not noticed them before.

She came in and quite mechanically she locked the papers up in her dressing-case. She asked Rosa what the time was, and whether dinner would be at the usual time. Yes, dinner would be at eight o'clock as usual, and it was now past seven. Rosa asked if the gracious lady would like to change her dress.

The rest of the evening was like a dream. Elza presided at dinner and she and Jasper did most of the talking--that is to say, Elza asked innumerable questions to which Jasper gave long replies, with forced cheerfulness. Maurus, it seemed, was better. The doctor was coming again the last thing at night, but the patient was much calmer, had taken some nourishment in the way of milk, and had slept for an hour. Elza, self-possessed, wonderful as usual, lingered over dessert. She poured out coffee, offered liqueur and cigarettes. For her hospitality and its duties were a religion; she would as soon have neglected them as a devout Catholic would neglect confession. The very fact that they cost her an effort made them all the more imperative and in a way comforting.

At ten o'clock Rosemary found herself once more alone in her room. Jasper had kissed her tenderly when he bade her goodnight. Only when she did find herself alone did Rosemary realize how much she had dreaded this goodnight. She knew that she had no reserve of strength left to stand one of Jasper's savage outbursts of passion; tonight of all nights she would have gone down under it like the tuberoses below her window under the lashing of the storm.

The rain beat against the window-panes, terrific crashes of thunder followed one another in close succession, and every few minutes the sky seemed rent right through with blinding flashes of lightning. The heat was nearly intolerable through this almost tropical storm. Rosemary had dismissed Rosa. She undid her hair, which clung damp against her forehead and the back of her neck, and clad only in chemise and petticoat, with bare arms and neck, and bare feet thrust into slippers, she sat down at the table with Jasper's notes before her, and read them through once more.

After that she searched through the chest of drawers for a bundle of manuscript paper, and taking up her fountain-pen she began to write. She had Jasper's notes in front of her, and she put them, as he had suggested, into her well-known, picturesque language. She enlarged upon them, amplified them, always keeping his suggestions as a background for her own statements.

For hours she sat there writing. It was the longest spell of uninterrupted work that she had ever accomplished, but she was not even conscious of fatigue. The storm raged for a while longer, but she did not hear it. Only the heat worried her, and from time to time she mopped her forehead and the back of her neck with her handkerchief.

The storm passed by, and the air became very still as slowly the dawn chased away the night. The waning moon peeped through the clouds, only to melt away in the translucent ether; one by one the birds awoke, shook their wet feathers and called to their mates. But not until she had written the last line did Rosemary rise from the table. Then she put her papers together, put a clip through them, arranged Jasper's notes separately, and locked up both sets in her dressing-case.

After that she put on a wrap and threw open the window. The clock in her room struck five. She had been writing for six hours! The task was done. There it stood ready, and Elza should decide. In this Jasper had been quite right-wasn't he always right? It was for Elza to decide. Her son's life on the one hand, her people's welfare on the other. It was for her to decide. Philip was her son; the oppressed people of Transylvania her kindred. Jasper was quite right. Let Elza decide.

And after Rosemary had saturated her lungs with the pure air of the morning, she went to bed and slept soundly, heavily, until Rosa came into her room later on with her breakfast.

And when, presently, Jasper came in, Rosemary was able to greet him with a smile which was not altogether forced. She was able to return his kiss, and after awhile to tell him what she had done.

"The articles are written," she said, "and ready for publication. I have even written a covering letter and addressed the envelope to the editor of The Times, asking him kindly to arrange for their publication at the earliest possible date. But before I put the articles in the post, I shall give them to Elza to read. She shall decide if they are to go. You were quite right, dear," she added, and looked Jasper quite frankly, unwaveringly, in the eyes. "It is a matter for Elza to decide."

CHAPTER XXX

Rosemary found herself alone with Elza in the early part of the afternoon. The doctor had been over in the morning to see Maurus, and on the whole the bulletin was satisfactory: "The patient was doing well. If he was kept very quiet there would be no complications. He was no age, and on the whole had led an abstemious life. The most important thing was to keep all worry, all agitation from him, both now and in the future."

Both now and in the future! Elza dwelt on those words when she told Rosemary just what the doctor had said.

"The future!" she murmured with a weary little sigh. "Of course, the doctor does not know. Perhaps I ought to tell him what the future holds in store for poor Maurus."

The nursing sisters had arrived overnight. Rosemary had caught sight of them about the house during the course of the morning, with their white-winged caps that made them look like doves with outspread wings. Their felt shoes made not the slightest noise as they walked. They were very sweet and very restful, entirely incompetent but exceedingly kind, and full of gentle pity and kind advice to the patient, who became terribly irritable as soon as they ministered to him.

After lunch Rosemary persuaded Elza to come out with her into the garden. It was the first bright moment in the day. Neither morning nor early afternoon had kept the promise made by the dawn. Storm clouds hung, heavy and leaden, over the mountains, and dull rumblings proclaimed the return of thunder. But about three o'clock there was a break in the clouds, and a pale sun shot fitful gleams of silvery light upon park and garden. It was oppressively hot. Rosemary led Elza to the summer-house and made her sit down. Elza was fidgety. It almost seemed as if she did not want to be left alone with Rosemary. She made one excuse after another: Maurus! the chef! the stables! But Rosemary insisted.

"Listen to me, Elza, darling," she said firmly. "I want your full attention for two minutes."

Elza turned her big blue eyes upon Rosemary and murmured like an obedient child: "Yes, dear! What is it?"

Rosemary had the papers in her hand: the newspaper articles which she had written during the night. The hand that held the manuscript shook ever so slightly, but her voice was quite steady.

"I want you," she said to Elza, "to read very carefully what I have written here. They are newspaper articles which General Naniescu would like to see published in England and in America. When you have read them you will understand why. He wants this so badly that on the day these articles are published Philip and Anna will receive a full pardon, Kis-Imre will not be taken from you, and, if you wish, you can all leave the country for a time until things settle down and better times come for you all."

She thrust the papers into Elza's hands and turned to go.

"I will leave you to read quite quietly," she said.

But Elza's round blue eyes were still staring at her.

"I don't understand you, dear," she murmured vaguely.

"Of course you don't, darling," Rosemary rejoined gently; "but you will when you have read what I have written. The gipsy was quite right; it is in my power to save Philip and Anna, but only to a certain extent, because it is you alone who can decide if I am to exercise that power or not. God bless you, darling!"

She put her arms round Elza and kissed her tenderly. Thank Heaven all self-pity, all selfish introspection had gone from her. Her thoughts, her love, her pity were all for Elza. But it had to be. Elza must decide. Her people! Her son! She must decide!

When Rosemary hastened across the lawn she turned once more toward the summer-house. Elza was still sitting there, staring with big blue eyes into vacancy. Every line of her attitude indicated bewilderment. She had the packet of paper in her hand and was tapping it against her knee. Poor Elza! A heavy sob rose from Rosemary's aching heart.

CHAPTER XXXI

Rosemary did not Elza against that day. Just before dinner Rosa came with a short scribbled note from her. "Maurus is very restless," it said; "I don't like to leave him. Will you and dear Lord Tarkington forgive me if I don't join you at dinner?"

The evening was dreary. Jasper said very little, and Rosemary felt thoroughly out of tune with him; he had a meek air about him that irritated her. Hers was not a nature to sympathize with remorse, and Jasper's manner gave the idea that he regretted having forced her into a decision. So she gave curt answers when he spoke to her, and after dinner he retired into the smoking-room with the excuse that he had some business letters to write. She sat reading most of the evening, her nerves on edge, hearing all sorts of mysterious sounds through the apparent stillness of the house.

When Jasper came to say good night she felt sorry for him. He looked forlorn and miserable, and reason told Rosemary that he of all people ought not to be allowed to suffer through a situation that was none of his making. Poor Jasper! She, his wife, had dragged him, unwillingly enough, into this impasse wherein his quiet habits of a wealthy English gentleman were hopelessly perturbed and his outlook outraged at every point. So, after she had returned his last kiss and saw him going upstairs, slowly, dragging one step after another, almost like an old man, she ran after him and linked her arm in his, and gave him an tender and sympathetic smile. The look of gratitude which he gave her in return warmed her heart. Here, at least, was no divided duty. In a moment of pique--it was nothing less than that--she had linked her fate with Jasper Tarkington, accepted from him all the lavish gifts that wealth could buy, and which he so generously bestowed upon her. In exchange for that he only asked for her love; and if the love which he gave and demanded did not reach that sublime ideal of which Rosemary had once dreamed, at any rate it was loyal and ungrudging and she had no right to let her caprice stand in the way of his happiness.

It was perhaps strange that these thoughts should come to her at a moment when her whole soul was torn with a terrible sorrow and a racking anxiety; perhaps they came because on this very day she had made the greatest abdication of her will that she had ever done in all her life. She had always acted for herself, judged for herself, set herself a high standard of straight living and straight thinking, and lived up to it. To-day she had left a decision which should have been hers in the hands of another. She knew that she had done right, but her pride was humiliated, and to soothe that pride she set herself a fresh standard of duty to Jasper and determined to live up to that.

But ever afterwards she turned away with a shudder from thoughts of this evening, when she probed the full depth of Jasper's passion for her, and saw before her like a row of spectres the vision of an endless vista of years, during which every caress would mean for her an effort, and every kiss a lie.

The new standard of duty which she had set herself would be very difficult to live up to. She had never loved Jasper, only hoped that she might learn to love him one day, but on this fateful evening she realized that she might in time learn to hate him.

When at last she was alone she found herself unable to rest. Through the open window the sounds of the oncoming storm became more and more insistent. It was rolling in on the bosom of the clouds from over the mountains in the west. Already one or two vivid flashes of lighting had rent the sky, and now and then great gusts of wind swept across the valley and sent a soughing and whispering through the trees. The poplars bowed their crests, and the twisted branches of the old acacias shivered and cracked in the blast. It was insufferably hot, and there was a smell of sulphur in the air. Rosemary in a thin lace wrap could not succeed in keeping cool. She stood by the open window, longing for the storm to break in all its fury, so that she might be rid of this feeling of oppression which was so unendurable, because the storm, far or near, had gone on almost uninterruptedly for over twenty-four hours. Rosemary's thoughts now were with Elza. She pictured to herself the unfortunate woman wrestling with a decision which either way must mean the breaking of her heart. Elza, who outwardly seemed just a soft, futile, pampered doll, with thoughts fixed on her menus and her servants, was a veritable heroine, strong and tenacious, proud without vanity, loving without weakness, the type that represented everything that was finest and best in a woman. She was of the stuff that religious martyrs were made of in the past, and she would not come to a decision without a terrible struggle. If in the end her heart overruled the dictates of justice and of right, her remorse would be as devastating as her courage hitherto had been sublime.

If Elza had been a religious woman she would not have suffered nearly so cruelly. The pagan knows nothing of the comfort of prayer, of diving blindly from the rocks of care into the ocean of God's love. And Elza was only a pagan from whom the thin veneer of Christianity laid on in early life had been rubbed off long ago. She would not now be on her knees, murmuring with heaven-born resignation: "Lord, not my will, but thine be done!" she would be fighting a tough battle, wrestling with her heart, castigating her tenderest feelings, fighting alone, unaided, unconsoled.

Poor, poor Elza! Rosemary, looking out into the storm, seemed to see the pretty round face distorted by grief, the big, child-like eyes gazing bewildered on the immensity of the puzzle which the Fates had set for her to solve. And while Rosemary gazed the storm became full of pictures, each lightning flash revealed a face. Elza! Philip, dark-eyed, enthusiastic, the idealist! Anna, gentle and resigned. Maurus, the man, the head of the family, the trunk of the tree weaker than its branches. And then Peter. Oh, Peter filled the night with his presence. There was Peter in flannels, a boy with bright eyes and curly head, fighting life's battles with a cricket bat and a joke. Peter home on leave from that hell in Belgium, receiving from his king the supreme reward for an act of almost unequalled bravery, of which, in his boyish way, he would often look quite ashamed. And Peter that night in June, long ago. Peter's strong arms round her shoulders. Peter's impassioned words, vying in melody with the nightingale. Peter's kiss that opened wide the portals of Heaven; and, lastly, Peter the mysterious, the sub-tle, unseen influence in whose wake strode sorrow and disaster. And the rumbling of the thunder brought back to Rosemary's ears Jasper's words of warning: "I only wish I had your belief in coincidences;" and "Ever since Peter's arrival I have seen nothing but one calamity after another fall upon these wretched people here." And then that awful, awful indictment which she had been unable to refute: "Don't you know that Peter Blakeney is a paid spy of the Roumanian Govern-ment?" The thunder brought the echo of those terrible words. Louder and louder, for the storm was drawing nearer, and the echo of those awful words drowned the very sound of thunder.

All at once the storm broke in all its fury; there was a deafening crash and a flash of lightning so vivid that for the space of one second the garden stood revealed as if in broad daylight before Rosemary's gaze, clear-cut in every detail, every tree, every leaf, every flower, every ripple upon the lake, each pebble upon the garden walk; and in that one second Rosemary had seen Peter standing on the gravel walk, not fifty yards from her window, and looking up at her--gazing. She caught his eyes in that one flash. He was dressed in a dark suit, his cricketing cap was on his head. It had been an instant's flash, but she had seen him, and he was gazing up her window. And their eyes had met in that one flash, right through the storm.

After that all was darkness, and though from time to time the night was rent by lightning flashes, Rosemary did not see Peter again. And when later on the storm subsided, and, wearied out, she went to bed and slept, she dreamt that all her suspicions of Peter had been proved to be wrong. She dreamt that she was a few years younger, that they were on the river together, in a punt, and that the nightingale was singing. She dreamt of the lapping of the water against the low-lying river bank, of the scent of meadow-sweet, and of the honey-coloured moon that painted long lines of golden light upon the reeds. She dreamt that Peter kissed her, and that she was free to give him kiss for kiss.

CHAPTER XXXII

When Rosemary woke the next morning she felt quite convinced that the vision which she had had in the night, of Peter standing on the gravel walk and looking up at her window, was only a creation of her own fancy. Rosa had opened the curtains and the volets, and Rosemary saw a dull, grey sky before her. The storm had certainly abated, but it was still raining. Rosemary thought of the cricket match, which would probably have to be postponed owing to the weather, and of the disappointment this would mean to many, especially to Peter, who had set his heart upon it.

During breakfast Jasper told her that he had received a note from his agent de change at Cluj, and that the latter said in his letter that the cricket match which should have been begun yesterday had to be postponed owing to the weather.

"Steinberg goes on to say," Jasper continued, "that he had heard that the cricket pitch--the playground he calls it--was like a swamp. The storm seems to have been very severe the other side of the frontier. It went on for twenty-four hours without a break, and was still raging at the time of writing. Unless the weather improves very much, Steinberg says that the match will have to be abandoned altogether, as Payson and several of his team have to be back in Budapest in time for work on Monday morning, which means leaving Hódmezö on the Sunday."

Then, as Rosemary made no comment on the news, only stared rather dejectedly out of the window, Jasper went on after awhile:

"I am afraid it will mean a disappointment all round, as the weather can hardly be said to have improved, can it?"

Rosemary said: "No, it cannot," after which the subject was dropped. Somehow the idea of the postponed cricket match worried her, and there was one insistent thought which would force itself into the forefront of her mind to the exclusion of all others, and that was the thought that the postponed cricket match would have left Peter free yesterday to come over to Kis-Imre, and that therefore it might have been himself in the flesh who was standing during the storm in the garden last night.

Why he should have chosen to stand in the garden in the rain rather than come into his aunt's house was a problem which Rosemary felt herself too wearied and disheartened to tackle.

When she went downstairs soon after ten o'clock she met Elza in the hall, dressed ready to go out. She looked more tired, more aged, more ill than the day before; obviously she had spent another sleepless night. But she kissed Rosemary very tenderly. "Come into the smoking-room, darling," she said. "I want to say something to you."

Rosemary followed her into the smoking-room and at once asked after Maurus.

"He has had no sleep," Elza said, "and at times his brain wanders. But physically he seems no worse-rather stronger, I think, than yesterday, and he enjoyed his breakfast. If we could only keep him quiet!"

She opened her handbag and took out the papers which Rosemary gave her yesterday.

"I read your articles through very carefully, dear," she said, "but I did not have to pray for guidance. I knew at once, that none of us, not Maurus or I, or Anna's people, would accept the children's safety at such a price. The children themselves would refuse."

With a perfectly steady hand she held the papers out to Rosemary. "Take them, darling," she said. "Thank you for letting me decide. This is the one thing which we none of us would have forgiven, if you had published these articles without consulting us."

CHAPTER XXXIII

Half an hour later!

Rosemary thought that Jasper was still in his room, and she had a longing to get away from his nearness and out into the open. It was still raining and the sky was the colour of lead. She threw a cape over her shoulders and opened the door of her room. She was dreading to meet Jasper again, so she listened intently for awhile for any sound that might betray his presence. From Maurus' apartments at the opposite end of the gallery there came a buzz of voices, and from down below where the servants were laying the table in the dining-room for luncheon a clatter of crockery. Otherwise silence. And no sound from Jasper's room close by, so Rosemary ran quickly downstairs.

She had just reached the hall intending to go out into the garden when she heard a strange clatter coming apparently from the smoking-room. It sounded like a scuffle. Of course it could not be, but that was just what it sounded like. She stood still to listen. And then she heard quite distinctly a smothered cry. Something like a curse. And she thought that she recognized Jasper's harsh voice. At once she ran to the door of the smoking-room and threw it open.

Jasper was on the ground, struggling to get back to his feet. He appeared dazed, and to be moving with difficulty. His hand was tearing at his collar, as if he were choking; his clothes were disarranged, his face looked pallid and blotchy, and his eyes bloodshot. But Rosemary did not scream when she caught sight of him. Something else that she had seen had paralysed her limbs and seemed actually to be holding her by the throat. The tall window which gave on this side of the garden was wide open, and in a flash, just as she entered the room, Rosemary had seen Peter in the act of getting over the window-sill. The next second he had disappeared over the ledge, and she heard his footsteps crunching on the gravel as he ran in the direction of the main gates.

A moment or two later Jasper had recovered his voice and the use of his limbs.

"Call to the servants!" he cried in a raucous voice. "Curse that devil--he will get away."

But Rosemary could not move. She could only stand where she was in the doorway and stare at the open window. Jasper had struggled to his feet, lurched forward and tried to push past her. He tried to call out, but the words were choked in his throat. He put his hand up again and tore at his collar, then he tottered and would have fallen backwards if Rosemary had not been quick enough and strong enough to catch him and to guide him to the nearest chair, into which he sank, half fainting. One of the servants came across the hall from the dining-room. Rosemary called to him to bring some brandy.

"The gracious lord feels faint," she said. "Be quick, Sàndor, will you?"

As soon as Sàndor had brought the brandy, Rosemary sent him peremptorily away. Fortunately neither he nor any of the other servants had heard anything of the scuffle, and Rosemary, for very life, could not have said anything to them just then. She knelt down beside Jasper and made him swallow some of the brandy. Obviously he had not been hurt, only scared, and the scared look was still in his eyes when he came to himself.

"You haven't let him go?" were the first words he uttered.

"Let whom go, Jasper?" Rosemary asked quietly. She rose to her feet and offered him an arm to help him get up.

"That spying devil," Jasper replied, with a savage oath. "Peter Blakeney."

"What in the world do you mean?"

"You know quite well what I mean. You must have seen him--I told you to call the servants. Are you in collusion with him, then, that you did not do it?"

"I heard a scuffle," Rosemary rejoined coldly, "when I reached the hall. I opened the door and saw you lying on the ground. I only had enough presence of mind to send for some brandy. Perhaps you will tell me what else happened."

"What else?" he retorted, with a sneer. He had risen and gone over to the mirror to readjust his clothes. She could see his face in the glass, livid with passion, his eyes fixed upon her reflection, while he fumbled with his tie and collar. But even while she watched him she saw a change come slowly over his face. The colour came back to his cheeks, his eyes narrowed, and an indefinable expression crept into them. Perhaps he did not know that Rosemary was watching; certain it is that she had never seen such an expression on his face before--the lips parted above the teeth, which gleamed sharp and white and gave the mouth a cruel, wolfish look. It was all over in a moment, the next he had swung round and faced her, apparently quite himself again, with just the habitual expression of high-bred weariness which he always affected.

"I was obviously wrong," he said coolly, "to suggest that you were in collusion with that young devil, and for this I beg your pardon."

"Wouldn't it be best," she retorted equally coolly, "if you were to tell me what did happen?"

"Peter Blakeney sneaked in through that open window. My back was turned that way and I heard nothing, as I was intent on reading your manuscript. He attacked me from behind. I was taken unawares, but I tried to put up a fight. However, he is younger and more athletic than I am, and he knocked me down. He had already snatched your manuscript out of my hand, and he disappeared with it the way he came, through that open window, at the very moment that you entered the room."

Rosemary had listened to this without moving a muscle. She stood in the middle of the room as if she had been turned to stone, alive only by her eyes, which were fixed with such an intensity of questioning on Jasper that instinctively he turned away, as if dreading to meet her glance.

"That is all, my dear," he said, with a sudden assumption of meekness. "I was certainly to blame for allowing that precious manuscript to be taken from me. I should, I know, have guarded it with my life, and so on, and I have probably sunk very low in your estimation as a coward. But I was taken entirely unawares, and one is not usually prepared for daylight robbery in a house filled with servants. So that must be my excuse--" He paused a moment, then added drily: "That and the fact that I warned you more than once that Peter Blakeney was working against you. Now perhaps you are convinced."

At last Rosemary recovered the use of her tongue, but her voice sounded strange to herself, toneless and distant, as if it came from beneath the earth. "You are quite sure, I suppose," she said slowly, "that it was Peter Blakeney who--who did what you say?"

"Aren't you?" he retorted with a harsh laugh.

She made no reply to the taunt. Outwardly she did not even wince.

"You are quite sure that he got away with the manuscript?"

He shrugged his shoulders. "I am quite sure," he replied.

"What do you supposed he means to do with it?"

"Sell it to Naniescu, of course."

"In exchange for Philip and Anna's freedom?"

Jasper looked at his wife keenly for a moment or two, and the corners of his lips curled in a satiric smile. He took out his cigar-case, carefully selected a weed, struck a match, lit his cigar, and blew out the flame. Then only did he reply.

"Hardly that, I think, seeing that he was instrumental in getting them locked up. More probably, I should say, in exchange for a few thousand pounds."

This time the shaft struck home. Rosemary had some difficulty in smothering the cry of protest which had risen to her throat. But she recovered herself in less than a second and said coolly:

"The manuscript must be got back, of course."

Once more Jasper shrugged his shoulders.

"It might have been done at the moment; but I was helpless, and you were so concerned for my welfare that you did not raise hell to send the servants after the thief."

"I did not know then--about the manuscript."

"You know now," he retorted, "and have not called the servants yet."

"This is not the business of the servants. I look to you to get me back the manuscript."

"To me?" he rejoined with a harsh laugh. "Are you not putting to great a strain on my allegiance? You know my views. Should I not rather be wishing that damnable spy God-speed?"

"Jasper," she said earnestly, "you must get me back the manuscript."

"How is that to be done, my dear? From all accounts our friend Peter is as elusive as his ancestor, the Scarlet Pimpernel. He has ten minutes; advance of us already . . . a car probably waiting for him in the village. Are you quite sure you can't hear the whirring of a motor now?"

"You could try, at any rate." And now there was a distinct note of pleading in her voice. "General Naniescu--"

"Give yourself no illusion in that quarter, my dear," he broke in quickly. "Once Naniescu is in possession of those precious articles of yours he will send a courier flying across Europe with them. Remember that with the manuscript there was your covering letter to the editor of The Times, asking for immediate publication. Let me see," he went on slowly, "this is Saturday. I believe we shall see the first of those wonderful articles in print in The Times on Wednesday."

"I don't care how it's done," she replied impatiently. "If you won't help me I'll manage alone."

"What can you do, my dear?"

"Telegraph to The Times, for one thing, and start for London this evening."

"Plucky!" he remarked drily; "But I doubt if you'll succeed."

"Will you put obstacles in my way?"

"I? Certainly not. But Naniescu will." Then, as without attempting further argument she turned to go, he added blandly: "And Peter."

To this final taunt Rosemary made no reply. Her thoughts were in a whirl, but through the very confusion that was raging in her brain her resolution remained clear. She would wire to the editor of The Times not to act on any letter he might receive from her until he heard from her again, and in the meantime she would start for London immediately. Even if her wire were stopped by Naniescu's orders, she would be in London in time to stop the publication of the articles. Though she had a great deal of influence in the journalistic world, it was not likely that so important a paper as The Times would be ready to print her articles the moment they were received. Yes, she had plenty of time. And the whole conspiracy, whatever it was, had been clumsily engineered and would certainly prove futile.

The conspiracy! Rosemary could not think of that. Yet when she did it would mean such a terrible heartache that the whole world would become a blank. Peter blotted out of her life. That is what it would mean to her probably in the train, travelling alone across Europe, hurrying to nullify work done by Peter--shameful, despicable work that would sully the reputation of a pariah. The work of a spy, of hands tainted with ill-gotten wealth! Rosemary's gorge rose at the thought. The conspiracy would prove futile-there was plenty of time to subvert it--but it was an evil, noisome thing that had been. It had existed--and Peter had given it birth!

Peter!

Never again could the world be bright and beautiful. The thing was so loathsome that it would taint with its foulness everything that Rosemary had up to this hour looked on as sweet and sacred and dear. She herself would remain noisome: a body to execrate, since it had once lain passive and willing in Peter's arms, since her lips still retained the savour of his kiss.

Rosemary went out into the village as far as the post office. She wrote out her telegram to the editor of The Times and asked whether it could be sent out immediately. In order to stimulate the zeal of the postmistress she emphasized her instructions with a hundred lei note. The post-mistress smiled and thanked the gracious lady for the note, and she promised that she would send the telegram off within the next few minutes. Then, as soon as Rosemary had gone out of the stuffy little office and disappeared down the village street, the woman rang up at the Imrey Palace at Cluj and asked to be allowed to speak with His Excellency the General.

CHAPTER XXXIV

Rosemary's wire was repeated over the telephone to General Naniescu, who promptly gave orders that it should not be sent. When he put down the receiver he was very much puzzled. Something had apparently happened at Kis-Imre which had greatly disturbed the beautiful Uno. It seemed indeed as if she had actually written those articles which Naniescu wanted so badly that he was prepared to pay ten thousand pounds sterling of Government money for them. And having written the articles, the lady seemed first to have sent them off, then to have repented.

Well, well! It was all very puzzling. Even M. de Kervoisin, experienced diplomat though he was, could suggest no solution. He advised the obvious: to wait and see.

"We shall see our friend Number Ten soon," he said. "If I am not mistaken he has at least one key to the puzzle in his possession."

But it was not Number Ten who presented himself at the Imrey palace that afternoon. It was ce cher Monsieur Blakeney, who had come all the way from England in order to preside over a game of cricket that had not come off because of the weather. His Excellency was delighted to see him, and so was M. de Kervoisin. This charming, most unexpected but most welcome visit was due no doubt to the cricket and the bad weather. So tiresome! Mais hélas! Man proposes and the rain disposes.

His Excellency was most sympathetic. Would M. Blakeney have a cigar and a glass of fine? No? Then what could His Excellency do for M. Blakeney.

"Pray command men, my dear Monsieur Blakeney. We are all so grateful to you for the kind interest you are taking in our young athletes. It will be such a happy recollection for them in after years that so distinguished an English champion as yourself has helped them with their games."

Peter let him talk on. He thought it a pity to stem this flood of eloquence, and he was looking forward to the moment when Naniescu's complacent effusions would turn to equally comic puzzlement first, and subsequently to amazement and delight.

"Shall I tell your Excellency now," he said as soon as he could get a word in edgeways, "why I have come?"

"Mais comment donc?" the general replied suavely. "I am hanging on your lips, mon cher Monsieur Blakeney."

"Well," Peter said, quite slowly and speaking in French since M. de Kervoisin did not know English. "Well, it's just this. Lady Tarkington has written certain newspaper articles, which you, general, very much desire to see published. That's so, isn't it?"

But though this opening almost betrayed Naniescu into an exclamation of surprise, he had enough control over his nerves not to give himself away. Fortunately he was a great adept at expressive gestures and his cigar also helped to keep him in countenance.

He leaned back in his chair, was silent for a moment or two blowing rings of smoke through his full, red lips.

"Articles?" he queried at last with an assumption of perfect indifference. "I don't know. What articles do you mean, cher ami?"

"Those," Peter replied with equal indifference, "for which you were prepared to pay a deuced lot of money to your spy-in-chief."

Naniescu waved his podgy hand that held the cigar, then he deliberately dusted away a modicum of ash that had dropped upon his trousers.

"Ah!" he said innocently. "Lady Tarkington, you say, has written such articles?"

"Yes. She has."

"Then no doubt she will honour me by allowing me to see the manuscript. She knows how deeply I am interested in her work."

"No, general," Peter broke in drily. "Lady Tarkington has no intention of allowing you to see that particular manuscript of hers."

"Ah! May I be permitted to inquire how you happen to know that?"

"I happen to know--no matter how--that Lady Tarkington only wrote the articles tentatively; that after she had written them she repented having done so, and that her next act would have been to throw the manuscript into the fire."

"Very interesting. But, forgive me, my dear Monsieur Blakeney, if I ask you in what way all this concerns you?"

"I'll tell you," Peter said coolly. "I also happen to know--no matter how--that you are prepared to pay a large sum of money for those articles, so I thought that I would forestall your spy-in-chief by driving a bargain with you over the manuscript."

"But how can you do that, my dear young friend, without the manuscript in your possession?"

"The manuscript is in my possession, Excellency," Peter said coolly.

"How did that come about, if I may ask the question?"

"You may. I stole it this morning from Lady Tarkington."

"What?"

Naniescu had given such a jump that he nearly turned himself out of his chair. The cigar fell from between his fingers, and the glass that contained the fine was upset and its contents spilt over the table. Even M. de Kervoisin had given a start; and his pale, expressionless face had flushed. Though the report of the post-mistress of Kis-Imre had given Naniescu an inkling that something unexpected had occurred, he certainly had not been prepared for this.

He looked up at Peter and frowned, trying to recover his dignity which had been seriously jeopardized. Peter was laughing--very impolitely, thought His Excellency. But then these English have no manners.

"You'll forgive my smiling, won't you, sir?" asked Peter quite deferentially.

"Go on with your story," Naniescu retorted gruffly. "Never mind your manners."

"I can't very well mind them, sir," Peter rejoined, with utmost seriousness, "as I don't possess any. And I can't go on with my story because there is none to tell."

"You have got to tell me how you knew that Lady Tarkington had written certain newspaper articles; how you knew that I wanted them; how you came to--to steal them--the word is your own, my dear Monsieur Blakeney--and where they are at the present moment."

"None of which facts, I am thinking, concern your Excellency," Peter retorted coolly, "except the last. The manuscript of Lady Tarkington's newspaper articles is in my pocket at the present moment, together with her letter to the editor of The Times, asking for these articles to be published at an early opportunity. So, you see, sir, that I am bringing you a perfectly sound proposition."

"I'll have to read those articles first."

"Of course," Peter agreed, and took the sheets of manuscript out of his pocket. "At your leisure."

Naniescu thrust out his podgy hand for them, his large, expressive eyes had lit up with a gleam of excitement. Peter gave him the manuscript, and as he did so he remarked casually, "They are no use to your Excellency without the covering letter."

Which remark seemed to tickle M. de Kervoisin's fancy, for he gave a funny, dry cackle which might pass for a laugh. Naniescu, however, appeared not to notice the taunt. His white, downy hands shook slightly as he unfolded the manuscript. He leaned back in his chair and began to read, the excitement of his nerves was chiefly apparent by his stertorous breathing and his almost savage chewing of the stump of his cigar.

M. de Kervoisin remained silent. He offered Peter a cigarette, and while the Englishman struck a match, lit the cigarette and smoked it with obvious relish, the Frenchman watched him through his half-closed lids with an expression of puzzlement upon his keen, wrinkled face. No sound disturbed the silence that had fallen over the actors of the little comedy, only the ticking of an old-fashioned clock and now and then the crisp crackling of paper as Naniescu turned over the sheets of the manuscript. From time to time he nodded his head and murmured complacently, "C'est très bien! C'est même très, très bien!" And once he looked across at his friend and asked: "Would you like to read this Kervoisin?" But the Frenchman only shrugged and replied with a slightly sarcastic smile: "Oh, my dear friend, if you are satisfied--"

Peter said nothing. He waited quite patiently, seemingly completely indifferent, and smoked one cigarette after another.

When Naniescu had finished reading, he carefully folded the manuscript, laid it on the table beside him and put his hand upon it.

"What do you want for this?" he asked.

And Peter replied coolly: "The title-deeds of the Kis-Imre property."

Naniescu stared at Peter for a moment or two, then he threw back his head and laughed until the tears trickled down his cheeks.

"You are astonishing, my friend," he said. "The property is worth fifty thousand sterling."

"I have paid an option on it of five thousand," Peter retorted, "and the rest of it wouldn't come out of your Excellency's pocket, I take it."

"Not out of my pocket, of course," Naniescu was willing to admit, "but out of that of my Government. We are going to sell Kis-Imre for the benefit of the State."

"And won't your Excellency be purchasing these newspaper articles for the benefit of the State?"

"These articles are not worth it," Naniescu retorted gruffly.

"Very will, let's say no more about it. I'm sorry I troubled your Excellency."

Peter rose as if to go and put out his hand toward the sheets of manuscript.

"Don't be a fool," Naniescu broke in. "I'll give you a good price for the thing, but a property worth fifty thousand sterling--hang it all--it's a bit stiff."

Peter smiled. "How tersely you put the matter, general," he said. "I dare say it is a bit stiff, but I am not prepared to bargain--only to sell. And if you are not satisfied--"

"Easy, easy, my impetuous young friend. Did I say that I was not satisfied--or that I refuse to consider the matter? But there are considerations."

"What considerations?"

"To begin with, how do I know that the English newspaper would accept these articles as the genuine work of Lady Tarkington?"

"I told you that I had Lady Tarkington's own covering letter to the editor of The Times, asking him to publish the articles as soon as possible."

"Let me see it," Naniescu retorted.

"With pleasure."

Peter took the letter out of his pocket, but before handing it over to Naniescu he said drily: "May I in the meanwhile refresh my memory of the articles?"

The eyes of the two men met across the table. Naniescu's flashed with resentment, but Peter's face wore a disarming smile. He looked for all the world like a schoolboy bartering marbles for stamps. But the situation appeared to tickle Kervoisin's fancy. He gave a dry chuckle and said:

"You are quite right, mon ami. They are astonishing, these English."

The exchange was effected without Naniescu losing his sense of resentment or Peter his pleasant smile, and Peter held on to Rosemary's manuscript while the general read the letter through.

While he read, the look of resentment vanished from his face and a complacent smile rose to his full, sensuous lips.

"Il n'y pas à dire," he murmured; "c'est très, très bien."

When he had finished reading he looked up at Peter.

"Now then, Monsieur Blakeney," he said curtly, "your last price?"

"I have told you, sir-the title-deeds of Kis-Imre."

"You are joking."

"I was never more serious in my life."

"But, hang it all, man, if I make the property over to you, how are we to get rid of the Imreys?"

Peter shrugged his shoulders, and, still smiling, said coolly: "That, Excellency, is your affair, not mine."

"But the Countess Imrey is your aunt."

"What has that got to do with the whole thing, Excellency?"

"What has it got to do with it? What has it--?" Naniescu was gasping with astonishment. He was something of a rascal himself, but never in all his life had he come across such callousness or such impudence. He turned to Kervoisin as much as to say: "Have you ever seen such an unmitigated young blackguard?" But the Frenchman's face was inscrutable; his keen, pale eyes rested with obvious puzzlement on Peter.

"Then you want me," Naniescu asked, as soon as he had recovered his breath, "you want me to turn the Imreys out of their home?"

"It won't be the first time, Excellency, that you have done that sort of thing, will it?" Peter retorted, with his most engaging smile.

Strangely enough, Naniescu was losing his temper. He wanted those articles and wanted them badly, and if this preposterous deal went through he could have them without putting his hand in his pocket. But this young blackguard exasperated him. Perhaps professional pride was wounded at meeting a man more corrupt, more venal than himself. To further his own ends Naniescu would have plundered and bullied to an unlimited extent, but he would not have robbed and bullied his own kith and kin; whereas this handsome young athlete with the engaging smile did not seem to have the slightest scruple or the least pricking of conscience. It would be a triumph to get the better of him in some sort of way. Unfortunately the scamp had not yet given up the manuscript, and Naniescu only had the letter, whilst de Kervoisin was in one of his abstracted fits when he wouldn't open his mouth to give friendly advice.

The general, sitting back in his chair, and blowing smoke rings through his pursed lips, had a swift but exceedingly pleasant day-

dream. Those articles were just what he wanted. They were so beautifully written! So convincingly! What a stir they would make! They
were a complete vindication of his administration here in Transylvania. The country prosperous. The people contented. Only a small
minority grumbling without the slightest justification. Oh, those articles! Published in the English Times and signed by the illustrious
"Uno"! Naniescu, closing his eyes to enjoy this wonderful day-dream,
saw himself summoned to Bucharest, there to receive the personal
thanks of his King and a substantial reward from his Government,
whilst all he need do now to obtain these glorious results was to hand
over to this young rascal a property that belonged to that fool Maurus
Imrey.

It was a lovely day-dream. A stroke of the pen would make it reality. No wonder that General Naniescu swore loudly when the crackling
of paper woke him from his short trance. The young rascal was quite
unconcernedly stowing that precious manuscript away in his pocket.

"Halt!" Naniescu exclaimed, on the impulse of the moment. "I ac-
cept--" Then he added guardedly: "On principle, I mean."

"And in fact?" Peter queried, without making the slightest movement towards taking the manuscript out of his pocket again.

"Yes, yes!" Naniescu replied impatiently. "But, curse you for a
jackanapes, these things take time--"

"They need not," Peter rejoined curtly. "All you need do is to give
me an official receipt for forty-five thousand sterling, the balance of
the purchase-money for the Kis-Imre property. The British Consul and
your lawyer will do the rest."

"And when do you want possession?"

"At once."

Naniescu made a final appeal to his friend: "What do you say,
Kervoisin?"

But the Frenchman's face remained inscrutable. He was watching
the smoke that curled upwards from the tip of his cigarette, and only
from time to time did he throw a quick, indefinable glance at the tall,
athletic figure of the man who was driving such a contemptible bargain. When Naniescu appealed directly to him, he only shrugged his
shoulders to indicate his complete detachment from the whole affair.
Peter, on the other hand, showed not the slightest sign of impatience.
He even went to the length of buttoning up his coat.

"Would you like to think it over?" he said coolly. "I can leave my
offer open for another few hours."

Pimpernel and Rosemary

"No! damn you!" Naniescu exclaimed, and jumped to his feet. "Wait for me here. I'll have the receipt ready in five minutes."

After which, from sheer force of habit, he swore in several other languages before he finally strode out of the room.

202

CHAPTER XXXV

Peter met de Kervoisin's shrewd eyes fixed searchingly upon him. He gave a quaint, good-humoured laugh.

"Are you trying to make up your mind, sir," he asked, "just what kind of a blackguard I am?"

M. de Kervoisin's thin lips curled in a wry smile. "I am not sure," he said, "that you are a blackguard. But I confess that I do not understand you."

"Which is very flattering, sir. But isn't it natural that a man should covet a beautiful property and seize the cheapest means to become possessed of it? That sort of thing has been largely done by the conquering nations since the war. Then why not by individuals?"

"Why not, as you say? But I was not thinking of that side of the question, chiefly because I do not believe that you stole Lady Tarkington's manuscript in order to drive a bargain with our friend here over the Kis-Imre property. I may be wrong, but you don't look to me the sort of man who would do this dirty trick for mere gain. I am giving you the credit of desiring above all to save your kinsfolk, young and old, from certain highly unpleasant eventualities."

"You are very generous, sir, in your estimate of me."

"The question is," Kervoisin mused, "whether after all this they will be grateful to you for what you have done, or will they hate you, do you think, for what the publication of those articles will mean to their people? Lady Tarkington must at one time have intended to publish those articles, since she took the trouble to write them. Something turned her from the purpose: either her own conviction, or the desire of the Imreys themselves."

"I suppose so," Peter said, with a shrug of complete indifference.

"Whereupon you, my dear friend, stepped in like an unwanted deus ex machinâ, and settled the business to your own satisfaction, if not to theirs."

"I never was good at Latin," Peter said, with his most engaging smile, "but we'll leave it at that if you like."

De Kervoisin was silent for a moment or two, his attention being seemingly riveted on the rings of smoke that rose from his cigarette.

"I wonder," he murmured after a while.

"Don't trouble, sir. I am not worth it."

"Ah! but youth always is a perpetual wonder to me. It is such a long time since I was young myself. And I was wondering which of the two levers youth pulled in order to make you act as you did."

"Two levers?"

"Love or hate."

Then, as Peter was silent in his turn, M. de Kervoisin went on: "You know, we in France always look for the woman in every case. Now here we have not far to seek. And yet love would seem to me to have gained nothing by this adventure, whilst hate, on the other hand--"

He paused abruptly, his keen eyes narrowed, and his lips curled in a sardonic smile.

"Ah!" he said. "I think I understand, after all."

"That's more than I do, sir," Peter retorted ingenuously.

M. de Kervoisin would no doubt have pursued the subject, which seemed greatly to interest him, had not Naniescu just then made a noisy re-entry into the room. He had a large, official-looking document in his hand, which he threw down on the table.

"Have a look at this, my dear Monsieur Blakeney," he said curtly. "I think that you will find it in order."

Peter took up the paper and examined it at great length. It was a receipt for the sum of forty-five thousand pounds sterling, in full satisfaction for the sale of the estate of Kis-Imre here described as the property of the Crown of Roumania. It was signed with Naniescu's elaborate flourish, countersigned and stamped; it stated further that the sale would be duly inscribed in the Bureau des Hypothèques in accordance with the law, and the acte de vente and title-deeds handed over within one month to M. Peter Blakeney or his duly appointed representative.

It was all in order. Peter folded the receipt, but before putting it away he said to Naniescu:

"The whole thing, of course, is conditional on a free pardon being granted to Philip Imrey and Anna Heves, with permission to leave the country immediately. That was the original bargain between yourself and Lady Tarkington."

"They can clear out of the country the day the last of these articles is published in The Times," Naniescu rejoined gruffly. "I'll arrange for that fool Maurus Imrey and his wife to clear out at the same time. The sooner I am rid of the whole brood of them, the better I shall like it."

"I am sure you will," Peter said blandly. "Then perhaps you won't mind letting me have passports for them. You can post-date them, of course. I shouldn't then have to intrude on you again."

"You are very kind. The passports post-dated, say, a week from to-day will be in the bureau at your disposal whenever you like to call for them. You understand that I should revoke them if at least one of these articles has not appeared within the week."

"I quite understand," Peter concluded. Everything now being in order, he slipped the receipt into his pocket-book, then, without further words, he handed Rosemary's manuscript over to Naniescu.

"You have the covering letter," he said simply.

Naniescu nodded, and he took the papers with a sigh of satisfaction, which he did not even attempt to disguise. His ill-temper had vanished. The day-dream was coming true: the journey to Bucharest, the thanks of his King, the reward from a grateful Government! Naniescu felt at peace with all the world. He would even have hugged Peter to his breast.

"We part the best of friends," he said suavely, "my dear Monsieur Blakeney."

"Oh! the very best," Peter assented.

"And when you come to take possession of Kis-Imre you will command my services, I hope. "

"I shall not fail to do so."

"I will see to it that you can do it at the earliest possible moment. By the way," Naniescu went on with some hesitation, "the furniture--and other contents of the château--they are not included in the sale, of course."

"Of course not."

"You won't mind the Imreys having those? It might create an un-pleasant impression--if we were to--er--"

"It might," Peter assented.

"I was sure you would agree with me about that," Naniescu rejoined unctuously. "Then what would you like us to do in the matter?"

"Leave everything as it is until you hear from me again. The British Consul will look after things for me."

"Ah!" Naniescu concluded with perfect affability, "then I don't think I need detain you any longer, my dear young friend. May I express the wish that you will spend long and happy years in this beautiful country."

"Thank you."

Peter did not shake hands with either of the two men, but he caught Kervoisin's glance and gave him a pleasant nod. To Naniescu he said just before leaving:

"I suppose you have realized that Lady Tarkington will probably wish to start for England immediately."

"Yes, my dear young friend," Naniescu replied blandly. "I had realized that, and I have taken measures accordingly. But how kind of you to remind me!"

And when Peter finally went out of the room the general, breathless, perspiring, nerve-racked, threw himself into a chair and exclaimed:

"Il n'y a pas à dire! They are astonishing, these English!"

He poured himself out a glass of fine and drank it down at one gulp.

"Did you ever see such an unmitigated young blackguard?" he exclaimed.

But de Kervoisin had remained thoughtful. His shrewd, pale eyes were fixed upon the door through which Peter had just disappeared. Naniescu had taken his handkerchief and was mopping his streaming forehead and his neck round the edge of his collar.

"I feel quite sick," he murmured. "Ah, these English! mon ami. You don't know them as I do. I firmly believe that they would sell their fathers, their mothers, their sisters, or their wives if they saw money in the transaction."

Kervoisin made no comment on this tirade; after a while he asked abruptly: "What are you doing to prevent the lovely Uno from putting a spoke in your wheel?"

Naniescu gave a complacent laugh.

"Doing?" he retorted. "Why, I've already done everything, my friend. My courier starts to-night for London with Lady Tarkington's letter and manuscript. He will be in London on Monday evening. On Tuesday he will call on the editor of The Times. Ostensibly he is Lady Tarkington's messenger. When he has delivered the letter he will ask for a reply. That reply he will telegraph to me. Then we shall know where we are."

He drank another glass of fine, then he went on:

"I have no doubt that the fair Uno has already got her boxes packed and is ready to start for England by the express to-night, but--"

Naniescu paused. He stretched out his legs, examined the toes of his boots and the smoke of his cigar; his face wore an expression of fatuous self-satisfaction. "I think," he said, "that you will be surprised at what I have done in the time. And so will the incomparable Uno," he added with an expressive twinkle in his fine, dark eyes.

"What about friend Number Ten?" Kervoisin remarked drily.

"Well," Naniescu retorted with his affected smile, "I imagine that friend Number Ten will be the most surprised of the lot."

CHAPTER XXXVI

At Kis-Imre the day dragged on leaden-footed. Luncheon, then a long afternoon, then dinner. Time wore on and Elza had not returned.

Rosemary was ready, dressed for the journey; her suit-case was packed. She was only taking a very little luggage with her as she had every intention of returning as soon as her errand in London was accomplished. She would not for the world have left Elza alone too long with her troubles. She made herself no illusions with regard to the telegram which she had sent from the village. It would, she was sure, be intercepted, and Naniescu would not allow it to go. Rosemary's intention was to send another directly she was the other side of the frontier. This would prevent the articles being published hurriedly, and, of course, she would be in London thirty-six hours later.

Indeed, the odious deed which Peter had planned and carried through appeared to her now not only in its hideousness but in its futility. What did he hope to accomplish? Did he know her so little as to imagine that she would merely call the occurrence an adverse blow of Fate and quietly sit down under it--be content to send one wire which would be intercepted? It was futile! Futile! She was a British subject. She had a British passport. No power on earth could stop her from going to London or to the outermost ends of the earth if she had a mind. No one. Not even Jasper. Least of all Jasper!

But in the meanwhile Elza had not returned. Time went on, slowly but certainly. Eight o'clock--nine o'clock--ten o'clock. Unless Elza was home within the next half-hour Rosemary could not start for London before the next night. There was only one through train to Budapest every twenty-four hours, the midnight express! Any other slow train would be no help for getting the communication with the Orient Express.

And Rosemary could not go to London without knowing what Elza's wishes were. Elza was to decide--not she. And Elza had not come
back from Anna's mother. Soon after ten Rosemary sent Rosa round to
Maurus to ask if she might see him. She hoped that he could perhaps
tell her something definite about Elza's movements. Rosemary found
him very much altered since last she had seen him. He looked well in
health, but his whole expression, even his appearance, seemed strange.
The gipsy strain was more apparent--the eyes seemed darker and more
restless, the mouth redder and fuller, and the nose more hooked and
narrower across the bridge. But he talked very quietly about Elza, because he had not really expected to see her back this evening.

"She was going to Cluj first," he said, "to see Philip and Anna.
Probably it took time to get permission to visit the children in prison.
Then after that she was going to Ujlak. I suppose she wanted to let
Charlotte know how little Anna is getting on. Poor child! Poor child!"
Maurus went on slowly, wagging his head. "Isn't it pitiable? She is
such a nice little girl. And my Philip--my Philip--"

He rambled on, and his speech became thick and unintelligible. The
sister in charge gave Rosemary a hint that it would be better for her to
go. Rosemary rose at once.

"Well, my dear Maurus," she said, "I don't want to tire you. I
thought perhaps you might know something definite about Elza. But if
you are not anxious about her I am sure it is all right."

"Oh, yes, yes, it is all right. You see, she went to visit the children.
Then she was going to Ujlak. It is a long way for the horses--"

"You don't think she would stay in Cluj for the night?"

"I don't know. I don't know. She was going to Cluj first to see the
children--then she was going to Ujlak. It is a long way for the horses--
Elza will stay with Charlotte for the night. A hard woman, Charlotte.
But Anna is such a nice child. And my Philip--my Philip--"

The mind was obviously wandering. Maurus, while he spoke was
staring straight out before him. Rosemary tried to explain to him that
she had to go away on business for a day or two and she hoped to start
this evening, but she could not go, of course, without seeing Elza first.

"Ah! you are going away, dear Lady Tarkington?" the invalid said
with a quick gleam in his restless, dark eyes. "I wish I could go with
you. I am so sick of this place, and now that my Philip has gone. . . .
But how can you go to-night, dear Lady Tarkington?"

"I won't go before I have seen Elza."

"No, no, you must not go before Elza comes. I have only the one
comfortable carriage now. They have taken everything from me, my

horses, my cattle, my carriages, and my motor-cars--I can't send you to Cluj in comfort until Elza comes back in the carriage. I have another pair of horses--but no comfortable carriage. They took everything away from me. Soon they will turn me out of this house--"

"Don't worry about that, dear, my husband has the use of a small car and a soldier-chauffeur. We can get to Cluj all right."

The sister in charge interposed again, more peremptorily this time. Rosemary took as cheerful a farewell of the invalid as she could.

"You must arrange," she said, "As soon as you are well enough, to come over to us in England for a visit. It would be such a change for you, and Jasper and I would make you and Elza very welcome."

But Maurus shook his head, and stared straight out before him. "That, dear Lady Tarkington," he said, "can never be now." And slowly the tears gathered in his eyes and trickled down his cheeks. Broken-hearted, Rosemary bade him a final good night.

There was only one more chance of getting in touch with Elza to-night, and that was to ascertain if she were staying at any of the hotels in Cluj. And this Jasper did at Rosemary's request. He telephoned to the "Pannonia" and to the "New York", the only possible places where Elza might have put up for the night. True, when the Roumanian Government took over the Imrey palace two or three rooms were allowed to remain in possession of the family if they required them, but it was not likely that Elza would elect to sleep under the same roof as General Naniescu. Both hotels replied on the telephone that the gracious Countess Imrey was not there. Ujlak, unfortunately, had not the telephone installed.

There was, then, nothing to be done.

But the next day was even more trying than the one before. The morning wore on and there was no news of Elza. Anxiety for her friend was added to the heavy load which Rosemary had to bear. Anxiety and this unexpected uncertainty, which was positive torture.

Jasper, on the other hand, had become both helpful and sympathetic. Already the day before he had announced his intention of accompanying Rosemary to London. At first she had protested, but he looked so contrite and so abashed that she relented, and said more graciously:

"It is more than kind of you, dear, to suggest it, but I really am quite capable of looking after myself."

"I don't doubt it," he had replied with a sigh, "but I, too, have certain privileges, chief of which is looking after your welfare--and your safety."

She laughed. "I am perfectly safe. No one is going to run away with me."

"You might have trouble on the frontier."

"Not very likely," she retorted, "with a British passport."

Jasper had made no further remark just then, and the subject was dropped. But Rosemary knew from his manner and his look that he intended to accompany her. It would be no use protesting, though she had the feeling that she would so much rather have travelled alone.

But when the morning of the next day went by without news of Elza, Jasper was ready with a fresh suggestion. "Let me go to London for you," he said. "I could see the editor of The Times and ask him in any case to withhold publication until he heard from you. Then after that, if Elza's decision went the other way, you could always wire or write again."

Rosemary hesitated for a moment or two. She could not very well put into words the thought that was in her mind. But Jasper presently did it for her.

"You do not trust me," he said quietly.

For another fraction of a second she hesitated, then with a frank gesture of camaraderie she put her hand out to him: "I think I ought to carry my own business through myself," she said, and added softly: "You understand, dear, don't you?"

She could always win any man over with her smile, and at the soft tone of her voice Jasper captured her hand and buried his face in the soft, smooth palm.

"Tell me how I can serve you," he said, "but, in God's name, don't go away from me."

He was once more all kindness and consideration, more like the charming companion of the early days of her brief married life. With utmost patience he discussed the whole situation with her: the possibility of getting in touch with Elza and the advisability of communicating with The Times in any case, leaving it open for an ultimate change of tactics.

But though he was so kind, so unselfish, so generous, Rosemary could not respond in the same way as she had done in the past. Her confidence in him had been wavering for some time, whenever those wild outbursts of ungovernable passion, when he claimed her body and her soul as he would a slave or a chattel, had outraged as well as mystified her, and she could not free her mind from that vision which she had of him in the mirror yesterday, with his mouth parted in a cruel, wolfish grin. The dual nature in him puzzled her. She would not admit that she feared him, because she had never in her life been afraid of anyone, but she did own to a certain vague dread which would creep into her heart whenever she found herself alone with him; she had accepted his kisses at first, hoping that in time friendship and confidence would turn to warmer feeling, but she had a horror of them now, and knew that the last shred of friendship was being torn to rags by all that was violent, passionate and cruel in him. At the same time she did admit quite readily that he was very helpful and kind in the present emergency, and gladly did she accept his final offer to motor straightway to Cluj to see if he could find out something definite about Elza.

"If she was not at Cluj," he said, "I would go on to Ujlak; and, in any case, I can be back by about eight o'clock. If in the meanwhile, as I hope and think, Elza has turned up, we can make our plans in accordance with what she has decided, and either start for England at once, or leave matters as they stand."

The suggestion was so practical that Rosemary felt really grateful. She walked with him to the village where he garaged the car that Naniescu had lent him. It was a powerful little car, of a well-known French make and built for speed. The soldier-chauffeur was fortunately on the spot, and with a friendly handshake Rosemary wished her husband God-speed.

"I don't know how I shall live through this day!" she said to him at the last.

Jasper was very self-contained and practical. He satisfied himself that everything about the car was in order, then only did he get in. He took the wheel and waved Rosemary a last farewell, and very soon the car disappeared down the road in a cloud of dust.

CHAPTER XXXVII

General Naniescu was enjoying himself thoroughly. He had his friend Number Ten sitting there opposite him, and Number Ten was looking as savage as a bear. Naniescu had offered him a cigar, a glass of fine, even whisky and soda, but Number Ten had declined everything and remained very truculent.

"You had no right," he said, with a savage oath, "to go behind my back."

But Naniescu was at his blandest. "What could I do, my dear friend?" he asked, and waived his white, downy hands to emphasize by appropriate gesture, both his perplexity and his contrition. "What would you have had me do? Decline to deal with that young Blakeney? Then those precious articles would have been lost to me for ever. Lady Tarkington would not have written them all over again."

"I told you the other day that I would get those articles for you. Ask M. de Kervoisin here if I have ever failed in anything I have undertaken. I had the manuscript in my hand when that young blackguard snatched it out of my hand. Curse him!"

Naniescu leaned back in his chair and gave a guttural, complacent laugh: "I do agree with you, my dear friend," he said. "That young Blakeney is an unmitigated blackguard. I have had to deal with some in my day, but never with such a corrupt, dirty scoundrel. Yes, dirty, that's what he is. But you know, you English, you are astonishing! Everything big with you--big fellows, big Empire, big money, big blackguards! Yes, big blackguards! Oh, là, là!"

"Yes," Number Ten assented drily. "And the big blackguard who is also a big fellow, got big money out of you, for you have been a fool, as well as a knave, my friend. I only asked you ten thousand sterling for the manuscript."

"Are you pretending that you know what I paid Blakeney?" Naniescu asked, with his most fatuous smile. "Because, my friend, in picturesque poker parlance--I am very fond of a game of poker myself--and in poker language, we call what you are doing now 'bluff.' You don't know what I paid Blakeney for the manuscript. But I don't mind telling you that I paid nothing at all. Yes, my dear friend, nothing at all."

And with the tip of his well-manicured little finger, Naniescu emphasized every syllable with a tap on the table.

"I am glad to hear it," Number Ten retorted curtly, "because that will make it easier for you to pay me the ten thousand now."

But this idea amused the General so much that he nearly rolled off his chair laughing.

"Ils sont impayable ces Anglais!" he said, when with streaming eyes and scanty breath he found words to express his sense of the ludicrous. "Why in the name of Tophet should I pay you ten thousand pounds sterling?"

"Because if you don't, those newspaper articles will never be published."

"Ah, bah!" Naniescu exclaimed with a mocking grin, "who will prevent it?"

"I, of course."

"You, of course? How, I should like to know?"

"That's my business."

"You can't do it, my friend," Naniescu rejoined complacently. "You can't do it. I defy you to do it."

"Is that a challenge?"

Number Ten had said this very quietly. He was in the act of lighting a cigarette when he spoke, and he finished lighting it, blew out the match, and threw it into the nearest ash-tray before he glanced at Naniescu. Then he smiled, because Naniescu's face expressed arrogance first, then bewilderment, and finally indecision.

"Is it a challenge?" he reiterated sardonically. "I don't mind, you know, one way or the other. There are at least three governments--neighbours of yours, by the way--who will pay me ten thousand pounds apiece for certain services which they require, and which I can render them. But you have behaved like a knave and a fool, my friend, and it will amuse me to punish you. So listen to me! Unless you give me a cheque for the ten thousand pounds which you promised me, and which I can cash at your fusty old bank over the way this very afternoon, I guarantee you that Lady Tarkington's articles will not be published in any English newspaper."

He smoked on in silence for a little while longer, blowing rings of smoke through his pursed lips, and in the intervals laughing softly, mockingly to himself, or throwing an occasional glance of intelligence in the direction of Kervoisin, who apparently immersed in a book had taken no part in the conversation. Naniescu's bewilderment had become ludicrous, and at one moment when he took his perfumed handkerchief out of his pocket and mopped his streaming forehead, the face of his spy-in-chief became distorted with that look of ferocious cruelty which was so characteristic of him.

"I haven't a great deal of time to spare," Number Ten remarked drily, after a few minutes' silence; "if you accept my challenge I start for London to-night."

"You'll never get there in time," Naniescu rejoined, with an attempt at swagger.

Number Ten smiled. "Don't you think so?" he asked simply.

"The frontier is closed--"

"Would you rather risk it than pay me the ten thousand pounds?"

Naniescu appealed to his friend.

"De Kervoisin--" he said, almost pitiably.

But M. de Kervoisin, with a shrug, indicated that this was no concern of his.

"M. de Kervoisin," Number Ten said, still smiling, "knows my methods. During the war I had other and more dangerous frontiers to cross than this one, my friend--and I never failed."

In Naniescu's puny mind, obviously a war was waging between greed and avarice. He was seeing his beautiful day-dream vanishing into the intangible ether--whence come all dreams--and he was not prepared to take any risks. Those articles which a reliable courier was even now taking to London with all speed were the most precious things he, Naniescu, had ever possessed. They meant honour, security, money--far more money than Number Ten was demanding with such outrageous impudence. And Naniescu was afraid of Number Ten-- afraid of his daring, is courage, his unscrupulous determination to carry through what he had set out to do.

Ten thousand pounds! It was a great deal, but it would come out of secret service funds, not out of Naniescu's own pocket. There was only that slight desire to get the better of Number Ten, to win this battle of wits against so crafty an opponent. But what was amour propre when weighed in the balance with the realization of Naniescu's wonderful daydreams?

Nevertheless he made one more effort at a bargain.

"If I pay you that the thousand," he said, with a savage oath, "what guarantee have I that the articles will be published?"

"None," was Number Ten's cool reply; "but if you don't pay me the ten thousand, I guarantee that they will not be published."

At which M. de Kervoisin put down his book and indulged in a good laugh.

"Take care, my friend," he said to Number Ten, "our friend here is beginning to lose his temper, and you may find yourself under lock and key before he has done with you."

"I wonder!" Number Ten retorted drily "It would mean raising hell in the English press, wouldn't it? if a British subject--what?"

He did not pursue the subject. Even Naniescu himself had put such a possibility out of his reckoning.

"All that our friend could do," Number Ten went on, speaking over his shoulder to M. de Kervoisin, "would be to have me murdered, but he would find even that rather difficult. Ten thousand pounds of secret service money is considerably safer--and cheaper in the end."

Then at last Naniescu gave in. "Oh, have it your own way, curse you!" he exclaimed.

"The money now," Number Ten said coolly, raising a warning finger. "You may as well send one of your clerks over to the bank for it. I prefer that to taking your cheque."

Then he turned to Kervoisin, and picked up the book which the latter had thrown down on the table "Ah!" he remarked, with a total change of tone, "Marcel Proust's latest. You are an epicure in literature, my friend."

He fingered the book, seemingly as indifferent to what Naniescu was doing and saying, as if the whole matter of a ten thousand pound cheque did not concern him in the least.

The general had gone across to a desk which stood in the farther corner of the room. He had written out a cheque, rung the bell, and was now giving orders to a clerk to fetch the money from the Anglo-Roumanian bank over the way.

On the whole he was not displeased with the transaction. The articles signed by Uno and published in The Times would redound to his credit, would bring him all that he had striven for all his life; and, after all, they would cost him nothing--nothing at all.

Number Ten and de Kervoisin were discussing Marcel Proust; he, Naniescu, was savouring his day-dreams once again; and presently when the clerk returned with a bundle of crisp English bank-notes in his hand, Naniescu handed the money over to his spy-in-chief without a qualm, and certainly without regret.

"This being Monday," Number Ten said, after he had stowed the money away in his pocket-book, "and your courier having started last night, you will probably see the first of the articles in Thursday's Times. By the way," he went on casually, "what are you doing about young Imrey and the girl?"

"What do you mean by that? What should I be doing with them?"

"Well, when these articles appear--"

"I send them packing, c'est entendu. I never go back on my word," Naniescu said, with a grandiose gesture.

"It would not pay you to do that in this case, my friend. Lady Tarkington has your written promise and she would raise hell if you played her false. But I wasn't thinking of that. I only wished to warn you to keep an eye on those two young firebrands."

"Oh," Naniescu retorted, with a shrug, "once I have them out of the country they can do what they like. They no longer hurt me. Especially after the publication of those beautiful articles."

"That is so, but you are sending Count and Countess Imrey out of the country aren't you?"

"What makes you say that?"

"Well, you paid Blakeney for the articles with the title-deeds of Kis-Imre, didn't you?"

"How did you know that?"

"I didn't," Number Ten replied drily. "I guessed, and you gave yourself away."

"Well, and if I did--what is it to you?"

"Nothing, my friend. Nothing. I come back to my original warning. Keep a close eye on young Imrey and Anna Heves, and above all keep a close eye on Blakeney."

"That young blackguard?"

"Yes, that young blackguard! He may be playing a double game, you know. I suppose he is still in Cluj?"

"I thought of that," Naniescu broke in curtly, "so I have had Imrey and the Heves girl transferred to Sót."

"Sót? Isn't that rather near the frontier?"

"Thirty kilometres."

"But why Sót?"

"We have commandeered a château there, which we use as a prison for political offenders. We chose it because it stands alone in an out-of-the-way part of the country, and it saves the nuisance of public manifestations and disturbances when a prisoner who happens to have been popular is condemned. We try them by a military tribunal which holds it sittings at Sót, and if an execution is imperative--well, it is done without any fuss."

"I see. Well," Number Ten went on, as he rose to take his leave, "I need not detain you any longer. Let me assure you," he concluded, with his habitual sardonic smile, "that I shall not now think of interfering with any of the measures which you have adopted to stop Lady Tarkington from running after her manuscript."

"I don't believe that you could have interfered in any case," Naniescu retorted gruffly.

"It is not too late, my friend. I would rather like to pit my wits against yours. So if you have repented of the bargain--" And Number Ten half drew his bulging pocket-book out of his pocket.

"Oh, go to the devil!" Naniescu exclaimed, half in rage and half in laughter.

"And I hope soon to meet you in his company," Number Ten replied, and he finally took his leave from the two men.

As soon as the door had closed on him, Naniescu turned and looked at his friend. But de Kervoisin had picked up his book, and gave him no encouragement to discuss the intriguing personality of Number Ten.

His face, too, was quite inscrutable. Marcel Proust was engaging his full attention. For a moment it seemed as if Naniescu would fall back on his stock phrase, or else on a string of cosmopolitan oaths; he even drew his breath ready for either; then it seemed as if words failed him.

The intriguing personality was above comment.

CHAPTER XXXVIII

Rosemary had never before welcomed her husband so eagerly as she did that afternoon. As soon as she heard the whirring of his motor she ran to the gates to meet him.

"What news?" she cried when he had brought the car to a standstill.

As usual, his dark eyes flashed with joy when he saw her. He jumped down and raised both her hands to his lips.

"Very vague, I am afraid," he replied. "And some of it a mere conjecture."

"Tell me."

"To begin with, young Imrey and Anna Heves have been transferred to Sót."

"Where is that?"

"Between Cluj and the frontier. It seems that there is a château there that is being used as a prison for political offenders."

"Who told you that?"

"Naniescu. I saw him for a moment. He was very busily engaged with the Minister for Home Affairs who was over from Bucharest, so he could only give me a few minutes."

"Had he seen Elza?"

"No. But she had applied for permission to see Philip and Anna, and he gave the permission. He supposed that she had gone on to Sót by train."

"Even so," Rosemary mused, "she would be back by now, or else she would have wired."

Jasper appeared to hesitate for a moment or two, and then he said: "I don't think that she has been allowed to do either."

"Why not?"

"It is mere surmise, my dear," Jasper went on quietly, "but one thing Naniescu did tell me and that was that he had on behalf of his government definitely made over the Kis-Imre estates to Peter Blakeney."

They were walking round the house towards the veranda when he said this. Rosemary made no response; indeed, it might be thought that she had not heard, for the next question which she put to Jasper appeared irrelevant.

"Does the midnight express stop at Sót?"

"It does," Jasper replied.

"Then, I can see Elza there. I am sure that is where she is. You inquired at Ujlak?"

"Yes, Elza went there first and then to Cluj."

They had reached the veranda now, and Rosemary went up the steps and then into the house.

"You still wish to come with me to-night?" she asked her husband before she went upstairs.

"Why, of course."

"You are not too tired after all this running about?"

"I?" he exclaimed with a laugh. "Tired? When it is a question of being near you!"

He tried to capture her wrist, but she evaded him and ran quickly through the hall and up the stairs. Before going into her room she called down to him:

"If we use your motor we need not start before eleven o'clock, and there is still a chance of Elza being home before then."

It was just before dinner that the culminating tragedy occurred. Rosemary was in her room, when she heard loud commotion coming form the hall--harsh, peremptory voices, a word or two from Anton, and then Jasper's voice raised as if in protest. She opened her door, and to her horror saw a squad of soldiers in the hall, and between them an officer, and a man in civilian clothes who had an official-looking paper in his hand, and was apparently explaining something to Jasper.

"I regret, my lord, but these are my orders," the man was saying, "and I cannot enter into any discussion with you."

Jasper tried to protest again. "But surely--" he began. The man, however, cut him short.

"If you like," he said, "I can allow you to see Count Imrey first, but this order I must deliver into his own hands."

Rosemary in the meanwhile had run downstairs.

"What is it, Jasper?" she asked quickly.

"An order of eviction," Jasper replied curtly, "against that wretched Maurus."

"Whatever does that mean?"

"That he must quit this place within twenty-four hours."

"Impossible!" she exclaimed hotly.

She turned to the officer and the civilian who had brought this monstrous order.

"The whole thing is a mistake," she said coolly; "some error in the name. Count Imrey is a loyal subject of the King. There has never been a hint of disloyalty levelled against him."

The officer in charge gave a curt laugh and shrugged his shoulders, and the civilian said with a sneer:

"They all say that, milady. They are all wonderfully loyal after they have been found out."

"But General Naniescu himself is a friend of the family. And Lord Tarkington and I can vouch--"

"Pardon, milady," the civilian broke in coldly. "This affair does not concern you or Lord Tarkington, and the order of eviction is signed on behalf of the present owner of Kis-Imre by His Excellency the Governor himself."

"On behalf--"

It was Rosemary who spoke, but the sound of her voice might have come out of a grave. She had never been so near to swooning in her life. The walls around her, the woodwork, the stairs, all took on distorted shapes, and moved, round and round and up and down, until everything was a blur through which the faces of the Roumanian officer and the civilian stared at her and grinned. "On behalf of the present owner of Kis-Imre!" But that was Peter! Peter! And the world did not totter, the earth did not quake, and engulf all these monstrous crimes, this cruelty and this shame!

Luckily none of the Roumanians appeared to have noticed this sudden weakness in her; the civilian was consulting with the officer whether he should allow milord Tarkington to break the awful news to Maurus. Neither raised any objection, and Jasper pronounced himself ready to go. Rosemary turned appealingly to him:

"You will be very patient, Jasper," she begged, "and very, very gentle?"

"Leave it to me, dear," he responded; "I'll do my best."

When he was gone, Rosemary mechanically asked the officer and his companion to come into the smoking-room and sit down. She offered cigarettes. They made her ceremonious bows, and were as polite and conventional as circumstances demanded. She tried to talk; she even asked questions; but they were diplomatically ignorant of everything except of their duty. They explained that this consisted in seeing Count Imrey personally, and giving the eviction order into his own hands.

"It will kill him," Rosemary said, with conviction, "or else send him out of his mind."

Both the men shrugged. They had seen so much of this sort of thing, one of them said, people always threatened to die or to go mad, but nothing of the sort had ever happened.

"Are you quite sure of that?" Rosemary retorted.

Somehow the episode had brought back into the forefront of her consciousness her responsibility with regard to her newspaper articles. Not that conscience had been dormant, but Peter's infamy had been such an overwhelming shock that every other emotion had slipped away into the background. But now it all came back to her. Those articles of hers if they were published would bring a justification of all this--of these orders of eviction, the sort of thing that men died of, or went mad over out of grief, while officials shrugged their shoulders, having seen it all so often.

A few minutes after Jasper returned and Maurus was with him. At sight of Maurus, Rosemary had risen from her chair as if drawn up by mechanical force, and she remained standing, staring at the man whom she had last seen as a fragile weakling, babbling incoherent words. Maurus had dressed himself with unusual care. It almost seemed as if he had been expecting visitors. Rosemary had never seen him with hair so sleekly brushed, or chin so smooth. The officer and the civilian had risen to greet him, and he went up to them with perfect calm, inquiring politely what they desired to say to him. Rosemary turned a questioning glance on Jasper. He, too, appeared puzzled, and followed Maurus' every movement as if he dreaded that something would happen presently, and all the man's self-possession disintegrate in a tempest of fury.

But nothing of the sort happened. Maurus took the order from the civilian, and read it through carefully. Not a muscle of his face twitched, and his hands were perfectly steady. For the moment Rosemary wondered whether this outward calm was not some form of madness.

"I can't understand it," she whispered to Jasper, while the three men were engaged together.

"I am just as puzzled as you are," Jasper replied.

"So long as he is not just putting a terrible strain on himself--in which case the reaction will be frightful."

Maurus was now taking leave of the officials.

"I quite understand the position," he said quietly. "If I had bought a house, I, too, would wish to take possession of it as soon as possible. Perhaps," he added, with a smile, "I should not have been quite in such a hurry, but we all know that with the English time is money, eh, messieurs? And now all I need do is to thank you for your courtesy. I will comply with the order, chiefly because I have no choice."

It was almost unbelievable. Rosemary thought that her eyes and ears must be playing her a trick. The two Roumanians took their leave with their habitual elaborate politeness and Maurus himself saw them to his front door, where the squad of soldiers still stood at attention. When they had all gone, he came back into the smoking-room, and he was actually laughing when he entered.

"Did you ever see such swine?" he said lightly, and then apologized to Rosemary for his language.

"You are taking it so bravely, Maurus, dear," Rosemary murmured bewildered. "But what about Elza?"

"Oh, she prepared me for it; she knew all about it yesterday, and she sent me word what to bring along in the way of clothes for her. And, of course, there will be her jewellery, and one or two little things to see to. However, I have got twenty-four hours before me, and there will be Anton and Rosa to help me."

"But, Maurus, dear--"

"You are astonished, dear Lady Tarkington," Maurus broke in, with rather a sad smile, "to see me take it all so calmly. I was born in this house, and I always thought that I would die in it; but lately these walls have seen so much sorrow and so many villainies that I would just as soon turn my back on them."

"But what does Elza feel about it?"

"The same as I do. She writes quite calmly."

"When did you hear from her?"

"Early this afternoon--so you see I was prepared."

"But where is she?" Rosemary asked insistently.

"She was at Sót when she wrote to me. She had seen Philip and Anna. And she was on the point of leaving for Hódmezö. This was late last night. She is in Hungary by now--and in safety. Please God I shall be with her soon."

He still spoke quite quietly, in short, crisp sentences, with nothing of the rambling and babbling about his speech that had been so pathetic to witness yesterday. But though Rosemary ought to have felt reassured and comforted about him, she could not rid herself of a persistent feeling of dread: the same sort of feeling that invades the nerves at the manifestation of a supernatural phenomenon. There was nothing supernatural about Maurus certainly, but his attitude was so abnormal, so unlike himself, that Rosemary caught herself watching with ever-increasing anxiety for the moment when his real, violent nature would reassert itself.

A moment or two later the dinner-bell rang, and Maurus was full of apologies.

"My stupid affairs have prevented your getting on with your packing, dear Lady Tarkington. Can you forgive me?"

Rosemary could only assure him that all her packing was done. "And anyway," she added, "as Jasper has a car we need not start before eleven o'clock."

"Ah, then," Maurus said, and offered her his arm to lead her into the dining-room, "we need not hurry over dinner; and I shall have the pleasure of two or three more hours of your company."

Jasper all the while had been strangely silent. Rosemary could see that he was just as much puzzled as she was, and that he was studying Maurus very keenly while the latter was talking. During dinner and while the servants were about, the conversation drifted to indifferent subject. This was the first time that Maurus had a meal in the dining-room since he was taken ill four days ago, and he was like a child enjoying his food and delighted with everything. It was only when coffee had been brought in and the servants had gone away that he reverted to the important subject of his departure.

"My chief cause of regret, dear Lady Tarkington," he said, "is that I cannot welcome you here when you return from your journey. But perhaps we could meet at Budapest, not? Elza speaks about that in her letter to me. She is very anxious to see you."

"I shall break my journey at Hódmezö," Rosemary said, "and probably wait there twenty-four hours till you come."

She had it in her mind that she could wire from there to The Times office, and in any case she had to see Elza.

"There are two good hotels in Hódmezö," Maurus rejoined. "Elza is staying at the Bristol. A very grand name for a simple provincial hotel, but it is very comfortable, I believe. Peter Blakeney's cricket people stayed there last week, you know."

He even could mention Peter's name calmly; and a quaint old English saying came to Rosemary's mind, ever her professional activities brought her in contact with extraordinary people. "Nought so queer as folk!" She almost said it aloud; for never in all her life had she witnessed anything so strange as this metamorphosis of a violent-tempered, morbid epileptic into a calm, sensible man of the world, who takes things as he finds them, and Fate's heaviest blows without wearing his heart on his sleeve.

"I shall not forget the Bristol at Hódmezö," she said after a little while, "and I will certainly remain with Elza until you come. Perhaps I can help her to endure the suspense."

"Perhaps."

"How did the letter get to you? Through the post?"

"No; she sent a peasant over from Sót, a lad who lives in Kis-Imre and was returning home. You know him, dear Lady Tarkington--him and his brother--the two sons of János the miller."

"Those two brave lads who--"

Rosemary paused abruptly. The last thing she wanted to do was to bring back to Maurus' memory that fateful night of the children's abortive escape; but Maurus himself broke in quietly:

"Yes, the two fellows who helped us all they could that night when Philip and Anna tried to get out of the country. The attempt was unsuccessful, as you know. Philip and Anna were captured. They are in Sót now. But the two sons of János--I forget their names--got over the frontier safely. They joined the cricketers at Hódmezö, and are safely back at the mill now."

"Thank God," Rosemary exclaimed fervently, "they did not suffer for their devotion."

"No, I am glad of that," Maurus concluded, with obvious indifference. "But the authorities don't trouble about the peasants. It is the landed aristocracy and the professional classes who have to suffer, if they belong to the conquered race."

It was past ten o'clock before the small party broke up. During the latter part of the time it had been Rosemary's turn to become silent. Maurus started the subject of politics, and Jasper carried on a desultory argument with him on that inexhaustible question. In almost weird contrast to his previous calmness, Maurus' violent temper broke out once or twice during the course of the discussion, and it needed all Jasper's tact and Rosemary's soothing influence to steer clear of all that tended to aggravate him. It was the real man peeping through the armour of all the previous unnatural self-control, the gipsy blood reasserting itself-self-willed, obstinate, impatient of control, bitter against humiliation. Rosemary almost welcomed the change when it came. It was more like the Maurus she knew--a man eccentric and violent, walking close to but not over-stepping the borderland that separates the sane from the insane. It was only when Philip, or Elza, or Kis-Imre were mentioned that he seemed to step over that borderland, encased in an armour of impish indifference.

The soldier-chauffeur brought the car round at eleven o'clock. Rosemary took affectionate leave of Maurus.

"We meet very soon," she said. "In Hungary."

"Yes," he replied. "In Hungary. I shall be so thankful to be there."

He also shook hands very cordially with Jasper.

"I am afraid this has not been a very agreeable stay for you," he said.

"Better luck next time," Jasper responded, as he settled himself down in the car beside his wife.

The car swung out of the gates. Rosemary, looking back, had a last vision of Maurus standing under the electric lamp in the porch, his hand waving a last farewell.

CHAPTER XXXIX

Rosemary must have fallen asleep in the corner of the carriage, for she woke with a start. The train had come to a halt, as it had done at two or three stations since Cluj was left behind. So it was not the sudden jerk, or the sound of the exhaust from the engine, that had caused Rosemary suddenly to sit up straight, wide awake and with that vague feeling of apprehension which comes on waking when sleep has been unconsciousness rather than rest. Jasper sat in the other corner with his eyes closed, but Rosemary did not think that he was asleep. They had a sleeping compartment, but hadn't had the beds made up; it was perhaps less restful for the night journey, but distinctly cleaner. The carriage was in semi-darkness, only a feeble ray of blue light filtered through the shade that tempered the gas-light up above.

Rosemary pulled up the blind. They were at a small station dimly lighted by one oil-lamp above the exit door. A clump of acacia trees in full leaf effectually hid the name of the station from view. A couple of soldiers stood at the door through which a number of peasants, men with bundles and women with baskets, one or two Jews in long gabardines and a prosperous-looking farmer in town clothes and top-boots were filing out. Someone blew a tin-trumpet, a couple more soldiers stalked up the line in the direction of the engine. There was a good deal of shouting.

Rosemary drew the blind down again, and tried to settle herself comfortably in her corner once more. But sleep would not come. She looked at her watch. It was past two. This seemed an unconscionably long halt, even for a train in this part of the world. Rosemary peeped again behind the blind. The station appeared quite deserted now except for the two soldiers on guard at the door. Everything seemed very still- -of that peculiar stillness which always seems so deep when a train comes to a halt during the night away form a busy station, and all the more deep by contrast with the previous ceaseless rumbling of the wheels. From the direction of the engine there came the sound of two men talking. Otherwise nothing.

Rosemary reckoned that they should be over the frontier soon, but, of course, if they were going to have these interminable halts--

Half an hour went by. Even the distant hum of conversation had ceased, and the silence was absolute. Feeling unaccountably agitated rather than nervous, Rosemary called to Jasper. At once he opened his eyes.

"What is it, my dear?" he asked vaguely. "Where are we?" And he added, with a shake of his long, lean body: "These carriages are deuced uncomfortable."

"We are at a small station, Jasper," Rosemary said. "And we've been over half an hour. Have you been asleep?"

"I remember this confounded train pulling up. I must have dropped off to sleep after that. I wonder where we are."

"We can't be very far from the frontier. I thought at first they would turn us out for the customs, or passports or something. But nothing has happened, and we don't seem to be getting on. I do hope there has not been a breakdown on the line."

"My dear!" Jasper exclaimed, rather impatiently, "why in the world should you think that there is a breakdown on the line? There's a signal against us, I suppose. That's all."

But Rosemary was not satisfied. "Do you mind," she said, "seeing if you can get hold of anybody. I can't help feeling nervous and--"

At once Jasper was on his feet, courteous, attentive as always. "Of course I'll go and see, my darling," he said. "But it's not like you to be nervous."

He drew back the shade so as to get a little light into the carriage, straightened his clothes, then went out into the corridor. Everything was so still that Rosemary could hear his footstep treading the well-worn strip of carpet, then the opening of the carriage door, which sent a welcome draught of air through the stuffy compartment. Rosemary pulled up the blind, and leaned out the window. It was pitch-dark, though the sky was starry. The small oil-lamp still flickered over the exit door, and the two soldiers were still there. Rosemary saw Jasper's vague silhouette in the gloom. He stood for a moment looking up and down the line; then he walked away in the direction of the engine. A few minutes went by, and presently Rosemary saw Jasper coming back, accompanied by the guard.

"What is it, Jasper?" she called. "Where are we, and what has happened?"

The two men had come to a halt immediately beneath her window. The guard doffed his cap at sight of her, and scratched his head in obvious perplexity.

"We are at Sót, my darling, but I have bad news for you, I am afraid," Jasper said. "There has been a very serious landslide lower down the line. I suppose it is due to the heavy storms. Anyway, the line is blocked for a distance of nearly half a kilometre, and of course there will be considerable delay. I don't understand all the man says, but it seems to have been a terrible catastrophe."

But out of all this only two words had penetrated Rosemary's brain--"considerable delay." What did that mean? She asked the guard, but he only shook his head. He didn't know. He didn't know anything except that there had been a landslide, and that no train could get through till the line was clear. He supposed that a gang would come down in the morning, but he couldn't say. Rosemary wanted to know whether there would be any other way of continuing the journey and picking up a train the other side of the frontier. The guard again shook his head. He really couldn't say; he was a stranger to these parts, but perhaps in the morning---He suggested respectfully that the gracious lady should allow him to make up a couple of beds in two of the sleeping compartments. There was no one else on the train, so--

"No one else on the train?" Rosemary broke in curtly. "What does he mean, Jasper? There must be other passengers on the train. Where have they gone to?"

Jasper put the question to the guard.

"The last of the passengers got out at this station, gracious lady. When it was known that the line was blocked this side of the frontier, no one took a ticket further than Sót."

"How do you mean? When was it known that the line was blocked?"

"Before we left Cluj, gracious lady, and so--"

"But they sold us tickets to Budapest, and said nothing about a breakdown," Rosemary exclaimed. And then she turned to her husband: "Jasper, tell me, is this man a fool or a liar, or am I half-witted? You took our tickets to Budapest. Did the man at the ticket-office say anything to you about a block on the line?"

"No," Jasper replied, "he did not."

"But our luggage?"

"We have no registered luggage--only what we have with us in the carriage."

"Of course, how stupid of me! But when the man clipped your ticket?"

"He didn't say anything."

Rosemary, impatient, her nerves on edge, turned again to the guard. "You saw the gracious gentleman's tickets," she said, "when we got into the train. Why didn't you warn us?"

"I thought perhaps the gracious lady and gentleman would only go as far as Sót and sleep there. I thought everyone knew about the landslide, and that every passenger had been warned."

"Can we get a car here that will take us to Hódmezö?"

"Not at this hour, gracious lady."

"Or a vehicle of any sort?"

The guard shook his head. Rosemary could have screamed with impatience until Jasper's quiet voice broke in: "I think, my dear, that by far the best thing to do will be to let the man make up a couple of beds for us, and to try and possess ourselves in patience until the morning. There is nothing to be done--really, darling, nothing. And, after all, it may only mean a delay of eight to ten hours."

Then, as Rosemary remained silent, making no further objection, he slipped some money into the guard's hand, and told him to get the beds ready. After that he re-entered the carriage, and rather diffidently sat down beside his wife.

"I feel terribly guilty, dear one," he said humbly, "but you know I don't speak Roumanian very well, and when these sort of people jabber away, I don't always understand what they say. And I was rather anxious about you at Cluj. You seemed so agitated, so unlike yourself."

"Can you wonder? Twenty-four hours' delay may mean that Naniescu's courier will get to London and make arrangements before I have time to wire. I must see Elza first, and in the meanwhile--"

"My darling," Jasper put in, with a quick, wearied sigh, "it is not like you to be so illogical. Do you really suppose that events move at such a rate in a newspaper office? There is bound to be delay--and there's ample time for your telegram to reach The Times before the editor has even thought of inserting your articles. Even if we are held up here for twenty-four hours, you can see Elza and send your wire from Hódmezö before Peter Blakeney, or whoever Naniescu's courier happens to be, can possibly have made any arrangements with The Times ."

"Of course, dear, of course," Rosemary said, more calmly. "I am stupid to-night. This whole business has got on my nerves, I suppose. I don't seem to know what I am doing."

CHAPTER XL

On the narrow made-up bed, with the coarse linen and the heavy blanket, and the smell of sulphur and dust about her, Rosemary found it quite impossible to get any rest. At first there had been a good deal of clumsy shunting, the engine probably had been detached, the tin-trumpet sounded at intervals, and there was a good deal of shouting; but all these noises ceased presently, and the night seemed peculiarly still. Still, but not restful. Rosemary could not sleep. Fortunately the communicating doors between her compartment and the one which Jasper occupied were closed, so she felt free to fidget, to get up or to lie down as the mood seized her, to turn on the light to read or to meditate, without fear of disturbing him.

She could not help feeling desperately nervous. Jasper, of course, was quite right: there was plenty of time in which to see Elza, and then to send a telegram to London if necessary, so there was nothing in a few hours' delay to worry about. Nevertheless she, who had always prided herself on independence and level-headedness, felt a strange kind of foreboding--something vague and indefinite that nevertheless was terrifying. She tried to compose herself and could not. She forced herself into quietude, deliberately kept her eyes closed and her body still. It was torture, but she did it because she wanted to feel that she still controlled her nerves, and that she was not giving way to this stupid sense of fear.

And there was no denying it; the fear that beset her was on account of her coming interview with Elza. Maurus' attitude had been very strange, even abnormal, and it was consequent on a letter from Elza. And Rosemary, though she had not owned it to herself before, felt a growing conviction that Elza's lofty patriotism had given way at last to mother-love. Confronted with Philip and Anna, who no doubt had youth's passionate desire to live, with Anna's mother who was all for conciliating the tyrants, and with Maurus whose reason was threatening to give way, Elza had laid down her arms, had capitulated and decided that her son's life must be saved at any cost. Perhaps she knew that Rosemary's articles had fallen into Naniescu's hands, perhaps she and Peter had actually been in collusion over the theft, perhaps--perhaps---There was no end to conjecture, and no limit to Rosemary's dread of what the next four-and-twenty hours would bring.

Only now did she realize what it had meant to her to place the final decision into Elza's hands. With it she had given her professional honour, her very conscience into another woman's keeping. She had probably only done it because she was so sure of Elza, of Elza's patriotism and her sense of justice and honour. Poor Elza! Who could blame her for being weak, for being a mother rather than a patriot? She should never have been placed before such a cruel alternative. Self-reproach, the stirrings of conscience helped to aggravate Rosemary's racking anxiety. She got up in the early dawn, made what sketchy toilet the limited accommodation allowed, and went out into the open. The little station appeared quite deserted; only the two soldiers were still there on duty at the exit door. Rosemary marvelled if they were the same two who had been there during the night. They looked perfectly stolid, unwashed and slouchy in their faded, coarse-looking uniforms and dusty boots and képis.

Rosemary looked up and down the line. The train, consisting of half a dozen coaches, looked derelict without its engine, and there was no guard in sight. She had no eyes for the beautiful scenery around--the narrow valley bordered by densely wooded heights; the mountain-side covered with oak and beech that were just beginning to clothe themselves in gold and at the approach of autumn; the turbulent little mountain-stream; the small station nestling amidst gnarled acacia trees; and on the right the quaint Transylvanian village with the hemp-thatched roofs and bunches of golden maize drying in the sun, with its primitive stuccoed church and whitewashed presbytery. Rosemary saw nothing of this; her eyes searched the landscape for the château--now a prison for political offenders--where Philip and Anna were detained--those children whose safety would be paid for perhaps by countless miseries, by worse tyranny and more cruel oppression. But there was no large building in sight, and presently Rosemary caught sight of Jasper, some way up the line, walking toward her in the company with a man in very négligé toilet, who probably was the station-master.

At sight of Rosemary, Jasper hastened to meet her, while the man kept at a respectful distance.

"What news?" Rosemary cried eagerly.

Jasper appeared dejected. "Not very good I am afraid," he said. "The station-master here tells me that he has been advised that the line will take the whole of the day to clear--probably more."

"Very well, then," Rosemary said resolutely, "we must get a car."

"Impossible, my dear; you can't get across if the road is blocked."

"All the roads in Transylvania are not blocked, I imagine," Rosemary retorted drily. Then she called to the station-master: "I want," she said, "to get to Hódmezö to-day. Can I get a car anywhere in Sót?"

"But the roads are impassable, gracious lady," the man exclaimed; "the landslide--"

"Never mind about the landslide. There are other roads in Transylvania besides this one. I can go by a roundabout way, but I can get there somehow if I have a car. Or," she added impatiently, seeing that the man was looking very dubious, "a conveyance of any sort, I don't care what it is."

"Alas! gracious lady, that is just the trouble. The soldiers were here yesterday, and they commandeered all the horses and bullocks in Sót for military purposes. It is so hard," the man went on, muttering half to himself; "no sooner does a man scrape together a little money and buy an old horse, then the soldiers come down and take it away from him."

The man was full of apologies and explanations, but somehow Rosemary had the impression that he lied. He rambled on for a while in the same strain; Rosemary did not hear him. Her brain was at work trying to find a way to combat this net of intrigue that was hemming her in. She was quite sure that the man was lying--that Naniescu had ordered these ignorant yokels to tell the lies that suited him. She, Rosemary, Lady Tarkington, a British subject, could not be held up at the frontier, of course, but there could be a landslide, a block on the line, no conveyance available, horses commandeered by the military, two, three, perhaps four days' delay while Naniescu's courier was speeding to London with Rosemary's manuscript and her letter to the editor of The Times asking for early publication.

She turned with some impatience to Jasper.

"What shall I do?"

Gravely he shook his head.

"Accept the inevitable," he replied gently. "I understand that there is quite a clean little hotel in the place, and twenty-four hours' delay is not very serious, is it?"

"It would not be," she admitted, "if it were not prolonged."

"It can't be prolonged indefinitely."

"No," she retorted, "for I can always walk to the frontier."

"Over mountain passes?" he queried, with a smile.

But she only gave a scornful shrug. "Accept the inevitable?" How little he knew her. The more she saw difficulties ahead, the more she felt ready for a fight. Time was still in her favour. Hódmezö was not far with its telegraph service, and Naniescu's power did not extend beyond the frontier.

Always supposing that Elza did wish her to wire.

Rosemary thought things over for a moment or two; then she said to Jasper: "Very well! I'll possess myself in patience for twenty-four hours. Will you see about rooms at the hotel? And I suppose this man will see about our luggage being taken across?"

"Of course I'll see to everything, dear," Jasper said meekly. "But you would like some breakfast, wouldn't you?"

CHAPTER XLI

Meekly and obediently Jasper went off to see after the luggage, and Rosemary wandered away as far as the village. Her first thoughts as far as the village. Her first thought was to ascertain definitely whether indeed there was no chance of hiring some sort of conveyance to take her as far as Hódmezö. The first man she spoke to was the keeper of the inevitable grocery store. He had heard a rumour that there was a block on the railway line somewhere near the frontier, and this annoyed him very much because he was expecting a consignment of maize from Hungary, and he supposed that he would not now get it for two or three days. He had no horse. Hadn't had one since the beginning of the war, when his nag was commandeered. Now even an old crock was so dear it did not pay to buy.

Rosemary asked him if he knew of anyone in the village from whom she could hire a horse and cart to take her as far as the frontier, but the man shook his head. The Jew at the hotel had two horses, and the priest had one, but the military were down from the barracks yesterday and took those away. There were maneuvers in progress somewhere, it seems. The soldiers said they would bring the horses back in two or three days, but it was very hard and inconvenient for everybody when that sort of thing was done.

Rosemary asked, what about oxen? But draft-oxen and some buffaloes belonging to the mayor had also been commandeered. It was very hard. Did not the gracious lady think so?

Finally the storekeeper made a suggestion that with the help of a little baksheesh the gracious lady might succeed in getting the officer at the château to let her have what she wanted. The château was only a couple of kilometres from the village. It lay close to the road; the gracious lady couldn't fail to spy the great iron gates. It had belonged at one time to Count Fekete, but the family had been gone some time, and the château was now a cavalry barrack, and some prisoners of war were still kept there.

The storekeeper offered his son as an escort to the gracious lady, so that she should not miss her way. But Rosemary declined the offer; she purchased a few stale biscuits from the man, intending to ask for a glass of milk from some cottage on the way; then she set out at a brisk pace down the road. It ran along the mountain-side, and some fifty feet below the turbulent little stream tossed and tumbled over stones and boulders, its incessant murmuring making a soothing accompaniment to Rosemary's thoughts. At the last cottage in the village, where Rosemary had obtained a glass of fresh milk from a comely peasant woman, the latter had directed her to a mountain path which ran below the road, parallel with it, and close to the edge of the stream. Here it was perfectly lovely; the moist, sweet air, the occasional call of birds, the beech and oak and dense undergrowth, the carpet of moss, the oc-casional clearing where the grass was a luscious green, and the mauve campanula grew to a stately height. At times the path rose sharply, twenty feet or more above the stream; at others it ran level with the water's edge; and at one place the stream widened into a little bay, where the water was as clear as a fairy pool and of a translucent blue.

Rosemary lingered for a little while beside the pool, thinking how delicious it would be to bathe in it. When she went on again she came to a sharp bend in the path, and as soon as she had rounded this she saw some twenty yards farther on a man dressed in the uniform of a Roumanian officer, sitting upon a tree stump close by the water's edge. The man sat with his elbows resting on his knees, and his head was buried in his hands. He looked like a man in trouble. Rosemary walked on, a dry twig crackled under her tread, and the man suddenly looked up.

It was Peter.

The moment he caught sight of Rosemary he jumped up, and then made a movement as if he meant to run away. But Rosemary, with sudden impulse, called to him at once:

"Don't go, Peter."

It seemed as if the magic of her voice rooted him to the spot. He stood quite still, but with his back to her; and then he took off his képi with one hand, and passed the other once or twice across his forehead.

Rosemary felt strangely disturbed and puzzled. Why was Peter here? How did he come to be here? And in this uniform?

"Aren't you going to speak to me, Peter?" she asked, because Peter being here seemed so amazing that for the moment she thought that she was seeing a vision; "or even look at me?" she added.

"I did not suppose you particularly wished me to speak to you," he said, without turning round to face her.

"Why should you say that?" she asked simply.

"Because I imagine that you look upon me as such an unmitigated blackguard that the very sight of me must be hateful to you."

She said nothing for a moment or two. Perhaps she was still wondering if he was real, and if so, how he came to be here--just to-day and at this hour. Then she went deliberately up to him, put her hand on his arm, and forced him to look at her.

"It is true, then?" she asked, and her eyes, those pixie eyes of hers, luminous and searching, were fastened on his as if seeking to penetrate to the very soul within him. But a look of dull and dogged obstinacy was all that she got in response.

"It is all true, Peter?" she insisted, trying with all her might to steady her voice, so that he should not hear the catch in her throat.

He shrugged his shoulders, indifferent and still obstinate.

"I don't know what you mean," he retorted, almost roughly.

"I mean," she said slowly, "that these last few days have not just been a hideous nightmare, as I still hoped until--until two minutes ago. That things have really happened--that you--that you--"

She paused, physically unable to continue. It was all too vile, too hideous to put into words. Peter gave a harsh laugh.

"Oh, don't spare me," he said, with a flippant laugh. "You mean that you did not believe until two minutes ago that I was really a spy in the pay of the Roumanian Government, and that you did not believe that I had intrigued to have Philip and Anna arrested, stolen your articles for The Times, and bought Kis-Imre over Aunt Elza's head, and turned her and Maurus out of their home. Well, you believe it now, don't you? So that's that. And as I am on my way to meet a friend, you'll excuse me, won't you, if I run away? Is there anything else I can do for you?"

"Yes," she said. "You can look me straight in the eyes and tell me what has brought you down to--to this. Is it money?"

Peter shrugged. "The want of it, I suppose," he replied.

"I have no right to ask, I know. Only--only--we were friends once, Peter," she went on, with a note of pleading in her tone. "You used to tell me all your plans--your ambitions. You used to say that you did not want to--to bind me to a promise until you had made a name for yourself. If you had told me that you were short of money, and that you were actually thinking of taking up this--this sort of work, I could have helped you. I know I could have helped you. I know I should have found the right words to dissuade you. Oh, Peter!" she went on almost wildly, unable to hold her tears longer in check, or to control the tremor in her voice, "it is all so horrible! Can't you see? Can't you see? We were such friends! You used to tell me everything. You were taking up your father's work. Some of your scientific experiments were already attracting attention. And you were a sportsman, too! And your V.C. And now this--this! Oh, it is too horrible--too horrible!"

Her words were carrying her away. The murmur of the water grew louder and louder in her ears, and in the trees the soughing of the wind among the leaves grew almost deafening. She felt herself swaying, and for a few seconds she closed her eyes. But when she put out her hand she felt it resting on Peter's arm. There was the feel of the rough cloth of his tunic. So she opened her eyes and raised them slowly until they met his. Her glance had wandered on the ugly uniform, the livery of his unspeakable shame. Her eyes expressed the contempt which she felt, the loathing which was almost physical. But Peter's glance now was not only dogged, but defiant. In it she read the determination to follow in the path of life which he had chosen for himself, and a challenge to her power to drag him away from it. This was no longer the Peter of Kis-Imre, the irresponsible young English athlete, whose thoughts would never soar above the interest in a cricket-match. It was more the Peter of olden times--the tempestuous lover, the wayward creature of caprice, the temperamental enthusiast capable of heroic deeds, and always chafing under the restraint imposed by twentieth-century conventions; the Peter whose soul had once been equally great in virtue as it was now steeped in crime; the gallant soldier, the worthy descendant of the Scarlet Pimpernel. It was the Peter of olden times, but his love for her was dead. Dead. If one spark of it had remained alive, if something of her image had remained in his heart, he could never have given himself over to this vile, vile thing. But while she had been battling bravely to banish from her mind all memories of their early love, he had torn her out of his heart, and turned to this ig-nominious calling to help him to forget.

Rosemary felt giddy and ill; even the sweet woodland air seemed to have turned to poisonous fumes of intrigue and venality. She roughly pushed away from Peter's arm that supported her, but she was still swaying; her hat fell from her head, and her glorious hair lay in a tumbled mass of ruddy gold around her face.

"Better sit down on this old stump," Peter remarked drily. "You'll have to lean on me till you get to it."

But Rosemary did not really know what happened just then--she had such a gnawing pain in her heart. She certainly tottered forward a step or two until she reached the tree-stump, and she sank down on it, helped thereto, no doubt, by Peter's arm. The next thing of which she was conscious was a flood of tears that would not be checked. It welled up to her eyes, and eased that heavy pain in her heart. Great sobs shook her bowed shoulders, and she buried her face in her hands, for she was ashamed of her tears. Ashamed that she cared so much.

And the next thing that struck her consciousness was that Peter sank down on his knees before her, that he raised her skirt to his lips, and that he murmured: "Good-bye, sweetheart. My Rosemary for re-membrance. God bless and keep you. Try to forget." Then he jumped to his feet and was gone. Gone! She called him back with a cry of des-pair: "Peter!" But he was nowhere to be seen. He must have scrambled up the incline that led to the road. She certainly heard high above her the crackling of dry twigs, but nothing more. Peter had passed out of her life, more completely, more effectually, indeed, than on the day when she became Jasper Tarkington's wife. Peter--her Peter, the friend of her girlhood, the master from whom she had learned her first lesson of love, was dead. The thing that remained was a vague speck, a crea-tion of this venal post-war world. It was as well that he should go out of her life.

CHAPTER XLII

A minute or two later Rosemary was startled out of her day-dream by the sound of Jasper's voice calling to her from somewhere in the near distance. She had barely time to obliterate the traces of tears from her eyes and cheeks before he appeared round the bend of the path. The next moment he was by her side. Apparently he had been running, for he seemed breathless and not quite so trim and neat in his appearance as he usually was.

"I heard a scream," were the first words he said, as soon as he came in sight of her. "It terrified me when I recognized your voice. Thank God you are safe!"

He was obviously exhausted and, for him, strangely agitated. He threw himself down on the carpet of moss at her feet; then he seized her hand and covered it with kisses. "Thank God!" he kept on murmuring. "Thank God you are safe!"

Then suddenly he looked up at her with an inquiring frown. "But what made you scream?" he asked.

Rosemary by now had regained control over her nerves. She succeeded in disengaging her hand, and in smiling quite coolly down upon him.

"It was very stupid of me," she said, with a light laugh. "I saw a pair of eyes looking at me through the undergrowth. It startled me. I thought that it was a wild cat--I had heard that there were some in these parts--but it was only a homely one."

She tried to rise, but Jasper had recaptured her hand. He was engaged in kissing her finger-tips one by one, lingering over each kiss as if to savour its sweetness in full. Now he looked up at her with a glance of hungering passion. Rosemary felt herself flushing. She was conscious of an intense feeling of pity for this man who had lavished on her all the love of which he was capable, and hungered for that which she was not able to give. He looked careworn, she thought, and weary.

"You were not anxious about me, Jasper, were you?" she asked kindly.

He smiled. "I am always anxious," he said "when I don't see you."

"But how did you find me?"

"Quite easily; I went to the hotel, you know. Not at all a bad little place, by the way; rather primitive, but with electric light and plenty of hot water. In engaged the rooms, and had a mouthful of breakfast. Then I sallied forth in quest of you. A man in the village told me you had been asking the way to the château, and I knew you would never stand the dusty road. So when I found that there was a woodland path that went through the same way as the road, I naturally concluded that you would choose it in preference. You see," Jasper concluded, with a smile, "that there was no magic in my quest."

Then he looked up at her again, and there was a gleam of suspicion in his dark, questioning eyes. "You must have walked very slowly," he said. "I started quite half an hour, probably more, after you did."

"I did walk very slowly. This path is enchanting, and this is not the first time I have sat down to think and to gaze at this delicious little stream. But," Rosemary went on briskly, "I think I had better be getting on."

But Jasper putout his arms and encircled her knees. "Don't go for a minute, little one. It is so peaceful here, and somehow I have had so little of you these last days. I don't know, but it seems as if we had taken to misunderstanding one another lately." Then, as she made an involuntary movement of impatience, he continued gently: "Do I annoy you by making love to you?"

Rosemary tried to smile. "Of course not, dear. What a question!"

"Then tell me if there is anything in the world I can do to make you happier. You have not looked happy lately. I have been tortured with remorse, for I feel somehow that it has been my fault."

"You are sweet and kind, Jasper, as always. But you must be a little patient. I have gone through a great deal these last few days."

"I know, I know, little one. Don't let us talk any more about it."

He was wonderfully kind--kinder and gentler than he had been since the first days of their married life. It almost seemed as if he had set himself the task of making her forget all that he had involuntarily revealed to her of his violent, unbridled temperament, and of that lawless passion that lay at the root of his love for her.

He talked of the future, of their return to England, the home that he would make for her, which would be a fitting casket for the priceless jewel which he possessed. Rosemary, who felt inexpressibly lonely, was once more conscious of that feeling of gratitude towards him which she had once hoped might be transmuted, in days to come, into something more ardent than friendship.

She had suffered so terribly in her love for the one man who, with all his faults, had come very near to her ideals, that she felt a desperate longing to cherish and to cling to the husband whom she had chosen half out of pique, the man on whom she had inflicted so much cruelty by becoming his wife.

CHAPTER XLIII

Rosemary was the first to remember that time was slipping by. She looked at her watch. It was past ten o'clock--over an hour since Peter had asked her to try to forget. She rose briskly to her feet, and arm in arm, like two good comrades, she and Jasper made their way together towards the château. When they came in sight of the great gates-a couple of hundred yards still ahead of them--Rosemary was the first to spy a motor-car standing there, and some half-dozen persons in the act of getting into the car. There were two sentries at the gates, and seemingly a few people on the other side.

"It looks like a man and a woman and three soldiers in uniform getting into that car," Rosemary remarked casually. And immediately, for no apparent reason, Jasper started to walk along more rapidly; a few seconds later he almost broke into a run. At that moment the car started off, and was soon lost to sight in a cloud of dust. Rosemary thought that she heard Jasper utter a savage oath.

"Is anything wrong?" she asked. But he did not answer, only hurried along so quickly that she was not able to keep up with him. He had passed through the gates when she reached them, and when she tried to follow she was stopped by the sentry. She called to Jasper, who apparently did not hear; pointing to him, she explained to the man on duty that she was that gentleman's wife, and if he was allowed to go in, why not she? They were as mute as if she had spoken in an unknown tongue, but they would not allow her to pass. In the meanwhile Jasper had disappeared inside the château. Rosemary had seen him go in by the main entrance, challenged by the sentry on guard at the door, but after a second or two allowed to pass freely in.

Fortunately she was provided with money, and her experience of this part of the world was that most things could be accomplished with the aid of baksheesh. A young officer was crossing the courtyard; he looked in the direction of the gates, saw an excessively pretty woman standing there, and, true to his race and upbringing, came at once to see if he could enter into conversation with her. Very politely he explained to her that no one was allowed to enter the château, or to visit any of the prisoners, without a special permit from the commanding officer.

Rosemary told him that she desired to speak with the commanding officer. This also, it seems, was impossible. But a hint from Rosemary as to reward if the matter could be managed simplified matters a great deal.

The young officer conducted her across the courtyard and into the château. It had been a fine place once, not unlike Kis-Imre in architecture, but its occupation by the military had stripped it of every charm. There were not carpets on the floors, and only very rough furniture in the way of chairs and tables in what had obviously been at one time a cosy lounge hall. The officer led the way through a couple of equally bare rooms en enfilade, and came to a halt outside a door which bore roughly chalked upon the finely carved and decorated panels the legend: "Major Buriecha. Private. No admittance." He offered one of the rough chairs rather shamefacedly to Rosemary, and said: "Major Buriecha will becoming through here presently. Will you wait, gracious lady? You will be sure to see him. I am afraid," the young man added, with a pleasant smile, "that it is the best I can do."

"Couldn't you announce me?" Rosemary asked. "I am Lady Tarkington. I am sure Major Buriecha would not refuse to see me."

The officer's smile became self-deprecating. "It is more that I should dare to do, milady," he said. "The major is engaged in conversation with an important government official. I would even ask you kindly, when you see him, not to tell him that I brought you as far as here."

"I couldn't do that, even if I wished, as I don't know your name."

"Lieutenant Uriesu, at your service, milady."

"I suppose," Rosemary went on, after a moment's hesitation, "you couldn't tell me what has become of my husband, Lord Tarkington. He went through the gates and entered the château, then I lost sight of him. But he seemed to be well known inside this place. Could you find out for me where he is?"

"I am afraid not, milady," the young officer replied politely. "I have not the honour of Lord Tarkington's acquaintance."

He stood at attention, waiting for a moment or two to see if the English lady had any further questions she wished to ask; then as she remained silent, he saluted gravely and went out of the room, leaving Rosemary to bear her soul in patience, and to wonder what in the world had become of Jasper.

At first only a confused murmur of voices came to her ears through the closed doors of Major Buriecha's private room. But gradually one of those voices grew louder and louder, as if raised in anger; and Rosemary, astonished, recognized that it was Jasper speaking--in French, and obviously with authority--to Major Buriecha, the officer commanding! . . . What in the world--?

She heard some words quite distinctly:

"You are a fool, Buriecha! No one but a fool could have been taken in like this."

And the voice that gave reply was humble, apologetic, decidedly tremulous with fear. Rosemary could not distinguish what it said.

Major Buriecha engaged in conversation with Jasper! And Jasper reprimanding him with obvious authority! What could it mean? At first she had only been puzzled, now a vague sense of uneasiness stirred in her heart. Uneasiness that almost partook of fear. With sudden impulse she rose and went to the door. Orders or no orders, she must know what was going on inside that room. Her hand was on the latch when she paused, listening. Was it mean to listen? Perhaps; but instinct was stronger than good conduct, and she had just heard Jasper's harsh voice giving a curt command:

"Get through to General Naniescu at once," and then the click of the telephone receiver being lifted from its hook and the whir of the bell-handle. What could she do but listen? There was silence inside the private room now, but Rosemary could hear Jasper's easily recognizable step pacing restlessly up and down. And one moment he paused quite close to the door, and Rosemary quickly drew back a step or two, ready to face him if he came. But he resumed his pacing and she her watch by the door. Presently she heard the other voice--the major's, presumably--saying: "Is that you, Marghilo? Ask his Excellency the Governor to come to the telephone, will you?" There was a pause, then Buriecha spoke again: "Tell him it is Major Buriecha. And, I say, Marghilo, tell him it is very important and desperately urgent."

Again there was a pause, a long one this time. Jasper was still pacing up and down the room. Rosemary could picture him to herself, with his habitual stoop and his thin hands held behind his back. Once he laughed, his usual harsh, mirthless laugh. "You'll get a fine dressing-down for this, my friend. I am thinking," he said. "Naniescu won't make light of it, I can tell you."

Silence once again. Then Jasper's voice speaking into the telephone, and always in French: "Hallo! Hallo! Is that you, Naniescu? good! Number Ten speaking."

Number Ten! What--? But there was no time to think, no time for puzzlement or fear. Jasper was speaking again.

"Buriecha has bade a complete fool of himself. He has allowed young Imrey and the girl Heves to escape! Hallo! Did you hear me? It's no use swearing like that, you'll only break the telephone. Yes, they've gone, and you've got to get them back. Went by car half an hour ago, in the direction of Cluj, but probably making for the frontier--what? Oh, a plot, of course, engineered by that damned Blakeney. No use cursing Buriecha; you are as much to blame as he is. Eh? Of course, for treating with that young devil behind my back! Yes, you--- Well, hold on and listen. Blakeney, I am sure it was he, came here with a forged order from you, demanding that Imrey and the girl shall be delivered to him for transference to an unknown destination. Eh? Well, of course he should have known, but he says your signature looked perfect; he thought it was all in order. The rascal was in officer's uniform, and had two men with him also in uniform. What can you do? Telephone all along the roads to your frontier police, of course. If they stick to the car they are bound to be stopped. Yes, five persons--three of the men in uniform, in an open car. The prisoners have probably taken on some disguise by now. Shoot at sight, of course, if the car does not slow down. Police the mountain paths as well. Blakeney can't know them well. I don't know who the other two men are. Hungarian, perhaps, or English. Don't delay. Yes, yes! What's that? Marghilo getting through? Good! Well, that's the best you can do. We'll have a reckoning presently, my friend. You should not have treated with him, I say. He has probably robbed your courier of the newspaper articles or else telegraphed in Uno's name to The Times not to print them, and then got the prisoners out of your clutches by this impudent trick. Oh, all right. Hurry up! You have no time to waste, nor have I. Yes! All right. Come along if you want to. I shall be at Sót all right enough. But you won't enjoy the interview, my friend, I promise you that. What?"

Jasper had ceased speaking for some time, but Rosemary still stood beside the door--a woman turned to stone. Her hands and feet were numb. She could not move; only from time to time a cold shudder travelled down her spine. She felt nothing, not even horror. It was all too stupendous even for horror. A cataclysm, a ball of fire, a flame that froze, ice that scorched. A topsy-turvydom that meant the kingdom of death.

And Jasper, her husband, was on the other side of that door, Jasper Tarkington, her husband! The spy of an alien government, Number Ten! A thing! A rag torn and filthy. The man whose name she bore. She could hear his footstep in the next room, his mirthless laugh, his harsh voice muttering curses or else invectives against the other man, who was only a fool. Then suddenly the footsteps came to a halt. The door was pulled open and Rosemary stood face to face with Jasper.

At sight of her he stood stock-still. An ashen hue spread over his face. The curse that had risen to his throat died before it reached his lips.

From the room behind him Major Buriecha's tremulous voice was asking if anything was amiss. Jasper closed the door and stood with his back to it, still facing Rosemary. His eyes, always hawk-like and closely set, had narrowed till they were mere slits, and his lips had curled up over his jaws, showing his teeth white and sharp, like those of a wolf. An expression of intense cruelty distorted his face. He was about to speak, but Rosemary put up her hand to stop him.

"Not here," she commanded. "Not now."

He gave a hard laugh and shrugged his shoulders.

"It had to come some time, I suppose," he said coolly. "I am not sorry."

"Nor I," she replied. "But will you please go now? We'll meet later--in the hotel."

He looked her up and down with that glance which she had learned to dread, and for a moment it seemed as if he would yield to that ungovernable passion in him and seize her in his arms. Rosemary did not move. Her luminous eyes, abnormally dilated, never left his face for one instant. She watched the struggle in the man's tortuous soul, the passion turned to hatred now that he stood revealed. She did not flinch, because she was not afraid. The man was too vile to inspire fear.

"Go!" she said coldly.

For another second he hesitated, but it was the banal sound of Buriecha spluttering and coughing on the other side of the door that clinched his resolve. This was neither the place nor the time to assert his will, to punish her for the humiliation which he was enduring. Once more he laughed and shrugged his shoulders, then he walked slowly out of the room.

CHAPTER XLIV

For over half an hour Rosemary waited in that bare, cheerless room, and gazed unseeing out of the window while she tried vainly to co-ordinate her thoughts. In the forefront of her mind there was a feeling of great joy which she hardly dared to analyse. Joy! And she also had the feeling, though she had come to the very brink of an awful precipice, though she was looking down into an abyss of shame and horror, with no hope of ever being able to bridge the chasm over, that yet on the other side was peace--peace that she would never attain, but which was there nevertheless, to dwell on, to dream of, when the turmoil was past and she be allowed to rest.

After about half an hour the young officer who had first conducted her to the fateful spot came back to see what had happened. He seemed astonished that she was still there.

"Major Buriecha has not yet come out of his room," Rosemary managed to say quite coolly. "It is getting near dinner-time. I don't think I'll wait any longer."

The young man appeared relieved. Anyway he was not likely now to get into trouble on the English lady's account. He clicked his heels together, expressed perfunctory regret at her disappointment, the offered to conduct milady out of the château. Rosemary accepted his escort and took leave of him at the gates.

"If milady, will write to the commanding officer," Lieutenant Uriesu said at the end, "I am sure he will give the permit milady requires."

"I will certainly take your advice," Rosemary assented cheerfully. "Good-bye, Lieutenant Uriesu, and thank you for your kind efforts on my behalf."

She walked back towards the village by way of the path. When she came to the spot where first she had seen Peter that morning, she sat down on the tree-stump and listened to the murmur of the stream. She would not allow herself to think of Peter--only of Philip and Anna, whom he was taking across the frontier by another clever trick--in disguise, probably--and over the mountain passes. Rosemary could not believe that they would stick to the car and be stopped by the frontier police. They would get away into Hungary-on foot. They were young, they knew the country, and they could scramble over the mountain passes and be at Hódmezö soon, where Elza would be waiting for them. Elza knew, of course, and Maurus knew too. That was why he had been so calm and so composed when he was told that he must leave Kis-Imre within four-and-twenty hours. The all knew. Peter had trusted them. Only she, Rosemary, had been kept out of his councils, because she might have betrayed them to Jasper, and Peter could not tell her that it was Jasper who was the miserable spy.

But no, she would not think of Peter, or of how he had worked to circumvent Jasper at every turn. She only wanted to think of Philip and Anna, those two children who were so ingenuously learning the lesson of love one from the other, and of Elza, so patient and so heroic, and of Maurus, who had played his part so well. Maurus would be coming through from Cluj some time to-day, and he, too, would be held up at Sót, and perhaps spend the night in the funny little hotel. Rosemary hoped that she would see him. His company would be very welcome whilst Jasper was still there. Then to-morrow she and Maurus would get across the frontier somehow, and join up with Elza and the children at Hódmezö. And there was always the British Consul in Cluj to appeal to. There was no desperate hurry now. The children were safe and those articles of hers would not be published in The Times. Peter would have seen to that.

But no, she did not want to think of Peter. Was she not still Jasper Tarkington's wife?

CHAPTER XLV

It was late in the afternoon when Rosemary at last made her way back to the small hotel in Sót. She had spent the day roaming about the forests, and eating such scrappy food as she could purchase at one or other of the cottages. Twice she had been to the railway station to meet the trains that were due in from Cluj. She hoped that Maurus might have come by one of them. Now there was not another due before the midnight express, which got to Sót in the small hours of the morning. The farce of there being a block on the line was still kept up. Passengers got out of the train, grumbling, and the small hotel was full to capacity. It was a low, irregular building, with a very large courtyard closed on three sides, and a wide archway, through which cars and carriages could drive in, intersecting the fourth. One side of the house was given over to stabling and cowsheds, another to kitchens and offices, the other two held the guest-rooms and one or two public rooms. Some of the bedrooms were level with the ground, and on the floor above a wooden gallery ran right round the courtyard. The courtyard itself seemed to be the principal meeting-place for cows and chickens, and even pigs, which roamed freely about the place and entered any door that happened to be conveniently open. The best bedrooms gave on the balcony above. On inquiry Rosemary was informed that the English milord had booked three rooms that morning for himself and milady who would be coming during the day. A buxom, bare-footed peasant girl then conducted milady up to these rooms.

Rosemary went along heavy-footed. She was more tired than she would have cared to admit. She had had very little food all day, and her nerves by now were terribly on edge. It had been a day packed full of emotion and there was more to come. There was the inevitable interview with Jasper. Horrible as it would be, she had no intention of shirking it. She would leave him, of course, with the hope never to set eyes on him again, but certain matters would have to be arranged between them, and Rosemary's moral courage would not allow her to have recourse to letter-writing or to the help of lawyers. She knew what she wished to say to Jasper, and would have despised herself if she had shrunk from the ordeal.

The hours went slowly by. Later in the evening she ordered some supper to be brought up to her room. She found it difficult to swallow any food, but she drank two cups of deliciously strong coffee, and munched some of the excellent and very sustaining maize bread for which this part of the country is famous. She had a book in her suitcase and contrived to read for a while, but she could not concentrate on what she was reading, and soon had to put the book away. Time hung very heavily. She was terribly weary and yet she could not sleep. And she could not understand what had become of Jasper. She had seen or heard nothing of him since they parted in that ugly, bare room, the picture of which would for ever remain graven in her mind as the place where she had experienced the greatest horror in her life. No one in the hotel had seen him. A vague sense of uneasiness began to stir within her. At the same time she dismissed from her mind any fear for his safety. She was quite sure that whatever he ultimately decided to do, he would not pass out of her life without a final struggle for mastery. She did not dread the interview. She knew it to be inevitable; but she longed passionately for it to be over--to know the worst--to feel certain of that measure of freedom for which she meant to fight.

And because she longed for the interview to be over she would not go to bed before Jasper returned. She sat in the narrow slip-room, grandiosely described by the hotel proprietor as the salon, which divided Jasper's room from hers. The one window, which was wide open, gave her a beautiful view over the mountains, and the evening sky studded with stars. Somewhere the other side of those mountain-tops Philip and Anna were speeding towards freedom-the freedom which Peter had won for them by dint of courage, resource and wit. Instinctively, memory recalled that other weary waiting at Kis-Imre, when she and Elza had watched and prayed together through the hours of the night. And torturing fears rose out of the darkness lest this second attempt at flight should prove as unsuccessful as the first.

It was past midnight when Rosemary heard Jasper's familiar step along the wooden balcony. He came straight to the door of the salon and entered, apparently without the slightest hesitation. He closed the door behind him, and throwing down his hat said coolly:

"I saw the light under the door, so I knew you had not gone to bed yet. I've been in some time, but stayed to have some supper in the coffee-room. Very good supper, too. They know how to cook in Hungary. That is the one thing the Roumanians might with advantage learn from them."

He threw himself into a chair and drew his cigarette-case out of his pocket. Having selected one he offered his case to Rosemary.

"Have one?" he asked. When she shook her head he shrugged and laughed, then he struck a match and lighted his cigarette. His hand was perfectly steady. The flame of the match brought for a moment into relief his narrow hatchet face, with the dark eyes set closely together and the harsh Wellingtonian features. Rosemary looked at him curiously. It was the first time she had really studied his face closely since she knew. Once or twice, before she had been repelled by a flash of animal passion in his eyes, and once she had caught sight of his face in the mirror in the smoking room at Kis-Imre, when it was distorted by a wolfish expression of cruelty. Now both the passion and the cruelty were there, expressed around his mouth and in his eyes which looked at her over the tiny flickering flame.

Deliberately he blew the match out, took a long whiff from his cigarette, and said calmly:

"How you are going to hate me after this!"

After a second's pause he added: "Well, I have had so much cruelty to endure from you in the past, a little more or less won't make much difference."

"I have never meant to be cruel, Jasper," Rosemary rejoined coldly. "But I know now that the cruellest thing I ever did to you was to become your wife."

"You only found that out, my dear, since you saw Peter Blakeney again."

To this Rosemary made no answer. She shrugged her shoulders and turned her head away. Jasper jumped up and gripped her by the arm, making her wince with pain.

"Before we go any further, Rosemary," he said with a savage oath, "I'll have it out with you. Are you still in love with Peter Blakeney?"

"I refuse to answer," Rosemary said calmly. "You have no longer the right to ask me such a question."

"No longer the right," he retorted with a harsh laugh. "You are still my wife, my dear. What happened this afternoon will not give you your freedom in law, remember."

"I know that, Jasper. What happened this afternoon has broken my life, but, as you say, it cannot give me my freedom, save with your consent."

He gave a derisive chuckle. "And you are reckoning on that, are you?" he asked drily.

"I am reckoning on it."

"Then all I can say, my dear, is that, for a clever woman, your calculations are singularly futile."

"I don't think so," she rejoined. "I know enough about the laws of England to know that they do not compel me to live under your roof."

"You mean that you intend to leave me?"

"I do."

"And create a scandal?"

"There need be no scandal. We'll agree to live apart; that is all."

"That is not all, my dear," he retorted drily, "as you will find out to your cost."

"What do you mean?"

"I mean that Peter Blakeney chose to follow you to Transylvania; any number of witnesses can testify to that. I mean, that we are now in a country where money will purchase everything, even such testimony as will enable Lord Tarkington to divorce his wife, and raise such a hell of scandal around Mr. Blakeney that no decent club would have him as a member, and he would have to live out of England for the benefit of his health."

Rosemary had listened to him without attempting to interrupt. She even tried hard not to reveal the indignation which she felt. When he had finished speaking, and once more threw himself into a chair, with a sigh of self-satisfaction, she said quite quietly:

"I thought that this afternoon I had probed the lowest depths to which a man's nature could sink. But, God help me! I have seen worse now!"

"That is as it may be, my dear. A man fights for what he treasures with any weapon that comes to his hand."

"For what he treasures, yes! But you--"

"I treasure you beyond all things on earth," he broke in hoarsely. "You are my wife, my property, my own possession. You may love Blakeney and hate me, but I have rights over you that all the sophistries in the world cannot deny me. I am alone," he went on--and in one second he was on his feet again, and before she had time to defend herself he had her in his arms--"I alone have the right to hold you as I am holding you now. I alone have the right to demand a kiss. Kiss me,

Rosemary, my beautiful, exquisite wife, with the pixie eyes! Though you hate me, kiss me--though you love him, kiss me---Mine is still the better part."

He pressed his lips against hers, and for these few horrible moments Rosemary, half swooning, could only lie rigid in his arms. But horror and loathing gave her strength. With her two hands she pushed against him with all her might. "Let me go," she murmured. "I hate you."

But he only laughed. "Of course you hate me. Well, I like your hatred better than the cool indifference I have had from you up to now. You hate me, my dear, because you don't understand. With all your vaunted cleverness you don't understand. Women such as you--good women, I suppose we must call them--never would understand all that there is in a man that is evil and vicious and cruel. Yes, in every man! Deep down in our souls we are blackguards, every one of us! Some of us are what women have made us, others have vices ingrained in our souls at birth. Have you ever seen a schoolboy tease a cat, or a lad set a terrier against a stoat? Would you hate him for that? Not you! If he has revolted you too much, you may punish him, but even so you'll only smile: it is boy's nature, you will say. Well, boy's nature is man's nature. Cruel, vicious! Civilization has laid a veneer over us. Some of us appear gentle and kind and good. Gentle? Yes! On the surface. Deep down in our souls, grown men as we are, we would still love to tease the cat, or to see a terrier worry a stoat. Whilst men had slaves they thrashed them. Where wives are submissive their husbands beat them. Give a man power to torture and he will do it. Boy's nature, I tell you, but we dare not show it. We are gentlemen now, not men. And most of us have a false idea that women would despise us if they knew. And so we smirk and toady and pretend, and those of use who are not puppets writhe against this pretence. I was born a savage. When I was a schoolboy I was not content with teasing a cat, I loved to torture it; if a horse was restive I would thrash it with the greatest joy. Later I reveled in twisting a smaller boy's wrist until he screamed, in pulling a girl's hair or pinching her arm--anything that hurt. Boy's nature. Most women only smiled! Then came the war and the world was plunged in an orgy of cruelty. I was a very fine linguist and became attached to the secret service. I worked for the French army. I no longer pulled girl's hair nor pinched their arms, but I--the spy--tracked enemy spies down--women and men--dragged them out of their lair as a terrier would a stoat, and brought them before the military tribunals to be condemned and shot. But the women still smiled. Good women,

mind you! Those whom I was tracking down were Germans, and so I-
the spy--was a hero and they were only human refuse whom to torture
was a duty. When war was over and my uncle died I inherited a title,
and civilization threw the mantle of convention over me, imposed on
me certain obligations. My work was done. I became a puppet. I
smirked and toadied and tried to pretend. Oh, how I loathed it! Re-
strictions, civilization, drove me mad! If I had never met you I should
have gone off to a land where I could keep slaves and work my will on
them, or turned Moslem and kept numberless wives, whom I could
beat when the mood seized me. But I met you, and all my desires were
merged in the one longing to have you for my own. You were adulated, famous, rich probably. I had a title to offer you and nothing else.
My friend de Kervoisin, who knew my capabilities, spoke to me of
Transylvania, a conquered country where rebellion was rife. He spoke
to me of Naniescu, an ambitious man, unscrupulous and venal, who
wanted help to consolidate his position, to put himself right before his
government and before the world by brining to light intrigues and conspiracies that did not always exist. The work meant money. I took it
on. I made over £100,000 in three years, and there was more to come.
Already I was a rich man and the work satisfied the boy's nature in me.
Following up a clue. Disguises. Tracking a man down, or a woman.
Seeing their fear, watching their terror. Arrests, secret trials. Executions in the early dawn. Scenes of desolation and farewells. I had them
all! They helped me to endure the London seasons, the evenings at the
club, the balls, the crowds, the futility of it all. And the money which I
earned brought me nearer and nearer to you. Luck was on my side.
Peter Blakeney courted you, and like a fool he lost you. How? I did
not know and cared less. I won you because I was different from other
men, because you were piqued, and because I interested you. Because
I knew how to smirk and toady better than most. Then came the question of Transylvania. Naniescu entrusted me with the task of
discovering the authorship of certain articles that had appeared in English and American newspapers which impugned his administration. He
offered me ten thousand pounds if I succeeded in bringing the author
to justice, and ten thousand more if certain articles which you were to
write were published in The Times. The very first morning that we
were in Cluj the girl Anna Heves gave away her secret. Once I had her
and Philip under arrest it was easy enough to bring pressure to bear
upon you. I almost succeeded, as you know. At first it was difficult--
whilst Elza and Maurus Imrey were ignorant of the bargain that
Naniescu had proposed to you. I had only gained one victory, I was

not likely to win the other. So, while you thought me in Bucharest, I came back disguised as a gipsy and warned Elza that Philip and Anna were in danger of death. This brought everything to a head. Unfortunately Peter Blakeney already suspected me. It began probably in England--exactly when I shall never know--but he was my friend once, and then suddenly I felt that we had become enemies. I must have given myself away at one time, I suppose, and he is as sharp as a wild cat. He followed us to Transylvania--to make sure. . . . Then at Cluj Anna Heves confided in him. The children's arrest confirmed his suspicions, and that night at Kis-Imre he recognized me under my disguise as a gipsy. Curse him! After that the whole adventure became a battle of wits between him and me. I won the first round when I spied out the plan for Philip and Anna's escape; I won again when I persuaded you to place the whole bargain between yourself and Naniescu before Elza, and indirectly induced you to write the newspaper articles which he wanted. I thought I had won an easy victory then. But Peter Blakeney stole your manuscript, and I feared then that I had lost everything. The death of Philip and Anna Heves would have been some compensation, it is true, but I wanted that extra ten thousand pounds more than I did the joy of seeing those two children shot. I thought that Peter had stolen the manuscript in order to bargain with it for the lives of his two cousins, but I know better now. He sold your manuscript to Naniescu for the Kis-Imre property. It will stand in his name until he can hand it over to the Imrey's again. In the meanwhile by a clever ruse he has got Philip and Anna out of the country. And by now he will have sent a telegram in your name to The Times. He has won the battle hands down. I am beaten in all, except in one thing, I have you. Not all his cleverness--and he is as clever as a monkey, it seems--can take you away from me. If you leave me, you do so knowing the consequences. Remember what I said: we are in a country where money can purchase everything, even such testimony as will enable me to divorce you and to raise such a hell of scandal around Peter Blakeney that no decent man in England would shake him by the hand. So now you know. I have told you my history, and I have extolled Peter Blakeney's virtues--his heroism, if you like to call it so. And I have done it deliberately so that you may admire him, regret him, love him if you must, even whilst you feel yourself irrevocably bound to me. You are just as much my slave now, as if I had bought you in the open market. If you continue to hate me, I shall probably hate you too in the end. But that would not help to free you. On the contrary, I think it would rather amuse me. I was never content to tease a cat, I invariably tortured it."

Jasper Tarkington had been speaking without interruption for near-ly ten minutes, but he had not spoken without a pause. He was pacing up and down the narrow room with his hands held behind his back, but now and again he had come to a halt, quite close to Rosemary, either to emphasize a point, or to look her up and down with a glance of cru-elty or merely mockery. Rosemary withstood every glance without flinching. She was standing close to the table with her hand resting on it, to giver herself support. She did not interrupt him. She wanted to hear everything he had to say, right to the end. When he renewed his threat that he would call false witnesses in order to create deadly scan-dal around Peter, and warned her that she was as much his slave as if he had bought her in the open market, she had, quite instinctively, glanced down on the tray which contained the remnants of her supper. There was a knife on the tray; one with a broad blade narrowing into a sharp point. She shuddered and turned her eyes away, but Jasper had caught her glance. He had just finished speaking, and he went deliber-ately up to the table, picked the knife up by its point, and with a mocking smile held it with its handle towards her.

"Very dramatic," he said lightly. "Did you ever see La Tosca?"

When she made no reply he laughed and threw the knife back on the table. Then he sat down and lit another cigarette.

There was silence in the little room now. Rosemary had scarcely moved. The horror and indignation which she had felt at first when Jasper embarked upon the history of his life had given place to a kind of moral numbness. She had ceased to feel. Her body seemed turned to stone; even her soul no longer rebelled. She was this man's wife, and he had warned her of the means which he would adopt to bind her, unresisting, to him. Nothing but death could loosen the bonds which he had tightened by his threats against Peter.

Jasper smoked on in silence. Only the fussy ticking of the old-fashioned little clock broke the stillness that had descended like a pall over this lonely corner of God's earth. A little while ago Rosemary had been vaguely conscious of a certain amount of bustle and animation in the house, and subconsciously she had associated this bustle with the probable arrival of guests who had come off the night train. But that had been some time ago. How long she did not know; probably before Jasper had begun speaking. She looked at her watch. It was half-past two. Jasper jumped to his feet.

"It must be very late," he said coolly. "I really must beg your par-don for having kept you up so long. Reminiscences are apt to run away with one."

He put down his cigarette, deliberately went up to his wife and took her by the shoulders.

"Kiss me, Rosemary," he said quietly.

It seemed to amuse him that she did not respond, for he gave a mocking chuckle and put his arms round her. He pressed his lips upon her mouth, her eyes, her throat. Then suddenly he let her go and she almost fell up against the table.

He then walked across to the door of his room.

CHAPTER XLVI

Jasper Tarkington, on the point of entering his room, had switched on the light and then paused on the threshold, uttering a gasp of astonishment.

"Maurus!" he exclaimed, "what in the world are you doing here?"

Maurus Imrey was sprawling on the horse-hair sofa, apparently fast asleep. At Jasper's ejaculation he opened his eyes, blinked, yawned, and stretched his arms.

"Ah! my dear Tarkington," he said in Hungarian. "I thought you were never coming."

He rose and shook himself like a big, shaggy dog, and passed his fingers through his tousled hair.

"I must have been fast asleep," he said.

"But what are you doing here, my friend?" Jasper asked, frowning.

"Waiting for you to do me a little service. It is so late, I don't really like to ask you. But I should be badly stranded if you did not help me."

"What is it?"

"I left Cluj by the midnight express," Maurus explained. "You know that we have all been turned out of Kis-Imre. And, by the way, it is Peter Blakeney who has bought the place. Isn't it a scandal? I never thought he would be such a swine. You know he is a near relation of my wife's."

"Yes, yes!" Jasper muttered impatiently. "What about it?"

"Well, simply that those damned officials at Cluj station never told me that I could only get as far as Sót. So I arrived here with my luggage and Anton, and, of course, I found this beastly hotel full. Not a room to be had, my dear fellow. Did you ever hear of such a thing? In the olden days one would just have taken a man by the scruff of his neck and thrown him out of any room one happened to want for oneself. I don't know what it's like with you in England, but here--"

"Just as bad," Jasper broke in with a curse, "but in heaven's name get on, man."

"Well, then, I left my big luggage here, and Anton and I went on to another little tavern I know of in the village. There, as luck would have it, the proprietor whom I used to know is dead, and the new man is one of those Bulgarian agriculturists who come over every year, you know, for the harvesting. Some of these men do settle down here sometimes, and this man--"

"Well, what about him?"

"He doesn't know a word of Hungarian, my dear fellow, and he does not seem to understand much Roumanian either. You once told me that you had been in Bulgaria and that you knew a little of their beastly language, so I thought--"

"What is it you want me to do?" Jasper broke in impatiently. "Walk over with you and arrange with the man about your rooms?"

"If you would not mind. Or could you let me sleep on your sofa?"

Jasper had hesitated at first. It was close on three o'clock, and he did not relish the idea of turning out again at this hour; but the suggestion that Maurus should be his room companion for the night was far more unpleasant.

"Come along, then," he said curtly. "It isn't far, I suppose?"

"Five minutes' walk, my dear fellow," Maurus said with obvious relief, "just the other side of the stream. And Anton shall walk back with you afterwards."

"I don't want anybody to chaperon me," Jasper retorted roughly.

He had to go into the salon to fetch his hat. Rosemary was still standing there leaning against the table for support. She had very much wanted to see Maurus at one time, but now it did not seem to matter. Nothing probably would ever matter again. She heard Jasper's voice saying in a whisper, "You've heard what this fool wants. I suppose I shall have to go."

She nodded in response. And then Jasper added with mocking courtesy:

"Good night, Lady Tarkington."

CHAPTER XLVII

Anton saw it all, and it was he who broke the news to Rosemary.

He had been sitting up in the small slip of a room on the ground floor which had been assigned to him, waiting for his master and wondering why the gracious count should be so long upstairs at this hour with the English lord and lady, when he saw the gracious count and the English milord come along the first floor balcony, he heard them go downstairs, and saw them go out of the house.

Anton was rather anxious about his master because the gracious count had been very, very queer the last twenty-four hours. Sometimes he would be very hilarious; he would laugh and sing and shout "Hurrah for Peter! Bravo!" and so on; at others he would be terribly depressed and sit and cry like a child, or else tear about the place in a passion of fury. He had had a slight fit after the gracious English lord and lady had gone, and the sisters thought that probably the control he had put on himself when the Roumanian soldiers brought the expulsion order had been too much for his nerves.

So when Anton saw the gracious count go out with the English lord at this extraordinary hour he could not help but follow him. Though there was no moon the sky was clear and the darkness of the night was just beginning to yield to the first touch of dawn. The two gentlemen walked quite fast, but Anton was able to keep them in sight. When they came to the little wooden bridge that spans the stream the English lord was a few steps ahead of the gracious count. Suddenly, in midstream, the count sprang upon milord from behind, and in a moment had him by the throat. The English lord, taken entirely by surprise, fought desperately nevertheless. Anton had uttered a great shout, and ran to the rescue as fast as ever he could. Through the gloom he could just see the English milord forced down, with his back nearly doubled over the slender parapet of the bridge, and the gracious count bending over him and holding him by the throat. Anton's shout echoed from mountain to mountain, but all around there was the silence of the night, broken only by the howling of a dog outside a cottage door.

Then suddenly, before Anton set his foot upon the bridge, the catastrophe occurred. The parapet suddenly crashed and gave way under the weight of the two men, and they were hurled into the stream below. One awful cry rent the stillness of the night. Anton, half crazy with horror, waded into the stream, the waters of which at a point near a huge boulder were stained with a streak of crimson. The English milord in falling had broken his head against the stone. The gracious count had probably fallen at first on the top of him, and then rolled over on his back, thus breaking his fall. Anton dragged them both, single-handed, out of the stream, first his master, then the English lord. The latter was dead, but the gracious count was still breathing and moaning softly. Anton laid him down upon the grass, and made a pillow for him with his own coat, which he had taken off. Then he ran to the priest's house, which was quite close, and rang the bell until he made someone hear. The priest had been quite kind. He roused his servant, and together--the priest and Anton and the servant--carried the gracious count into the presbytery. But the English milord, who was quite dead, they laid upon the bier in the tiny mortuary chapel which was by the entrance to the churchyard.

The priest had already sent for the village doctor, who had done what he could for the gracious count, but of course, he was ignorant, and, anyhow, Anton was of the opinion that there was nothing that any man could do. But he had been to the station and roused the station-master and asked him to telephone to Dr. Zacharias at Cluj. Anton was just going to run back and see if the answer had come through. In the meanwhile he had come over to the hotel to see if he could speak with the gracious lady.

Rosemary had not yet thought of going to bed. For two hours after Jasper went out with Maurus she had sat, unthinking, by the open window. Time for her had ceased to be. She had heard the howling of a dog. At one moment she had heard a shout, and then a weird and prolonged cry. But these sounds conveyed no meaning to her brain. Her thinking powers were atrophied.

Then the bare-footed, buxom, very sleepy little maid came to tell her that Anton, the valet of the gracious count at Kis-Imre, desired to speak with her at once. She was fully dressed; she sent for Anton and he told her what he had seen.

Hastily seizing hat and wrap, she went with Anton out of the house and through the village to the priest's house. The soft, colourless light of dawn lay over the mountain and valley. On ahead the turbulent waters of the stream tossed and played around the projecting boulders, murmuring of the tragedy which had culminated within their bosom. Nearing the priest's house Rosemary could see the narrow bridge, with its broken parapet--

The priest met her at the gate. The gracious count, he said, had not regained consciousness. He still lived, the doctor said, but life only hung by a thread. Rosemary sat down by Maurus; bedside and watched that life slowly ebbing away. In the late afternoon Dr. Zacharias came over from Cluj. He only confirmed what the village doctor had said. The spine was broken. It was only a question of hours. He could do nothing, but at Rosemary's earnest request--or perhaps on the promise of a heavy fee--he agreed to come again in the morning.

Less than an hour after he left, the dying man rallied a little. He opened his eyes, and seeing Rosemary, his face was illumined by a great joy. She bent over him and kissed his forehead. Two tears rolled slowly down his wan cheeks. He murmured something, and she bent her ear till it was quite close to his lips.

"He was a monster," he murmured. "I heard everything. I had to punish him for the evil he did to my wife and the children. And I have made you free."

At sunset Maurus Count Imrey passed away into the Unknown.

Then only did Rosemary leave his bedside. Accompanied by the priest, she went to the little mortuary chapel to take a last look at the man who had done her such an infinity of wrong. Now that his stormy life was ended, and his hard features were set in lines of peace, Rosemary felt once more that aching sense of pity for him which so often before had prompted her to forgive. She was able to commend his turbulent soul to God without the slightest thought of hatred or revenge. He had said once that she would never understand; but the infinite pity in her heart was born of an infinite understanding. The man who had atoned for his sins by this tragic death was not wholly responsible for his actions. He was the victim of his temperament: more sinned against, perhaps, than sinning. Who knows? If some other woman had captured his fancy she might have made him happy, found what was strong and fine in him, and all that was cruel would perhaps have been submerged beneath a great wave of love.

CHAPTER XLVIII

Since then, nearly two years! And this was the season of 1924! Wembley! The Rodeo! Royalties from Italy and Denmark and Roumania! The Labour Government!

How far, how very far, seemed Transylvania and Sót and the little mortuary chapel wherein Rosemary had gazed for the last time on the enigmatic personality which had once been Jasper Tarkington--her husband.

Even in death he had kept his secret--the secret of the strange dual identity which she had never been able to reconcile one with the other, the cruel, wolfish nature so skillfully hidden beneath the mantle of super-civilization.

Rosemary had not seen Peter since then. After the tragedy at Sót she had at last succeeded, by dint of bribery, in entering into direct communication with the British Consulate at Cluj.

Arrangements for the conveying of Lord Tarkington's body to England took up some considerable time. She only met Elza in Budapest when she herself was on her way home. Peter had left by then for an unknown destination. He had conveyed Philip and Anna over the frontier. They had soon abandoned the car, fearing pursuit, and in disguise had made their way to the frontier over the mountains. They were young and strong, the hardships were not serious, and the dangers reduced to a minimum once they had reached the lonely mountain passes. It was the planning of the escape that had been so wonderful. Peter Blakeney, disguised as a Roumanian officer, and having with him Captain Payson and a young Hungarian cricketer, both dressed as Roumanian soldiers, had presented a forged order for the surrender of the two prisoners, Philip Imrey and Anna Heves. To the officer commanding the depôt the order appeared in no way suspicious, and he gave up the prisoners without question. After that the whole thing became just a delightful adventure, nothing more. But Elza spoke of Peter with tears in her eyes. They had all of them mistrusted him. Wasn't that strange? Did Rosemary guess? Elza wanted to know, and Philip and Anna plied her with questions.

These were sad days for them all. But still Elza was wonderful, as wonderful as she had ever been. Even Rosemary never actually found out just how much of the tragedy Elza knew or guessed. Anton did not tell her, and to their world the death of the two men who were known to have been friends was just a terrible accident. Darkness. A broken bridge. Fatality.

Rosemary never told, of course. She wondered if Peter knew. She waited on in Budapest for some days hoping for news of him. But none came. Captain Payson heard in an indirect way that Peter was still in Transylvania, but no reliance could be placed on the truth of the rumour. It was only when Rosemary was back in England that she heard definite news of Peter. Elza wrote to say that he was living in Kis-Imre. "He is administering the property for us," she went on. "Isn't he wonderful? I am sure he will make something more of it than poor Maurus was able to do. Of course, they dare not do anything to him, because he is a British subject, and he tells me in his last letter that he hopes in a very few years' time, when justice had been at last meted out to our unfortunate country, to hand over Kis-Imre to Philip in a better state than it is now. Then my poor Philip's dream will, I hope, come true. He and Anna have loved each other ever since they were tiny children. When he has once more a fine home to offer her they will be married with my blessing. And all this we shall owe to Peter Blakeney. Can you wonder, my dear, that we all worship him? When I look at him I seem to see my dear and beautiful sister gazing at me through his eyes, and in his smile I see something of hers, because, just like Peter, she was always ready to laugh, always smiling at the world, always doing great and kind things under cover of a joke. So Philip and Anna and I, we bless Peter and for some reason, which perhaps you can explain better than I, when we think of him we also think of you."

Since then nearly two years! Rosemary has resumed work. Her powerful articles in The International Review on the conditions obtaining in Transylvania under alien occupation have begun at last to arouse from its apathy public opinion in England and America. Time and her own perseverance, aided by the lovers of justice and fairplay who abound in Anglo-Saxon communities, would after a while, she felt, do the rest. Rosemary had seen the rampant evil with her own eyes, now she was conscious of her power to help in remedying, or, at any rate, mitigating it. She threw herself heart and soul into the work not only because she loved it and because it thrilled her, but because work alone could help her to forget. "Try to forget" were the last words which she heard Peter speak, there in the woods beside the turbulent mountain stream when she had thought him a spy, a vile and venal wretch, and he had not said one word to exculpate himself. How could he when this might have meant rousing her suspicions of Jasper?--or perhaps it was just pride that had caused him to hold his tongue. Pride, which so often has proved love's most persistent enemy.

Or perhaps he no longer cared, and that was why he thought it would be so easy for her to forget.

Since then nearly two years! Rosemary walking through the park that late afternoon in July. She had been to the Albert Hall to hear Kreisler, and she wandered up the Broad Walk under the trees, because she did not feel that she could stand the noise and bustle of streets at a moment when her whole soul was still full of the exquisite music conjured up by that great magician. It was very hot and she was rather tired, so she sat down on a chair in the shade. Then suddenly she saw Peter. He was coming towards her, quite naturally, as if to an assignation. He looked just the same as he always did--like a boy, clean and straight-limbed as a young god, his eyes shining with excitement, that quaint, self-deprecating smile on his lips that Rosemary knew so well.

"I've been to hear old Kreisler," were the first words he said. "Wasn't he wonderful?"

So like Peter! He dragged a chair quite close to hers and sat down. He threw down his hat and passed his hand through his hair. He did not attempt to greet her in any way. "I've been to hear old Kreisler!" So like Peter! The very first words . . . and she hadn't seen him for nearly two years.

After a second or two he went on: "I wouldn't speak to you in the Albert Hall. When you went out I followed you. I knew you would wander out here."

And Rosemary asked quite casually: "Have you been in England long?"

"Only a few hours," Peter replied with a laugh. "I crossed over by the night boat, via Havre. I always meant to sample that journey, and it was really rather nice." After that he was silent for a moment; then suddenly he seized her hand. She had no gloves on, and he held the soft palm to his lips. Rosemary did not move. She was not looking at

Peter; she was just watching a huge blackbird that had landed on the elm tree opposite and who was whistling away for dear life.

"Rosemary, when can we be married?" Peter asked abruptly.

She couldn't help smiling. It, too, was so like Peter. "I've waited two years, dash it all," he went on. "Two years in hell. Now I'm not going to wait any longer. When can we be married, Rosemary?"

Then Rosemary ceased to watch the blackbird and turned slowly to look at Peter.

"Whenever you like, dear," she replied.

THE END

**The Complete Richard Hannay - 39 Steps,
Greenmantle, Mr Steadfast, Three Hostages,
Island of Sheep.**
John Buchan
Benediction Classics, 2012
908 pages
ISBN: 978-1-78139-203-4

Available from www.amazon.com,
www.amazon.co.uk

The Complete Richard Hannay includes the five John Buchan novels that feature the hero: 39 Steps, Greenmantle, Mr Steadfast, Three Hostages, Island of Sheep. Richard Hannay was one of the first modern spy thriller heroes and has shaped the genre. Hannay is strong and silent, combining the Scottish dourness with the English "stiff upper lip". He is tough and shrewd, courageous and resourceful. However, unlike later spy thrillers he has a greater breadth of emotion. He is philosophical and refuses to demonise his enemies, he falls in love, he is dependent upon his friends and he is religious. These books are exciting, with Richard Hannay being chased over moor and glen, they are page turning thrillers.

John Macnab
John Buchan
Benediction Classics, 2011
208 pages
ISBN: 978-1-84902-423-5

Available from www.amazon.com,
www.amazon.co.uk

John Macnab is the second most famous
novel by John Buchan, published in
1925. It is a story of three successful
men - a barrister, cabinet minister and banker who are bored.
They decide to alleviate the boredom by anonymously informing
three Scottish estates that they intend to poach a stag or a salmon
and returning it to them undetected. It is about daring thinking
and high living set in the beautiful Highlands of Scotland and evoking images of the hunting, shooting and fishing lifestyle.

The Chronicles of Captain Blood
Rafael Sabatini
Benediction Classics, 2011
188 pages
ISBN: 978-1-84902-469-3

Available from www.amazon.com,
www.amazon.co.uk

First published in 1931, this new edition is
now available. It is a collection of short stories set within the timeframe of Sabatini's
best-selling novel 'Captain Blood'. A second collection of short stories 'The Fortunes of Captain Blood (1936) is also available.

The Fortunes of Captain Blood
Rafael Sabatini
Oxford City Press, 2012
162 pages
ISBN: 978-1-78139-128-0

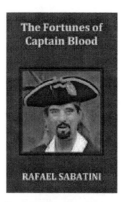

Available from www.amazon.com,
www.amazon.co.uk

Rafael Sabatini is a master storyteller. The
Daily Telegraph described him thus: 'One
wonders if there is another storyteller so adroit at filling his pages
with intrigue and counter-intrigue, with danger threaded with
romance, with a background of lavish colour, of silks and velvets,
of swords and jewels'. 'The Fortunes of Captain Blood' (1936) is a
collection of short stories. Captain Blood is handsome, brilliant
and skilled with his blade, always one step ahead of his enemies.
Perils upon perils challenge him but with his faithful crew, ever
willing to follow him into danger, he manages to be both chivalrous and victorious. 'The Chronicles of Captain Blood' (1931),
another collection of his short stories is also available.

Also from Benediction Books …
Wandering Between Two Worlds: Essays on Faith and Art
Anita Mathias
Benediction Books, 2007
152 pages
ISBN: 0955373700

Available from www.amazon.com, www.amazon.co.uk

In these wide-ranging lyrical essays, Anita Mathias writes, in lush, lovely prose, of her naughty Catholic childhood in Jamshedpur, India; her large, eccentric family in Mangalore, a sea-coast town converted by the Portuguese in the sixteenth century; her rebellion and atheism as a teenager in her Himalayan boarding school, run by German missionary nuns, St. Mary's Convent, Nainital; and her abrupt religious conversion after which she entered Mother Teresa's convent in Calcutta as a novice. Later rich, elegant essays explore the dualities of her life as a writer, mother, and Christian in the United States-- Domesticity and Art, Writing and Prayer, and the experience of being "an alien and stranger" as an immigrant in America, sensing the need for roots.

About the Author

Anita Mathias is the author of *Wandering Between Two Worlds: Essays on Faith and Art.* She has a B.A. and M.A. in English from Somerville College, Oxford University, and an M.A. in Creative Writing from the Ohio State University, USA. Anita won a National Endowment of the Arts fellowship in Creative Nonfiction in 1997. She lives in Oxford, England with her husband, Roy, and her daughters, Zoe and Irene.

Anita's website:
    http://www.anitamathias.com, and
Anita's blog Dreaming Beneath the Spires:
    http://dreamingbeneaththespires.blogspot.com

The Church That Had Too Much
Anita Mathias
Benediction Books, 2010
52 pages
ISBN: 9781849026567

Available from www.amazon.com, www.amazon.co.uk

The Church That Had Too Much was very well-intentioned. She wanted to love God, she wanted to love people, but she was both hampered by her muchness and the abundance of her possessions, and beset by ambition, power struggles and snobbery. Read about the surprising way The Church That Had Too Much began to resolve her problems in this deceptively simple and enchanting fable.

About the Author

Anita Mathias is the author of *Wandering Between Two Worlds: Essays on Faith and Art*. She has a B.A. and M.A. in English from Somerville College, Oxford University, and an M.A. in Creative Writing from the Ohio State University, USA. Anita won a National Endowment of the Arts fellowship in Creative Nonfiction in 1997. She lives in Oxford, England with her husband, Roy, and her daughters, Zoe and Irene.

Anita's website:
    http://www.anitamathias.com, and
Anita's blog Dreaming Beneath the Spires:
    http://dreamingbeneaththespires.blogspot.com

CPSIA information can be obtained at www.ICGtesting.com
Printed in the USA
LVOW07s0014171114

414026LV00001B/210/P

9 781781 392454